Neutrino Drag
Stories

Four Walls Eight Windows
NEW YORK

To Deborah, Queen of Lowbrow Delights.

*And to my brothers and sister, from
youngest to oldest: Bob, Frank, and Cathy:
thanks for all the love and support.*

© 2004 Paul Di Filippo

Published in the United States by:
Four Walls Eight Windows
39 West 14th Street, room 503
New York, N.Y., 10011

Visit our website at http://www.4w8w.com
First U.S. printing April 2004.

Library of Congress Cataloging-in-Publication Data on file:

ISBN 1-56858-300-1

10 9 8 7 6 5 4 3 2 1

Typesetting by Jerusalem Typesetting

Printed in Canada on 100% recycled paper.

Table of Contents

Introduction 1

Rescuing Andy 3

Yellowing Bowers 25

The Moon-Bonham Effect 47

Living with the Giants 67

Destroy All Brains! 81

The Ballad of Sally NutraSweet™ 89

Take Me to the Pilot 115

And Them, Too, I Hope 131

The Man Who Stole the Moon 141

The Square Root of Pythagoras 169

Stink Lines 197

Working for the U 229

Doing The Unstuck 243

Math Takes a Holiday 273

Neutrino Drag 303

What Goes up a Chimney? Smoke! 333

A Martian Theodicy 357

Weeping Walls 381

Seeing Is Believing 405

What's up Tiger Lily? 443

Credits 491

Table of Contents

Introduction

Welcome to *Fractal Paisleys II.*

No, you haven't been misled by an erroneous dust jacket. This collection is indeed titled *Neutrino Drag* (a title I continue to fear might inspire images of a cross-dressing particle physicist). But over the years since the appearance of my earlier collection, *Fractal Paisleys*, I continued to hope that one day I might amass enough similar stories for a companion volume, a volume I always mentally tagged with the Hollywood-sequel-style appellation. That day is now here. Thanks to the ongoing, invaluable support from many editors—and particularly from John Oakes and the whole staff at Four Walls Eight Windows—you hold in your hands a second collection of comic science fiction stories set mainly in the present, wherein average folks of less-than-sterling character get warped up in improbable events. Not your standard, space-opera material.

There are a few exceptions to this capsule description. The historical figure Pythagoras is neither average nor contemporary. Yet thanks to the humanizing touch of my co-writer, Rudy Rucker, this ancient mathematical savant steps down into the gutter with the rest of us, prey to lusts and bad judgment. Bash Applebrook is presented as a certifiable genius, but you'd never know it from the trouble he manages to get himself into. And the (not-so-far-of?) future inhabited by Sally NutraSweet™ is an unlikely scenario at best (I hope). Yet there's some undeniable thread of absurd wonders erupting into lives deemed staid by their owners that runs from story to story. And that's the only message or moral I have to present.

Not only is the universe stranger than we imagine, it's stranger than we *can* imagine.

These stories include some of the earliest I ever sold, nearly twenty years old, and some of the newest. They're arranged chronologically, to convey an illusion of improvement (fingers crossed). If you'd care to see me devolve into the formless slug I was when I first embarked on this destinationless journey, simply read this book from back to front.

This is either the first story I ever sold, or the second, or the third.

Let me explain.

Back in the seventies, I placed a Barry Malzberg pastiche with the magazine UnEarth. *Barely a full narrative, borrowing the style of another man, it was nonetheless my first real sale. It took me nearly ten years to make another. And then two came almost simultaneously. Ted Klein bought this piece for* Twilight Zone Magazine, *while Ed Ferman picked up "Stone Lives" for* The Magazine of Fantasy and Science Fiction. *I now cannot recall which letter of acceptance preceded the other. So I always nominate both men equally as my first literary godfathers.*

Soon after this sale, I went to New York to introduce myself to Ted Klein. The parent company of Twilight Zone Magazine *also produced its real moneymaker, a skinzine named* Gallery. *Showing up at their offices, I was greeted by a receptionist who was strikingly beautiful enough to have been a centerfold. She was sitting beneath a giant framed poster of a mostly nude woman, the printing of which must have exhausted the metropolitan area's supply of flesh-colored ink.*

All right! *I thought.* My crazy career choice is finally starting to pay off!

Rescuing Andy

Napoleon's ghost refused to play fair. Despite the entreaties and threats employed by Major Flood, it still persisted in misunderstanding the rules of the board game.

From across the large, cluttered room, flooded with August sunlight, Piers watched the argument with amused tolerance. Just two months ago, the whole affair would have struck him as bizarre and improbable, rather like seeing a horse atop a saddled man. But back then, he had been merely a jaded New Yorker, inured to instant death, garish spectacles, and a citizenry that ranged the gamut from eccentric to outlandish.

Now he lived in Blackwood Beach.

Things were much stranger here.

Piers rested his narrow rear on a big oak sideboard full of junk—a conch shell whose apparently natural color and pattern was that of the American flag; a rusted flintlock pistol; an object on which the eye could not quite fasten, that Major Flood claimed was a tesseract given to him by young Randy Broadbent. With his legs crossed at the ankles and arms folded across his chest, Piers enjoyed the sight of Major Flood arguing with his guest.

The major was a bulky man, florid but pleasant, who always dressed in khaki, now exemplified by a bush jacket and shorts. (His response to Piers' polite inquiry as to where he had soldiered had been to wink slyly and say, "The War of Independence, boy. The only one worth waging, and one I'm still fighting for all I'm worth." Further probing produced no more concrete answer.) He sat in a barrel chair at the head of a long, polished table. His face was as red as one of the good lobsters—once cooked—found in the waters off Blackwood Beach. He clutched a croupier's rake—which he had been using to move pieces—so tightly he seemed to be compressing its wooden handle. Midway down the table, an Avalon Hill strategy game was set up. The chair at the far end was occupied by a milky, man-sized whorl of oily gas, looking something like a giant's greasy thumbprint on the air.

"God damn it, your royal stupid eminence!" Flood shouted. "How many times do I have to tell you? Those red

4

markers represent tanks. Land ironclads! They cannot just roll blithely over the parts of the board that represent water. *L'eau! Comprenez?*"

The ghost replied in a buzzing that resembled French as it might be spoken by a praying mantis.

"No!" thundered the major, raising his staff and bringing it down upon the table with a resounding *thwack* that caused all the pieces to jump out of alignment. Piers was reminded of an angry Olympian stirring up the battlefield outside Troy. "They're not submarines. That was another game. If you can't keep things straight, I'll send you away and bring back Caesar to play. Even if he gets mixed up too, at least he's not insufferably pompous."

The ghost buzzed insultingly, and Major Flood let out a wordless roar. He launched himself across the slick table in his eagerness to throttle Napoleon, and the game board blew off in a spray of cardboard hexagons.

Piers chuckled nervously and turned to ascend the elaborate staircase on his right.

Although he enjoyed nothing more than visiting his neighbor, he always felt a little queasy watching him wrestle with the insubstantial emperor. The whole affair looked a bit too much like a scene from Bedlam, and Piers was still new enough to Blackwood Beach to occasionally doubt his own sanity.

On the landing halfway between floors, Piers passed a suit of armor. It seemed quite conventional, until one noticed it possessed a long articulated, caudal tube, evidently for the wearer's tail.

Flood had given Piers the run of his house early in their acquaintance, and now Piers used the privilege to retreat to the widow's walk until the major should cease his brawling.

In the square, hot, little room, with its windows on all four sides affording a grand view of the sea and countryside and town below, Piers paused. An archaic brass telescope on a wooden tripod occupied most of the space. Idly, Piers bent to the eyepiece and swung the glass out to sea.

Little Egg, the bald dome of rock a mile out into the Atlantic, popped into view. Piers studied its incommunicative face for a while, and then trained the scope on Big Egg, a few degrees away. Both were quite bland and featureless. Shifting his position, he brought the lens to bear on the rocky coast that stretched north of Blackwood Beach. Waves crashed with soundless fury against the tumbled, unpeopled boulders. The water was rough today. Why, look there: one wave seemed almost bold enough to touch the feet of that naked woman lying brazenly on the rocks—

Piers froze, as if captivated by Medusa. This was something new, at least to him. He had never seen this beautiful woman before, either on the rocks or in town. Who could she be? And why had she picked such an inconvenient place to sunbathe? Surely she could have found privacy without venturing to such an inaccessible spit.

Piers studied her as closely as the instrument allowed. Her skin was dusky, her thick, long, black hair spread out like a fleece around her head. Her limbs were long and muscular, her breasts full and firm. From Piers' head-on angle, her face was obscured, but she had a nice, expressive brow and a pretty, pink line defined the part of her hair.

Piers watched her for ten minutes, but she never sat up or turned her face to him.

He noticed, after a time, a bundle of her possessions beside her. Only then did he believe she had not just climbed from the sea.

At last he broke away and returned downstairs.

Major Flood sat on the floor. The chair the ghost had

been occupying was a heap of kindling, destroyed in their fight. Flood looked up when Piers approached.

"Sorry about the ruckus," Flood said contritely. Then, with bemusement, "I wonder if I'd have better luck with someone more modern. But, damn it, all the great generals were pre-twentieth century." He eyed Piers speculatively. "I don't suppose you'd reconsider—"

"No," Piers said. He was on good terms with the mercurial Flood now and was afraid to alter their relationship by getting involved with the man's passion for simulated warfare.

Piers extended a hand, and Flood took it. The heavy man got to his feet with surprising nimbleness.

"I've just seen something wonderful," Piers said. "A gorgeous woman tanning herself on the rocks."

"That's Andy," said Flood, bending over to adjust his olive knee socks. He added as an afterthought, "She's not tanning herself. She's waiting to be ravished."

Piers' jaw dipped before he could control it. "I beg your pardon."

"I said, she's waiting to be ravished."

All Piers could summon up were two words: "By whom?"

"That I couldn't tell you. But I believe Dr. Frostwig knows her whole story. If you'd like me to call him and arrange a visit—"

Piers nodded agreement.

"Fine, I will." Flood had rearranged his rumpled attire to suit his stringent standards. Now he looked Piers straight in the eye.

"Would Grant or Lee be more amenable, do you think?"

* * *

Three months ago, Piers had ceased to need to work, broken the bond between his belly and bankbook. A broker in Manhattan, he had overheard, while half drunk in a noisy bar, a conversation that enabled him to make a fortune trading in fish meal futures. Once he had invested his profits at a suitably high interest rate and quit his job, he realized he wanted nothing more to do with New York. It was not his native city; that was Boston. He had few friends in Manhattan and had come to dislike its uproar and grime and sundry subtle pressures. But neither did he wish to return to Boston and live uncomfortably close to his domineering, widowed father.

One day, riding the Amtrak train between the two poles of his indeterminate life, he spotted a weathered wooden road sign that passed almost too quickly for him to interpret:

BLACKWOOD BEACH

12 MILES

The name stuck in his mind for the rest of the trip, replaying itself like an insistent jingle. It somehow seemed to hint at a pleasant desuetude, a languorous decay, an atmosphere as far removed from the hurly-burly of New York as that of the Upper East Side was from Harlem.

When he arrived in New York, he immediately took his black Saab from its garage and headed north.

The town almost did not want to be found. When Piers finally located, after hours of hot driving, the sign he had seen from the train, he realized that it gave no direction as to which of two possible roads he should take.

Assuming from its name that the town fronted the shore, he headed east, toward the Atlantic.

The assumption was right, the choice wrong. The road petered out at an abandoned farmhouse, standing gray and desolate on a weedy lot, within sound of the breaking surf.

Only by taking the westerly road, which wandered through the New England landscape like a sun-addled snake, did he eventually arrive at Blackwood Beach.

Like happiness, the town seemed approachable only through indirection.

Blackwood Beach occupied something of a natural amphitheater, with the restless sea serving as the great tragicomedy on the east. The gently sloping sides of the bowl were laced with meandering, tree-lined streets, connecting huge Victorian and Edwardian houses, all in more or less conspicuous stages of comfortable disrepair. The houses, exerting themselves like circus acrobats, had managed to toss a few of their comrades up over the lip of the wide but shallow bowl. These houses sitting up atop the ridge commanded the finest views.

It was one of these crest-riding old sentries that Piers knew he had to have. Something ineffably right about the town had drawn him into its mustily welcoming embrace.

Traveling the ridge road—labeled rather perversely with an antique wrought-iron street sign as "Lower Avenue"—Piers came upon a sprawling, flaking, white house, its lower windows boarded with plywood, a faded lawn sign proclaiming it FOR SALE. From the stained-glass portrait of a kraken in its tower, to its warped porch floorboards, it was everything Piers wanted.

Within a week, he was living there, happy and relaxed. Two local carpenters—Ed Stout and his silent son, Jack— kept the place noisy during the day with repairs, so Piers took to exploring the town.

That was when he began to realize the kind of place his new home was. "Not ordinary" would be putting things in the most conservative light.

The events that led him to this realization were not dramatic, taken separately, and allowed him to preserve a belief that one day he would be rendered a logical explanation for them all. The glinting object behind Welcome Goodnight's eye patch; the chase through the hilly streets that Randy Broadbent gave in pursuit of the catlike thing; a strange phrase here, a half-glimpsed something there— He tried to ignore them at first. But they eventually mounted up to conclusive evidence that Blackwood Beach did not find it convenient to obey the same physical laws as the rest of the world.

The actions of Major Flood, his closest neighbor, were the most startling things he had so far witnessed. But that was perhaps only because the major was the sole citizen whose private life he was intimately familiar with. During the period when the Stouts had been working on his house, he had been invited by Flood to keep him company and share a drink. He had assented gladly, a bit lonely, unaware however of the other visitors the major entertained.

Even these he had been able to rationalize, though.

But this woman lying on the rocks, waiting to be "ravished"—for some reason such a situation was too much to tolerate. All his incipient bewilderment had been crystallized into an irksome pearl.

He resolved before leaving Flood's that he would have the answer at least to this one mystery.

* * *

The bobcat held Piers' gaze with its own unwavering one. Its head only inches from his, it snarled with silent yet malign fury, its teeth twin rows of needle-like instruments of pain and mutilation.

Piers gently patted the dusty head of the stuffed and mounted animal, while he watched Dr. Frostwig's bony back. The doctor was rummaging among some papers on his roll-top desk, muttering to himself all the while. Piers caught only snatches.

"Can't imagine . . . How did it ever . . . Why don't things . . . "

Piers sat in the study of Dr. Frostwig's house at 13½ Staghorn Road. (Many of the houses in Blackwood Beach were numbered with fractions, not for any particular reason Piers could determine—such as subdivision of older lots— but merely to express a certain contrariness. In keeping with the spirit, yet striving to be modern, Piers had painted his mailbox with the legend:

3.14159 . . . LOWER AVENUE

He had noticed approving glances from passersby, and felt he was fitting in.)

The doctor's study, a dark and shuttered room lit by a single sixty-watt bulb, was filled with stuffed animals. A fine repast for generations of moths, the creatures occupied every niche. An owl held its wings outspread atop a sideboard filled with mice in various comic poses. A fox stalked unseen prey across the terrain of a couch. In one shadowy corner, Piers swore he could detect the shape of an adult gorilla. These were only a portion of the indoor wildlife.

Without warning, a bang resounded, and Piers jumped.

The doctor turned from the desk whose top he had slammed shut.

"I can't find the damn magazine," Frostwig said. "But I'll manage without it. I'm not that senile yet. I still remember old friends like Professor Ramada, even if I can't recall every detail of his crackpot theory."

"Thank you for looking, Doctor," Piers said. He watched as Frostwig lowered himself slowly into a chair facing his.

The doctor was a collection of sinew and bones, outfitted in a baggy, blue shirt with acid stains and gray pants.

He was entirely bald, and his face resembled an ancient dry riverbed.

"Now then, Mr. Seuss. Exactly what would you like to know about Ramada and his daughter?"

Piers found himself slightly tongue-tied at the prospect of mentioning how he had spied on the nude woman. Using Frostwig's own words as a cue, he finally said, "Uh, I believe I once heard the professor speak, and I was curious as to what he did nowadays. And his daughter, also. That is, if you know anything about her."

Frostwig eyed Piers as if he were a transparent mannequin stuffed with falsehoods. But he must have decided his intentions were honest, since he began speaking in an unreserved tone.

"The professor does nothing these days, I'm afraid. He died a little over a year ago. Many people around here—the romantic fools, mostly—like to claim it was of a broken heart. But I suspect that falling twelve stories to the asphalt was what really did it."

"Suicide?"

"No, I don't believe so. Although I see how some could imagine it was. The professor did have a pet theory that was much disparaged by his fellow faculty members. He taught zoology at Brown University. He was on the top floor of the science library one day. Witnesses testify that he leaned out a window trying to examine a peculiarly speckled pigeon nesting on the ledge, when he lost his balance."

Piers knew the building and could visualize the accident all too clearly. He quickly asked, "What was Ramada's theory, doctor?"

Frostwig steepled his twig fingers. "That's why I was trying to find the magazine. I've been hunting for it since Flood called. You see, the professor managed to have his ideas published in some scientifiction rag as a speculative article. Which of course just brought more scorn from his colleagues. Basically, they amounted to this:

"Ramada believed that Big Egg was hollow, with an underwater entrance. He went on to assert that a long-lived creature inhabited the hidden interior. He linked the creature to a legend the Narragansett Indians had of an aquatic deity. It is a fact that the Narragansetts used to make an annual pilgrimage to Blackwood Beach—of course long before there was any settlement by Europeans. In any case, this marine Bigfoot did not sit well with Ramada's peers. But he maintained his belief in it up to the end."

Piers slowly digested the information. Frostwig still had not provided any explanation for the daughter's behavior, and Piers prompted him.

"And Andy, his daughter—?"

"Lovely girl," Frostwig said. "She lost her mother at an early age, and grew up something of a tomboy. She was naturally quite despondent over her father's death. I feel personally that she's brooded far too much over it. She hardly stirs from her house, except to shop for food. And—" Frostwig's severe gaze fell heavily upon Piers, who hung his head "—to lie sky-clad on the rocks, where, rumor has it, she is offering herself to the creature in some sort of obscure oblation, as if doing so could bring her father back."

"That's awfully sad," Piers said. "Not to mention a little daft."

Frostwig shrugged. "That's as it may be. As I stipulated, it's only a rumor. No one knows for sure what she's thinking, since she hasn't said. Perhaps she's merely trying to establish Blackwood Beach as the Saint-Tropez of New England. Remember also: we all work out our grief differently."

As Piers pondered the doctor's last statement, Frostwig rose creakily and removed a giant pair of calipers from under his seat cushion. He advanced on Piers.

"Now, young man, if you'll just repay my favor by allowing me to take a few measurements."

Piers, overcome by surprise, sat helplessly while the doctor ran the calipers along his skull, forearm, thigh, and other personal parts.

When the old man had finished, Piers stood to go. The doctor accompanied him to the study door.

As they neared the shadowed corner where the gorilla lurked, Piers' eyes, now dark-adapted, played that odd trick—so familiar to myopics, but not generally available to those with normal vision, such as Piers—whereby an object seen at a distance recoheres upon closer examination into something entirely different.

Piers started, and would have paused for a longer look, but Doctor Frostwig hurried him out.

As he walked home, he realized that it had been the big fur coat on the glass-eyed man that had deceived him.

* * *

They met face to face for the first time in the flour-and-sugar aisle at Rackstraw's Market.

Piers turned from examining an incomprehensible foodstuff—Kenyon's Johnnycake Meal—and found himself ensnared, melting into, almost subsumed, by Andy's arresting profile.

He knew at that moment that he had to speak to her. For starters. Then he would perhaps—if the coast seemed clear—grab her manfully by the waist, toss her over his shoulder, and ride off on some adventitious winged horse, to a secluded castle where they could lie abed twenty-three hours out of twenty-four.

Piers was not a brawny fellow, and Andy verged on goddess size, so the part about shouldering her weight gave him pause. Then instinct told him he could find the strength somewhere.

But for the moment, he neither spoke to nor abducted her, simply rested one elbow on the dusty, varnished-wood shelf of Rackstraw's Market (est. 1910) and contemplated Andy's face.

Her features were vaguely Castilian, or Lebanese, or Greek—one of those alluring Mediterranean races Piers found hard to tell apart. Her forehead was as fine as Piers had first thought. Hazel eyes induced vertigo. A prominent nose only made one imagine how best to position one's own head so as to kiss her ripe unpainted lips.

Piers let his look wander south. Andy wore a men's shirt, white and knotted at the waist, flower print cotton shorts, and sandals that laced up her inviting calves. She was filling a straw-handled basket methodically, if absentmindedly, with various staples. She tolerated Piers' adoration for perhaps thirty seconds before turning directly toward him.

Hastily, Piers straightened, realizing he must have looked like a regular layabout or lounge lizard (market-lizard?). He opened his mouth to disburden himself of his now fully blossomed worship, but Andy spoke first.

"Do I know you, sir?"

Her plangent yet melodic voice drove Piers into more dangerous depths of confusion. He wanted to say something like, "Although you do not, dear lady, we were fated to meet from the second I glimpsed your thrillingly naked bosom from afar." Instead, however, he sputtered out. "No, but I— That is— My name is—"

"Please stop right there," she cut in sharply. "I can't listen to anything you have to say, no matter how well meant. My life is too mixed-up right now. I haven't even time for my old acquaintants, let alone new ones."

She turned to leave, and Piers' heart sank.

"Wait. I'm new in town. I just want to introduce myself."

She faced him again. "My father was a firm believer in propriety, sir. No idle chatting with strangers was what he advised me. And although he's gone now, I still follow his advice. Please don't disturb a woman in mourning any further, or you'll make me angry."

Finished with him, Andy headed for soda-and-chips, with an irrepressible swaying of her hips. At the end of the aisle, she unexpectedly stopped and turned. An enigmatic smile contoured her lips.

"Perhaps when this is all over," she said, and then was gone.

Piers was left speechless and could not utter what he thought.

I'm not really a stranger—

And—

How can a body like that be in mourning?

* * *

The face in the mirror leered gruesomely. Its eyebrows shot up like those of a Groucho Marx on speed. The eyes themselves became crossed. The lips curled; the nostrils flared like those of a bee-stung bull. The total effect was one of a man simultaneously hearing a bad pun, sucking on a lemon, and having his ribs tickled.

Piers stopped mugging. He stood before his bathroom mirror, stomach pressed against the pedestal sink. He had been attempting to discern any incipient distortions of his countenance that perhaps might crop up in everyday social intercourse and frighten people. He had found none. In fact, he thought he had a rather pleasant face. Yet there must be some hidden flaw.

Why else would Andy react so coldly to him?

They had met two more times: once again in the market (silence), and once outside her house (a gabled and turreted monstrosity, whose salient feature was an enormous window shaped like an eye within a pyramid, above the front door; there, his reception had been positively Lucretia-Borgian, as Andy made a motion indicating she would gladly slit his throat).

The whole affair so far gave Piers scant reason for hope. Despondent, he studied his uncontorted features for the *nth* time.

A shock of nonaggressive brown hair fell across his brow. Tranquil blue eyes, an unassuming nose, a pleasantly well-defined jaw and chin. He saw no reason why such an assemblage should cause violent disgust. As for his body, all prior lovers had rated it at worst satisfactory.

The poor girl was mad not to at least talk to him. Her background, this crazy town—that was the only explanation. Obsessed with her father's death, she had no time for wholesome activities, but could only languish on the rocks, performing some arcane, totally useless penance for a death with which she had nothing to do. A monomaniac, that's what she was. He was well shut of her.

Piers dressed and went downstairs to read the *Blackwood Beach Intelligencer* and enjoy his breakfast, his mind made up to drop all thoughts of the infuriating woman.

His vow lasted until his third cup of coffee. Then, hating himself, he walked next door to Major Flood's.

Piers did not bother to knock, since the major never answered. He simply went inside and through several cavernous, high-ceilinged rooms to the one where the Major entertained his spirituous opponents.

There he found the usual tableau of Flood facing a churning pool of mist.

"Vizzkey," implored the mist.

"No, no whiskey," Flood yelled. "Not until we finish the game."

"Vat var?" the ghost inquired desultorily.

"Meade versus Lee at Gettysburg. You get to take the part of one of your own generals. Should be no problem. Now, move."

Without direct intervention, pieces began to slide about the board. Flood's face assumed a look of grim concentration.

Piers left him to his game.

The barrel of the telescope was warm to his touch. Piers swung it with practiced aim to the north. Soon he had captured Andy in his brass and glass contrivance.

It inflamed him beyond reason to watch her everyday in this remote and intangible manner. He had refrained from visiting her on the rocks only because he knew with dismal certainty that she would only hate him even more. (But did she hate him now? There was that smile in the market. If she hated him, life would not be worth living. Her granitic couch would serve to dash his brains out, as he hurled himself from the heights. Like father, like suitor.)

Piers' wild thoughts were suddenly truncated as neatly as if by a guillotine. What was she doing? She had sat up, taking something from her pile of clothing. It looked as if her fingers were clasped around air. No, a transparent bottle with transparent contents. Oh my God. It wasn't— It was. She wouldn't— She would.

With the deliberate economy so evident in her public gestures, Andy began to coat her honey-colored body with tan-enhancing baby oil.

Feeling like the most horrid voyeur, Piers watched her transform her upper body—arms, breasts, belly—into a shimmering paradise. When her hand strayed below her waist, Piers grew so agitated that he lost her from the restricted circle of the lens.

He stood erect, the telescope abandoned, a desperate plan forming in his frazzled brain.

*   *   *

Randy Broadbent looked curiously ageless. Although supposedly only twelve, his fat face radiated a Buddha-like timelessness. Even his food-spotted T-shirt and bulging bib overalls could not detract from his air of eternal introspection.

Piers and the boy sat in the basement of the Broadbent home. Randy's parents were both at work.

The cellar was Randy's workshop. Except for one corner grudgingly ceded to a washer and dryer, the dank expanse was filled with a bench full of chemicals and glassware, a set of pre-1900s *Encyclopedia Britannica*, and other such objects as had at one time or another retained Randy's interest.

"Now let me get this straight," Randy said. He sat on a high workbench stool that put his eyes level with Piers'. "You will provide me with a wetsuit, which you want me to alter into some sort of sea monster outfit."

"Correct," said Piers uneasily. "And don't forget the mask."

"Right. A mask to match. And all this is for Halloween. Which is two months away."

"Yes. But I'd like it as soon as possible."

Randy eyed Piers phlegmatically, as if reading his soul and preferring the synopsis. Piers thought he was about to refuse when he said, "A week okay?"

"Fine, wonderful," Piers babbled. He stood, relieved, and tried to make small talk. "What's this?" he asked, pointing to a cage-like apparatus.

"A matter transmitter," Randy said boredly. "But it's not perfected yet."

Piers chuckled accommodatingly. Ah, youth! What wild flights of imagination. But the boy was a good craftsman. Piers had seen a soft sculpture of Alexander the Great he had fashioned for Flood.

"Ah, I see you have a computer. I used to work with one, trading stocks."

Piers laid his fingers on the familiar keyboard. Randy said, "Be careful. That's not a normal machine. I've got some very sophisticated prognosticative software in there."

Piers started to smile. Without his having tapped a key, words began to scroll across the screen.

DON'T DO IT
IT'S DANGEROUS
YOU'LL BE SORRY.

Piers jumped back, as if the keyboard were electrified.

"Ha, ha," he said woodenly as sweat beaded his upper lip. "Good joke."

"I don't joke," said Randy. "And neither does it."

* * *

It had to be a day when the sea was calm. After going to all this trouble, Piers had no intention of letting heavy surf pound him against Andy's flat-topped boulder. At last one arrived. Piers left the house shortly after dawn, carrying the customized wet suit and mask in a duffel bag he had formerly used to carry his racquetball outfit and equipment.

He had picked the suit up several days ago, paying Randy a fair sum. Alas the boy had probably never gotten a chance to spend it. Piers had been as startled as the rest of the town to find the Broadbent home vanished one morning, water pipes cleanly sheared and visible in the empty pit from which even the foundation had disappeared. He recalled the matter transmitter and shuddered to think he had almost stepped inside the innocent-looking cage.

Piers did not really want to do what he was going to do. He felt truly small and mean. But what other choice did he have? He had to make Andy pay attention to him. There seemed no other way. And maybe, he thought in muzzy, pop-psychiatric terms, he could rid her of her obsession by actualizing it.

Down by the sandy public beach, empty at this hour save for peeling park benches and a rickety gazebo, Piers found a clump of perpetually leaning pines in which to change unseen. He stripped down to his undershorts and laid the suit out. Randy had done a good job, using epoxies, rubber, and plastic to achieve a warty, scaled look, with serrated fins at elbows and calves. The kid had even attached gloves. The mask—open at the back and fastened with elastic—looked something like the Creature from the Black Lagoon.

Piers donned the suit, mask, and flippers. The gasketed glass faceplate fit fairly well over his false face. A snorkel completed his gear.

Leaving his clothes amid the trees, Piers clumped clumsily down the beach and into the water.

As he began to swim north, he rehearsed his plan. He would discard his snorkel and diving mask while still unseen by Andy, as he floated out of sight. (He wouldn't need them to return, since the two of them would certainly walk off arm in arm.) After ditching the equipment, he would shoot up with the aid of a wave onto Andy's rock, uttering suitably grotesque noises. At this point, he foresaw several results.

Andy fainted, or turned and fled, or threw herself at his feet. Whatever eventuated, she would be cured. He would have rescued her from her delusions.

In his ridiculous suit, Piers paddled along, head down, flippers kicking. Every once in a while, he stopped and risked a brief look upward to orient himself. Everything looked different from this perspective, the shapes of the jagged coast all changed. He hoped to spot Andy's recumbent form, though.

And, eventually, he did.

His plan worked perfectly—to a point. A few yards from Andy's rock, her lovely toes in view, Piers doffed his mask and let it sink. The snorkel was likewise consigned to the sea. He snugged the clammy rubber face closer to his own, caught the next wave's impetus, and was thrust forward.

The flippers made for a few awkward, scrambling moments, but finally he stood at Andy's feet, a menacing figure risen from the depths.

"Urgh—" he began, seeing Andy sit up.

The cold webbed hand clutching his ankle took him totally unawares. As his right foot was jerked back, he fell forward, almost atop Andy, who crabbed sideways just in time. He got his hands braced as he toppled, but his jaw still hit the stone, and things flickered briefly.

When he looked backward, half-dazed, he saw the figment of Professor Ramada's theorizing.

Over seven feet tall, humanoid, with gray-green, barnacled, pebble-textured skin, it reared over Andy.

Without thought, Piers tried to tackle it.

It hardly rocked as he hit it. Its ankles smelled fishy. It bent and lifted Piers effortlessly above its head.

A brilliant flash, a pained grunt, and Piers was falling. He heard a splash just before he hit the rock and had every cubic centimeter of air knocked out of him.

He came to seconds later, a beneficiary of Andy's tender ministrations. She held a camera by its strap and was hitting him repeatedly across the back. Each blow was accompanied by a word.

"You—" *Whack*!

"stupid—" *Whack*!

"frigging—" *Whack*!

"idiot!" *Whack*!

Piers turned painfully over, and she stopped. She sat back on her heels, her lovely haunches quivering with rage. Then she started to cry.

"Wha—" Piers croaked. "Whazzamatta?"

"You've ruined everything," Andy said furiously. "Weeks spent luring that thing here, wasted. Today might have been the day it finally emerged, so I could get a good picture of it and prove my father's theory."

Piers sat up. His body insisted that every bone was broken. "You gotta picture," he managed.

"Oh, yes," she said through sniffles. "A fine picture, with you looking so obviously fake. Everyone will think the real one is a hoax too. And take that frigging mask off."

Piers did so. Andy had ceased to sniffle.

"I love you," Piers said.

Andy smiled cruelly. "If you love me, then go bring that creature back."

Piers thought a minute. He began to crawl off the rock and into the waiting sea.

The hand on his ankle this time was warm and soft. Piers stopped and looked back.

Andy said, "What is your goddamn name anyhow?"

In my previous story collection, Strange Trades, I mentioned that I, like many writers, had an abortive series, or three, in my past. The two Blackwood Beach stories in this volume represent an early failed hope. I wrote two others—"Captain Jill" and "Billy Budd"—which never found a home. I had conceived of pacing the stories according to seasonal changes. "Rescuing Andy" represented summer, while the entry below occurs during autumn. The events of "Captain Jill"—involving the ghost of a female pirate—take place in winter, while springtime brings a strange vegetal birth in "Billy Budd." I had dreams of turning out another cycle of four, then being deluged with requests from book publishers to collect all eight in a handsome volume. Alas, like most of my fancies during this apprenticeship, the notion was charmingly daft. Magazine niches were tight, and unenlightened book publishers regarded short-story collections as if such tomes were lepers.

Almost simultaneously with the first appearance of these two stories, Charles Grant began editing a series of anthologies about a mysterious town named Greystone Bay. The predictable confusion between Grant's better-publicized town and mine drove the final nail in the coffin of my dreams.

But then again, who needs sales to be happy?

Oh, yes: any resemblance between the opening scene and the exploits of a certain Harry Potter has brought me no credit whatsoever.

Yellowing Bowers

The twins made the mistake of believing the teacher wasn't looking.

Jason and Medea Hedgecock were inseparable and incorrigible. Inside Miss Empson's sixth-grade classroom at Abial Tripp School, they sat side by side in the back row, dual whirlpools of fidgets, giggles, and provocations. Outside of school, they were often seen running through the twisty streets of Blackwood Beach, giving vent to the most bloodcurdling shrieks. Their father, a teacher of Greek at an out-of-town prep school, was utterly unable to control them. No help in their upbringing was forthcoming from their mother, who spent all her time in the caves along the shoreline, collecting bats.

Now the two were up to something particularly devious. They huddled together over a pattern of scratches incised in Jason's wooden desktop. The pattern seemed to glisten redly, as if traced in blood. The twins whispered a series of cacophonous names *sotto voce*, immense concentration plain on their pug-nosed features.

Every other child in the class saw what they were doing. Each boy and girl ached with a mixture of fright and delicious anticipation. Would they get away with it? Were they going too far? Why didn't Miss Empson stop them? Miss Empson had her back to the class. She stood at the board, chalking a series of dates on it. Her spiky black hair had a streak of fluorescent pink down the middle. She wore a leather skirt and tiger-print top. It was rumored that Miss Empson, although a native of Blackwood Beach, found her excitement in the strange city of Boston to the north. The class was amazed that someone in her thirties—who ought to creak as she walked—could reportedly dance till dawn and still teach the next day.

But perhaps she had overdone things last night. She didn't seem to be on her toes today. She had never let the Hedgecocks step so far out of bounds as they were threatening to do right now.

A small cloud had formed over the twins' heads. Their chant increased in urgency, if not volume. All their classmates were perched on the edge of their seats, tension pulling them erect as a blind man pulls the cord that snaps open his collapsible cane. Unwittingly, Miss Empson wrote on.

Just as Medea and Jason reached the peak of their spell, and two small clawed hands poked out of the cloud, and the other children drew in one long, shuddering, collective breath, Miss Empson whirled and uttered a loud shout like Bruce Lee cutting an opponent down to size:

"Aiii-yah!"

From the piece of chalk in her extended hand shot a bolt of dusty white force that smote the twins.

The cloud with its contents disappeared with a small implosion of air.

The class fell back in their seats with relief.

Jason and Medea Hedgecock remained frozen in their conspiratorial attitudes, their skin a marmoreal white. No breathing disturbed their temporary repose.

At least the class assumed it was temporary.

Shad Stillwell wiped a hand across his sweaty brow. Wow, that had been close. He had always told the twins that it didn't pay to mess with Miss Empson. Now maybe they'd reform. Although he doubted it.

Shad checked his watch. (He was very proud of the watch, a twelfth-birthday present from his parents, and found occasion to study it at least once every ten minutes.) Nearly 3:00. Would Miss Empson go ahead with their history lesson after all the commotion, or would she relent and let them out early?

Shad got his answer with Miss Empson's next words

"Perhaps now we can focus on academic matters. We were discussing Colonial America yesterday, and I thought that perhaps we would all relate a little better to that period if we considered the history of our own town.

"In 1636, Roger Williams, fleeing persecution in Massachusetts, founded Providence. Two years later, one of his followers, Augustus Blackwood, whose views were too liberal for Williams, fled in turn: He came south down the coast, accompanied by his own people, and founded Blackwood Beach.

"The names of many of these original settlers are immortalized today in our streets and parks and public buildings. Staghorn, Tripp, Goodnight—"

At the mention of the last name, all the children shivered as the image of ancient Welcome Goodnight floated to the tops of their minds like marsh gas in a swamp. Tony DiChristofaro made a warding sign, index and little finger extended with middle two clenched by thumb.

"Unfortunately, hardly any of these families survive to this day, a result of the Spotted Plague of the 1750s. A second wave of immigration occurred after the American Revolution, when Blackwood Beach was discovered by freebooters and smugglers, who conducted a flourishing trade in, uh—" Miss Empson turned away for a moment—"lambskin contraceptive devices. Only when, at the urging of Benjamin Franklin, whose libertine nature was well-known to his contemporaries, the young Congress legalized these, ahem, devices, did Blackwood Beach fade from notoriety."

At the conclusion of Miss Empson's last sentence, as if she had timed it, the bell rang. Miss Empson said, "That will be all for today, class. Dismissed."

The children rose in an orderly and subdued fashion from their seats and filed from the room.

Except, of course, the twins.

* * *

Shad kicked through the fallen leaves that lay in deep drifts along the brick sidewalks of the town. His normal way home after school each day took him in a meandering path along a good percentage of Blackwood Beach's streets. Shad's house stood on Tipstaff Lane, rather high up in the natural crescent-shaped depression that the town occupied. From any of his home's tall slate-roofed turrets, he could gaze down over much of the rest of the town and out to sea. But before going home, he made his daily survey of Blackwood Beach's familiar attractions.

Shad ambled down the short block, known as Dyers Street, where the ostentatiously refurbished Starkweather mansion loomed like a clapboard image of its stiff-necked owner. Once past Rackstraw's Market, he headed uphill along Maiden Street, passing the pit where the Broadbent home had once stood and the round-topped, celestial observatory of Professor Scrimshander. After stopping to talk with some friends, whom he found patting Ed Stout's three-legged dog, he continued up to the street that ran along the high lip of the half bowl containing most of the town.

Up on Lower Avenue, he turned right at the neighboring houses of Mr. Seuss and Major Flood, then past the perpetually empty lot the kids called "the Burial Grounds"—although who or what resided there, they could not have said.

At last, Shad reached the Gully, one of his favorite spots.

The Gully was a deep crevasse through which ran a cold, swift, narrow river that eventually spilled over a cliff to drop in a spectacular fall, meeting the sea below in a frothing pool. Lower Avenue continued over it, carried by a cast-iron bridge decorated with leering faces.

Shad left the road by the side of the bridge and scrambled down the bank of the crevasse, dirtying both his jeans and hands. Down at the bottom, among the willows, birches, and poplars that filled the Gully, he stopped by the bank of the stream and scooped up a handful of stones, which he shied one at a time into the surging water.

Shad always felt happy and safe in the Gully. Not that he didn't feel that way at home. His parents were good sorts, as parents went. They gave him care, affection, and almost anything for which he asked. And school was okay, too. (Certain inexplicable feelings about Miss Empson's legs sometimes disturbed him, but he supposed they would disappear in time.) But the Gully was somewhere special. The clean tang of running water in the air, the thick carpet of mold and duff on the ground, the summertime canopy of leaves that shielded one from the outside world—these were vital, important things, good, Shad knew instinctively, for one's soul.

Now it was autumn, however, early November, and hardly any leaves remained, imparting a spectral feeling to the ravine. Birds' nests, formerly concealed, were now visible through the exposed skeletons of the trees, and at night, one could pretend the full moon was a small pearl, close at hand, caught in an aptly positioned crook.

Shad considered one tree in particular. A tall willow overhanging the river, it still possessed a full cape of incredibly sere leaves that clung somehow to the desiccated branches, rattling with each gust of air. Shad knew that willows, with their deep roots, often kept their leaves longer than other trees. But this tree was unique even among its nearby cousins.

Curious, Shad ambled over to study it.

Almost within the perimeter of the hanging withy branches, Shad halted.

A man was there.

Shad sucked in a sharp breath.

The man was only about as tall as Shad. He stood with his back pressed against the willow's bark, his right hand hidden. He had long hair and a beard of that yellowish-white-with-age color. His nose was crooked; his eyes shadowed. He wore a dirty old cardigan with a checked pattern, faded flannel shirt, musty wool pants, and broken-down work shoes.

Some bum, thought Shad. Harmless, he hoped.

The man saw Shad. He lifted an imploring hand toward the boy and moved away from the willow, as if to leave. It was then that Shad noticed the man's right hand was caught inside the tree, as if it had become wedged in a squirrel hole, preventing his escape. Shad felt sympathy for the bum, but also a certain inexplicable reluctance to go to his aid.

Yet despite himself, almost will-lessly, Shad stepped forward, entering the whispery circle of the willow's yellow leaves. Cautiously, he raised his hand to touch the man's outstretched fingers.

When his hand met the man's, his watch exploded with stinging force, the man tightened his fingers, and Shad fell backward, yanking the man with him, accompanied by a loud *pop!* as the tree freed its captive. They rolled a few feet together on the moist ground.

In seconds, they had untangled themselves and stood. Shad dug out a handkerchief and tightened it around his bleeding wrist. He looked back at the willow to see what, if anything, the man had been searching for inside its trunk.

There was no hole anywhere in the trunk.

"Wow," Shad said nervously, not knowing what else to say. "Guess the battery in my watch was defective. You okay, mister?"

The man said nothing, but merely nodded, regarding Shad with eyes as black as space. Shad found himself losing his unease. Despite the bum's odd silence, his unthreatening nature seemed evident in his slack stance and dangling arms.

"Say, what's your name, mister? Mine's Shad." He didn't offer to shake, considering they had, after a fashion, done so already.

The man remained speechless.

Suddenly Shad was reminded of something they had read in class a couple of weeks ago. A poem by Tennyson, it began:

> *A spirit haunts the year's last hours,*
> *Dwelling amid these yellowing bowers.*

Somehow it seemed to fit this stranger. Perhaps, if he wouldn't divulge his real name, he wouldn't mind Shad picking one for him.

"Suppose I call you Mr. Bowers?" Shad ventured.

Without actually smiling, the man conveyed approval.

"Okay, then, Mr. Bowers. Nice to meet you. But I have to be going now. Maybe if you're still here tomorrow, I'll see you again."

Shad turned and began to walk away. He reached a point about ten feet from Mr. Bowers—and suddenly hit an invisible barrier. It felt like falling into cotton candy, or treading ankle-deep in sticky taffy. No effort of his could penetrate it.

Mr. Bowers took a step forward. Shad found he could advance a step further.

Oh, Jesus, Shad thought. *What had he got himself into?*

He turned to the unspeaking, stony-faced man behind him. No help there.

Shad's mother had always said, "Try to make the best of a bad situation."

"How," said Shad, "would you like to come home for supper, Mr. Bowers?"

* * *

The hand lacked a finger. Where it had been was a blunt

pad of scar tissue. It was not a scary hand, but rather one with character. It was thick with calluses, and ingrained in its folds lay white powder like a permanent coat of talcum. The missing finger was the little one. The other four seemed competent enough to cope by themselves, yet there was an ineffable sadness about them, too, as if they indeed missed their brother.

Shad concentrated on his father's hand so that he would not have to look him in the eye. Granted eye contact, his father could always tell when he was lying. Of course, if he was denied eye contact, he could make a pretty good guess that Shad was lying. But he couldn't be sure.

And considering the enormity of his lies, Shad wanted that little edge.

Sam and Carol Stillwell sat at the table with Shad and Mr. Bowers. Supper that night had been meatloaf, mashed potatoes, and lima beans. No one had enjoyed it, except perhaps Mr. Bowers—but of this, they could not be sure. Shad was too nervous, and his parents too intrigued by their guest, to think of food. And the reason no one was certain of Mr. Bowers' enjoyment was that he had not precisely eaten his meal. He had laid his two crabbed hands on either side of the plate. The food had undergone a mysterious process that looked suspiciously like accelerated decay, soon disappearing completely. The plate—part of Carol's good set—had been left a cracked and worn thing, resembling some artifact just excavated from Nineveh.

Now the two elder Stillwells were studying Mr. Bowers. Often warned by his parents not to bring home any of the more obviously supernatural denizens of Blackwood Beach, Shad had been forced to lie. Shad knew they would never forgive him for freeing a spirit who, in hindsight, anyone could have seen was plainly bound to a tree. (He was still smarting from the ruckus he'd caused when he'd dragged home a talking cat that had turned out to be Welcome Goodnight's familiar.)

What he had told his parents, this time, was that he had seen a harmless old man soliciting passersby in the square downtown—a patently nonsupernatural beggar who'd displayed one of those little cards that said, I AM A DEAF-MUTE. PLEASE HELP IN ANY WAY YOU CAN. THANK YOU. MISTER BOWERS. This card had subsequently been taken by a sudden gust of wind and lost down a sewer. Shad did not explain that he appeared to be permanently linked to Mr. Bowers. Instead, he simply said that he felt obligated to help shelter such a helpless old man, and could he please stay for a couple of nights, Dad?

Sam Stillwell considered the request. He was basically a simple man. He worked in the limestone quarry outside of town. The quarry had long ago claimed his finger and his heart. Something about mining the detritus of the age of dinosaurs touched the romantic in him. His leisure time was spent fishing. (Only over Carol's protests had their son been christened Shad.)

But Sam Stillwell was also a lifelong resident of Blackwood Beach. Confronted with this bizarre figure brought home by his son, he sensed that the matter should not be pushed to a head by too-precipitous action. Better let it develop awhile longer. Strange forces were still building and massing. Mr. Bowers radiated a sense of purpose and resolve, a questing alertness, as if something or someone in Blackwood Beach had drawn him from illimitable distances.

Sam cleared his throat. It wouldn't do to look like too much of a soft touch on this matter, though. "It's a big responsibility to insert yourself into the life of another person, Shad. I want you to realize that, son, before we go any further."

"Oh, I know, Dad, I know," said Shad, as he thought of the invisible ties that bound him to Mr. Bowers.

"All right, then. With that in mind, and as long as your mother agrees, I give my provisional permission for your friend to stay as long as he wants."

"It's fine with me," Carol said, a small smile hovering lightly over her lips. Shad thought with relief that his mother never looked so beautiful or his father so noble.

"That's great, Dad. Can he have the room next to mine?"

Shad prayed that if he moved his bed next to the common wall, he could just remain within the sphere that enclosed him and Mr. Bowers.

"Sure," Sam said.

Shad rose, and so did Mr. Bowers. The chair in which the old man had been sitting quietly collapsed into a heap of dust.

Sam and Carol pretended not to notice to spare Shad further embarrassment.

Shad hurried off, Mr. Bowers at his heels.

* * *

The next morning, at breakfast (Carol served Mr. Bowers on a paper plate, and he sat on a primitive stool hastily cobbled together the previous night out of scrap wood), Sam was too incensed by a certain news item in that day's copy of the *Blackwood Beach Intelligencer* to think any more about their guest.

"Have you read the social column, Carrie?" he demanded of Shad's mother.

Shad watched the interplay between his parents with interest. Anything that promised to divert attention from Mr. Bowers was welcome.

"No," Carol replied. "Is it that Starkweather woman again?"

"Yes. Listen to this: 'Amanda Starkweather has announced the formation of the Blackwood Beach Improvement Society. She will be temporarily acting as chairperson, until elections can be held. The first item on their agenda, she told our reporter, will be attempting to convince the town council to tear down the old gazebo by the beach and replace it with a modern pavilion.'"

Sam tossed the paper down in disgust. "God damn it!" he yelled.

Amanda Starkweather raised that kind of feeling.

The woman was a newcomer to Blackwood Beach. She had inherited a house on Dyers Street when the last of the Blackwood Starkweathers passed away. Originally, she had lived in Boston. A tall, imperious woman, she dressed in severe blouses, plaid skirts, and brown loafers. She was never seen without her capacious Louis Vuitton handbag, which, rumor had it, contained mothballs and cans of aerosol antiseptic used to enforce her rigorous standards of cleanliness. Her two children attended the prep school at which Mr. Hedgecock taught.

Her husband was dead—some said of aggravation and spite, others of despair.

"Doesn't she understand the first thing about Blackwood Beach?" Sam demanded. "We're not interested in 'improvement.' We like our town run-down and sleepy. It has more character that way. You mark my words, she's messing with things that are bigger than her, and they'll have their way in the end."

* * *

Shad never before appreciated how lies tended to multiply and assume a life of their own. Whereas most information was subject to entropy, degrading and losing strength over time, lies seemed immune to such decay, instead spreading and growing in complexity and subtlety.

At school, he had been constrained by pride to formulate an entirely different set of lies from the ones he had told his parents. He couldn't have his friends think he liked dragging some old bum around, or that he had been so foolish as to become bonded to an inhuman spirit.

So instead he had told them that Mr. Bowers was his father's older, demented cousin, and that he was responsible for keeping tabs on him while his parents worked. He had even forged a note to Miss Empson from his mother, asking that Mr. Bowers be allowed to sit with him. Miss Empson, with a knowing tolerance, consented.

Now his head spun with a welter of fact and fiction.

The day dragged by like molasses through a funnel in Antarctica. The rest of the class eyed him curiously between lessons. At recess, Shad was forced to stand by himself with Mr. Bowers, not daring to run and perhaps come up short on the unseen tether. Luckily, Mr. Bowers sat complacently at the back of the classroom in the afternoon, next to the immobile figures of the Hedgecock twins, and made no fuss, save for consuming a box of Ticonderoga No. 2 pencils and two jars of paste.

At last the 3:00 bell rang, and Shad was free. He knew just where he was going, too—to Professor Scrimshander's, for some much-needed advice.

Out of the schoolyard, into Rackstraw's for a candy bar, past the statue inscribed C.D. WARD, and down Dyers Street in a shortcut to Maiden, where Scrimshander's observatory-cum-home stood.

On Dyers, Shad paused a moment in front of a large, many-gabled, three-story, Victorian house—the Starkweather mansion. Painted in bright, San Francisco pastels, it stood out from its decrepit neighbors. A broad, green lawn, immaculately raked and trimmed, contrasted starkly with the weedy lots on either side. The glass in the mansion sparkled like an ad for Windex. The whole assemblage was a bastion of order and enforced harmony.

Eating his Three Musketeers, Shad regarded the Stark-weather home in the light of his father's tirade. What was she trying to achieve, anyway? Didn't she like the town as it was? If not, then why had she moved here?

Some people just couldn't stand anything or anyone being not what they themselves wanted them to be, he guessed.

As Shad watched, the front door opened. Onto the wide porch that wrapped around the house stepped Amanda Starkweather. Her stiff skirt resisted the light breeze like sheet metal. She folded her arms across her chest and directed a biting gaze toward Shad.

"Don't toss that wrapper on my lawn," she called, "you nasty, dirty boy."

Then, from her omnipresent purse, she whipped forth a can of Lysol and sent a cloud of pungent spray billowing across the cut grass.

For a moment, Shad's wounded innocence made him forget completely about Mr. Bowers.

Then he felt the tug of the old man's forward motion.

Mr. Bowers had started up the lawn toward Amanda. He labored now at the limit of his leash, straining after the woman as if compelled by something stronger even than fate.

Shad felt Mr. Bowers' strength begin to drag him along. The cotton-candy border of their mutual envelope pushed against his back as Mr. Bowers steadily advanced. Shad dug his heels into the creviced brick sidewalk, knowing with utter certainty that he could not allow the old man to touch Mrs. Starkweather.

Shad's efforts were useless. Mr. Bowers pulled him forward inch by inch.

Frantically, Shad looked over his shoulder for help. There was no one nearby. Then he saw the street lamp.

Hurling himself backward with all his strength, he toppled, feeling his fingers graze the iron pole. Desperately he scrabbled his grip tighter, till he held it firmly.

Now Mr. Bowers must be straining with all his desire. Shad felt as if his arms would part company with his body at the shoulders. Or would the elbows give out first?

From up the lawn came the hurried slam of a door. Suddenly the strain was gone.

Shad stood, shaking. Mr. Bowers looked longingly at the empty porch, but made no move toward it.

Rubbing one sore arm, Shad sought to view the whole incident scientifically.

Here was one more datum for Professor Scrimshander.

* * *

Blazing galaxies pinwheeled in space, coruscating red, blue, yellow, and white. Gaseous nebulae expanded like octopi, engulfing whole civilizations over millennia. Black holes gulped down hapless cosmic wanderers, stretching them to infinite lengths.

Professor Scrimshander snapped off the monitor like a dissatisfied god. Shad shook his head, the spell exerted by the display broken without warning.

"Those idiots at NASA," the Professor complained. "They never look at anything interesting. I'm afraid I'm going to have take matters into my own hands pretty soon."

"You mean," asked Shad, "that you're going to try to direct the Hubble Telescope, instead of just tapping its telemetry?"

"It might come to that," Scrimshander agreed.

The Professor rose from his chair. Over six feet tall, he suffered from a stooped back that brought his head down almost six inches, thrust forward in an aggressive way belied by his normally mild demeanor. His large nose cleaved the air before him like some sort of remote probe. Thick eyebrows frequently shot skyward. At home, he wore a distressed lab coat over a set of red thermal underwear.

Scrimshander was the science teacher at Abial Tripp Elementary. His subject matter was wide-ranging and calculated to entice.

"So," Scrimshander said, nearing Mr. Bowers, who sat quietly atop a packing crate labeled ONE (1) DEAN DRIVE— ALL ENDS UP. "This is your problem, my lad? Let's see what sort of information we can get from him."

Scrimshander drew two wires from a metered device and hooked them to Mr. Bowers' forehead. The old being made no resistance. Flicking several switches on, Scrimshander watched the machine's dials.

All the needles swung to the far left and wrapped themselves several times around the stop posts. Smoke began to pour from the cabinet.

Shad watched in dismay. What could it mean?

Scratching his head, Scrimshander proceeded to run several more tests. At last, he appeared ready to give an opinion.

"My boy, this creature is composed of sheer entropy."

Shad studied Mr. Bowers, sitting in his shabby sweater and shapeless pants. He knew all about entropy, of course. The Professor had had the class read *The Crying of Lot 49* last semester. Everyone had enjoyed it, and they were all dutifully working on *Gravity's Rainbow* now. But could such a potent principle actually be embodied in this almost pathetic figure with its depthless black eyes?

Shad recalled Mr. Bowers' way with food and chairs, and thought it just might be true.

"I have," continued Scrimshander, "been anticipating a disturbance of some sort for the past few weeks. My entropy localizer—" here the Professor gave an affectionate pat to a gadget resembling the offspring of a blow-dryer and electric toothbrush—"has registered immense fluxes and spasm in the transubstantial etheric plenum lately. I was recently able to narrow the focus to the Gully off Lower Avenue. Evidently the precise locus was that strange willow of which you spoke. When you released this fellow from that tree, you crystallized the accumulating disorder that had been seeking entry into our universe. As the catalyst in the reaction, I regret to say, you are joined with him in sympathetic bondage. Just be glad he can apparently control his entropic powers to affect only that which he deems deserving of destruction."

The explanation, instead of relieving Shad, distressed him further. How could he ever get rid of this thing? Would he be saddled all his life with him? He had an abrupt image of himself grown old, shuffling along with Mr. Bowers beside him, an unearthly twin.

"What am I gonna do?" Shad wailed. "I don't want him anymore." An inspiration struck him. "Mrs. Starkweather—he seemed to be attracted to her. Let her have him."

Shad got to his feet, as if to rush out. The Professor laid a restraining hand on his shoulder.

"They can never meet, Shad. It's obvious why Bowers is drawn to her. It's the tug of opposites. She is pure order, discipline, negentropy. If they were ever to come face to face . . . the consequences would be unpredictable."

Shad relaxed his taut muscles. So—he was doomed. No normal life was foreseeable.

He wondered why he couldn't have been born someplace prosaic and sane.

Beirut, maybe. Iraq or Iran.

Even Boston.

* * *

His mother didn't mind losing that vase. Or the chaise lounge handed down from Mother Stillwell. At least she claimed she didn't. And that hole in the wall between Shad's room and Mr. Bowers'—well, as his father said, plaster was cheap.

Shad had told his parents nothing of what Professor Scrimshander had deduced about Mr. Bowers, and their patience was obviously wearing a bit thin. Though they didn't want to discourage the boy's natural sympathy for those less fortunate, and though they suspected there was much more to the whole affair than appeared on the surface, both Sam and Carol were beginning to get just a little bit weary of Mr. Bowers.

Shad knew this. How the hell did they think *he* felt? At least they were free for eight hours a day. He had to contend with this curse and burden every minute.

Weeks had passed. It was the day before Thanksgiving. Shad felt as if he'd been bound to Mr. Bowers for a year. His concentration at school had fallen precipitously, and with it his grades. Miss Empson appeared sympathetic, but there was nothing she could do. A tentative bolt from her stick of chalk, directed at Mr. Bowers after school at Shad's request, had had no effect other than to increase the luminosity of his black, energy-sucking eyes. Shad, having run out of ideas, now contemplated suicide. He envisioned tossing himself off the Lower Avenue Bridge into the Gully, where this whole mess had started. But the vision always ended with him suspended in midair, Mr. Bowers back on the bridge, arresting his plunge.

School was out till the Monday after the holiday, and Shad sat at home, watching his mother cook for the communal meal tomorrow. Each Thanksgiving, the residents of Blackwood Beach gathered on the Common in a festive mood and recreated the original meal. Normally, Shad looked forward to the event, but not this year.

Besides, how could he attend if Amanda Starkweather was there also? Too dangerous. He'd have to feign sickness.

That night, with the aid of a lit match held near the thermometer, Shad registered a high fever. His mock groans would have won him all the drama awards at school. In the morning he said he felt better, but not good enough to accompany his parents. After some convincing, they left him alone.

Alone save for Bowers, who sat still beside him, though with an aura of repressed energy.

Shad kept his resolve till about one in the afternoon. Then he began to feel sorry for himself. His stomach was rumbling, and the cold plate of food his mother had left looked totally unappetizing. Why should he be forced to eat this lonely meal seasoned with tears? He hadn't done anything wrong. It felt awful to be confined to bed in one's pajamas on such a beautiful day, when one wasn't even sick. And why was he so solicitous of such a mean and stubborn woman as the matron of Dyers Street? Let Amanda Starkweather watch out for her own damn hide!

Dressing quickly, Shad called for Mr. Bowers through the hole in the wall. The ancient being shuffled through, and together they set out for the Common.

A fringe of trees surrounded the open plot of land, where the settlers' sheep had once grazed. Hidden behind one wide bole, Shad peered out.

The inhabitants of Blackwood Beach celebrated Thanksgiving on November 26, regardless of whether it

was the fourth Thursday of November or not, in keeping
with George Washington's original proclamation. Also, they
dressed in costume, not of the Pilgrims, but of the first
President's contemporaries.

Memories were long in Blackwood Beach.

Tables surrounded by turkey-stuffed Blackwooders
occupied the middle of the lawn. A mild autumn sun shone
down. Where were his parents? Ah, off to the left there.
And Amanda Starkweather? Her loud, nasal, Brahmin voice
helped him spot her in the crowd. Clutching her leaden, can-
filled bag across her chest like a shield, she was discoursing
to a group of people who seemed fascinated by her alien
brazenness.

"And once that horrid shack by the waterfront is torn
down, we'll have the finest seaside pavilion between here
and Newport."

To emphasize her point, she withdrew an aerosol in-
secticide from her purse and unerringly shot dead the last
moth of summer.

Shad plotted a course to the turkey that would swing
wide of her. He set out across the grass.

As soon as he left the trees, he knew he had made a
mistake.

Mr. Bowers began to make a beeline for the Starkweather woman. Shad tried to change direction, but it was
impossible. And now there was nothing to hold on to.

Shad began to shout. "Help! Help! Everyone watch out!
Murder!"

All heads turned toward him. Amanda Starkweather
stopped in the middle of her peroration, seeing and knowing her doom. She turned to flee, but was blocked by the
line of tables.

Shad threw himself to the ground and dug his fingers

into the moist earth. No use. Mr. Bowers was unstoppable now.

The sight of the boy being dragged feet first by an invisible force across the lawn caused the crowd to scatter in alarm. For a moment, Amanda Starkweather stood transfixed, as if realizing that it was too late for her. To give her credit, everyone later admitted, she recovered from her paralysis long enough to swat the unstoppable Bowers with her heavy bag of sprays as soon as he came within reach. But although she connected with the might of a Monty-Python matron, the purse merely disintegrated.

In the next second, Mr. Bowers closed with her, enfolded her in his arms—

—and the sky was lit with the actinic light of their explosive embrace.

Shad's ears rang and his head swam. He couldn't see a thing, and he seemed to be floating as free as a bird. Was he dead? No! It was only that the sticky pull of Bowers was gone. Further evidence of life was the testament of his still-empty belly. He sat up, his vision gradually returning.

The steaming crater stopped half an inch from his feet. It appeared to descend at least halfway to the center of the earth.

His parents reached Shad first. He could see their lips asking if he was okay, but heard no sounds. He didn't care. He was free, free! No more Mr. Bowers! Only one important issue remained to be settled.

"Is there any cranberry sauce left?"

Here's an early attempt of mine to forge the hipster/pop-culture-saturated style that I would later employ in my novel, Ciphers. *Lots of silly misspellings and capitalizations and ungrammatical locutions, as well as song allusions and irreverent banter, a kind of sub-Pynchonian ironic street-speech. This affected style can grate or charm, sometimes within the same story. I hope the ratio of irritation to amusement here is weighted toward the latter.*

When I told my friend Charles Platt about the premise of this story, he asked me why it was necessary for two *ghosts to inhabit the drum machine. Wouldn't one have been sufficient? At the time, I had no ready answer for Charles, but nowadays, I'd merely quote ol' Billy Blake, about the road to wisdom running through the neighborhood of excess.*

The Moon-Bonham Effect

Skeezix Smash, born little Jimmie van Vleet during the Summer of Love, to Plain Folks who lived in a suburb of a suburb of a tentacle of Boston, until recently a retiring, albeit brilliant student at the Berklee School of Music, now simultaneously drummer, guitarist, keyboard player, singer, programmer, mixer, producer—in fact, sole member—of the immensely popular synth band known as Monkey Funk (which boasted two successive Number One Hits from their debut album: "Digital Thang" and "Baby Wears PVC"), had a Big Problem.

His favorite tool—his uniquely configured, irreplaceable, multi-boarded, hard-wired drum machine—was possessed.

It made his skin crawl like Coke Bugs just to think of it. Lately, whenever anyone asked him about his problem, he felt like screaming.

"Hey, Skeezer," said Harry "Hungry" Hartz, entering the studio. "How's the drum machine?"

"*Yow-wow-wow-wow-uhnh-uhnh-uhnh-uhnh-arr-arr-arr-arrooooo!*"

Hartz, wearing his traditional mohair suit and electric boots, sat himself unconcernedly down. He removed a banana from his hairy jacket pocket, peeled it leisurely, put the skin back in his pocket, took a bite of the banana, and began to chew.

"Am I to understand it's not fixed yet?"

Skeezix held his head in his hands. Wow, what a Mental Surge! They should make some kinda Suppressor for that. Felt like his cranium was gonna explode just then . . . . He was All Better Now, yeah . . . . Take it calmly boy.

"No, it is not fixed yet. It still will not accept any new programming. I have had every chip and wire replaced—except those parts that no one understands, which the Wandering Brujo Man installed. I have wiped its memory cleaner than a baby's powdered asshole a dozen times. I have hooked it up to twenty different speakers. I have kissed it, cursed it, and prayed to it. And it still will not perform as it should—as it once did. I am planning my imminent retirement from this business, before I reach Heartbreak City."

Hartz finished his snack and licked his fingers, before wiping them on his pants. "It can't be that bad, man. Won't it play anything?"

Skeezix laughed violently, his Krazy Kackles sounding more like Tina Turner's sobs than any expression of humor. "Oh, no, it plays all right—but only what it wants. Just listen."

Stabbing a button on the guilty machine with a rigid forefinger, Skeezix gestured for Hartz to pay attention.

From the speakers connected to the drum machine issued a three-minute storm of snares, traps, and cymbals, ending abruptly. When the machine had ceased playing, Skeezix eyed Hartz significantly.

"Boy," Hartz said, "was that hokey! Real moldy-oldy. Sounded kinda like Ginger Baker circa Cream or sumpin'. Not like your stuff at all."

"Tell me about it. Now watch. No obvious reprogramming, but it should play some different riffs."

A second poke, and the machine vented another elaborate sequence.

"I recognize that!" exclaimed Hartz. "It's something by Led Zep."

"Could be," agreed Skeezix. "I am not too keen on that ancient crap. All I know is, it is nothing I programmed."

"Where's it coming from then?"

"I do not give a shit about where it comes from. All I know is that I have a second album due next year, and I can not work on any new songs without my trusty drum machine. How am I going to recapture the sound of 'Lonely Pinhead' if my drum part sounds like 'Stairway To Heaven?'"

"You can't buy another?"

"This one's special, a Korg DDD5, modified up the kazoo, by me and others. Extradimensional sampling, quantum-drift correction, pan-African Juju talking drum effects—"

"Okay, okay, I get the picture. What about hiring a real drummer?"

Skeezix stared at Hartz with Googly Eyes. Hartz grew alarmed. His youthful friend's naturally thin face was becoming blood-engorged and swelling, like that of an ancient mating bullfrog. Skeezix opened his mouth once, twice, thrice, trying to utter a sound. Nothing emerged. Hartz stood, frantic. He looked desperately around the recording studio. A pitcher and tumblers stood on a table. Hartz ran for the carafe, grabbed it, scooted back to the choking Skeezix, grabbed him by his shag cut, tipped his head back, poured half the contents of the pitcher down his throat, and then dumped the rest over his head, completely soaking his T-shirt and jeans.

Skeezix blew a mouthful of orange liquid out. The treatment seemed somewhat to have alleviated Skeezix's symptoms of distress. Pushing the wet hair out of his eyes, he seemed to have regained The Power of Speech.

"Harry, you moron! That was a pitcher of Tequila Sunrise. Why did you do it?"

"You needed it, man. You were asphyxiating."

"And why should I not be, after what you said?"

"What was that?"

As if each word were something awful tasting—a doggie-chew, say that had somehow materialized in his mouth, Skeezix spat them out. "A. Real. Drummer."

"What's so bad about that? It might do you good to work with someone besides yourself for a change. Give you a different creative slant on things. I betcha Phil Collins would jump at the chance—"

Skeezix picked up a box of Kleenex and began dabbing at his clothes and face, trying vainly to cleanse himself of Sticky Mixed Drink. "I do not wish to work with another—another *person*. That is the Old Way. Other persons do not follow my orders, nor do they deliver the perfection I demand." The tissues had begun to disintegrate under the unwonted treatment, and Skeezix looked down to find himself spotted with bits of wet Floral Prints, like a Giant Shaving Cut. He tried to pick off tissue without much success.

"There's some on the end of your nose too," Hartz helpfully offered.

"Shut up. Listen, what am I going to do?"

Hartz thought. "Try building an exact duplicate of your old machine with all new parts—?"

"Okay," said Skeezix excitedly. "Now you are onto something. I will begin immediately."

Two weeks later, Skeezix summoned Hartz for the first trial of the new drum machine.

Expectantly, they gathered around.

Skeezix pushed the PLAY button.

The machine delivered the "mouth percussion" part from John Mayall's "Room To Move."

"This is even worse than the original problem!" lamented Skeezix. He launched an angry kick at the substitute machine, cracking its readouts. Then he began to cry.

Hartz placed an arm over the young pop star's shoulder.

"Skeezix, my lad."

"Snrgh?" snuffled Skeezix.

"There is only one recourse."

"You don't mean—"

"Yes, I'm afraid so."

"Not him—"

"Yes, Skeezix, yes. Him."

"Not that madman—"

"Yes, that madman. Doctor—"

"Oh my God!"

"—Silicon!"

* * *

Dr. Silicon lived and worked in an abandoned meat-packing plant. The cavernous interior retained its overhead system of hooks and tracks. Only now, from where raw, bloody fat-striped slabs of beef once used to hang, there depended various keyboards, empty plastic cases, naked CRT's, reels of magnetic tape, floppies spiked through their center holes, disk drives, add-on boards, printers, plotters, and other assorted digital components, all within easy reach of the Doctor's questing hands. Interlaced with this Damoclean Debris were many coaxial and fiberoptic lines, snaking in long caternaries like Jungle Lianas.

Naturally, all this overhead clutter cut down considerably on the ambient light that issued from the scattered fluorescents mounted on the hidden ceiling. The resultant illumination level approximated a twilight dotted with the amber/green fireflies of the active displays.

The vast room was filled with a mingled scent of electricity and ancient animal blood, the latter scent seeming to emanate from the faded stains on the mottled concrete floor. These brown blots were visible only in the narrow alleys formed by stacks of cartons and crates. This peculiar mixture of smells had been known to cause visitors to run gagging from Dr. Silicon's lair.

Not our two Stalwart Friends, tho, who were determined to be heroes, if just for one day.

A door creaked open. Sneakers slapped concrete. The unseen door thudded shut with a dull resonance. Muffled voices filtered into Silicon's Sanctum were automatically sampled, digitized, algorithmically distorted, and then played back as warped echoes.

From around a tall pile of boxes tentatively stepped Skeezix and Hartz.

"I do not like this, Harry," declaimed Skeezix. "In all my admittedly short yet meteoric career, I have avoided dealing with the Doctor as much as possible."

Hartz removed a Twinkie from his pocket and began to unwrap it. The crinkle of the cellophane was fed back by the Doctor's machines as alien thunder. Hartz replaced the empty wrapper in his pocket.

"Skeezer, relax. The Doc ain't such a bad sort. I've had

dealings with him before. He supplied us the lasers for our light show, remember?"

"They punched a hole in the auditorium roof."

"That was my fault. Too much power."

"I just am not comfortable with someone who is not fully human."

"The Doc's history is a sad one, Skeezix. You gotta take that into account."

"Who knows what percentage of the Doctor is still mortal by now? Why does he keep replacing his various parts anyway?"

Hartz spoke around mouthfuls of Fluffy Kake with Kreamy Filling. "It all began after his failed love affair with Jean Djinni. First she blinded him with science, then made him cry 96 tears. When she djilted him, he began to prune away the parts that had betrayed him, starting with his heart. The Doc's been running on a Jarvik-100 for years now. You can really empathize when you know the background . . . "

"I am not convinced. And another thing: why does he keep all this junk around?"

Skeezix and Hartz had stopped by a jumble of beige plastic cases topped with dust covers. Skeezix laid a hand on the stack to indicate the junk whereof he spoke.

"Yeow!"

The stack had stirred beneath Skeezix's hand and now stood up, revealing itself to be Dr. Silicon.

The Doctor had short fiberoptic threads for hair, each tipped with a bead of light. His eyes were concealed by over-sized square spectacles, whose lenses were twin diffraction gratings. His skin seemed waxen. Clad in a boxy injection-molded suit, he wore a dust cover across his shoulders like a mantle, and one around his waist like a skirt.

"Hello, boys," synthesized the Doc. His lips did not

move as he spoke, and his voice emanated from a speaker at sternum-level.

"Hu-hu-hullo, Doctor. How-how-how are you?"

"Fine, fine, I was just off-line and juicing up. Allow me to unplug, and I'll be free to give you my undivided attention."

The Doctor reached down to a wall socket and yanked out a power line that led to his left armpit. A take-up reel quickly sucked the cord back into the Doc.

"There, that's that. Now, what can I do for you two?"

"Harry, the machine."

Hartz handed over to Skeezix the recalcitrant original drum machine, which he had been carrying slung in a pack over one shoulder.

"Doctor, this is my pride and joy, an essential part of my success and—dare I dignify it with such a term—my art. It is fucked-up. I need you to put it right."

Silicon received the machine with appropriate respect. "An attractive device. I sense a certain headstrong complexity in its circuits . . . . Gentleman, let us adjourn to my study, where I can devote myself to this capricious little gadget."

The trio set out for a distant corner of the warehouse, which was isolated from the rest of the interior by chin-high, office-style partitions. The space thus cordoned off held a refrigerator (on which was taped a picture of an IBM 370 labeled MOM); a physician's examining table with crinkly tissue feeding over it from a roller mounted at the head; and a couple of chairs seemingly rescued from a junk heap, all scattered across a dirty rug.

Dr. Silicon set the drum machine down on the examining table. He unzipped its case and removed it.

"Make yourself at home, boys, whil e I hook this little lady up to a power source."

Skeezix sat down uneasily. Hartz moved to the refrigerator.

"Hey, Doc, there's nothing in here but some kinda goop. Whadda ya expect to serve your guests?"

Dr. Silicon's voice emerged from beneath the table, where he had crawled in search of an outlet. "That is my amino-acid concentrate. One hundred percent life-supporting. At least to one in my state. You're welcome to try some."

"I believe I'll just lick this Twinkie wrapper . . . "

The Doc emerged from beneath the table. He hovered over the drum machine, whose ruby power light now glowed. "Ah, my pretty baby, let's get a look at those boards of yours . . . " Silicon cracked the case. "What's this . . . ? Quantum-drift correction . . . Nth-dimensional tuner . . . Hybrid patches . . . Hmmmm . . . " Silicon looked up at Skeezix, who flinched from his rainbowed gaze. "You've really built yourself a stacked babe here, son. A regular prima donna, more skittish than a thoroughbred race horse. No wonder she's giving you grief."

"Gee, Doctor, she has never acted up before."

"These women are temperamental, son. Well, I've learned all I can from a visual examination. It's time for the probe."

So saying, the Doctor climbed on the examining table with the drum machine. Kneeling before the helpless device, he opened a door in his crotch. He reached in and, with a series of clicks, pulled out a telescoping phallic rod whose end bristled with sensors like a French Tickler.

"Oh my Christ," said Skeezix. "I can't watch this!"

"Buck up, Skeezer," said Hartz, laying a hand on his buddy's shoulder. "The Doc has his ways."

"Yes, but he is going to have his way with my poor liddle drum machine!"

"Where is the MIDI port on this sweet darling . . . ? Don't be shy, girl. Ah, there it is. Open up for papa, baby. Ahhhhh!"

"This is awful!" wailed Skeezix. "I really can't look anymore."

So he didn't.

From the Doctor's chest speaker now poured forth a bizarre series of crackles and static, like an overloaded transformer: "Zzzrt. Krzkk. Bzzz. Pzzzt." The sounds allowed Skeezix to imagine all too well what dreadful prongings his drum machine was undergoing.

At last the horrid noises culminated in a satisfied guttural exclamation, then ceased. Skeezix dared to look up.

The Doctor had climbed off the table. His lips still remained stolidly composed. He had retracted his Penile Probe and was shutting his hatch. A trickle of oil ran down one plastic-encased leg.

"That's some hot semiconductor chippie you've got there, son. You should treat her right."

"I do! It is her—I mean it—that has let *me* down."

"It's not her fault, Mr. Smash. You see, all those circuits you've added have created a synergistic effect. You now have—A Ghost In The Machine!"

"What am I going to do?"

"I'm afraid it's outside my domain. You've passed from physics to metaphysics. There's only one man who might help you now."

"And that is—?"

"The Hoodoo Guru!"

* * *

De Hoodoo Guru, he got no shoes. He count by ones, and he count by twos. He say: "One and one and one is three." Got to be good lookin' cuz he's so hard to see. He come from the south, down Jamaica way. Maybe Haiti, me no can say. An Exiled King, he is here to stay, altho he ain't Born in no U.S. of A. He got sea water in his veins, and Beatbox Brains.

He pull the Royal Scam, he sing, "Wop-bop-sha-bam," he never surface cuz he always on the lam. This man is one stone Def Jam . . .

Hartz kicked chunks of fallen plaster aside. Exposed lathwork sagged from the leprous ceiling. Blooms of mold and fungus grew from the walls, feeding on the Depression-vintage wallpaper and glue. A patchy twilight filled the hallway. The door onto the street was missing, but the portal was blocked by the reluctant form of Skeezix, who hung back from entering.

"Skeezer, please come in."

"Harry, I have followed you from lovely Boston to this festering cataclysm known as New York."

"Yeah?"

"Once here, I have further ventured from the relative safety of Columbus Avenue, down to this hellhole known as the Lower East Side."

"Yeah?"

"But I definitely draw the line at entering this derelict structure, inside which might lurk assorted needle-nasties, razor-boys, brainsuckers, crotch-emasculators, and decomposing bums. And large arthropods."

So saying, Skeezix folded his arms defiantly across his chest.

"Are you completely finished?"

"I have had my say."

"Then I'll have mine. Do you think I wanna be here either? I've got better things to do. The only reason I'm here at all is to help you in your stupid quest to have this ridiculous drum machine fixed. The carrying chores for which, by the way, I notice I was somehow delegated. I didn't pick out this dump on a whim. It's the address Dr. Silicon gave us, where we could find the Guru. He's our last hope. If you want to give up now; however, and try to finish the second album with your precious overgrown Casio in the condition it's in—"

Skeezix unfolded his arms and stepped inside the building. "Enough. I have seen the error of my ways. I am not too proud to beg. Let us get this over with."

"Would you carry this schizophrenic machine a while?"

"No. It is estranged from me."

Harry sighed. "Let's go."

Moving deeper into the building, they looked for signs of the Hoodoo Guru. As they explored, Hartz reached into his jacket pocket for sustenance. He withdrew what looked like an ordinary Slim Jim: beef jerky in its wrapper. Peeling back the plastic, Hartz pulled the Spicy Meat Treat toward his lips. The Slim Jim continued to emerge from his pocket until approximately three feet of Beef Rope trailed from his lips.

"What the hell is that?" demanded Skeezix.

"One hundred feet of Slim Jim on a reel. I got the idea from Dr. Silicon's power cord."

Cautious but thorough exploration of the aboveground three floors of the ancient tenement revealed no trace of the Hoodoo Guru. The frustrated duo found themselves at last on the ground floor again, standing at a gaping, black basement door.

"I suppose we must go down here," said Skeezix.

"Yeah," enthused Hartz.

No one had thought to bring flashlights, natch, so they were forced to proceed with groping caution down the splintery stairs. At the foot of the staircase they paused, letting their eyes adjust to the blackness. From what seemed an incredible distance away diffused a soft light, barely distinguishable from phosphenes. They set off shufflingly toward it.

After what seemed miles, they came upon a tent of hanging blankets nailed to rafters, from which nest the radiance seeped. Skeezix laid a hand on one flap, looked doubtfully at Hartz, then pulled it aside.

The Hoodoo Guru looked up.

De Guru, he be seated on a pillow in the Lotus, chargin' up his Kundalini Energies. He just a young man, it seem, got the shoulder-length dreadlocks matted with clay and straw, look like a compost heap on his head. His skin the color of licorice, his nose fill half his face, and big smile when he see visitors fill the other. His fingernails long as letter openers, his outfit raggedy-ass green workpants and flannel shirt with the sleeves rip off. He smell like a sack of dirty laundry, from his bare feet to his thatched crown.

In one corner of de Guru's space was a slatted crate holding a live, despondent chicken. On scavenged shelves were ranged miscellaneous bottles full of potions, packets of powders, amulets, and charms.

"Frenz," said Guru, "come in 'n' be welcome."

"Uh, okay, H.G.," essayed Skeezix. "If you are sure we are not interfering . . . . "

"No way, mon. I long time see you guys coming, but I na help, since anyone come here must make it on own."

Hartz and Skeezix were now seated on pillows also. "Whatcha mean, H.G.?" inquired Hartz. "That trip was short and easy."

De Guru, his smile growed. "You think so, boys? You think you know where you are? I gonna clarify your brains for you right now."

Standing, H.G. moved to a blanket. He pulled it aside to reveal a cement wall with a door in it. He opened the door.

Caribbean sunlight illuminated a golden-sanded beach that curved away in a palm-dotted crescent. Salt breezes wafted over the stunned visitors.

59

"Those are some special effects—" began Skeezix, then stopped.

A huge wave was rolling in. Closer, closer, closer— It crashed on the sand, climbed the beach—

—and creamed at the feet of Skeezix and Hartz, soaking their Adidas.

De Hoodoo Guru shut the door and returned to his seat. "Now how I help you boys, since you come so far?"

Hartz wordlessly laid the drum machine before de Guru. Skeezix spoke.

"Our instrument here appears to be, like, possessed. It has got a will of its own or sumpin'. We want you to exorcise it or communicate with the spirits inside it. Whatever. Just make it work like before."

Guru rested his big two-toned hands on the case. "Oh, mon, I should say there's some powerful *ghommids* inside here. This gonna require some Big Medicine. Everyone please to get bare."

Unwillingly, Hartz and Skeezix stripped, as did de Guru. The black man then slathered them all with an orange salve that smelled like fish paste. De Guru next produced from nowhere an enormous ganja-cigar, which he ignited and passed around. Pretty soon the tent was thick with aromatic haze, and everyone's Third Eye was open.

Somehow de Guru was holding the apathetic chicken. As the white boys watched, he sliced its throat with a knife-edged fingernail and drank some of its warm blood. With the remainder, he aspersed the congregation. Making contact with the drum machine, de Guru began to chant.

"Papa Legba 'n' Holy Bob Marley,

"You come me help, now me get gnarly.

"Gross bon ange 'n' ti bon too,

"Come up thru de earth inna foot with no shoe.

"Evil houngan what put on de hex,

"You must flee now, or me gonna vex!"

All had been smooth sailing up till now. Skeezix began to really hope that ol' H.G. could restore his drum machine to normality. But at the conclusion of de Guru's invocation, things began to go queer.

First de Guru's dreadlocks all stood up on end, like Buckwheat's always did when he got scared. Then he fell over and began to writhe, as if wrestling an invisible opponent. His body began to twitch like a hooked fish. Sparks shot out his ears and nose. All his joints popped like a string of firecrackers. A corona of energy wreathed his body.

Cowering helplessly, Skeezix and Hartz clutched each other slimily and waited for whatever might happen next.

Finally, the fight seemed over. Eyes shut, de Hoodoo Guru lay motionless for a time. Wearily, he rose.

"Boys, I am whipped. There be two exceedingly mighty *anjonu* inside your toy of Babylon, and they na wanna leave."

"*Anjonu*? What are they?"

"Spirits of de dead."

"Do they have names?"

"Dey be called 'Keith' and 'John.'"

Hartz looked at Skeezix.

Skeezix looked at Hartz.

"Oh, no," said Skeezix.

"Oh, yes," said Hartz.

* * *

So it has come to this, thought Skeezix. I am utterly and contemptibly screwed, blued, and tattooed.

Two weeks had passed since the heroic struggle by de Hoodoo Guru to separate the Ghosts from the Machine. (One of those weeks was spent just trying to get out of that Lower East Side cellar. Skeezix and Hartz had wandered footsore in the immense darkness without boundaries, smelling of Magic Fish Paste beneath their clothes and bewailing their Krool Fate. They had subsisted on Hartz's reel of Slim Jim, washed down with stagnant water from deep puddles, in which swam luminescent blind fish that spoke in tongues. They had climbed mountains and descended deep valleys. They had bopped their noggins on icy stalactites and stumbled on pebbled strands. Never did they think they would emerge. The very idea of junkie-littered Avenue D seemed like heaven. They were saved in the end only by the appearance of Baron Saturday, a demiurge sent by H.G., which led them glowingly to the foot of the tenement stairs without a word.)

Once Skeezix returned from New York, he moved into his studio, determined to finish the album he owed his label without the aid of his demon-infested drum machine.

He had since accomplished nothing. Skeezix Smash, the man who had once written a song a day for a month, was utterly destitute of ideas. All inspiration had fled—ennui and despair had set in. It was more than just losing his favored instrument. He had begun to doubt the whole possibility of making music, especially rock 'n' roll. What was it all anyway but a big joke, stokin' the star-makin' machinery . . . ? He was a bell-less horn, a keyless piano, a stringless guitar, a synthesizer without chips. He had been buggered by Entropy . . . .

It was four in the morning, Skeezix had just woken up from his clammy California dreamin'. He pushed aside the sweaty blankets and climbed off the cot in the studio. He felt like dying. He didn't know what to do.

So he fell to his knees before the Master Mixing Console and began to pray, as best he knew how.

"Dear Lord, would you buy me a Mercedes-Benz—"

No, that didn't sound quite right. Better try again.

"Bodhisattva, would you take me by the hand? Bodhisattva, can you show me the shine of your Japan, the sparkle of your China? There must be a higher love. Jesus is just all right with me. If you believe in something you can't understand, that's superstition. Spirit in the Sky, I'm one toke over the line. I can't drink this blood and call it wine! Plowmen dig my earth! I'm the King of Pain! Everybody's lookin' 4 the ladder, everybody wants salvation of the soul . . . . I'm 2,000 miles from home. Help me, Rhonda, help me get her out of my heart!"

Skeezix fell to the floor, weeping.

When his tears ceased, he felt a Presence behind him. Presences, actually. He levered himself up and turned.

From the traitorous drum machine emanated two tendrils of slippery ivory ectoplasm extending upward. After a few inches, the trailers resolved themselves into twin apparitions.

Two crucifixes fashioned from giant crossed drumsticks supported the sagging, nailed bodies of Keith and John. They were naked, save for loincloths made of Union Jacks. From their hideous wounds dripped a clear liquid that smelled like gin. It plopped into growing pools on the floor. Their bodies were pierced with hanging hypodermic needles, like Saint Sebastian's. They each weakly clutched smaller drumsticks in their hands.

"Who are you? Who, who are you?" Skeezix stammered.

"You know very well who we are," Keith intoned.

"Where did you come from?"

"Down the stairway to heaven, into your drum machine," John answered.

"But why? Why now, why me?"

"Because," said Keith mournfully, "of the sorry state of rock today, and because you are one of the guiltiest offenders."

"But what did I do? I was only trying to rock out in my own way."

"That's okay as far as it goes," John explained, "but you let your ego get too big. You wanted to do everything alone. You and your *machines!* Rock ain't machines. It's people, a community. It's human drummers, like us. Why did we die?"

"Too much drugs, booze, and sex?"

The spirits looked somewhat sheepish. "Well, could be. But that ain't all. It was because we burnt ourselves out on our music, creating greatness. Will a *machine* do that for you?"

"I do not know. I thought I had a handle on things, but I just do not know anymore."

"You must go back to using human musicians," Keith demanded.

"My Sweet Lord, do you two know what kind of money good session players command nowadays? I will not pay it. And my sound! What about my distinctive sound?"

"Change it!"

"I can not! You guys are behind the times. You just are not hip no more. People demand a different beat today. If I don't supply it, my sales will plummet. Then where will either you or I be? Nowhere!"

"Things mighta changed for the worse since we croaked. But it's your obligation to turn this mess around. Maybe we're a little out of date. But we know what's real rock and what's not!"

"You are demanding the impossible! I will end up in the cutout bins, whether I do what you say or I do not. The only way out is to satisfy both me and you simultaneously, and that is plain imposs—"

Skeezix stopped.

Impossible? Why?

Did they call him Mr. Smash for nothing?

Skeezix got to his feet. "Listen, boys, I believe we can do a deal!"

Skeezix explained.

John and Keith exchanged glances (awkwardly, considering their crucified positions). Then John said, "This had better work. We are not Fools In The Rain."

"And We Will Not Get Fooled Again," Keith added.

"No, I am sure, it will fly, trust me, boys, trust me."

"Okay. But remember, we'll be watching every move."

The spirits of Music Past began to fade away, retracting into the drum machine. When they were all gone, Skeezix began madly to dance.

"I am free, I am free, and freedom tastes of reality! It has been a long time since I have rock 'n' rolled, but now I can see for miles and miles!"

* * *

Hartz entered Smash Studios happily, clutching copies of *People*, *Musician*, *Rolling Stone*, and *Spin*, all with Skeezix's face on their covers.

"Skeezer, you are a genius!"

Looking up from the slide-controls of his console, Skeezix smiled. "It was nothing, Harry, nothing. Any brilliant polymath could have accomplished the same."

Hartz sat down. He reached into his pocket. No Slim Jim today! During the Week of Wandering, Hartz had grown heartily sick of that Former Fave. Today he removed a Dove Bar, miraculously unmelted, for Hartz had had refrigerator coils hooked up to his electric boots, installed in the pocket of his mohair suit.

"But really, Skeezer—*three* albums in Billboard's Top Ten simultaneously! One as artist, and two as producer—"

"And naturally, my own Monkey Funk music sits comfortably at Number One. I told those two superannuated spooks that their stuff would never sell as well as mine. Although I must admit that I never expected them to get even this high on the charts."

"And as long as no one knows that those two names who got drum credits on the new albums by the reunited Who and Led Zep don't exist, but are merely masks for your drum machine—which has never sounded better or more lifelike and passionate, by the way—then everyone is satisfied."

"Well, yes," said Skeezix, looking somewhat uneasy.

"What is it, Skeezer?" demanded Harry worriedly. "Are the ghosts making new demands?"

"No. They do not mind letting me use their machine for my own kind of music anymore, and are quite happy with their new mode of expression. It's only—"

"What, Skeezer, what!"

"I have just learned today that the record companies want all three groups to tour separately right now!"

Like my novella "Victoria," this story was directly in-spired by a song. Not, of course, one by the Kinks, as earlier, but one by Peter Gabriel: "Big Time." Seeking to replicate the giddy satirical bounce of that tune, I turned to one of the oldest of SF models, Swift's Gulliver. I seasoned that classic with our obsession with tabloid fame, and the resulting tale practically wrote itself.

Jeffrey Ford, a superior fantasist, seems to have indepen-dently stumbled on this same recipe, in his fine story "Exo-Skeleton Town." But have our mutual assaults on the cheap thrills of mediagenic notoriety had any curative effect on the enslaved public? Of course not! But I bet Swift also felt pretty down about Gulliver's chastising influence, or lack thereof.

Living with the Giants

I was sitting in a soda fountain when I was discovered by the giant who called herself Jayne Mansfield.

She pulled up in her big car, a red convertible Corvette with white leather interior. Each tire was the size of a normal subcompact vehicle. From my vantage point in the soda fountain, the cherry-colored hood was as big as Texas. The idling motor sounded like Niagara Falls.

Jayne gripped the steering wheel with one enormous hand, her huge, tanned arm resting easily atop the lowered window. She wore a low-cut gypsy blouse that revealed cleavage like the Grand Canyon. Platinum earrings and necklace the color of her hair.

"Hello, handsome," she said. "What's a nice boy like you doing in a place like this?"

At first, I didn't know how to answer. I had never spo-ken to one of the giants before. Of course, they were all as familiar to me as my own face. Like everyone else, I had seen them endlessly depicted on television, in newspapers, magazines, and movies, on billboards, and at some distance in real life. But the giants seldom spoke to us little folks, and I was unaware of the protocols one might have to employ when answering them.

And besides, the media had now arrived in their dish-topped vans, hot on the scent of their product, the giants. That really made me nervous. I knew that whatever I said would be instantly broadcast around the world, printed in a hundred outlets by evening, analyzed and scrutinized tomorrow by all those eager mortals, just like me, who longed for one of the giants to approach them . . . .

So I just sat there for a minute in the soda fountain, wondering what to say, while Jayne smiled expectantly, her perfect teeth big as small shovel blades.

Finally, I decided. Hell, I thought, she had approached me, not the other way around, so I'd be damned if I'd fall all over myself answering her. I'd treat her just as I would one of my own kind.

"Just hanging out," I said with what I hoped was the proper insouciance.

"Do you do this kind of thing often?" she shot right back, the cameras tracking like palsied spectators between us.

I was just as sharp. "If you mean talking to giants, the answer's no. If you mean sitting in soda fountains—well, yes, whenever I'm feeling down."

Jayne's face crinkled in an expression indicative of mixed interest and mild revulsion. "Isn't it sorta—icky?"

She had a point. I lifted one hand up out of the frothy, brown pool to wipe the Coke out of my eyes, but the falling droplets from the forty-foot spray re-wet my face the very next instant.

"Yeah, I guess. But it sweetens up my disposition."

"Cute, cute." She paused to regard me with her enormous head cocked to one side. "So. Why are you depressed?"

"Why are you happy?"

"Because I have everything I want."

"Good reason." I didn't volunteer anything more. I was waiting to see what else she had to say to me.

Jayne then blew a pink bubble, using what had to be four tons of gum. The rosy sphere was as big as one of Malcolm Forbes' hot air balloons. I mean, the size of one of his old ones, not the ones he needed to carry him now. It popped with a sound as loud as a cannon, and she sucked the gum back in between her silvered lips.

"What's your name, kid?"

"Marion."

"First or last?"

"First. Unfortunately."

"It won't do, won't do at all," Jayne decisively said.

I didn't ask for what.

"You're kind of rugged-looking. Stand up, please."

What the hell. She had said please. I stood, caramel liquid runnelling my soggy clothing.

"You're big," she said and smiled. I realized how inapt that word was when applied to one of us little folks. "For your kind, that is."

She was silent again, sizing me up speculatively. "Okay, Marion, listen close. I'm a staunch believer in coincidences, destiny, the stars, stuff like that. Let's take a chance. I say you can be John Wayne."

I shrugged. "Okay, I'm John Wayne. So what?"

"Why don't you get out of there, so we can talk better?"

"All right. I was just about done anyway." I wasn't going to let her think she could order me around. No sense in letting this relationship get off on the wrong footing.

One leg over the fluted rim of the stone basin, I stopped short.

Relationship? What relationship?

Shit, why was I kidding myself? I knew this was my big break. As a hundred lenses zoomed in on me, as shutters clicked and electronic flashes discharged, as reporters scribbled and spoke into mikes, I could practically feel myself starting to grow.

I couldn't get too close to Jayne's car, or I wouldn't have been able to see her above the cliff-like chassis, so I stood back some distance from her vehicle, dripping on the elevated terrace around the soda fountain.

"Now what?" I asked politely, but, I hoped, not obsequiously.

"Get in the car."

"But my clothes—I'll ruin your upholstery. Hell, look at what the spray's doing to your paint job." I pointed to the Corvette's hood, where Coke was eating pits into the cherry lacquer.

"Forget it," she said. "I'll have it fixed. Just shut up and climb in, before I change my mind."

She levered open the passenger door. It swung out like some Ali Baba mountainside to my unspoken "Open, Sesame." I had to jump back so it wouldn't knock me flat.

"C'mon," admonished Jayne. "Hop aboard."

Easier said than done. I walked with squishing noises over to the car, conscious all the time of the cameras on me. When I stood beside it, I had to reach up fifteen inches over my head to grasp the aluminum ridge of the door frame. I chinned myself, flexed my arms, caught a toehold, and then stood on what seemed to be an acre of dirty auto carpet. I had to repeat the sequence to get into the cowhide-smelling seat.

I looked up at Jayne towering beside me. It was like staring at the Colossus of Rhodes. Her bust was mountainous. I tried to picture her bra.

"Good start," she told me, reaching across to shut the door. Her arm resembled a freckled wall. The sound of the door slamming nearly deafened me.

Then she peeled out. The acceleration forced me back deep into the seat.

I could see there was going to be a lot to get used to in my new life.

* * *

Jayne's mansion occupied a part of the city that had formerly comprised an entire residential subdivision. The whole plat had been taken by eminent domain and allocated to the giants when they had first manifested themselves. We had thought it might be enough space for all of them to live in. It took hundreds of men six months to demolish all the existing structures, cart the rubble away, level the ground, and lay fresh green turf over an area as big as Central Park.

The giants had then come in and built precisely one enormous structure on the land.

Other parcels around the nation were quickly appropriated and given to the giants, whereupon they built more titanic mansions fit for their kind.

No one except a few cynics minded all that much. We had quickly found we couldn't live without the giants. They added so much luster to our drab lives. We gloried in their shadows, as if in the brightest sunlight. They were the talismans that gave ultimate meaning to our own humble existences.

Jayne opened her garage door with a remote control as big as a refrigerator, and we drove in. It was like entering NASA's Vehicle Assembly Building.

Once inside the hanger, Jayne said, "Okay, John, follow me."

For a second, I didn't know to whom she could be referring. Then I remembered: it was my new name; I was now to become John Wayne.

I hoped I was up for the role.

Reversing the procedure I had used to enter Jayne's car, I soon stood on the concrete floor. Jayne was striding toward a door leading into the house, and I had to run to keep up with her. The oil stains on the floor were as big as lakes, and involved wide detours. By the time I reached the portal, she had vanished. Luckily, she had left the door open, and I was able to get inside.

The interior of Jayne's mansion was vistas of brocade and crystal, lustrous woods and shiny marble, velvet curtains and silver fixtures. It was all half-familiar to me, and I was surprised not be more in awe of it until I realized the reason why. I had seen it a hundred times before, on TV and movie screens, the myriad rooms filled with the laughing, passionate figures of Jayne and her kind.

I don't know if I've mentioned that Jayne was wearing perfume. She smelled like a whole greenhouse full of freesias. Thus I was easily able to follow her scent through the house whose topography was not totally strange to me—until I found her in the bedroom.

Jayne had kicked off her high heels and was unsnapping her toreador pants when I walked in, panting and exhausted from my alpine expedition up her stairs.

"Hurry up, John, we have to have sex now."

I tried to catch my breath. "Is that part of the job description?"

"Don't be silly. Your new life could hardly be called work. You're just supposed to enjoy yourself." Jayne had her slacks down over her hips. She wasn't wearing any panties. I was riveted by the sight of her pubic bush: it was as thick and extensive as what was left of the Amazonian rain forests.

"I hardly see how we'll be able to do anything together," I ventured.

"Oh, it'll be awkward at first, but things will get easier as you start to grow. Having sex with a giant is, in fact, one of the ways you begin to grow. This is the commencement of your new life, John."

I lifted my shoulders sheepishly. I had no one to blame for this but myself. If I was uncomfortable now, it was only because I had succumbed to the lure of the giants and placed myself in this situation. I would have to do what Jayne said from now on. There was no turning back.

I began to undress, tossing my wet, tiny garments to the floor.

Jayne's pants were down around her ankles. She bent at the waist to remove them completely.

It had been pointless to try to visualize Jayne's bra, for she wasn't wearing one. Her breasts spilled out of her blouse, exactly as those of the original Jayne had tumbled forth in that famous picture that graced the cover of that book about an earlier generation of giants, more nearly our own size.

I stared like a fool. They were big as whales.

"Hurry up," Jayne repeated.

I hurried. Jayne already lay in the bed. I stood helplessly on the rug. Finally, I spotted the bedside lamp's electric cord. I began to climb hand over hand up its slippery length.

Perched on the bed table's edge, I surveyed the recumbent form of Jayne, which seemed to stretch for miles.

This would not be making love, I knew.

This would be exploring a continent.

I jumped down, landing softly on the mattress.

Like Lewis and Clark, I began to chart unknown territory. I ranged from mountains to valleys and was almost swept out to sea when I ventured down to the delta. I don't know what, if anything, Jayne got out of my travels, but it was certainly an experience I had never imagined and was glad I had not refused. Halfway through doing what I was doing, I stopped, stricken with a new thought.

"Jayne—are there cameras watching us now?"

"Of course. There are always cameras."

"Do they have to be on?"

"Do you want to grow?"

I considered what Jayne and I might do when I got more nearly her size. "Yes."

"Then they have to be on. You don't grow except on video."

If I had been leery before of becoming what Jayne proposed, I was now utterly bent on it. I realized anew that I would do whatever she said.

It turned out to be pretty reasonable, considering a giant's needs.

* * *

Life with Jayne and her fellow giants wasn't bad, considering I wasn't yet their peer. During most of the day, Jayne and I shopped, or ate in public, or made our peculiar kind of love. The "shopping" was just show, of course, since there was nothing in any of the tiny stores that Jayne could possibly use. The ritual consisted of promenading up and down the sidewalks, oohing and aahing at the unseen contents of store windows down around her shins, letting the public feast their eyes on us. It was hard work keeping up with Jayne's pace, but mostly I managed. Occasionally, I got to ride Jayne's pet leopard when she took him out. He was commensurate with Jayne, and I was frightened of him at first, until Jayne explained that he would no more design to eat me than a cat would bother with a crumb.

I recalled some of the cats I had owned and was not re-assured. But eventually, I got used to sitting up on his broad furred back, just behind his rhinestone collar, beneath the arc of a leash that was as thick as a cable on the Brooklyn Bridge.

Several times everyday, I checked myself in the mirror for signs of growth. After several weeks, I imagined I could detect an increase in my stature. I asked Jayne what she thought.

She frowned and said, "Yes, you're definitely growing. But not fast enough. There seems to be some problem. I don't know if the public is quite ready to believe in you as John Wayne. We need to get you some more publicity. Are you practicing your drawl?"

"Waal, dang it, Missy," I attempted. "Ah'm shore tryin' to get this here way of jawin' down."

"Not so broad, please."

"Sorry."

Jayne's frown was replaced by a look of concentration. "We're going to have to throw a gala affair in your honor. That should help you grow. I'll get busy calling people right away."

I had already been to many parties with Jayne, but none of them had ever been held specifically for me. I hoped it would work.

A date was arranged for a week from that day, and the engraved invitations—each big as a billboard—were sent out.

Meanwhile life continued as before, an endless round of photo opportunities: charity galas and nightclub appearances, theater openings and celebrity banquets, awards ceremonies and film festivals . . .

At one such occasion, I was approached for the first time by a reporter. I can't even remember now what questions were asked of me; all I recall is babbling blithely into a microphone while the cameras closed in tightly on my face. But the contact with the media had its effect.

The next time I laid myself naked across Jayne, I found that, by dint of stretching to my utmost, I was now simultaneously able to reach each nipple with the tips of my index fingers.

It was a historic moment in my life. I was convinced that true giant status would soon be mine.

There was one funny thing about the size of the giants though. It fluctuated.

When I initially noticed this fact, I was inclined to believe I was hallucinating. Nothing in the public knowledge about the giants had ever prepared me for this possibility. Eventually, however, I was forced to accept it as truth.

Sometimes, the giants would seem utterly Gargantuan, their heads in the clouds, their feet planted as solidly as islands in the sea. These times seemed to coincide with the focus of media attention, the adoration of the public. At such times, the giants positively seemed to radiate a kind of glory borrowed from their audience.

At other times, the giants seemed big, but not cosmic in scale. They were more like occupants of the extreme end of the permissible human spectrum than like Olympian immortals. This was the stature, in fact, that they most often held in my eyes.

And sometimes, they even looked strictly mortal, or even less than human. When, very rarely, a giant stumbled, or made a faux pas . . .

I remember once when Jayne caught some kind of flu. She lay groaning and moaning in bed, clutching her stomach, before she had to jump up with a case of diarrhea.

When she finally came out of the bathroom, I could almost look her level in the eyes.

But that didn't last long.

The glamour always returned.

And I must confess that I was hoping the upcoming party in my honor would confer some on me.

*   *   *

My big day arrived at last. Jayne insisted that I dress in my Stetson and chaps, boots and spurs. She'd be wearing a clinging white cocktail dress with spaghetti straps, calculated for maximum exposure of her assets.

I could hardly contain myself until evening. I spent the day in front of my mirror, dressed in my John Wayne outfit, practicing my accent, watching for any sudden spurts of growth. It was a long way from hanging out in soda fountains, I told myself.

Around 6:00 the caterers arrived, little people like I had once been. They were equipped with a whole fleet of vehicles needed to carry around the giant canapés and trays of drinks. This fleet was airlifted by choppers to the tabletops, where the troops deployed themselves and began unloading Ritz crackers as big as manhole covers. A team of engineers erected a huge silver champagne fountain, and a convoy of tanker trucks arrived to fill it. Soon, bubbly was tumbling down into the terraced basins.

I supervised the operation with an air of superiority, noting with pride how I towered over these former kin of mine, easily twice as tall. After tonight, I was sure, I would utterly dwarf them.

The musicians arrived at 8:00. They, however, were giants. I recognized Hendrix, Lennon, Morrison, Joplin, Holly, and Redding. And, of course, Elvis. Lord, this was gonna be one hell of a party. I was so excited. Jayne had spared no expense for me. At the same time, I was as nervous as a Victorian bride. I hoped I would be able to live up to her expectations.

I helped the tiny roadies to deploy the enormous microphones, cumbersome as battleship cannons, hoping to exhaust some of my nervous energy. All I succeeded in doing was getting so sweaty that I had to go upstairs and change my spangled shirt.

Around 9:00, the guests began to stroll in.

I had never seen such a glittering galaxy of giants. Practically everyone who was anyone was there. Warhol, Onassis, Princess Grace, Montgomery Clift, Liz, Lisa, Mick, Gable, Madonna, Charles and Di, Malcolm Forbes, Donald Trump, Carl Icahn, Mailer, Updike, King, Kubrick, Scorsese, Newman, Fonda (Henry and Jane), Picasso (Pablo and Paloma), Schnabel . . .

Each one of them greeted me personally as they came in: the men shaking my little hand with care not to crush it; the women launching air-kisses over my head as they pressed me to their tremendous bosoms. It was all too much for me. My head began to whirl. I barely managed to utter the requisite perfunctory pleasantries. I felt my limbs and torso lengthening, enlarging, with every embrace and handclasp.

When Brando walked through the door, having jetted in unexpectedly from his tropic hideaway, I almost fainted. (His jet was as big as the Empire State Building. It needed a runway the size of Rhode Island.)

After the majority of guests arrived, I left my post by the door and plunged into the heady social vortex, circulating among the giant glitterati.

Everything went fine until midnight. That was when I made my fatal mistake.

I had had too much to drink and snort. (The giants laid lines as thick as standard-gauge rails across mirrors as big as the Rockefeller Center skating rink. Their rolled-up bills were the circumference of mighty oaks.) I got into an argument with Dennis Hopper about just how good an actor James Dean had been. I had to stand on a chair to maintain eye contact with Hopper, but I thought I was holding my own.

Then Dean himself walked up, invariably attracted by the sound of his own name, as most giants were.

He poked me in the chest with a finger as big and stiff as a telephone pole.

"Hey, you asshole pygmy, who are *you* to be puttin' *me* down?"

I tried to summon up some John-Wayne-style bravado, but could think of no rejoinder save a stammered, "Who, me?"

"Yeah, you," said Dean, exhibiting no more wit than myself. Unfortunately, this was not a contest of wit, but of sheer size.

Before I could react, Dean picked me up and, with a minimum of ceremony, dumped me in the champagne fountain.

The whole room went dead silent, all attention focused on me. But it was the wrong kind of attention. Hostile and from my superiors, it did not make me grow. Instead, it began to have the opposite effect. I could feel myself shrinking, shrinking . . .

From nowhere, Jayne appeared.

"Well, you can take the boy out of the soda fountain, but you can't take the fountain out of the boy . . . "

The giants burst into harsh laughter, the men roaring and women tittering.

"All right, *Marion*," Jayne said. "Haul ass and clear out."

I didn't even bother to try to protest. I knew the broadcast of my shame had already been seen by the whole world, and the public would never accept me as John Wayne after such a disgrace. I didn't even bother to pack any of my new clothes, which I knew would be too big in just a few days. I just pulled myself out of the champagne and slogged wetly over to the door.

A few weeks later, I was back to my normal size. I didn't mind too much. It felt more comfortable somehow. I didn't return to hanging around soda fountains though. Those days were over. Instead I found a job, met a nice girl my own size, got married, settled down, had kids, got older . . .

I never followed the lives of the giants much after my exile from their midst. It was just too painful. But every once in a while, I will admit, I did daydream about the days when I was almost one of them.

And you know—I could've sworn at such moments I actually shot up an inch or two.

This little jape probably stems from too much viewing of the work of the seminal Monty Python troupe, specifically their "killer joke" routine. It amused me to use my friends as victims of my imaginary fiendish film, so you can picture Bruce (Sterling), Rudy (Rucker), Marc (Laidlaw), and Liz (Hand) as the hapless unfortunates.

Curiously enough, however, the science-fictional notion of "bad memes"—audio or visual—which I employed in throwaway fashion, has recently attracted a lot of serious attention. Such writers as John Barnes, Dave Langford, David Foster Wallace, and others have employed this trope. I return to this subject at greater length and more depth elsewhere in this collection, specifically in "Seeing Is Believing." I trace the whole notion back to Fritz Leiber, and his "Rump-Titty-Titty-Tum-Tah-Tee" (1958), about a song that could not be eradicated from memory once heard.

What's that, you say? You're humming the theme to Gilligan's Island *right this minute?*

Destroy All Brains!

I first heard of the movie *Destroy All Brains!* from my friend Bruce.

He phoned me at 3:00 in the morning. I wasn't sleeping, so I answered on the first half of a ring.

Without preamble, he spewed out a torrent of Texas jive.

"Man, I just seen the best goddamn movie! *Destroy All Brains!* Real cheesy Technicolor, buncha half-familiar character actors from sixties sitcoms, script by that guy who used to write for *Ramparts*—you know, he killed himself in '72—and the plot!"

Here Bruce paused. I prompted him. "The plot?"

I could hear Bruce scratching his stubble over the long-distance line. His voice was petulantly doubtful when it returned, like that of a man who had misplaced his car keys, and was, moreover, unsure of the location of the car itself.

"The plot—well, yeah, man, there was a plot, sure there was. I just can't put it into words. Something sorta James-Bondish, about a scheme to take over the world by a cabal of Secret Masters employing insidious, diabolical Red Chinese psychopharmaceutical mesmerization techniques." His voice gained a little conviction. "But it was really, really well-done. Sincerely twisted, you dig? Highbrow trash. Catch it if you can. Later, man!"

Bruce is a software engineer. He works at home and keeps odd hours. A cable-ready Watchman rests atop his monitor, placed so he can scan it from time to time while he hacks. No wonder he hadn't been able to tell me the plot.

I got up from my seat in front of the softly glowing tube of my own TV and went to a shelf of reference books. I review media for my local newspaper. I had been watching bad movies since age five and thought I had heard of all of them. The title Bruce had mentioned didn't ring any bells.

I checked *Psychotronic Films: Destroy All Brains!* was not mentioned. I looked in the *Re/Search Incredibly Strange Films* issue. Nothing. I thumbed through Halliwell and Katz. Zip. Likewise for the Maltin, Martin, and Ebert guides.

I tried to call Bruce back, to make sure I had heard the title correctly.

His line was busy. I figured he had his modem plugged in. I went to bed.

Two days later I got a postcard from Bruce. The card depicted a water buffalo in a rice paddy. It was postmarked "somewhere in southeast Asia." This is what it said:

Yo—Gone to live in Burma. Got a job building a data-

base for drug warlords. Send all correspondence via diplomatic pouch.

* * *

The next time I heard about *Destroy All Brains!* was from my buddy Rudy.

Rudy was a professor in California. He taught semiotics and pop culture. His best and most popular course was entitled "The Myth of Single-Valued Narratives in the Work of Ernie Bushmiller." I had a text I wanted him to deconstruct.

When he was done with that simple chore, he said, "You ever heard of a movie called *Destroy All Brains!*?"

"Once."

"Well, you should track it down. It's a rather disturbing little gem. I didn't spot the copyright in the credits, but I'd peg it around '38. Probably from one of the independent studios, like Republic. Black-and-white of course. From the sloppy editing, I'd guess it might have even been originally issued as a serial. Anyway, the director was one of those half-forgotten guys. Not Lewton or Browning, somebody even more obscure. The cast was anonymous—though I thought I saw Einstein in a crowd scene."

"The physicist?"

"No, the rabbi! Of course, the physicist. But forget that. They could've been using stock newsreel footage to save money. No, the important thing was the plot—"

"The plot."

"Yeah. It's kinda hard to summarize. It was mostly about a cult of voodoo-crazed Louisiana Negroes trying to enslave America's political leaders by obeah rites. I could swear one of the scenes of them worshipping featured full-frontal nudity. During the big dance around the fire. Is that possible?"

"Precode," I said. "Maybe. Especially if it was done *National-Geographic*-style."

Rudy sounded worried. "If you ever see it, I'd appreciate your thoughts on its relevance."

Kinda weird phraseology, I thought.

The next day, I was in my office at work when the bulletin came in. Rudy had taken out the governor of California with a radio-controlled model airplane packed with Czech plastic explosives. The lifestyles commissioner had been a collateral fatality. Rudy had escaped the scene of the carnage disguised as the ambassador from Burkina Faso.

* * *

When I met Marc on the sidewalk a few days later, I told him all about Rudy and Bruce.

"Far out, man. I seen that movie too. Just the other night, in fact. But nothing bad's happened to me so far."

"How could you tell?" I asked.

"Funny, man, *muy jubiloso*."

Marc lived in a squat, an abandoned building that used to be a coat hanger factory. His clothing was assembled from items refused by the Salvation Army. He was always hungry. He had been a famous criminal lawyer until he had gotten unprofessionally involved with the murderous widow of a perfume magnate. Falling in love with her white shoulders, he let her become his obsession, his opium. But she turned out to be poison in the end. His current roommates were a tribe of Puerto Rican separatists who were sending most of the money they made by selling mimeographed Romanian pornography back to their colonized island, while using the rest to amass sophisticated weaponry. They had tapped into a nearby power line and stolen a television from a local bar named The Three-Pound Sponge.

"You saw *Destroy All Brains!* over the air?"

"Yup. Channel 68 last Wednesday, after midnight."

"I checked the *Guide* that day. It wasn't mentioned."

"Last minute substitution."

"What was it about?"

"It was this totally 1950s sci-fi thing. Alien invasion of Earth. The hero was Ward Cleaver, or someone who looked just like him. The aliens were organically shaped just like TVs! Big, clunky, console models with those old-fashioned separate rabbit ears with felt pads on their bottoms. State of the art for the time, I guess. It was great the way they made the legs move. And their saucer—! Anyway, I don't remember much more than that. I'm not even sure how it ended."

"Color, or black-and-white?"

"I can't be sure. The color's not working on our set."

"Here's a twenty, Marc. Take it easy."

"Dope."

"Don't spend it that way, Marc."

"No, I just meant cool."

"Oh."

The lead story on the 6:00 news was all about Marc. He had apparently used my twenty to illegally purchase a clip of ammo for one of the automatic weapons the Puerto Ricans were stockpiling, whereupon he had gone down to our town's old-line department store—where all the clerks were twenty years-of-service lady veterans with clip-on earrings—and sprayed a six-by-fifteen-foot display of televisions. No one was hurt except a state senator browsing among the nearby CDs—when they wheeled him out on a stretcher, I could see he was still clutching *Destroy All Brains!—The Soundtrack,* but when I went down to the store for it, they told me there was no such title in inventory—who was gashed by flying, phosphor-coated glass.

I felt Rudy would have been pleased by the lucky accident of such a political victim.

I called up Channel 68: they claimed not to own a copy of *Destroy All Brains!*

* * *

For the next two weeks, I checked *TV Guide* religiously. But *Destroy All Brains!* was not slated to appear. I figured that having played here recently, it would not show up in my market anytime again soon, but should surface elsewhere in the country.

Liz woke me at noon one day with a call from Chicago. She works for an ad agency there.

"I know how you're always searching for a good column topic. You should try to rent this movie I saw last night. It's called—"

"*Destroy All Brains! . . .*"

"Right! You've seen it already?"

"No. But it seems like everyone else I know has."

"They must've told you then how it's above-average for a made-for-TV flick."

"Made for TV?"

"Sure. Mid-seventies, I'd guess. I think it was by Aaron Spelling, but I could be wrong. Anyhow, it starred what's-his-name, the pop star who was on a soap-opera. Or was it a western? And that kid actress, the one who later got into porn films. They were recruited by the government and sent as special agents to break the Arab oil embargo."

"Which one?"

"The first. I think. But the interesting part came when they met Lawrence of Arabia and Richard Burton."

"Taylor's Burton?"

"No, the one who discovered the Nile. The two Englishmen were still alive and, like, the immortal masterminds behind everything that happened in the Mideast. After that, it gets a little hard to explain."

"I can imagine."

"Well, I gotta run."

"Liz—"

"Yes?"

"Nothing. Just take care of yourself."

"Sure."

When Liz married the king of Jordan—whose wife had recently died in a joint Israeli-PLO terrorist attack while she was consecrating a McDonald's—I wasn't surprised.

After that, I read about a frat party during Spring Weekend that turned into a six-day riot with hundreds of casualties and millions of dollars worth of property damage. The expendable last paragraph of the article mentioned that the night's entertainment, screened just before the riot, had been a showing of "an old eight-millimeter stag film about gangbangs called *Destroy All Trains!* (sic)."

I found a film catalog that listed, among its educational offerings:

DESTROY ALL BRAINS!: B&W, 40 min. 1948. Department of Agriculture feature about the dangers of mad-cow disease. Mature audiences only.

Joe-Bob Briggs saw *Destroy All Brains!* at a drive-in that summer and reported on it in print, describing it as "the first gore 'n' garters intergalactic thriller of the nineties!" Later that same month, he was filmed by camera crews while disappearing through the gates of a Zen Buddhist monastery in Kuala Lumpur, his head shaven, begging bowl in hand.

When the tenth friend called me up to tell me about *Destroy All Brains!* I quit answering the phone. I figured I'd read about them one place or another anyway, or catch them on the late news.

I kept waiting for *Destroy All Brains!* to show up on

a local station or appear in my neighborhood video rental store. When it didn't immediately manifest itself in the next few months, I reminded myself that this was a big country.

One day recently at work, when I wasn't particularly thinking about the film, I got a small package delivered to my desk. I opened it up.

Inside was a toy: a red plastic case with an eyehole fitted with a plastic lens and slide-switch. I cracked the case at its seam. Inside was a single AA battery, flashlight bulb, small electric motor, tiny spool of film, and its takeup reel.

I closed the case. I took it home.

Private showing.

Product placement: it's a way of life for the savvy artist. Fay Weldon and The Bulgari Connection *have nothing on me. If I had had a good agent at the time I wrote this story, I'd be typing this introduction right now from poolside at my mansion in Beverly Hills.*™

The Ballad of Sally NutraSweet™

On the day that was to change her life forever, Sally Nutra-Sweet™ awoke, as always, to yet another perfect FDA-approved morning in the bedroom of her apartment in the NutraSweet™ skyscraper rearing high over the glorious city of Productville.

Through her bedroom window, the sun poured its muted bounty. Lying still for a moment as she came fully awake, Sally had a direct view of the dim, low-hanging orb, which at this hour of the morning was emblazoned with the logo of Pepsi.™ (A huge fleet of satellites, each equipped with an enormous, translucent, programmable filter-screen, blanketed Earth with their protective advertising shadows, compensating for the nonexistent ozone layer.)

As she did first thing every morning, Sally recited the special little prayer of the NutraSweet™ clan, her heart full of gratitude and joy at her happy station in the communal life of Productville.

"May I bring the sweetness of aspartame into the lives of everyone I meet today, without the calories or cavities of sucrose. Amen."

Her heart brimming with good feeling toward all mankind—an emotion that found an outlet in a big unfocused smile—Sally hastened to rise. Throwing back the puffy blue coverlet emblazoned with the red-and-white NutraSweet™ swirl, she swung her feet to the floor, finding the comfort of the shag carpet bearing multiple iterations of the Nutra-Sweet™ crest, and slid into her NutraSweet™ logo slippers. Wrapping herself in the NutraSweet™ robe, which had hung overnight on the bedpost, Sally shuffled into the bathroom for a pee.

The toilet flushed in a perfect swirl of red and white, as self-organizing nanomachines in the water cohesively maintained the NutraSweet™ image.

Looking into the digital mirror above her sink, Sally saw the same playful trademark reflecting back. Living under the skin of her brow, almost where Hindu women had once worn caste marks, was a horde of nanodevices similar to those in the toilet water, forming the familiar shining blazon, a corporate third eye to complement her two genetic ones, each as blue as Windex.™

Summoning one of her images from last week into a corner window of the mirror's display, Sally was pleased to see no new lines in her current face. She knew it was silly of her to worry about such things—after all, she was only twenty-two—but still, it was much easier to catch such incipient wrinkles with nano-Oil of Olay™ as rapidly as they occurred.

Sally activated the taps and scrubbed her face with Ivory,™ before heading into the blue, white, and red breakfast nook.

There, she fixed her usual breakfast RDA of Kellogg's Corn Flakes,™ Sunmaid™ raisins, and Hood™ milk—the dish liberally sprinkled with, of course, NutraSweet,™ and accompanied by a cup of Maxwell House.™ Then she tuned her Nakamichi™ multimedia set to the NutraSweet™ channel to catch up on the latest infotainment.

The narrowcast was specifically tailored to the interests of the NutraSweet™ clan, most of whom held similar jobs and interests. NutraSweet™ people tended to gravitate into posts such as receptionists, dental assistants, cashiers and clerks, airline attendants, public relations figures, sales reps, and fashion models. Occasionally on the Nakamichi™ flatscreen, Sally would catch the portrait of a NutraSweet™ anomaly: a scramjet pilot, say, or a lawyer, bearing the NutraSweet™ logo on his or her forehead. At such times, Sally felt vaguely uneasy, as she tried to imagine herself in such a role.

No, she was quite content, even proud, of her lot in life.

Personal secretary to Mr. Gameboy,™ CEO of the Fun and Duty Administration.

As Sally ate her breakfast, one eye on the parade of self-help and feel-good features flowing across her screen, she noticed a trailer scrolling across the bottom of the display.

CONSUMERS ARE ADVISED TO AVOID USING AISLE SEVEN UNTIL FURTHER NOTICE, AS A TERRORIST ACT HAS RESULTED IN DAMAGE TO THE BRIDGE OVER OVALTINE™ RIVER. A SPOKESPERSON FROM THE FOX COPS™/ AMERICA'S MOST WANTED™ CHANNEL HAS STATED THAT THE PRIME SUSPECT IN THIS HEINOUS DEED IS THE GANG OF ZEBRA AGITATORS LED BY THE INFAMOUS "LUNCHMEAT."

As the message began to repeat, Sally uttered a curse she seldom employed.

"Sugar!"

This news meant she would have to take a detour to her job in the FDA Tower. Unless she left immediately, she'd be late. And if she were late, Mr. Gameboy™ would probably make her work through her lunch hour, and she'd be unable to share it with her fiancé, Dan, as they had planned.

Gulping down her Maxwell House™ and scorching her tongue in the process, Sally rushed to dress, not even stopping long enough to brush her teeth with Crest.™

Soon, wearing her NutraSweet™ frock, she was riding the Otis™ express elevator down with her fellow clan members, some of whom seemed similarly agitated by the unexpected need to scramble.

"What the heck is the matter with those Zebras?" asked a young blonde man as the Otis™ dropped. "Don't they know that they're only hurting themselves in the end?"

An older man, with a large potbelly that distorted the trademark swirl on his shirt in a manner Sally found rather unbecoming, said, "Maybe they were wired on too much *coffee*!"

Someone else chimed in. "Or ate some bad *food*!"

"Or mixed up their *toothpaste* with their *muscle rub*!"

The use of these generic terms—arguably justified by the stress everyone was feeling—still made Sally a bit queasy. Despite her earlier use of such a "swear," she wasn't easy with such rough language. Certainly, neither Mr. Gameboy™ nor Dan would ever use such coarse phrases around her.

So Sally was grateful when the young fellow who had first spoken said, "Hey, guys, there's a lady on board . . . . "

The men who had spoken so crudely now stared embarrassedly at the floor.

"Thank you very much!" said Sally with her traditional NutraSweet™ verve. She made a mental note to have her Nakamichi™ multimedia node's agents track down the man and Hallmark™ him.

Outside the NutraSweet™ building, waiting at a unaccustomed stop for an unfamiliar Greyhound™ maglev, Sally turned to cast a backward glance at her home, seeking some comfort in its reassuring mass.

Like every building in Productville, Sally's home was sheathed in nanocladding that regulated the interior environment. Aside from the transparent windows, the semi-intelligent exterior of the structure was programmed to depict, on all four sides, a package of Equal™ approximately fifty stories tall.

Sally's Greyhound™—the Cross-Store Express via Aisles Nine and Ten—pulled up silently in its banked chute, as seemingly weightless as Patagonia Capilene Underwear.™ Climbing aboard, Sally eyed her home briefly one last time. It suddenly seemed remote and unapproachable, a refuge now denied to her. A strange feeling, like that time she had taken too much Halcion,™ swept over her.

Bravely shrugging off her temporary disorientation, Sally found a Lay-Z-Boy™ seat and dropped gratefully into it without noticing her companion.

"Hello, Sally," her seatmate said.

Sally turned and saw her friend and co-worker, Crystal Light,™ an attractive black woman with long braided and beaded hair.

(Actually, Sally's friend's full name was Crystal Crystal Light,™ but everyone tended to abbreviate it. The Crystal Light™ clan was closely affiliated with the NutraSweet™ clan—sisters, so to speak—and they intermingled frequently, at clan picnics, rallies, and aerobic exercise nights devoted to Soloflex™ and Nautilus™ workouts.)

Sally was glad for the company of such a close friend on a disturbing morning like this.

"Oh, hi, Chris. I suppose you've heard about the damage in Aisle Seven . . . ?"

"That's why I'm on this Greyhound™ with you, girl. I'll take my oath as a Jehovah's Witness™ that one of these days those Zebras are gonna kill someone!"

Sally had never contemplated this likelihood before. Was it actually possible that any member of their global society, however lowly and degraded their exiled subhuman status might be, would resort to the taking of human life to make some theoretical point or highlight a hypothetical injustice? She felt compelled—both professionally and personally—to dispel the pall Chris' words had cast.

"Now, Chris, don't go wishing for trouble. Remember: 'Accentuate the positive!'"

Chris almost spat. "Positive! Sometimes I just wanna be nasty! There are days I regret ever being born into the Crystal Lights.™ I'd like to marry me a Colt™ man, or even an Uzi!™ Then you'd see this girl get down!"

"Marrying outside the clan is an awfully big step, Chris. Much as I love Dan, I still have second thoughts now and then about mixed marriages. Moving to your husband's tower is traumatic enough, but switching jobs as drastically as you're contemplating—!"

"I'm up for it!"

Sally could tell that there was no point in discussing the topic further with Chris, so she changed the subject.

"Nice dress!"

"It just felt like a Lemonade kind of day . . . ."

The Greyhound™ zipped along through relatively unfamiliar neighborhoods that Sally seldom visited. She was in CEO territory now, and the buildings were more luxurious and exotically shaped. She gaped at the Kool-Aid™ Kondominiums, Marlboro™ Mansions, Cadillac™ Co-ops, and Lexus™ Lodges. Somewhere in this district, in the Gameboy™ Gazebo, lived her boss.

As she checked her Swatch,™ Sally prayed that he too would arrive late.

The women had to change to Trailways™ Down-Store Number 54, which took another twenty minutes to deposit them at their destination: the terminal outside the FDA beanstalk.

Surrounded by a plaza some several hundred acres in area, the Fun and Duty Administration building was really and primarily a giant cable that extended into low-earth orbit, where it was tethered by a satellite. Magnetic pods—known as Chevys™—rode the outside circumference of the massive synthetic, nano-maintained stalk, ferrying passengers and materials into space. The lowest few miles of the stalk were honeycombed with offices accessible by internal Otis™ elevators.

As always, Sally experienced a shiver of awe and pleasure and pride (comparable to biting into a York Peppermint Patty™) at the sight of the gargantuan structure where she was privileged to work. If only the Ancients had had the technology and foresight to build such a safe and ecologically sound device, before their innumerable NASA Shuttle™ flights had destroyed the ozone layer (a disaster that all of current technology could still only ameliorate) . . . .

A sudden change of shadow flickered across the plaza. Sally looked up at the sun, which was now advertising Tampax.™

"Quick," Chris urged. "It's 9:00!"

The women trotted through the enormous portals and into the Carrier™ coolness of the building along with the crowds of their co-workers. At the bank of Otis™ elevators, they separated.

"See you on the Greyhound™ home!" Sally called out.

Even as she said the familiar words, she had a sinking feeling that they would not come true.

Ascribing her unease to guilt at being late, Sally waited impatiently for her particular Otis™ to arrive.

The ascent to the vertiginous offices of Mr. Gameboy™ took over two minutes. Now she was truly and royally late.

Outside the office door, Sally straightened her Leggs Sheer-to-the-Waist™ pantyhose and primped at her Vidal Sassoon™ hairdo. Thank goodness her nano-Ban™ was hard at work to keep her fresh! Satisfied she looked as presentable as possible, she parted the kelp-like circulatory ribbons of the door and entered the familiar office.

Seated at her OfficeMax™ desk was another woman!

And not just any woman!

It was that tramp from the secretarial pool, Linda Lurex!™

The intruder at Sally's post wore an outfit in keeping with her clan's totem: a skintight sheath of glittering silver Lurex™ that ended immodestly at her upper thigh, along with Lurex™ stockings and Candies™ high heels. Linda's hair was in an elaborate coiffure, her jewelry big and gaudy.

"Well, good afternoon!" Linda sneered.

Sally struggled to maintain her composure. She wouldn't give Linda the satisfaction of seeing how upset she was.

"What are you doing at my *desk*?" said Sally coldly, putting all the disdain she could muster into the harsh generic term.

Linda took a Coty™ emery board from the middle drawer of the OfficeMax™ desk and began unconcernedly to sharpen her claw-like nails.

"I'm your replacement. Mr. Gameboy™ called the pool this morning and had them send me up."

"My—my replacement? But why?"

"I don't know, and I don't care. All I know is that Mr. Gameboy™ wants to see you immediately."

"I'll—I'll go see him then . . . . "

Linda sneered. "How clever of you. Let me buzz him."

Sally's replacement depressed the call button on the Radio Shack™ intercom. "Oh, Mr. Gay-hame-boy,"™ lilted Linda Lurex.™ "It's that person you wanted to see . . . . "

"Send Miss NutraSweet™ in, please."

Taking heart from the neutral tone of her boss' voice,

Sally bucked up her courage and entered Mr. Gameboy's™ inner office.

Seated behind his Ethan Allen™ execudesk, Mr. Gameboy™ was playing his shirt. The garment was a Microsoft™ nano-driven flexi-display, its buttons the controls. Currently, the shirt was running Tetris.™ With his fleshy chin tucked into his chest, Mr. Gameboy™ seemed intent on breaking through to some hitherto unreachable screen.

"Have a Naugahyde™ chair, Miss NutraSweet.™ I'll be right with you."

Savagely twiddling his cuff buttons, swiveling from side-to-side in his chair, lunging and darting, Mr. Gameboy™ eventually succeeded in beating the game, causing a cacophony of celebratory computer noises to emerge from his collar speakers.

Mr. Gameboy™ vigorously shot his cuffs and straightened up his bulky frame. His patrician, smooth-shaven features had reverted to their usual imperturbability. Sally could smell his Aramis™from where she sat.

"Now, what can I do for you, Miss NutraSweet?"™

Mr. Gameboy's™ apparent unconcern was too much for Sally. After the unsettling morning, she simply broke down.

"Muh-muh-mister Gameboy,™ I'm so suh-suh-sorry! I puh-puh-promise I'll nuh-nuh-never be late again!"

Immediately, Mr. Gameboy™ was by her side. "Please, Miss NutraSweet,™ don't cry. Were you late this morning? I never even noticed. Here, have a Kleenex™ and stop crying."

Sally accepted the Kleenex.™ She wiped her tears, blew her nose, and attempted a wan smile.

"You didn't notice I was late? Then why is that—that *woman* sitting at my desk?"

"Now, now, Miss NutraSweet,™ I know you and Miss Lurex™ have never been the best of friends. But there's no need to employ such language with regards to her."

"I'm sorry. But I was hurt to see her there."

"Miss Lurex™ is merely filling in for you for an indefinite period. You see, I have a new temporary assignment for you. Something much more challenging than your usual work. If you're willing to take it, and if you succeed at it, you'd be doing an inestimable service to the whole FDA and all your fellow consumers."

Sally was puzzled. "Why, what could it possibly be?"

Mr. Gameboy™ returned to his Ethan Allen™ desk but remained out front, resting one haunch on a corner. He folded his arms across his chest, thereby warping his Microsoft™ shirt display into a weird rainbow of patterns.

"Miss NutraSweet.™ I assume you keep up with the news and are aware of the activities of those dissidents know as the Zebras."

"Tom NutraSweet™ just did an infomercial on them last week. 'Those Rogue Generics: Growing Threat or Hollow Bogeymen?'"

Leveling an intense gaze at her, Mr. Gameboy™ said, "Let me assure you, Miss NutraSweet,™ that whatever conclusions your channel's reporter reached were carefully vetted and approved by the Fun and Duty Administration with an eye toward keeping consumer confidence stable. It's no mark of distrust toward your clan in particular, or any clan at all. It's just that the FDA has an obligation toward society as a whole that supercedes an individual's right to full-label disclosure."

Mr. Gameboy™ continued to regard Sally with a fervent frankness that made her giddy as a double shot of Finlandia.™ She wondered where his talk could possibly be leading.

"I'm now about to reveal several things," continued

Sally's boss, "which are unknown to the average consumer. I must have your assurance these facts will not go beyond this room."

"Of course, Mr. Gameboy.™ Whatever you say."

"Very well. First, I will confide in you that the Zebras are not the small group of anarchists portrayed by the multimedia. They are, in fact, a large, well-organized and well-funded group of malcontents whose roots strike deep into the very heart of the FDA."

Sally gasped. "No! I can't believe any sane consumer would even *sympathize* with the Zebras, never mind *help* them!"

"It's sad, but true. For whatever perverted reason, certain high-placed officials have thrown their lot in with the renegades. And this, Miss NutraSweet,™ is where you come into the picture."

"I don't see—"

Mr. Gameboy™ held up a hand to interrupt. "Miss NutraSweet™—Sally if I may—don't be frightened at what I'm about to tell you. The Zebras are planning new villainy, infamy of a magnitude hitherto unthinkable. They plan to topple the FDA beanstalk, this magnificent structure we sit in at this very moment, symbol of our society's wonderful accomplishments and sane stability."

Sally felt on the verge of swooning. This strange day seemed to have a never-ending supply of shocks in store.

Seeming to sense her confusion, Mr. Gameboy™ rose and moved to Sally's side. He took one of her hands reassuringly in both of his.

"Sally, the FDA and all the clans need you to help avert this tragedy. I'm asking you to go undercover, to infiltrate the Zebras, and return to me safely with the details of their plot."

"But—but—I'm just a NutraSweet,™ a secretary! Why

can't a professional handle this? Someone from the Brinks™ or Wells Fargo™ clan?"

"They're compromised, Sally. We have no way of being certain that any given agent is not a secret Zebra sympathizer. They're the first ones the generics targeted. But someone like you—thanks to your low profile and humble station and spotless record—is absolutely trustworthy."

"Mr. Gameboy,™ I'm honored that you would consider me for this assignment. But I don't have any training—"

Releasing her hand, Mr. Gameboy™ straightened his spine and assumed a stern mien.

"Miss NutraSweet.™ One hundred years ago, when the whole world was on the verge of collapse, reeling under the onslaughts of gang violence, ozone holes, overpopulation, starvation, techno-hip-hop music, religious wars, rising sea-levels, disintegrating infrastructures, and weak consumer spending, a group of brave men and women—possessing no more special abilities than either you or I—saw what had to be done and did it. They instituted the clan-product system and the Fun and Duty Administration. Through fire and storm, riot and rebellion, against all odds and all benighted opponents, they built the system we inherited, a system that insures each individual has a place in a happy, extended brand-name family. For a whole century, the globe has been peaceful and productive. Now, a group of deviants threatens our inheritance, and the times call for the average members of society like yourself to do extraordinary deeds.

"Miss NutraSweet™ are you going to let the Founding Trademarkers and the Global Warranty down? Or are you going to live up to their shining example?"

Sally found that her eyes were wet at the end of Mr. Gameboy's™ paean to brand-name loyalty. She was certain they were red as well and wished for some Visine™.

"Mr. Gameboy,™ I—it's an honor. I'll do my best. How do I begin?"

"Excellent! First, you're to visit the Mary Kay™ offices on the ninety-ninth floor. They'll arrange your disguise. Then, you'll be exiled to the Bargain Bin just as if you were a regular criminal. As far as returning goes, you'll have a special Bristol-Meyers™ organipass coded to your genotype. Simply present it to the border guards, and they'll see you safely back to me."

"And how do I learn about the plot?"

"I'm afraid I can't help you there, Miss NutraSweet.™ You'll have to play it by ear."

Sally could sense that Mr. Gameboy™ was ready for her to leave. She got to her feet and turned to go, then stopped.

"Mr. Gameboy,™ there's one last thing. Could I—could I at least tell my fiancé where I'm going? He's totally trustworthy. There's not a better man or a more faithful consumer around!"

"Hmmm. Your boyfriend is Dan Duracell,™ isn't he? Yes, he's not a security risk. You may confide in him. But no one else!"

"Oh, thank you, Mr. Gameboy!"™

"Thank *you*, Miss NutraSweet."™

Sally left. Outside, Linda Lurex,™ despite her haughty arrogance, looked somehow pitiable to Sally. *She* couldn't be trusted with this assignment!

Sally interpreted Mr. Gameboy's™ permission to talk to Dan as taking precedence over reporting to the Mary Kay™ division, so she headed directly to where they had planned to meet for lunch. By now, it was almost noon!

It took Sally fifteen minutes to walk a quarter of the way around the beanstalk, to the first Chevy™ loading station. Once inside the bustling terminal, she headed straight for the Kentucky Fried Chicken™ megaplex.

Here it was that fate had first brought Sally together with the handsome and rugged Dan Duracell.™

Sally had been in the terminal on one of her days off, waiting to embark on a day trip to an orbiting Caesar's Palace™ casino, when she decided to have an Original Recipe™ lunch. The restaurant was crowded, and she had been forced to sit at a table occupied by a group of rowdy Duracell,™ Energizer,™ and Everready™ techs, those workers responsible for the smooth functioning of the beanstalk.

One of these men—their boss, as it eventuated—had been different. Quiet, calm, with a knowing smile, he had been particularly courteous to Sally, drawing her out with much more than merely cordial interest. He seemed to want to know everything about her and her job in Mr. Gameboy's™ office.

From that chance meeting, their romance had bloomed through a succession of dates—visits to the Showcase Cinema™ and Chuck E. Cheese,™ among other venues—and into a solid commitment to eventual marriage.

Now, her heart beating with excitement, Sally saw Dan across the crowded restaurant. In his black-and-gold coveralls and cylindrical foil cap topped with a fake anode, he was the most striking figure in the place.

Soon, Sally was in Dan's manly embrace. When he finally released her from the warm clinch, she spoke.

"Dan, I have the most exciting news to tell you. I've got a new job!"

"You haven't left Mr. Gameboy's™ office?" asked Dan concernedly, as he escorted her to an empty table.

"Well, in a way . . . . "

Sally explained her mission.

Dan's face assumed a worried look. "Gosh, Sally, I just don't know. It sounds awfully dangerous."

By now, Sally had come completely around to Mr. Gameboy's™ way of thinking. "Not at all! Those Zebras wouldn't dare hurt an official representative of the FDA. And besides, I don't plan on ever letting them find out I'm anything but a hardened criminal like themselves!"

Dan laughed. "My little Sally, a Zebra! It seems impossible, not to mention extremely risky."

"But I told you how the Zebras plan to destroy the beanstalk unless I discover their plans!"

"I think Gameboy's™ worried without reason, though I can't blame him for playing it cautious. Why, it would take at least four Martin-Marietta™ laser cannons of at least ten billion candlepower each, equipped with Hughes™ repeaters and positioned at precise ninety-degree intervals around the base of the tower to cut through. And how could the Zebras possibly arrange such a thing, unless they had suborned the entire tech crew?"

At that moment, a large Siemens™ robot made of Legos™ politely approached their table.

"Could you please sign for this delivery of four crates, Mr. Duracell?"™

"Certainly."

After the robot had left, Dan said, "Well, I can't say I'm not awfully proud of my little girl, playing the spy like this. Just take care of yourself and come home safe to Mama Duracell's™ favorite son."

"I will, Dan. Oh, I'll be ever so sly and tricky!"

Dan swept Sally up in his arms for a final embrace, and then they parted.

Hastening to her appointment with the Mary Kay™ representative, Sally was already envisioning her successful return. Mr. Gameboy™ would be so proud of her that he would give her a raise; perhaps, if security allowed, the multimedia would do a feature on her, detailing her daring exploits. And Dan—Dan would be so relieved and happy! Perhaps he would even want to push up the date of their marriage. She would finally have to make up her mind about her gown. Last month's online *Brides*™ magazine had featured, at her request, several possible choices. But it was so hard combining the NutraSweet™ and Duracell™ motifs into a tasteful pattern. (And how in the world would she ever get used to being known as "Sally Duracell?"™)

Soon, Sally was knocking at the door of the cosmetics division of the FDA and had to put all such frivolous thoughts from her mind.

I must concentrate on my mission, she reminded herself.

The door was opened by a Mary Kay.™ The man wore the traditional hot pink jumpsuit and requisite Kabuki-thick makeup. His false eyelashes were at least two inches long, and Sally wondered how he could even see.

"Hi," said the Mary Kay™ in a pleasant baritone. "I'm Mark, and you must be Sally. Mr. Gameboy™ told me you'd be coming in for a makeover. Step right this way."

Soon, Sally was seated in front of a digital mirror wall.

"First," said Mark, "we've got to remove your trademark."

Sally flinched, although she had known such a step would be involved in her subterfuge. She had no idea how she would feel with her trademark removed, since she had had it literally since birth, but she expected the sensation would not be pleasant.

Mark put the barrel of a Squibb™ nanoperfuser against her brow and pulled the trigger.

It took only seconds for her trademark to dissolve. Mark increased the magnification of the mirror, and the nearly obscene image of Sally's naked face filled the wall. Her heart began to beat wildly.

"There, there," Mark said. "Don't worry. I know just how you're feeling. I've seen a hundred brides go through such a spell when I change over their trademarks to their husband's . . . . "

"But I'm not getting married today! This is something I never counted on!"

"Don't fret, dear." Mark picked up a second gun and shot her in the arm. Almost instantly, Sally was Zebrafied.

Where her lovely NutraSweet™ trademark had been now flared a hideous symbol of moral, financial, and social degradation.

A barcode!

And not only was it on her brow, but the Un-Person Code was replicated like measles or leprosy all over her body!

"You're UPC now all right," said Mark with unseemly glee. "For all anyone knows, you could be Lunchmeat herself, merciless leader of the rebels."

Although Sally felt only like wailing, she steeled herself not to. She had a mission to complete, and this was a necessary part of it. The sooner she finished her task, the sooner she could regain her lovely aspartame swirl.

Mark tossed a pair of shapeless black-and-white-striped coveralls into her lap. "You can change in the dressing room while I call Hertz™ transport."

Sally did so, discarding her pretty frock and pumps and Victoria's Secret™ undies in favor of the scratchy coveralls and a pair of green foam hospital slippers she found in the changing booth. (Her Bristol-Meyers™ organipass, she was relieved to find, was secreted in one pocket, and she blessed Mr. Gameboy's™ legendary attention to details.)

When she emerged and saw herself in the mirror, she almost cried again. But before she could, two Hertz™ men had surrounded her. Both carried Glock™ sidearms and exhibited a cruel indifference to her condition.

"Okay, Zebe," one said. "Let's shake it. It's a good half hour ride to the Bin."

The men hustled Sally out the door.

"So long!" called out the Mary Kay™ rep cheerfully. "Remember—you only feel as good as you look!"

Sally drew what comfort she could from the motto.

The Hertz™ transport was a Textron™ copter whose passenger seats were separated from the pilot's compartment by a wire screen. The men strapped in Sally, and they were soon airborne.

Thankful that no other prisoners were riding with her, Sally used the time alone to compose herself and adopt the hardened persona she would need to survive in the cruel, generic world of the Bargain Bin. She was aided in this by the coarse language the Hertz™ men would occasionally toss at her.

"Look at that getup! It's probably made of *cotton*!"

"*Cotton*! Are you kidding? The FDA wouldn't waste *cotton* on a Zebe! I bet it's pure *polyester*!"

Attempting to get into her new role, Sally shot back, "Fuh-fuh-*fish*! You guys can just eat *fish*!"

The roughnecks only laughed. "That's just what you'll be doing soon enough, sister!"

In all too short a time, the Blue Lights of the Bargain Bin could be seen below them.

The Bargain Bin was a 1,000-square-mile enclave that had once been the Ancients' largest landfill. Rising up like an artificial butte from the surrounding plain, it was sur-mounted by a thick, high wall, topped with razor-wire and the symbolic Blue Lights. Armed guards patrolled the entire rampart.

Sally knew the authorities never ventured inside the Bin, only dropping in supplies. Anarchists and dictators fought for control of the prisoners' lives and existence was precarious at best . . . .

The copter landed atop the wide wall, Sally was trans-ferred to the care of the guards, and the copter took off.

One of the Brinks™ men gestured with his Smith and Wesson™ crowd-control shotgun. "Down the stairs, Zebe."

Sally entered the indicated door and found herself in a dimly-lighted, circular stairwell.

The door slammed behind her.

With no choice, she began to descend.

Before she reached the bottom, her calves had begun to ache. All those hours on the Stairmaster™ had not prepared her for this torturous descent.

Finally, she stood before the exit. Hesitating a moment, she pushed on the panic bar and stepped out into her new home.

It was 3:00 in the afternoon, and lonely shadows adver-tising Purina Dog Chow™ slanted across the Bin. Sally could hardly believe it was still the same day that had begun so beautifully with Pepsi™ radiance pouring into her faraway bedroom . . . .

A big black man was waiting for her. His barcoding, Sally noticed, was done in white.

Extending his hand, the man said, "Hi. My name's Harry."

Sally shook hands. "Harry what?"

Harry laughed ruefully. "We don't use last names here,

it's too painful. But if you must know, I used to be a Wetnap.™ I'm the Welcome Wagon,™ so to speak. If you want me to show you around, I charge a day's food."

The way Harry uttered the noxious noun was so straightforward that Sally knew no offense was intended. She pondered his offer while she took a longer look around.

Crowds of Zebras circled her vicinity like vultures, plainly waiting for her to refuse Harry so they could move in on her. In the doorway of one generic cinderblock building, a scarred man cleaned his teeth with a homemade knife . . . .

Sally shivered and turned back to Harry. "Sure. It sounds fair."

"Great. C'mon."

Sally was glad for her escort. The desperadoes and ne'er-do-wells stepped aside from Harry's path, and she noticed how he kept one hand in his pocket at all times.

"We'll get you your meal ticket, and a berth in one of the nicer ladies' dorms. Then I'll show you around a bit."

Harry led her across the grassy mesa to a large building from which wafted the odors of cooking. Inside its lobby, he secured her a smartcard from a Zebra female who apparently had somehow finagled the concession, and who demanded another day's food from Sally.

After the transaction, Harry explained. "Your card's good for three meals a day. I know you've gotta eat too, so you don't have to pay me or that gal all at once. I'll take a meal a day for the next three days, and so will she. You can get by on one."

Sally's knees had grown weak at the smell of the food. She had not eaten since breakfast . . . .

Harry noticed. "Say, what am I thinking of? Want something now?"

"I could use a little bite . . . . "

Harry conducted her into the big open refectory. They took scratched, plastic trays and battered, stainless-steel utensils and joined a line.

There was no choice of anything. One simply took an already prepared salad, main dish, drink, and dessert from among a dozen identical plates.

Sally had never felt more humiliated. Even her new clothing had not been as painful as this ritual.

Proffering her card at the end of the line, Sally paid for both her meal and Harry's. Then they carried them to a table.

Staring at a square, pink hunk of unidentifiable processed meat, Sally asked, "Is that, uh, Spam?"™

Harry roared in laughter, and everyone looked. "You'll never see nothing fine as Spam™ again, honey! This here is mystery meat!"

Sally braced herself and choked it down, along with the pasty instant mashed potatoes, imitation orange drink, and chocolate-flavored pudding.

Afterwards, Sally followed her guide as he secured her the promised dorm space in a hall where the bunks ran in endless tiers twenty high. Unfortunately, only top ones were vacant. Sally massaged one calf wistfully.

"Now I'm gonna take you to the church I go to. Then you're on your own."

The notion of a church in the Bin struck Sally as odd. She could hardly imagine any of the Official Religions maintaining a mission here, although maybe the Mormons™ . . . .

Harry led her to an innocuous building that looked like all the rest. Inside its anteroom, he paused.

"I know a lotta folks abandon all respect for the trademarks when they find themselves here. But there are a few of us who still keep the faith, no matter how bad society has treated us. I hope you'll be one of them."

With that, Harry led her into the half-lit interior of the church.

On an altar at the front of the room, dozens of empty cans, bottles, packages, and actual products, all of which were yellowed, grimed, aged, and distressed, were arranged. Yet here and there the beautiful trademarks still shone through.

There was a Campbell's Soup™ can and a package of Birds-Eye™ peas. The wrapper from some Charmin™ bathroom tissue was draped over a Sears Diehard™ battery. A Sara Lee™ cakebox stood next to a jar of Tang.™ A used Huggie™ emitted the odor of petrified baby shit over the congregants.

Respectful of the assembled kneeling worshipers, Harry whispered, "Down in the basement, we've dug into the old landfill. The cops would stop us if they knew. But as long as we keep a low profile, we can still be close to the sacred trademarks . . . . "

The sight of the venerable brand-names brought a tear to Sally's eye and inspired her with courage. Even amidst such despair and squalor, some ideals remained . . . .

"Thank you for showing me this, Harry. If I'm here very long, I promise I'll attend."

Harry hustled her out of the church. Once outside, he said, "What do you mean, if you're here long? You've been sentenced for life, girl!"

Sally adopted a conspiratorial tone. "I'm only here as long as the FDA's in power, if you get my drift."

"You don't mean . . . . "

"Yes! I want to hook up with the one they call Lunch-meat!"

Harry shook his head. "You don't know what you're getting into . . . . "

"Please, Harry!" Sally played a sudden hunch. "I ask you as a former NutraSweet™ speaking to a former Wetnap!"™

The invocation of the old clan names seemed to decide Harry. "All right. But don't say I didn't warn you!"

Now the two set out on a twisting and devious path across the face of the old landfill. Down back alleys and across rooftops they went, until Sally was thoroughly lost.

At last they stood in front of a chipboard door seemingly like any other.

Harry knocked, and a panel slid open.

"Does your car use Mobil?"™ asked the anonymous person on the other side.

"No. It runs on *gasoline*."

"Enter, friend."

Harry said, "I'm leaving you now, girl. Politics ain't my thing. Good luck."

So saying, Harry hastened away before Sally could even thank him. Meanwhile, the door had opened.

Sally went in.

A motley group of Zebras awaited her, hard-faced men and women all.

One, a short gray-haired woman, spoke.

"Why are you here?"

"I—I want to join you. I've heard a rumor that you plan something big, something that involves the beanstalk. I—I used to work there, and I thought maybe I could help you with some inside information . . . ."

The woman smiled. "What kind of information?"

"I'll only tell that to Lunchmeat himself."

The woman approached Sally and grabbed the fabric of her coveralls. "Why should we trust you? What makes you hate the FDA so much you'd go against them?"

Sally gulped. "Well, they sent me here—"

"For what?"

"Yeah," said another Zebra. "What are you in for?"

Sally thought fast. "I—I drew a mustache on a billboard of Aunt Jemima!"™

The Zebras gasped, and the one holding Sally released her. "You're okay, kid. Let's bring you to the boss."

The inner sanctum of the rebel's HQ was windowless and illuminated only by a single generic 25-watt bulb. Behind a desk sat a figure with his back to the door.

Sally was left alone with him. After a long, tense time that seemed to stretch like Silly Putty,™ he turned.

Sally shrieked. "Mr. Gameboy!"™

Mr. Gameboy,™ Zebrafied like Sally, stood. He advanced on Sally, who cowered back against the closed door.

"Are you really so surprised, Miss NutraSweet?™ I'm flattered that my masquerade was so seamless."

Sally bit a knuckle. "But—but why?"

Mr. Gameboy's™ face assumed a malevolent look. "Did I never mention to you, Miss NutraSweet,™ that I was not born into the Gameboy™ clan, that my high status in life is the result of purchasing a false identity, a borrowed past?"

"What—what clan were you born into?"

Mr. Gameboy™ leaned into Sally and spat out the name.

"The Ty-D-Bowls!"™

His face purpling, Mr. Gameboy™ launched into a vituperative speech the likes of which Sally had never heard.

"Do you have any idea, Miss NutraSweet,™ what it's like to be born into such a vile clan? To grow up enduring the taunts of all the little Nissans™ and Saltines™ and Oscar Meyers?™ 'Bobby Blueface' they called me! And other names too horrid to sully your virginal ears with. Even the Ajax™ kids looked down on me. Eighteen years of such torment I endured, until I made my escape. Do you have any real notion of the depths of my anger? No, of course you don't! Because you had the good fortune to be born into your sticky-sweet clan! Well, I made a vow to topple the system that warped me so, and now I'm on the verge of accomplishing it!"

Sally had begun to cry. "But why involve me in your schemes?"

"Because I hate you! I've hated you since the moment you came to work for me! You represent everything I despise about our society. The thought of your ultimate degradation was all that kept me from puking at your every word!"

An inner door opened, and Linda Lurex™ emerged.

"Oh, Bobby, I love it when you talk that way! Can we do it now?"

"You bet! I've waited long enough!"

With this, Mr. Gameboy™ pinioned Sally's wrists together in a grip like Krazy Glue™ and marched her through the second door.

The next room resembled a high-ceilinged warehouse space, its upper reaches accessible by catwalks.

Halfway across the room, a giant metal vat loomed. Sally was urged toward it.

At its edge, she was fitted with a harness under her arms, which were then bound. A stout rope was attached to the harness, and soon Sally found herself lifted off the floor.

Joyfully, Mr. Gameboy™ hauled away on the tackle while Linda Lurex™ watched. Sally found herself hoisted above the middle of the vat, whereupon her captor secured the rope to a stanchion.

Looking down, she saw a seething blue liquid in the cauldron.

Sally gasped. "Not—"

"Yes," Mr. Gameboy™ roared. "Boiling Ty-D-Bowl™ water!"

The villain—whom she could only think of now as Lunchmeat—took a knife from his pocket.

"Prepare to die, Miss NutraSweet!"™

Slowly, the knife bit into the rope. A strand popped audibly.

"Not so fast!"

Sally looked up.

Dan Duracell™ stood on the catwalk! And he held a gun!

Linda Lurex™ yelped. Sally's ex-boss seemed bewildered. "No, Dan. We—"

Before he could speak further, two shots rang out. The evildoer and his moll crumpled to the floor where they lay like used Scott Towels.™

In a trice, Dan vaulted to the floor, lowered Sally and unbound her.

When she could speak again, she said, "Dan, Dan, I don't understand anything!"

"Don't worry, dear," the valiant Duracell™ said. "I won't let anyone harm you."

Sally relaxed a bit. "Oh, Dan, tell me we'll get married and raise a family and everything will be fine . . . . "

"Well, it might be a little different than you imagine. But, yes, everything will be fine."

Dan reached into a pocket of his gold-and-black coveralls and miraculously removed a condensation-beaded can of Coke,™ which shone in Sally's eyes like the Holy Grail.

"You look like you could use some refreshment, dear."

"You're so thoughtful, Dan. I—"

"Hush. Just sip your *soda*."

Yet another in my catalog of stories bearing titles stolen from pop songs. In this case, however, there's a definite disjuncture between the tone of Elton John's gospel-tinged tune and my foray into comic ontology. I was trying to achieve something of the feel of the cult film Buckaroo Banzai *here: the wacky adventures of a swinging polymath, with an immense implied back story. And telling the story from the "average-guy" buddy's viewpoint is always a safe bet when your protagonist is supposed to be an off-the-scale genius.*

Take Me to the Pilot

It had been one hell of a week.

Not for me personally so much as for the world.

On Monday, Mount Fuji, dormant since 1707, had come alive in a cap-shattering explosion, spewing ashes and cinders over Tokyo like a choking smoker the size of Godzilla. As a red carpet of lava crept closer to the city, millions were being hastily evacuated.

On Tuesday, a mile-wide, mile-long crack in the earth appeared in a tectonically stable area of Mongolia, swallowing hundreds of yaks and a dozen mounted herdsmen. The Russians still weren't quite sure how deep it was because their expedition to investigate had been wiped out by a freak tornado.

From Wednesday through Friday, a global epidemic of cancer remissions had doctors chewing on their stethoscopes and discharging terminal patients by the thousands. The vacated beds were promptly taken by hundreds of women with spontaneous midterm pregnancies, some of them occurring in certified virgins.

Late Friday evening, something invisible clipped the spire off the Chrysler Building as neatly as a gardener trims a rose. The detached spire floated across Manhattan until it was over the Central Park Reservoir, whereupon it plunged into the water tip-first, sending a tidal wave to flood the basement of the Metropolitan Museum of Art.

On Saturday, the full moon rose, colored lime-green.

On Sunday, it didn't rise at all.

Naturally, the world's population was in a panic. Religious leaders of all stripes were proclaiming their various revelations. Politicians were urging calm while they raced for their hardened shelters. Scientists were holding forth with contradictory theories and asking for billions to learn more. Desperate people in the street were turning to bookies, bartenders, shrinks, and mystics for solace and answers.

As for me, I went to see my friend Darwin Vroom.

I had a hunch he might know what was going on.

Might even have a hand in it.

You see, ever since Darwin came back from discovering Atlantis—that was right after the trip into the interior of the sun, but before the incident with the intelligent ants—he hadn't been quite himself. I could tell that something big was bothering him, some riddle whose handle he couldn't quite grab.

And when Darwin got like that, there was no telling what might happen as he flailed around creatively for a solution.

Darwin lived in a converted carriage house in the Elmhurst section of town—a very nice district. I remembered when he first moved in. The neighbors soon raised quite a ruckus. Understandably, of course. That forty-foot-tall robot, the nonhuman languages employed by the nocturnal visitors, the tunneling machines, the inertialess aerial dogfights— Enough of that would make anyone who didn't know Darwin a little nervous.

My buddy had responded by buying out the entire

neighborhood at twice its valuation. Sixty acres. Paid the city twenty years' property tax in advance to grease the deal. Now there was an intelligent fence around the entire property, and Darwin was the only resident.

I stopped my car by the front gate. It wasn't really a gate, naturally, but a kind of glistening, synthetic web with a cybernetic spider hanging in the center

The spider wiggled its palps in a creepy way. "State your name and purpose."

"Burnett Thompson, and I—"

"Burn!" exclaimed the spider in Darwin's voice. "You're just in time! C'mon up!"

The spider began eating its web, and soon I was able to drive through the entrance.

The neighborhood certainly had changed since the last time I had been here.

The splendid houses of Elmhurst were being disassembled by swarms of mechanical termites. The houses closest to the fence were just giant piles of dull-colored dust. I knew that Darwin had big plans for the land. For starters, he intended some kind of weapons emplacements against his temporarily quiescent enemies, like the neutron-star creatures. And he had made an offhand comment once about an orbital-transfer stalk . . . .

But deconstruction had to precede these schemes, and so Darwin had loosed his insect disassemblers first.

I pulled up in front of the carriage house located at the center of the enclave, and got out of the car. I had to squint against the sharp sunlight reflected off the building's titanium sheathing, but once I was standing under the shade of the floating, laser-equipped defense platforms, I could easily see again.

I rang the doorbell, and much to my surprise, Darwin himself appeared. I say "appeared" rather than "opened the door," since Darwin used the teleport disk built into the front porch.

It had been ten years since we had attended college together. Me, Darwin, and Jean. It was Jean who, in a moment of drunken insight, altered Darwin's last name from "Froom" to "Vroom," permanently rechristening him in tribute to his hyperactive mind and mannerisms.

I often wondered how Jean was doing these days, married to the Galactic Overlord. A sleazy character, if you ask me. Just that goatee— But there's no predicting who a woman will fall for. Anyway, I never let myself dwell too long on her choice—painful for all concerned—to leave Earth behind for life as Queen of the Greater Cosmos.

In that busy decade since Darwin had graduated with his three and a half degrees (the half was in Provencal poetry), my friend had not altered one whit. The unruly hair, the face that always reminded me of Harold Lloyd's, the knobby wrists, the inside-out T-shirts, the childlike fondness for kelp-flavored ice cream (made expressly for him by Ben and Jerry's)— He was the same brilliant, albeit slightly unfocused genius who comes along only once in a geological era that he had always been.

Nothing seemed to leave its mark on him. Not earning his first billion. (I had helped a little with that; a small matter of cheap biomimetics; the "Love Trousers" alone had brought us one hundred million apiece.) Not battling the lobstermen. Not getting lost in the underground Martian ruins. Not mistiming that nova. Only lately had he seemed a little different, troubled by a puzzle he hadn't yet seen fit to share with me.

After Darwin stepped off the disk and we shook hands, I broached the subject of my visit. "Darwin, have you been following last week's news—?"

Holding up a hand in a stop gesture, Darwin interrupted me as was his wont. "I own up to the cancer cures and pregnancies, but the rest of the stuff is the work of someone else."

"I knew it! I just knew you'd have the answers the whole world was awaiting! Why, this reminds me of that time with Antimatter Earth . . . . "

"It's even more serious than that. And there's a lot worse to come. Unless we act fast. Follow me!"

Darwin employed the transport plate and vanished. So did I.

We emerged in a long, windowless room filled with strange devices. I recognized a Kalvonic transmogrifier and a rack of gluon torpedoes, but much else was new to me.

"You've redone the attic," I guessed.

"Hardly. We're half a mile below the surface. I designed this as a haven from most of the folks who bear me a grudge. But it's proven useless against what I'm contending with now. This hidden chamber with all its defenses is as open as a pup tent to the guy I'm chasing—if he should turn his attention on it. But it's as safe—or unsafe—as anywhere else, and all the equipment's here, so I'm continuing to use it."

"I don't get it, Darwin. What are we up against?"

Darwin sighed. I knew he hated explaining things to someone who thought as slow as I did—my IQ was only in the low 500s—but he also valued our friendship. After all, I had saved his life at least a dozen times, not the least of which was last year when his pressure suit failed on Jupiter. So he made the extra effort to phrase things so I could understand.

"Have you ever felt, Burn, that our world is not the real one? That there might exist a higher level of reality somewhere?"

"You're not talking about hyperspace or the Funny Zone, are you?"

"No, those are merely topological quirks of our own universe, integral pieces of our space-time continuum. The kind of thing I have in mind is another order of existence entirely. This transcendent plane would stand in relation to our universe as our universe stands in relation to cyberspace. Our whole plenum would be nothing more than an information shadow, so to speak, contained within this higher realm. And just as you or I can easily manipulate the contents of virtual reality in a godlike manner, so would the inhabitants of this plane be able to manipulate all reality, should they choose to do so. Nothing we can do on this level can affect them, but they can reach us simply by extending a hand."

Even my puny brain was able to put two and two together. "This is not all just empty speculation, is it, Darwin? You've actually visited this incredible realm?"

"Right you are, Burn. It's taken me some time to learn the ropes there. Not that I'm totally confident even yet. Hence the little mix-up with all those pregnancies on our Earth. But unfortunately, I've run out of time for experimentation. You see, I've alarmed someone—or something—that lives there. And he—or she, or it—is the one who's been causing all the trouble like the disappearance of the moon. I've got to stop him before he wreaks further harm. I think that between the two of us we've got a good chance to neutralize him. Are you game?"

"Game? For the biggest adventure of our career? You've got to be kidding, Darwin. I wouldn't miss this one for all the living jewels in the Galactic Overlord's slave mines!"

Darwin clapped me on the shoulder. "I knew I could count on you, Burn! Let's go!"

"How do we get there, Darwin? Do we use the Photon Clipper? The Phantosphere? The X-Crawler? The Neutrino Tube?"

"You're still stuck in our universe with any of those conveyances, Burn. You haven't made the mental leap yet. This new place—call it 'the oververse'—is simultaneously as close as your own skin, yet further away than the Silent Quasar. No, we can only reach this new plane by a combination of psychic and sensory adaptations."

A mechanical valet wheeled up on its quiet treads just then. Two of its arms held what looked to me like full-body VR rigs, while its third appendage supported a tray bearing two drinks.

"Get dressed," Darwin ordered, and I did without further questioning. (The last time I had bothered to doubt Darwin, we had ended up lost in the jungles of Venus, circa one million B.C.)

Once clad head-to-toe in our rigs, with our helmet visors still raised, Darwin picked up a glass, and I did likewise. "This is a recipe I worked out with Terence McKenna and Sandoz Labs. Psilocybin, lysergic acid, and nitrous oxide encapsulated in micronodules, among other constituents. Along with the biomimetic circuitry built into these suits, it will transport us to the oververse."

"Can we take any equipment?"

"Negative, pardner. In fact, you're in for a small surprise when we get there."

So saying, Darwin quaffed his drink. I followed suit.

"We'd better lie down," Darwin advised.

Dropping our visors, we reclined on luxurious couches I recognized as salvage from the kingdom of Opar.

I waited for the glory of the oververse to burst upon me.

Slowly, like a mountain of sugar melting under the kiss of a rainbowed mist, the familiar universe in which Darwin and I had experienced all our thrilling adventures began to dissolve. My stomach felt kinda like that time the Space Pirates from the Magellanic Cloud had shot us with their

Distress Pistols. Luckily, I hadn't eaten any breakfast aside from a Miracle Pill.

Everything got dark. Much to my surprise, I felt the transport rig vanishing right off my body, along with my street clothes. Amoeboid blobs of light began to float and bob, weave and interlace, finally coalescing into something that might have been a coherent scene.

I blinked twice, and things snapped into focus.

Trimmed grass striped like peppermint canes stretched away infinitely on all sides. The pink-and-white turf was broken at intervals by multi-branched trees that resembled cotton candy cones, fluffy tops on trunks that tapered to a point where they entered the lawn. Scattered across the grass were trillions of grazing floppy-eared rabbits. Only they were colored zillions of different colors, some of which I had no names for. It was like a bunny Manhattan.

The sky— The sky was a vivid, Tartan plaid and appeared to be stretched taut only slightly above the fuzzy treetops. Illumination came from the red stripes in the plaid.

Back in the subterranean room, Darwin had been standing on my left.

I turned to look for him.

All I saw was a creature that looked exactly like My Little Pony: a midget, neotenic, pastel-blue horse with an exaggeratedly long-and-flowing-styled mane.

"Darwin . . . ?"

The horse spoke. "Right you are, pard. Now, let's get cracking. There's no time to waste!"

I lifted what I meant to be my hand. Into my field of vision came a butterscotch-colored hoof and fetlock.

The pony that was Darwin began to caper away. I did not immediately follow.

"Darwin, hold on a minute, please. I've got a couple of questions."

It was hard for a My Little Pony to look irritated, but Darwin managed. "Okay. But hurry up. Every minute we dilly dally here, something awful could be happening on Earth."

Trying to rank my concerns in order of importance, I first asked, "You're sure, aren't you, Darwin, that this is really the oververse, the sublime realm that exists on a transcendent level of reality greater than anything we're accustomed to?"

"Yes."

I digested that for a moment. "And this is what humans look like in the oververse?" I waved a hoof to indicate myself.

"No. The humans are those rabbits, which I call 'smerps.'"

I studied the vast herds of rabbits—or smerps—for a moment. "Each of those creatures represents a particular human back on Earth, perhaps even an individual we know and love?"

"Only the olive-green ones are humans. Any smerp of a different color belongs to another species. All living things coexist harmoniously side-by-side in the oververse. Beetles, cacti, whales, Ganymedean slime worms . . ."

"And these forms we now inhabit—?"

"They appear to be a reaction of the oververse to our unnatural intrusion. We're unique. We shouldn't see any others like us—except perhaps for the evil one we're after. Although he may well have learned how to alter his oververse shape after all these years."

"Where are our original bodies right now?"

"Still back where we started, lying unconscious under the influence of the drugs and travel-rigs."

I took another long look around. The oververse reminded me of a child's board game. Candyland. Uncle Wiggly. Chutes'n'Ladders.

"Everything we experience in our old universe, all the glories and terrors, holy mysteries and vile sacrileges, springs from this—this crayon scribble?"

"Burn, you're making value judgements again. Why shouldn't something simple give birth to something complex? It happens all the time, even in the regular cosmos. I mean, hydrogen atoms are the basic building blocks of suns, right? Anyhow, I kind of like this place. It has the virtue of uncluttered simplicity."

"It's brain dead!"

"Ours is not to criticize, Burn. Just because you or I would've designed things differently is no reason to get all worked up. Now, let's go. We've still got to find the Pilot."

"The Pilot?"

"That's what I call the one who's messing up Earth. I tried dubbing him 'Dr. Strange,' but it didn't seem to fit. He's no master magician. More like the guy who crashed the *Exxon Valdez*. Even though I suspect he's been resident in the oververse for an unimaginably long time, he appears to be retarded. As gods go, he's definitely tenth-rate."

I was starting to feel like Darwin's personal echo, but I couldn't help it. "God? Does he really deserve that title?"

The My Little Pony who was Darwin assumed an expression of serious concern. "I'm afraid so, Burn. There's very little doubt that the majority of acts attributed to God are really the work of the Pilot."

I must've looked dubious, because Darwin continued.

"Haven't you ever wondered why—if there was a God—he seemed so arbitrary and capricious, overactive one century and inactive the next? Well, here we have the answer. God is a clumsy trespasser, like us. He's only arrived in the oververse during recent semihistorical times. Say the last quarter of a million years. Before then, the oververse ticked smoothly along, and so did Earth. But with the arrival of the

Pilot and his blundering ways, things got out of kilter. Oh, there were always disasters and a general tendency toward entropy. But the Pilot has introduced a whole new level of irrationality. It's quite possible, for instance, for him to back both sides in the same war! And it's up to us to stop him. Let's move it!"

Darwin started to trot toward one of the cotton candy trees. I caught up and asked another question.

"Am I right in saying that everything in the oververse has a one-for-one relationship with something in the regular universe?"

"It's a little more complicated than that, but basically, yes."

"Well, what kind of havoc are we causing back on Earth by trampling this grass?"

"Luckily, this grass represents the cosmological constant, the invisible energy inherent in the vacuum between worlds. So our passage has little effect, other than to deplete the space-time continuum slightly."

All around us, the smerps continued to nibble contentedly on the peppermint grass, ignoring us. I noticed other types of plants growing down among the stalks. For instance, a small-leafed thing with a cluster of purple berries and one with a yellow clover-like flower.

"What about these?"

"The ones with the berries are pregnancy makers. I accidentally stampeded some green smerps among a concentrated patch of them. They started eating, and you know the rest."

"Holy cow!"

"And the clover ones are cancer causers. I shooed some other smerps away from those."

"Darwin, this is too big a responsibility. I mean, I know that we've held the fate of whole planets in our hands before.

Even a dozen solar systems at once, like when the Eater of Darkness got loose. But this is something else entirely. Those other times, we always knew the capacities of our machines and the limits of our enemies. Here, one slight miscalculation and we could wipe out, I'm sure, an entire galaxy."

"Oh, easily. But we can't just let the Pilot hang in here, now that we know about him, can we? It's our duty to rid the world of him."

"I guess . . . "

We reached the base of a fluff-topped tree, and Darwin spoke.

"Each of these trees represents an entire class of objects. This is the 'natural planetary satellite' tree. It was by manipulating this tree that the Pilot caused Earth's moon to go green and then disappear."

I backed up nervously. "So we're going to restore the moon now?"

"Better than that. I suspect the Pilot is still here."

The crown of the tree was so airy that I didn't see how anything could be hiding there and said so.

"At the top of each tree is a gate into the tree's 'metaphysical control room.' That's where I believe the Pilot is hiding. I couldn't reach any of the gates alone, which is why I couldn't undo any of the changes. But with your help—"

I saw what Darwin meant. The lowest branches would just be attainable if he stood on my back.

So I sidled up against the tree and let Darwin clamber atop me. Four My Little Pony hooves dug into my back, then I felt just his rear ones, and then his weight was gone.

I watched as Darwin climbed awkwardly one stage at a time. At the top of the tree, a hole opened in the plaid sky, and Darwin leaped upward into it.

The hole closed.

I waited.

126

The hole suddenly reopened.

Out tumbled the Pilot, followed by Darwin. They both fell to the ground, landing on the cosmological constant with a solid thud.

I had just a few seconds to size up the Pilot.

What I saw was a Neanderthal. A hairy, stocky, pugnacious caveman with an overhanging brow and prognathous jaw, an escapee from one of those prehistoric sabertoothskinrippers. Then the Pilot was up and running.

Darwin got painfully to his feet.

"Quick! After him!"

We began chasing the surprisingly speedy bandy-legged Pilot. Innumerable smerps scattered left and right out of our path, causing who-knew-what havoc back in the real universe.

As we ran, I managed to gasp, "How—how did he ever get into the oververse?"

A moderate gallop was no impediment to Darwin's lecturing abilities. "The ingredients of our travel cocktail are all found naturally on Earth. And I suspect that the sensorium alterations one would experience amid dimly lit cave paintings would be a crude substitute for our biomimetic circuitry—"

"How—how has he lived all these millennia?"

"He appears to eat smerps. I've found gnawed bones . . . "

"Yuck!"

The Pilot was plainly loping toward a certain tree.

"We can't let him reach that one!" Darwin yelled. "It's the tree for 'planet-busting, rogue asteroids!'"

Darwin sped up and cut the Pilot off from his goal. The caveman who was the only god our world had ever known gave an apelike howl of frustration and changed course.

I found myself tiring. This chase couldn't go on all day.

How long could we keep the Pilot away from any and every tree? Sooner or later, with his superior knowledge of the oververse, he was bound to outmaneuver us, getting free to cause unthinkable chaos.

Darwin must have realized the same thing. He put on a final burst of speed, catching up with the fleeing Pilot and butting the legs out from under him.

The Pilot rolled head over heels through a flock of olive-green smerps.

And when he regained his feet, he was clutching two of them, one in each gnarly hand.

"Oh boy," Darwin resignedly said.

"What, what? Who's he holding?"

"It's us. Those are the smerps from which Darwin and Burnett emanate. I identified them the last time I was here."

Before we could do anything, the Pilot had crushed the windpipes of both smerps and tossed them lifeless to the ground.

Darwin pawed the ground. "Now you've gotten me really angry," he announced, and then charged.

Me too.

If you've never seen someone trompled to death by two My Little Ponies, you're a lucky person. It's not a pretty sight.

When we were done licking the Pilot's blood from our hooves, I said, "So, we've saved the world again, Darwin. But this time we died doing it."

"I'm afraid so, Burn. Our bodies back on Earth suffered the same fate as our smerps. But just as the Pilot obviously survived the dissolution of his original cave-bound corpse here in the oververse, so did we."

"And there's no return for us now? We're doomed to inhabit this boring stick-figure landscape?"

"Well, I wouldn't say that . . . . "

As Jean later told us, she was really surprised when the asteroid belt in the Overlord's home system rearranged itself to spell out a message from her two college buddies. After all, she hadn't heard from us in over a sidereal year, not counting a hyperspatial birthday card. It was only the work of a few minutes to break out the frozen clones we had given her for safekeeping. (The blank bodies, of course, were represented by two healthy smerps in the oververse.) Old Mr. Goatee unbent enough to loan her his Imperial Subspace Yacht, and Jean showed up on Earth just a few days later. (Darwin and I spent that time in the oververse setting right all the damage the Pilot had recently done, as well as fine-tuning a few cosmic parameters. People should notice the disappearance of sexually transmitted diseases, for instance, real soon.)

Naturally, the teleport plate on Darwin's front porch was keyed to Jean also. After she took the rigs off our corpses and put them on the clones, she fed our force-grown, mindless duplicates a small dose of the transport drug—just enough to put them in sync with our manifestations in the oververse—and when it wore off, why, there we were, good as new.

"And just in time," were Jean's first words to us.

I let Darwin ask why.

Many, many years ago, I read a great story by the late George Alec Effinger, entitled "And Us, Too, I Guess." This wry, despairing tale revealed that the ongoing extinction of various species, a phenomenon we all lament, had nothing to do with mankind's depredations, but was a simple cosmic reality. Every now and then, a species would simply be squeezed instantaneously out of existence by a heretofore hidden law of the universe. The narrator closed on the realization that mankind was not immune, and we all had to live now with the threat that our turn could be next.

For a long time, I wanted to write the flip side to Effinger's thesis. He was still alive by the time I finally did, but I avoided sending him my published "answer-story," out of some kind of inertia or humility or misguided deference to his tragic condition. (GAE had many health issues that preoccupied him during his life.) Now, of course, it's too late, as Effinger died in 2002, lost to that personal extinction we can all count on.

Of course, in retrospect I wish I had sent him my tale. Maybe he'll be reincarnated one day as a Yellow Snout, and we'll have a good laugh together over the whole cosmic mess.

And Them, Too, I Hope

I saw the first of the New Creatures on my way to work one Tuesday morning. Of course, I didn't know then what I was looking at, or what it all meant or portended, no more than the rest of the world did.

Having just gotten off the First Avenue bus, I was walking down the sidewalk toward my office building when something in the gutter caught my eye. At first I thought it was a discarded length of rubbery yellow garden hose, about six inches long, or some other bit of anonymous industrial debris.

But then it moved. Like a headless snake, it writhed and rooted among the papers and trash, apparently questing for something good to eat. I surmised this motivation on the part of the lemon-colored hose because it was making a snuffling noise one could easily associate with hunger.

I don't remember being frightened at all, just curious. There wasn't any sense of menace emanating from the flexible yellow organ; no horror-movie shiver swept down my spine. I felt only the same sense of dispassionate interest your typical city dweller takes from watching pigeons or squirrels feed. It all seemed surprisingly normal.

I moved to the edge of the curb and looked down. The rubbery texture of the hose was still dominant close-up, but mitigated by what were plainly pores, some of which had short black hairs growing from them. As I bent down for a closer look, the hose briefly curled upward, as if sensing me. I saw two contracting and dilating nostrils sheened with moisture. Then my eyes traveled to the other end of the hose—or snout, as I was beginning to think of it.

That end vanished down a storm drain. Plainly, the snout was attached to something.

I stepped into the street and tried to make out the rest of the body hidden in the darkness of the sewer. But the snout must have been quite long, for nothing bulked immediately behind it.

On an impulse then, I grabbed it.

I still don't know why. I just did it. The first person ever to touch a New Creature.

And thank goodness it was one of the harmless ones.

The slim trunk stiffened like a board. It was warm and tough. A pair of red eyes with black, diamond-shaped pupils, set amid a swatch of gray fur, suddenly appeared behind the grating of the sewer.

I yelped and let go of the snout, and it retracted as fast

as if it had been on a mechanical take-up reel. Then the eyes vanished too.

Well, of course I was stunned. I looked around to see if anyone else had witnessed my encounter with this strange new addition to urban subterranean life. But all the pass-ersby were too busy, wrapped up in their own worlds.

So I continued onward to work. Despite some deep reservations as to how my story would be taken, at coffee break I told my co-workers about the incident. They all laughed, naturally. Someone mentioned the old urban myth about crocodiles in the sewers. Then we all went back to our desks.

But later on, I was glad I had mentioned it. Because when all the various early sightings of the New Creatures worldwide were eventually correlated, it turned out that my encounter had been the first one!

I knew it was sheer luck and that I hadn't done anything special except to keep my eyes open and not dismiss what I saw. Still, being first did make me feel kind of special, as did all the attention from the media.

But of course, my story paled next to the New Creatures themselves. It was just a sidebar in the biggest event of his-torical times. But it was my personal brush with greatness, the only unique thing that ever really happened to me in my whole life.

Anyway, that evening I went home as always. As I ate supper, I watched the early news, but there was nothing on it about the Yellow Snout, as I had named it in my head.

But the next morning that was practically all the media could talk about.

The city was inundated with Yellow Snouts.

They seemed to like the dank darkness of the under-ground tunnels lacing the metropolis. But many had been seen scuttling across streets and parks, apparently from one lair to another. They were indeed gray-furred, about as big as a wild hog, but more sinuous, with short fly whisk tails. Their snouts were a good eighteen inches long and kept coiled close to their heads when not in use, almost like a butterfly's proboscis. The Yellow Snouts appeared to be omnivorous scavengers, as they had been observed consuming an immense variety of edibles, ranging from carrion and hotdogs, to lettuce, peanuts, French-fries, and pretzels.

People were being advised that morning by the media not to approach the Yellow Snouts, although the animals had exhibited no hostility yet, and in fact seemed skittish around people. (It was not even certain if they possessed teeth or claws, venom or barbs.) Specimens both living and dead had been secured by Animal Control authorities, and local, national, and global experts were examining them already.

When I went to work that day, I was something of a celebrity already. People who had heard of my encounter yesterday—and soon that was everyone in the building—tended to regard me as an expert on the Yellow Snouts and asked me lots of questions about them, mainly where they could possibly have come from.

This was the main question everywhere, of course. Public opinion was about evenly split between two theories: the Yellow Snouts had been dropped by a UFO, or they had been manufactured in a secret lab.

But as things turned out, both of these theories were wrong and much too tame.

Of course, I had no insights that anyone else didn't possess, and I was reduced to listening to the radio for further information.

Around noon, news of the Yellow Snouts was eclipsed or supplemented by a new event.

In Ohio, another New Creature had surfaced.

That was what the announcer called it, and we all instantly knew that term was going to be the collective name for the Yellow Snouts and this other visitor.

The Ohio New Creature was something like a giraffe, except twice as tall. There was a troop of several thousand outside Des Moines. The average body of one of these individuals was shaggy like a mammoth's, but striped blue and orange. It seemed specialized to browse on some crop at the height of its head, since its unjointed legs made it unable to bend and reach the ground. A local mayor had started calling it the Dali Llama, and the name seemed to stick.

This second sighting made the world sit up and really take notice. One New Creature, however odd, was an anomaly, but two were a disturbing trend.

Were we undergoing a planned invasion? Was some mad bioengineer letting loose the creations of his vats? No one knew, but everyone had an opinion.

The next sighting came from Texas. A kind of flat desert burrower like a manta ray was sighted by hundreds of people. These New Creatures were dubbed Sandfish.

Hard upon this sighting came reports from California of a kind of small centaur, six-limbed in the classical manner, with a wolf's lower body and a monkey-like torso. Some reporter christened them Lobochimps.

By now it was plain that whoever was depositing these creatures or whatever was making them appear was working westward. Ships in the Pacific were alerted to be on the watch for anything peculiar breaking the surface of the sea.

Productive work at my office, of course, and pretty much across the world, had more or less come to a halt. A group of us had adjourned to a bar with a television, where we could wait for the latest New Creature to appear.

Around 6:00, all local programming was interrupted for a nationwide broadcast, which was also being fed by satellites around the world.

On the screen came the bearded face of a scholarly looking man. The crawl across the bottom of the image identified him as a famous Harvard naturalist who had written many books on popular science.

Basically, as best as I can recall, with only four New Creatures with which to work, this expert had correctly devised the same theory that later scientists would confirm. He was a very smart guy.

This is what he told us.

The New Creatures were not extraterrestrial in the common sense of the word. They were carbon-based life using the same DNA as our familiar dogs and cats, spiders and snakes, with the same kinds of proteins and amino acids and other biological stuff. Their proteins even exhibited the same "chirality" as ours, whatever that was, and even interbreeding was possible. The odds against organisms from other worlds being so similar were astronomical. (The famous man smiled at his pun.)

Also, it was not likely that they were artificial, for they were too randomly complex. No sane person would have bothered to design such creatures, full of anatomical quirks and dead-end organs as they were. It was obvious from dissection that they were the result of evolution. An evolutionary track parallel to ours, but just as valid, given some unknown set of environments and circumstances.

This word "parallel" was the key, said the naturalist.

The New Creatures were from another earth. Modern physics now permitted such alternate dimensions, he said. How they had crossed from their dimension to ours, he would leave to the physicists also. But he could hazard the guess that a single crack in space, a wormhole or flaw in the continuum, was sweeping across our globe as the planet rotated, depositing New Creatures wherever it touched.

What was happening on the other side of the flaw, how

it was managing to hoover up whole flocks of creatures from obviously radically distinct environments, was even less apparent.

It was possible, he continued, that this strange phenomenon had even happened before. The ancient explosion of life forms, some of them quite bizarre, recorded in the fossil record of the Burgess Shales, for instance, could be explained in this way.

In any case, said the naturalist, it was now up to people whether they would allow the New Creatures to take their place in the world. Many of them, such as the Dali Llamas, might be unfit for our world and starve without human aid. The New Creatures could possibly bring new diseases and parasites with them, and wreak ecological havoc, displacing native species. Yet the deliberate slaughter of so much new life, in a world that had already seen so much extinction and which was suffering from dwindling biodiversity, was not a step to be taken lightly.

And with that, the naturalist concluded his speech, and we all went home, slightly tipsy or outrageously drunk, numb or wondering.

Well of course, we all know now that slaughtering the New Creatures soon proved to be impossible, thanks to their sheer numbers. As the Cosmogonic Locus—for so it was dubbed—circled the globe once, twice, a dozen times, it deposited vast herds and swarms, prides and packs, flocks and schools of New Creatures in widely scattered locations. (The first amateur videotaper who caught a stampede of Gnashtusks emerging from thin air sold the tape to CNN for a cool half million.)

This parallel earth seemed even more fecund than our own, a whole alien ecology we could only decipher in bits and pieces, host to a thousand exotic breeds that made our world look like a primitive Galapagos Island.

Nothing short of a nuclear attack could have eliminated, say, the hundreds of thousands of Snuffleupaguses in Montana or the millions of Sneetches in Mongolia, not to mention the zillions of Flutterbyes in Mexico.

To say nothing of the thankfully benign but embarrassing Polkadot Virus that took up residence in that securest of homes, the human body.

After all, look at how little success we had had trying to stem the migrations of killer bees or fire ants. There were minor successful local massacres, true, authorized and unauthorized; and some natural predator-prey pairings of New Creatures were imported intact, helping to stabilize things. But on the whole, any human attempt to eliminate the New Creatures was like trying to bail the ocean with a spoon.

As the years went by, the arrival of more and more New Creatures became just a fact of life. People and societies and institutions and ecologies have either adjusted or failed. The NRA has disappeared: but that's because now everyone goes around armed. We don't hear much from either Hawaii or the Sierra Club these days. And Australians almost wished they could have their overabundant rabbits back, in place of the Weaseldillos that eliminated them.

Life certainly is richer and stranger though. That's for sure. For a while there, it was rather like inhabiting the Garden of Eden and getting to name all the animals for the first time once more.

Scientists these days seem to feel that the influx is slowing, although they're not really sure, since it's hard to pick new faces out of the crowd, so to speak. When I think back to that day when I first grasped the Yellow Snout's snout, it sometimes seems as if I personally formed the bridge that let the New Creatures cross into our world. I know it's silly, but that's just how I feel sometimes.

I guess the only big question remaining now is one that

was brought up by the famous Harvard naturalist in a recent interview. None of the New Creatures to date, he noted, had exhibited anything like human intelligence. He went on to speculate whether any such intelligence had ever evolved on this parallel earth, and whether such sapient beings were smart enough to stay out of the path of the Cosmogonic Locus, or might be caught up in it one day. The interviewer asked, Mightn't they even be controlling the whole process, and the naturalist admitted that it might be possible, although he couldn't see why.

It made me wonder if we might get a visit someday from our smart or smarter cousins next door, and how they'll fit in. Maybe they're even tailoring our world to their own specifications before they arrive. Who knows?

I know lightning seldom strikes twice. But I'm keeping my eyes open.

Maybe I'll be the first to spot them, too, I hope.

Here's my attempt at creating a protagonist I'd have no interest in hanging around with in real life. As someone whose reactions to sports range from loathing to extreme indifference, I have no jock buddies to draw on firsthand as models. Yet getting inside the psyche of Horty Lopenbloke proved surprisingly easy. Unbeknownst to myself, I must have been subliminally storing up every example of boorish athlete behavior I glancingly encountered in the media, just waiting to decant them all into a single character. Whether I created an accurate portrait or not, I leave up to those with more experience in the field of football to determine.

This is the first story in this volume to feature a date rape scene. (The second occurs in "What Goes Up a Chimney? Smoke!") The politics and esthetics of including such scenes in an otherwise comic story is problematic. Yet much of comedy, classic and modern, features incidents that would horrify us out of context. Would you laugh at someone who fell down an open manhole if you witnessed the fall in real life? That both Horty and the protagonist of "Chimney" get their comeuppance might mitigate the employment of such a motif. Men drool, women rule.

The Man Who Stole the Moon

Hawthorne "Horty" Lopenbloke missed many fine things once extant during his glory days as a quarterback for the multi-Superbowl-winning Sausalito Satellites. He missed the adulation of fans and the media. He missed hearing his teammates protect him by crunching the bones of his opponents. He missed rifling the pigskin ovoid many yards further than any of his peers. He missed the parties, the copious free drugs, and the constant travel. But most critically, he missed the endless stream of beautiful women eager to consummate sexual relations with a famous sports star. In veritable droves, assorted gorgeous women of every age, race, creed, and educational status had once lined up on a nightly basis for a chance to perform—alone, in tandem, or in packs exhibiting the astounding coordination of trapeze artists—enthusiastic deviltries upon his iconic body, asking nothing more in return than an autographed football, a wax impression of his victory ring, or a simple plaster casting of the object of their lust.

But cruel fate in the form of a severely busted-up shoulder (experienced ignominiously not on the playing field but while horsing around poolside) had unexpectedly put an end to this easy, carnal cavorting. Once mustered out of the ranks of professional Monday Night warriors, Lopenbloke had found the glamorous women no longer quite so accessible. It appeared that the magnitude of ex-sports stars diminished more quickly than that of a nova. And like a nova, retired athletes, having violently blown off everything that sustained them in a short, extravagant display, were frequently reduced to mere pitiful cinders.

None of this sat well with Horty Lopenbloke, resettled now in California. Still fairly well-off monetarily, thanks to the forceful advice of his financial advisor, Horty had not immediately felt compelled to find a real job after his retirement. But this fiscal cushion was not as beneficial as one might think, for leisure gave Horty too much time to ponder what he termed "the injustice of it all." By this phrase, Horty basically meant "the fact that I can't instantly have everything I want anymore." And as mentioned, the area of his life where he felt this sting most potently was sexual relations.

Professional sports had unfitted Horty Lopenbloke for more than the mundane workplace. The ex-quarterback had completely forgotten how to conduct himself with a woman whom he desired. The unnatural ease with which he had plucked feminine fruit from the vine of life had destroyed any previous skills he might have had along those lines (skills that had already begun to atrophy, it should be duly noted, in college). Moreover, Horty had lost patience for the ritual maneuvers of the mating dance. He wanted what he wanted immediately and without niceties. As for monogamy, finding the perfect soul mate and marrying her—why, Horty would have laughed in the face of anyone who dared to suggest such a limiting proposition.

Which is why Horty Lopenbloke became a serial date rapist.

Oh, nothing violent. Horty always maintained complete control of his bulky, muscled frame, no matter how impulsive his urges. Not for him was the assault by a stranger in a darkened alley or even the threat of physical violence face-to-face with a victim. No, Horty was not a crude fellow, despite his former, mindless avocation. He prided himself on a certain level of subtlety and discretion. That and some seriously illicit and devastating pharmaceuticals pretty much always did the trick.

* * *

In the Sausalito night sky above the disco called Cory Thalia's Hunt Club, the new moon reigned. Its blank, black face could just faintly be discerned as rimmed with the minutest ring of diffuse amber, offering implicit promise of tomorrow's rebirth as a thread-like sickle. This mysterious and awe-inspiring sight was lost, however, on Horty as he emerged from his sporty two-seater BMW Z3 and strode across the club's parking lot. Horty had no attention to spare for astrological phenomena: he was on the prowl for sex.

Recalling the days when clubs infinitely classier than this one would have paid *him* to enter, Horty disdainfully forked over the cover charge. Inside the crowded, noisy disco, oblivious to the techno music and faddish moves of the dancers, Horty immediately applied the same quick perceptions that had once allowed him to spot holes in the opposition's defense to zero in on unattached females. Grading and cataloging the available talent, Horty began his circuit at the bar. Drink in hand, he moved swiftly toward his number one choice.

Instinctively, like an experienced safari guide testing the trigger of his elephant gun, he fingered the vial of roofies in the breast pocket of his 44L sports jacket. All set to dissolve in the drink of his chosen "date." (After one or two bad experiences with animal tranquilizers, Horty had switched to Rohypnol. The drug left his victims pliable, yet somewhat aware, and had wonderful memory-erasing properties. Of course, the active participation and delightful initiative Horty had once enjoyed from his partners was nowadays utterly lacking, causing him further to lament "the injustice of it all," but a philosophical fellow took what he could get.)

The first woman Horty approached, despite a killer body, proved on closer inspection to be treacherously concealing very blotchy facial skin beneath a surplus of makeup. Horty was mildly outraged at the deception. Didn't people have any standards of honesty these days? After some *pro forma* banter, he moved on to choice number two.

The woman sat alone at a round-topped table the diameter of an extra-large pizza. Slimmer than Horty generally approved of, yet not without the requisite curves, she was dressed entirely in white: sleeveless silk blouse and billowy linen pants tucked into the tops of ivory boots of soft leather. Her skin exhibited an opalescent purity, a milky depth. Most startling, cascades of platinum hair broke on her shoulders. As the colored lights of the club played over her, she seemed to fill with the various tints of the gels: orange to rose to green. Only in the occasional moments when a brilliant colorless spotlight lanced the mirror ball could Horty be sure of her real complexion.

Horty snagged an empty chair from a neighboring table and carried it over to the woman, ostentatiously employing a single finger to balance the chair's not insignificant weight. He spoke loud enough to be heard above the music.

"Mind if I sit down?"

The woman had been focused intently on the dance floor scene, absorbing the unexceptional antics of the dancers as if she had seldom witnessed such a relatively common sight. Her right hand rested on the stem of the glass holding her drink, and Horty noticed that her nails were painted silver, to match her eye shadow. For a moment, the woman's uniformity of skin, clothes, and makeup sent a queer shiver through him. Was she some kind of freak or psycho? Horty put the suspicion aside. What practical difference would it make if she were? He wasn't planning to have any kind of *relationship* with her.

The woman looked up at Horty and blinked, and Horty observed that her eyelashes were white too. Was she an albino? No, for her irises gleamed not pink, but—silver. Some kind of contacts, of course.

The woman smiled—her teeth, it went without saying, were practically radiant—and spoke. Horty heard elfin bells in her voice, but disregarded their charm. A dulcet voice meant little, for this gal wouldn't be doing much talking tonight.

"Mind if you sit? Not at all," she said. "Especially since you were thoughtful enough to bring your own chair."

Horty arranged himself close beside her. "What's with your get-up?" he bluntly asked. Rohypnol afforded a suitor the rare luxury of offering deliberate social offense, as all transgressions would be wiped clean chemically. "Are you like one of those Goth types? I thought they dressed all in black. Or maybe you're into vampires."

The woman continued to smile. "Neither. I've just always dressed this way. You could say it's who I am."

"What's your name?"

"Selena. What's yours?"

"Troy. Troy Stag. No last name, Selena?"

"None that I care to use."

"Kinda like your pop star namesake, huh?"

"You could say that—Troy." Selena resumed her study of the dance floor, her silver eyes assuming a hundred-yard stare.

The woman's cool imperturbability irked Horty, and his remarkably scant silo of patience leaked further grains. He had been planning to waste as much as an hour dancing with this broad and chatting her up, but her failure immediately to fall all over him made him say screw it. He'd move right into Mickey Finn territory.

"Whatcha drinking, Selena?"

Selena returned her attention to her tablemate. "White zinfandel. It's from a Sonoma winery named—"

"Yeah, yeah, all those fancypants, rip-off artists share the same grapes. They just mix it all up in a big vat and drain it off into bottles with their own labels. Knock that one back, and I'll get you a glass of the house brand."

"How generous of you, Troy."

"That's just the kinda guy I am, babe."

At the bar, Horty slyly decanted the knockout drug into Selena's new drink while the bartender's focus was elsewhere. He returned to the white-clad woman and was somewhat surprised to see she had obligingly finished her first drink. Usually he had to cajole his victims to some degree, as most women tended to meter their liquor intake to avoid getting smashed and the risks that condition entailed. This pigeon was making things almost too easy. A vague foreboding peeped up in Horty's back brain, but he squelched it. With nonexistent *savoir faire*, he set the glass down before Selena. Lifting his own, he proposed a sentimental toast: "Down the ol' pie-hole, kid."

Selena sipped her wine. "Not bad, but the bouquet—"

"You want a bouquet, visit a florist. The kick's the thing."

"That's one way of looking at oenology, I suppose." A curious smile graced Selena's face. "Where are you from, Troy?"

"Oh, I've kicked around some."

"No roots? Where were your parents from?" Selena swallowed more wine, and Horty answered her truthfully just to keep her drinking. Telling the truth was easier than making stuff up, and what could it hurt?

"My folks raised me up in Jersey, small town named Luna Park."

"Did your family always live there? Previous generations, I mean."

"'Course not. Who has roots like that these days?"

"You'd be surprised. Some people seem to stay in one place forever."

"Well, that sure don't describe my situation. Like practically everybody else in this goddamn great country, we were pretty recent immigrants. My great-grandparents came here from England through Ellis Island."

"And before that?"

"Jesus, what is this, Genealogy 101? If you gotta know, the family line goes way back to France. The ones that moved to England even changed their last name. But enough of this crap, let's get stewed."

Selena obediently finished her drink. Was this chick simpleminded or what? Within minutes, her eyes seemed to be moving independently of each other, her speech grew slurred, and she was slumping ever lower in her seat. Horty gathered her up with a big arm wrapped around her waist and with one of her arms draped over his broad shoulders. He looked around for Selena's purse, but saw none. Weird, but the hell with it.

"Gotta get the missus home," Horty offered to the one or two onlookers curious enough to cast a speculative glance at him and his shuffling burden. "She just can't handle the ol' juice."

Outside, the new moon cast its impassive negative light over the parking lot. Horty dumped his "date" into the passenger seat of the z3, then climbed behind the wheel.

Horty owned a small but impressively situated pastel-colored house on the Headlands with a view of San Francisco Bay. He parked at a hasty angle near the front door and soon had Selena's weight in his arms.

In the bedroom, undressing Selena took only minutes. Horty had become well-acquainted with this fairly intricate procedure. He even insured that his victim's clothes would remain unwrinkled by carefully draping them over a chair. Naked, recumbent on the bed, his latest conquest mumbled and twitched. Horty, naked also, sized up her attractive form as he rummaged in a bureau drawer for a pack of condoms. No point taking any chances, Horty always felt.

You just couldn't safely assume anything about strangers these days.

* * *

Mornings after one of Horty's conquests generally progressed according to a fairly predictable pattern. Waking from her drug-induced sleep, the ravished woman of the moment would exhibit varying degrees of embarrassment, confusion, alarm, and anger. Imperturbable, Horty would emphasize three angles: her shameful inebriation that had left events muzzy in her mind, his trusting sensitivity, and their mutual consent. Matters of considerate venereal protection would be stressed. Horty would be dressed, the woman naked, and the balance of power would be skewed, especially since they occupied his house, not hers. After a short period of either muted distress or feminine histrionics, the victim would in all likelihood accept Horty's invitation either to deliver her back to her parked car or call a cab. And that would be that, until the next such postcoital parting. Ninety-nine percent of the time, Horty managed to hit the gym by noon.

This time belonged among the one-percent anomalies.

For one thing, Selena failed to awaken at a reasonable hour. Horty had tried everything to rouse her: subtle tactics such as brewing fragrant coffee, flushing the toilet, taking a loud shower, and whistling; followed by cruder measures like cranking up the radio, slamming doors, and even shaking her. But Selena slept deeply on, as if her constitution had reacted uniquely to the roofies. Unwilling to leave his guest alone in the house, Horty chafed and fretted, growing more irritated with Selena by the minute. What nerve this woman had!

Around 2:00 P.M., just when Horty was beginning to worry that the administration of the Rohypnol had unaccountably plunged Selena into some kind of coma, she opened her silver eyes. Horty had placed the small bed table clock on her stomach while she slept on her back, and her gaze now fell naturally enough on its dial. The afternoon hour, verified by the sunlight pouring in through the bedroom window, had the predictable effect of causing a shocked look to materialize on Selena's pale face. She leaped out of the bed, casting the covers and clock to the floor. But her first uncanny words bore no resemblance to any exclamation Horty had ever heard from any of his overnight guests.

"The Man in the Moon! He's locked me out by now!"

Horty held Selena's clothes, crumpled in one big hand, out toward her. "Listen, babe, whatever nickname you call your main squeeze, he's gotta take you home, cuz I sure ain't having you hanging around here any more. You've already put a crimp in my schedule. Get dressed now, and I'll bring you back to the club parking lot."

Selena ignored her clothes and despondently sat back down on the bed. Horty felt a stir of arousal as his look wandered over her splendid breasts—two generous scoops of French vanilla ice cream—and her creamy thighs. (Her nipples were the color of pewter, and her pubic bush—well, as Horty liked to phrase it, "the carpet matched the drapes.") Quickly, he repressed the lustful feelings. Violation of his one-night-stand policy was unthinkable. And Selena's next words just hardened his heart further, for they indicated that she was plainly a mental case.

"Oh, never in 10,000 years has such a thing happened! To betray my lunar office for a single night of mortal pleasure!" Selena curiously looked up at Horty. "We *did* have some pleasure last night, didn't we, Troy? Events are so hazy . . . . "

Horty didn't bother to offer his correct name. "Yeah, yeah, you were super duper. Now cover your butt. We've got to get a move on before my favorite Nautilus machine is all sweated out."

Reassured about her prowess as a bed partner, Selena resumed her mournful recriminations. "What could I have been thinking? Now who will light the moon through all its phases? How will humanity fare without its immemorial, marmoreal shining beacon?"

Selena's elaborate phraseology made Horty's head hurt,

and he lost patience. "Honey, you'll have a different kind of shiner to worry about if you don't hustle your pretty ass."

Selena reacted to the threat in an unexpected manner. She shot to her feet, quivering with rage. Her beautiful face assumed a bloodless, wrathful look similar to what one might see on the tusked mask of a cornered warthog. Her expression actually made Horty stumble backward a step.

"Do you have any idea whom you're addressing in your impudent fashion, mortal? Do you?"

"Nuh-no. Who, uh, who do you think you are?"

"I am the Goddess of the Moon! And if I were back home at this moment, your arrogant carcass would be buried beneath the Mare Imbrium by now!"

At this exact moment, Horty realized the true dimensions of his unwise choice of a bed partner. He had unintentionally saddled himself with a genuine psycho, a looney-tune who could not be brushed off as cavalierly as the majority of his used-up, disposable women. Getting rid of this one was going to take some finesse.

"Uh, Selena, I'm totally behind all this kind of empowerment bullshit. You're a moon goddess, I'm a centaur, whatever pushes your buttons. Far be it from me to get between someone and their fantasies. But being in charge of the moon must be like a full-time job, right? You certainly don't have any time to spend goofing off around here. So why not get dressed, and I'll bring you wherever you want to go."

Horty offered Selena her clothes once more, and this time she snatched them away. Donning them with contained fury, she said, "Weren't you listening to me? Although I have a car, I have no place to go. I was only visiting Earth on my one free night of the month, and I overstayed my return. I'm sure the Man in the Moon has locked the door against me now. He's threatened to do it often enough. You don't know him, what he's like. He's insane!"

A sinking feeling growing in his gut, Horty sat down on a chair. The more Selena talked, the more complicated things became. He knew that responding to her nutty babbling was a mistake that would only drag him deeper into her psychosis, but he found he couldn't resist interrogating her.

"If you're the moon goddess, the babe in charge, then who's this other guy? What's he do?"

Clothed now and mellowed somewhat, Selena grabbed Horty's hairbrush from his dresser top and began pulling it through her long, platinum tresses. "I control the machinery that lights the moon. He controls the machinery that darkens it."

"Machinery?"

"Oh, yes, caverns upon caverns full of very ancient and intricate equipment."

Horty squeezed his brow with the same talented throwing hand that had brought victory out of defeat so many times in the past. He hoped for similar results now. Trying to recall basic astronomical facts gleaned from one of the few college lectures he had attended, he formulated another question. "Doesn't the moon shine because of reflected sunlight?"

Selena laughed brightly. "What a foolish notion! Of course not. It's all my hard work that brings the moon's light your way. Starting with today's new moon, I'm supposed to be notching my controls forward a little bit each night, illuminating bigger and bigger pieces of the moon's surface from the inside, while my co-worker backs off on his darkness levels. Eventually we reach the full moon. That's *his* night off-duty, of course, although he hasn't made use of the time to visit Earth for millennia, that antisocial *jerk*! Anyhow, the night after the full moon, he begins to bump his levels up while I diminish mine—in a symmetrical patterning, naturally, to create the waning shapes that differ from the waxing ones. Although the procedure's second nature to me now, it's all quite complex, and it took me a long time to learn. Why, when I recall the mistakes I made when I first began—I think I drove several species of hominids so crazy they went extinct!"

Horty's skull felt as if compressed under several line-backers. "Honey, you've got a major problem, and I don't mean how to fly back home. I really think you believe everything you've told me. And that makes you choice bait for the guys with the big butterfly nets."

For the moment, Selena seemed tolerant of Horty's criticism. "Oh, Troy, I know you don't place any faith in what I've told you. But I'll show you by tonight that it's all true."

Horty gained his feet in one convulsive motion. "Tonight! I can't have you around here tonight!"

Selena laid a lily-pale hand on Horty's arm. "Really, Troy, was I that disappointing?"

He shrugged her off. "Quit calling me Troy! My name's Horty, Horty Lopenbloke."

Selena giggled. "What an unlikely name. Are you entirely sure?"

"Of course I'm sure! I'll show you a dozen trophies if you don't believe me!"

"That won't be necessary—Horty. I'm certain that we'll practice complete honesty between us from now on. And in that vein, let me tell you that I'm famished. What's for breakfast? Or should I say lunch?"

Horty's indignation faded. He had experienced too many emotions in too short a span to sustain any of them. This intractable problem left him despairing. "You're not leaving then?"

Selena firmed her silver lips in a tight line and firmly shook her head no.

"Uh, well, then, let's see— Um, in training camp I learned

from our chef how to make a mean batch of chocolate chip pancakes."

Selena's handclap expressed her delight vividly. "That's perfect! We have no chocolate on the moon. It's one of the wonderful things I try to sample each month on Earth. What brand?"

"Huh?"

"What brand of chocolate chips?"

"Ghiaradelli?"

"Perfect!"

* * *

Much to Horty's surprise, the remainder of his unconventional day passed pleasantly enough. Selena was not a chatterbox, the kind of loquacious broad that got on Horty's nerves. During the meal of chip-spotted, cocoa-tinted pancakes—round and dark as the new moon—she simply ate appreciatively, offering only a few wordless exclamations of delight. Afterwards, she even insisted on doing all the dishes, washing each plate and cup and utensil as if she were handling the crown jewels.

"You don't know how much fun this is, Horty! I so seldom get to do such simple chores. I have an entire army of servants that won't let me lift a finger."

"Servants, huh? Like butlers and maids?"

"Well, not exactly . . . . "

Around 4:00, Selena asked if they could drive into the city. "With my visits to Earth limited to twenty-four hours, I don't ever get a chance to really explore San Francisco, which is about as far as I dare venture anyway. Maybe you could show me a few sights."

Horty ignored the insane portion of her speech. "Okay, I guess. You like strip clubs?"

"What are they?"

"Well, you see—oh, just forget about it. We'll go look at the stupid bridge or something."

In the city, they hit the standard tourist spots. Exhibiting a bored indifference he hoped would drive Selena away, Horty improvised implausible anecdotes and local history, all of which Selena received with naive expressions of delight. By 7:00, they were seated in the restaurant at Cliff House, looking west over the Pacific. As the horizon bit into the sun, Selena grew excited.

"If I had made it home, when the sun went down tonight you would have seen the first small crescent after the new moon, low in the sky. But with my lesser half at the controls, who knows what will happen?"

"Yeah, sure. Are you gonna eat that last shrimp or not?"

The sun drowned in an oceanic pool of blood, and the sky gradually assumed nocturnal hues: violet, teal, lilac. Selena's attention was riveted on the western reaches of the celestial dome. Finished with Selena's appetizer, Horty looked up as well. He was just in time to witness a startling display.

Like the round lens of a flashlight instantly powered on, the full moon suddenly snapped into view. In the space of three seconds, it cycled through a number of colors: gold, blue, green, and cinnamon. Then the schizophrenic orb vanished, whelmed by darkness.

Horty's fork dropped to the floor with a melodious tinkle. His jaw seemed intent on popping its hinges. Several other diners who had noticed the brief spectacle were reacting likewise.

Selena was fuming. "That moron! He's tweaking me deliberately. If I ever get my hands on him—!"

Horty found his voice hiding somewhere in the vicinity of his jockstrap. "Holy shit! You weren't kidding about any of this!"

"Why, of course not. Would a Goddess ever stoop to lying?"

* * *

To say that the world went wild at the moon's misbehavior would be to overstate the cumulative reactions of the average sensation-jaded citizen. First of all, only the nighted half of the globe played host to the capricious chromatic behavior of Earth's satellite. The bulk of the Oriental masses experienced nothing untoward until the next day, and their night brought only the moon's forewarned absence. In Horty's hemisphere, the majority of potential observers failed to have their eyes on the sky during the critical seconds, and so were spared the paradigm-shattering vision. Astronomers, of course, went mad in herds. Coincidentally captured in amateur and professional photographs, the moon's disturbing fan dance gained solidity and could not be written off as an episode of mass hypnosis. Disseminated to the media, these photographs engendered a twenty-four-hour crisis, pushed from the headlines at last only by new revelations concerning an ongoing sex scandal involving the Canadian prime minister and the costumed host of a children's television show. (Apparently the host's costume, an icon to millions of kiddies, played a morally challenging part in the prime minister's affections.)

Truth to tell, the disappearance of the moon meant little to the average late-twentieth-century urbanite, suburbanite, and edge-city resident. Most people never noticed the moon in its nightly course anyway. Ask the mythical Man in the Street prior to this trouble what phase of the moon was currently showing, and you'd receive a stony look of incomprehension. So in short time, reassuring hypotheses for the moon's altered albedo began to surface and gain uncritical acceptance: a cosmic dust cloud, alien intervention, an act of God. So long as the tides still rose and fell—the moon's gravity being unperturbed—and so long as the artificial satellites on which Earth's communications were so dependent remained unaffected by whatever had cancelled out the moon, people were content to do without a visible satellite. Save for the reminders of a couple of instant novelty songs and some topical jokes on late-night TV, within two days of the vanishing of Earth's old friend, most people had thrust the anomaly from their minds.

Not so for Selena and Horty.

* * *

Heading north on Route 101 out of Sausalito, Horty sat back in the passenger seat of Selena's car, terrified. He tried to remember why he had ever consented to her doing the driving. Her mode of handling her car precisely characterized the type of motorist she represented herself to be: a self-taught driver who had gotten behind the wheel only one day every month ever since the invention of the automobile. Her style was a unique mix of enthusiasm, false confidence, and skittishness. As they narrowly avoided one titanic smashup after another, Horty prayed for deliverance to the only deity he knew, other than Selena: the Supreme Coach, a figure he always pictured as a skyscraper-sized Bear Bryant, complete with trademark fedora big as a blimp.

For thirty-six hours after the moon's convulsive display, Selena had brooded in Horty's home. Bereft of her vocation, locked out of the moon by her shadowy doppelganger, she seemed enervated and despairing. Horty refrained from questioning her about her future plans or from delving deeper into her past, tiptoeing quietly around her brooding form with exaggerated caution. He had never drugged and seduced a supernatural or nonhuman woman before and felt somewhat appalled by the cosmic repercussions of his actions. Finally, though, Selena transcended her funk.

"Stop that pacing, Horty! We're going to pay a visit now to the door that brought me here. I've thought of a way I might be able to override the lock."

Horty felt a trifle irked by Selena's air of command and her assumption that he'd be accompanying her. True, he supposed, he bore responsibility for her plight. But how much did a guy have to do in the way of payback? Hadn't sheltering and feeding her for a couple of days while neglecting all his own vital concerns been enough?

"And where the hell might this door be? I hope it's not too damn far away."

"Not at all. We just have to drive to the Valley of the Moon."

And so a mild, sunny Tuesday morning found Selena and Horty back in the parking lot of Cory Thalia's Hunt Club. Selena's car, a drab Jeep with federal plates, awaited them untouched.

"How come you're driving a government car?" Horty suspiciously asked. He suddenly imagined that all the confusing events of the past few days represented an elaborate setup to bag him for that extra-large cocaine purchase back in '93.

"This vehicle belongs to the Park Service. I bribed a Ranger to make me a set of keys and let me use it once a month."

"Bribe? What does a Goddess use for folding money?"

Selena looked at Horty as if he had asked the result of two plus two. "Do you have any idea what the Exploratorium in San Francisco pays for genuine chunks of lunar rock?"

"Oh."

The Valley of the Moon, Horty knew, was a picturesque

part of Sonoma County. It featured many wineries, resorts, and recreation areas. Other than that, he knew little about the region. So as Selena conducted them now at alarming speeds through such towns as San Rafael, Novato, and Petaluma—she had insisted on staying together and on using the Jeep, not Horty's BMW ("My Ranger friend could get in trouble if I don't return his car.")—Horty listened to Selena's history about the area with gratitude, as a means of diverting his attention from imminent accidents.

"Before Europeans arrived, the Miwok and Pomo Indians inhabited Sonoma, which in their language means 'Place of Many Moons.' I was their incarnate Goddess, of course, appearing once a month on Earth in their midst. They were such a nice group of people, but limited in what they could offer a girl in the way of entertainment. Blackened salmon dinners and music heavy on the drumbeats get stale awfully fast—although when I encountered a similar mix just recently in a fancy restaurant, I became *so* nostalgic. I certainly began to miss the Old World pleasures I had enjoyed for so many millennia in Greece and Rome, Avignon and Camelot, Ur and Babylon. But the portal had refocused itself here in what would one day become California, and I had no choice in the matter."

"What do you mean? You're the Goddess who controls all these moon gadgets you've told me about. Couldn't you make your doorway pop up anywhere you wanted?"

"Not really. You see, I didn't create all the moon machinery and a lot of it is beyond my understanding. I'm just a caretaker established by those known as Almost the Oldest Ones."

"And who're they?"

"A race of incredibly antique—but not ultimately ancient—beings from somewhere else in our galaxy. They're the ones who decided mankind needed a luminescent satellite to help in their development. They plucked me from my home world, while humanity was still dragging their knuckles, and put me in charge of the moon. They brought the Man in the Moon from elsewhere, as well as our servants."

"So your bad-ass partner up there's not as human as you?"

"Not in certain respects, no."

Horty pondered this information, while Selena continued her story and the intermittent horns of angry drivers assailed them. "When western civilization arrived, I became friends with various prospectors and settlers and farmers, showing up at my regular times. But only once since then have I revealed my true identity to a certain special man."

Horty felt irrational jealousy. "Who was this jerk?"

"Jack London."

Dim college memories surfaced in Horty. "The guy who wrote stories about wolves?"

"And much more. Jack owned a farm some 800 acres in extent in the Valley of the Moon. His land included my portal. It would hardly be polite to materialize in someone's parlor without introducing yourself now, would it?"

"So we're heading for his house now. Is this London guy still alive?"

Selena sighed. "Alas, Jack died in 1916. And his house now stands in ruins."

Selena's incredible talk of visiting savage Indians had affected Horty less than the suddenly vivid picture of her consorting with some geezer, dead nearly a century, whose very house unforgiving time had crumbled. He regarded her pale profile in silence for many miles thereafter.

In the town of Santa Rosa, they turned east on Highway 12. The Mayacamas Mountains loomed to the north, paralleled by Sonoma Mountain to the south. Vineyards stretched away on either side of the road. They traveled now through the extravagantly lush and splendid scenery of the Valley of the Moon.

A sign advertising Jack London State Historic Park advised them to turn off onto Arnold Drive some two miles outside the town of Glen Ellen. Selena drove this familiar road with more confidence, soon bringing them to a gravel parking lot. They left the Jeep, paid a small fee, and entered the grounds of the park. On this weekday, very few other people roamed Beauty Ranch, the former estate of the famous writer. For a time, however, until they could be certain no witnesses would observe them, Selena and Horty ambled innocently among the ruins and restored structures: a cottage, barns, stone silos, a winery. Selena paused by London's grave for a moment of silence, while Horty fidgeted. Then, seemingly alone on the property, they moved illicitly inside the posted ruins of Wolf House. In the corner of one shattered room, Selena approached an innocuous fragment of wall and began fooling with unseen features on its surface.

Horty nervously looked back over his shoulder, concerned some Ranger would intrude. "Are you sure—" he began to ask, turning back to Selena. And then he saw what the Goddess had wrought.

A person-sized oval of silver mist had replaced a portion of the wall. And out of the fog stuck the head and shoulders of an alien abomination.

Comic books were Horty's favorite reading material. He preferred either violent ones involving ill-mannered and heavily armed vigilantes or risqué ones featuring big-bosomed and immoral teenagers. But once Horty had accidentally purchased a black-and-white reprint of some space cartoons by Basil Wolverton. What goggled at him now from the doorway to the moon recalled a Wolverton drawing. From scaly shoulders broad as any found in the NFL emerged a plucked-looking, scabby neck as long as Horty's arm. The neck supported a disproportionate, blocky head topped with a shaggy mat of orange hair partially obscuring saucer-like eyes. A nose like a warty cucumber protruded out four inches. The creature's lower jaw hung open, revealing rows of squarish teeth looped with green saliva.

"Jesus!" Horty shouted. Instinctively, he stepped forward and swung his fist at the creature. Hitting the alien felt like punching a rotten, moss-covered plank. He connected at the same moment that Selena managed to shut the door to the moon. The closing of the portal severed the monster at the neck, and its head thumped to the floor amidst a gout of green blood.

Selena regarded the remnant of the alien somberly. "Poor Pretzel," she said.

"You *recognize* this hideous thing?"

"Of course. Pretzel was the Man in the Moon's chief servant. He must have been sent to guard the door against my possible return. Pretzel had no choice but to obey, but he never would have hurt me. And now he's dead."

Horty sized up the repulsive features of "poor Pretzel," then asked, "Are *your* servants this ugly?"

"Oh, no," Selena replied. "Much less handsome."

* * *

In the early part of the twentieth century, a traveling salesman for the Chattanooga Bakery in Tennessee, a man named Earl Mitchell, continually sought new ways to please his customers, mostly rough-and-ready coal miners in his home state and the bordering ones of Kentucky and West Virginia. The brawny, grimy workers frequently expressed a desire for a snack that would withstand the rigors of the miner's life, something filling, sturdy, and tasty. Earl was stymied by their demand and sought clarification at least on size.

"How big this here snack's gotta be?" he asked a miner

one day. Seeing the full moon rise over the company store, the anonymous hillbilly kobold framed the orb with his hands and said, "Jest like thet." Back at the bakery, Mitchell, like some confectionery Edison, experimented with graham crackers, marshmallow, and chocolate in the appropriate dimensions. And eventually at one Eureka moment, the enormously popular Moon Pie was born, a legendary Southern delicacy invariably washed down with an RC Cola.

The Moon Pie, of course, in its round, chocolatey darkness, paradoxically ended up representing not the full moon, but the new. And it was in the Moon Pie Factory that the Man in the Moon had established or found *his* doorway to Earth.

"He doesn't believe I know the location of his door," Selena told Horty after the debacle at Jack London's house. "As I told you before, he hasn't used the portal in so long, I think he's almost forgotten about it himself. All his attention and all his guards will be focused on my door. He'll never expect us to enter through his."

Thus it was that Horty now drove himself and Selena in their rented car through the streets of mountain-girt Chattanooga, heading toward the premises where Moon Pies were created. His head still spun from the encounter a day ago with the nightmarish Pretzel, and he tried to trace the steps that had led him to this moment. How was it that his life had become so entangled with Selena's? What spell had she cast on him? Did she represent the only real excitement he had experienced since his NFL career ended? How far was he willing to go with this adventure? Possibilities and limits swirled in his fevered brain, and he could barely concentrate on the road.

They parked in the factory lot and emerged to join a line for the visitors' tour. Sweet odors of chocolate and marshmallow and cracker flour wafted over them, and

Horty began to salivate. The double stack of pancakes and half pound of bacon he had consumed for breakfast—while Selena watched and sipped at her tea—hadn't stood by him as well as he might have wished.

As if sensing this hunger, Selena said, "We won't sneak away from the tour until after the free samples."

A guide assembled the group and led them inside. Horty paid little attention to his industrial surroundings. The scents of baking were driving him crazy. At last the pastry samples materialized. Selena took a Moon Pie and broke it open to reveal the dark cake's white interior. She fed a piece to Horty, and Horty gratefully devoured it as if it were a strange communion. A blissful satiation filled him, and he felt in control again. He congratulated himself on putting up with Selena so patiently; a much wiser strategy than storm and bluster. Soon now he'd be shut of her forever, thanks to his devilish slyness.

As they were being conducted out, Selena hung back. With a whispered "Now!" she pulled Horty into an alcove.

Within minutes, they had worked their way, unobserved, to the basement level of the factory. Selena zeroed in knowingly on an unlocked storeroom door. And in that dimly lit bunker, amidst burlap sacks of flour, she unhesitantly opened up the Man in the Moon's doorway.

The Moon Goddess paused at the silver oval. She blinked her mesmerizing eyes and said, "Farewell, Horty, and accept my thanks! I go now to battle for my kingdom!"

Selena stepped into the matter-transmitter and was gone. The portal began to shrink uniformly from its edges inward. A feeling of loss and despair filled his guts, and Horty yelled, "No!" He dove through the dwindling gate as if between a narrow gap flanked by opposing tackles.

The breathable air below the surface of the moon smelled faintly like moldering hay. And the dusty illumination in these enormous, high-vaulted caverns of the moon resembled moonlight itself as received by Earth. Everything from the rough-hewn floor to the distant walls and lofty ceiling, from the spectacle of an infinite corridor to the gargantuan, towering masses and ranks of complex machinery seemed painted by some master of chiaroscuro. The stark palette of black, white, and grays made Horty remember an old film he had watched once called *Forbidden Planet*, especially the scene when the visiting Earthmen toured the relics of the Krel with that dame in the short skirt.

Awed, Horty regained his feet with the nimbleness conferred by one-sixth gravity, not even feeling the pain of his scuffed hands. Selena stood a few yards off.

"So, my champion has decided to accompany me. Very well, let us confront our nemesis without delay."

Selena let Horty come up alongside her, and then she led the way down the long corridor.

Horty lost all track of time. It seemed they marched for weeks, past a plethora of strange sights. Huge lever arms that ceaselessly rocked, bellows big as houses that inflated and shrank, monitors that showed terrestrial and intergalactic scenes, deep, bubbling, fume-wreathed pits filled with something like mercury and rimmed with catwalks along which Selena and Horty hurried. The marvels saturated him until he grew numb and moved in a fog. Once Selena had to pull him back with a shouted warning: "Don't fall over those klystron tubes!" Her voice reinvigorated Horty, and he moved with renewed mindfulness.

Eventually they reached their destination: a room as big as several football stadiums. The space was half-filled with hordes of aliens like Pretzel and half-filled with another race that Horty realized must be Selena's minions. Her servants resembled human-sized, bipedal turtles with scorpion tails and beaked faces. They did indeed win the Wolverton

Draw-Alike Ugly Contest, thought Horty. On a control dais in the center of this assemblage sat a hunched figure whose features Horty could not discern at this distance.

Selena and Horty had entered the amphitheater at a point high up one of its curving walls, where a balcony turned into a flight of steps. Now Selena bellied up to the balcony's rail and vented a defiant rallying cry.

"Servants of the Goddess! Your mistress has returned!"

Chaos erupted immediately, as the two aliens races began struggling in hand-to-hand combat in a scene that quirkily fused the pummeling of a *Three Stooges* fracas with the surreal inhabitants of a Bosch canvas. Selena grabbed Horty's hand and started down the stairs.

"Quickly! We must stop the Man in the Moon before he escapes!"

On the floor, they wove their way through the tumult, Horty bulling through in the lead. None of the Man in the Moon's servants dared lay a hand on Selena, and the advancing pair simply had to avoid getting accidentally bowled over. Soon enough, they attained the edge of the control platform.

The Man in the Moon stood up from a bank of switches, and Horty staggered backward at his appearance.

From the neck down, Selena's dark partner was human enough. But his head destroyed any illusion of normality. Consider first that his head measured as long as his body. Second, that it was shaped like a pockmarked crescent and colored a waxy yellow. Third, that it was approximately two inches thick. Bulbous eyes occurred a third of the way down on either side, a needle-like nose at the halfway point, and a grinning split of a toothless mouth in the lower third. Horty was instantly reminded of the foam-rubber headgear worn by rabid football fans.

"Get him, Horty!"

At the sound of Selena's voice, Horty mastered his emotions. He leaped onto the low dais. The Man in the Moon raised his arms—in defense or attack, Horty could not be sure. So he launched a roundhouse swing.

Horty's fist went in one side of the Man in the Moon's thin head and out the other. The alien's whole lunar cranium crumbled into fragments, like a hunk of bad cheese, and Selena's ex-partner collapsed to the floor.

Bringing up his fist to his nose, Horty sniffed. Cheese indeed.

Upon the destruction of the Man in the Moon's fragile head, the fighting among the servants stopped. Selena jumped up beside Horty.

"The battle is over! Welcome your new master, the White Rabbit!"

Horty was baffled. "What are you talking about, Selena? Who's this White Rabbit?"

"You are, of course. Your family's French name, Horty, was *Lapinblanc*. Your ancestors were my loyal devotees for generations. Many cultures see in the moon's mottlings not a man, but a White Rabbit, my preferred symbol. I chose you to replace my old consort. He grew wearisome to me some centuries ago, but none of your line appealed to me till now."

"*You* chose *me*? But, but—I drugged you and kept you from getting home!"

Selena laughed in an eerie peal, and Horty realized he had known nothing about her till this moment. "Your drugs had no effect on me, nor did the Man in the Moon truly lock me out. Poor Pretzel was only stationed at my door to welcome me home. No, the old cheesehead still loved me and wanted me back, provided I returned alone. Alas, Horty, I confess now, I played you like a helpless mooncalf! But don't be angry—not that it would do you any good. I've elevated you far above your kind, both literally and figuratively. In exchange for a few small mechanical responsibilities, you possess me and my charms, a vastly extended life—as long as you keep me amused—and dominion over half the moon."

Horty could barely believe his fate. "But how will I stay busy up here?"

Selena snuggled up sinuously to her new consort. "That shouldn't be a problem. And don't forget, you get to visit Chattanooga once a month."

"But what about from day-to-day? What will I do with myself?" Horty looked out over the sea of grotesque yet obedient aliens waiting expectantly for his reaction like two rival teams—

Two rival teams. Suddenly inspired, Horty reached down for several hunks of the Man in the Moon's head. He wadded them up into a torpedo shape, then pitched the mock football into the audience. In the moon's light gravity, several aliens soared high to catch it.

Smiling, Horty turned to Selena. "Call me Coach White Rabbit, and you've got a deal."

I hope readers won't feel cheated because they can also find this story in Rudy Rucker's fine collection entitled Gnarl! *(Four Walls Eight Windows). But I did want to proudly lay claim to my half of the writing here (and to the title as well).*

I never would have chose Pythagoras as a protagonist on my own. But once directed toward this intriguing figure by the ever-questing, off-center mind of Mr. Rucker, I quickly got on the Pythagoras bus. We began this story one snowy winter afternoon when Rudy was visiting Providence and finished it over the ether shortly after he returned to sunny California. Somehow, out of the two climates, we distilled the weathers of an ancient Greece that probably never existed. That's what collaboration is all about.

The Square Root of Pythagoras
[co-written with Rudy Rucker]

The Crooked Beetle spit a number form into its cupped claws, the number a black, oozing mass almost ten stadia in length if uncoiled, now intricately folded into and through itself. The creature's oddly articulated arm joints creaked as it urged the prize upon the human standing cowed before it.

"Take it now," the *apeiron* Beetle said in a richly modulated drone. "You're almost ready for it. The fifth and the last of our gifts." The prize's weight was immense, and the human staggered, lost his balance, seemed to fall sideways out of the dream universe—

Morning sunlight fell across Pythagoras' face, and he woke. For a few moments, his mind was blessedly empty, free of the crooked, the infinite, the irrational, the unlimited—free of the *apeiron*. Pythagoras sat up, pulling a musty sheepskin around his shoulders like a mantle. Looking out of the mouth of his cave, he could see down the rocky slopes to the orchards and fields that nestled in the curve of the river Nessus.

The river. Sight of the gleaming, watery thread brought back the weight of his knowledge. Pythagoras' little store of five worldly numbers included the river's number, which, like the others, was inconceivably long. The knowledge of the River Number had come to him from the Braided Worm, the first of the *apeiron* beings who'd appeared to him, half a year ago.

Now there were five of these grotesque, unclean, raggedly formed creatures haunting his nightly dreams. A terrible psychic burden, yes, but there was gain in the encounters with the Tangled Tree, the Braided Worm, the Bristle Cat, the Swarm of Eyes, and the Crooked Beetle, for each of them had made Pythagoras a gift of a magical power number. The Crooked Beetle had been disturbingly portentous in granting of its boon. The new number surpassed all the others; it was of a crushing size. Clearly it meant something important.

Pythagoras sometimes wished that he could still believe his old teachings: the world was a simple pattern of small, integral numbers; it would be nice to once again have a soul as innocently harmonious as two strings tuned to the ratios of five and three. The *apeiron* dream creatures and their terrible gifts had begun to undermine everything Pythagoras had once believed.

Thank Apollo the Sun was back with its respite from the dreams. It was a fresh day, a good day, with students to teach and, perhaps, come late afternoon, a noblewoman with whom to dally.

There was a large stone ledge outside the cave, Pythagoras' public space. Stooping to the hearth there, Pythagoras assembled a rough cone of twigs and prepared to invoke the Fire Number he'd obtained from the Bristle Cat. This number was not the skeletal "four" of the tetrahedron, which some took to be the form of Fire; no, thanks to the demons of the *apeiron*, Pythagoras had experienced the *gnosis* of one of the true and esoteric numbers for physical Fire in this fallen world of Woman and Man. The magically puissant numbers for physical things were so huge that of all men who had ever lived, only Pythagoras had the mind to encompass them.

Pythagoras formed the Fire Number in his soul and projected it outward.

The sheaf of twigs, really no cone at all, became covered over with coarse red/yellow triangles and pyramids, mere simulacra of flames, for Pythagoras' Fire Number, in the end, was but a workable approximation. Now the divine nature of the world intervened, cooperating so that the lithe, curvy forms of actual fire sprang up from the twigs. The Fire Number kindled the true Fire inherent in the organic wood, activated the particles of elemental Fire placed in the wood by the beneficent rays of the great One shining Sun.

As the fire heated the water for Pythagoras' morning ablutions, the philosopher pondered his dream of the Crooked Beetle and the vast new pattern gained at such costs from his dreamworld familiar. The new number form corresponded to some object or quality to be found in the mundane world—the *peras*—in which Pythagoras was now once more firmly enmeshed. But the crucial identity of the pattern would remain a mystery until he actually experienced the shock of recognizing the physical form to which the number was attached in the higher realms. Pythagoras had learned patience and was content for the time being simply to revolve the number in his powerful mind.

Soon Pythagoras had finished washing and was intent on assembling, like any common hermit, his simple breakfast of honey, dates, and almonds. How useful it would have been, Pythagoras thought as he enjoyed his meal, to have the numbers for these staples. But the creatures of the Unlimited granted their gifts capriciously, and when for his second gift he'd asked the Tangled Tree for the signifier for honey, he'd instead received a Sheepskin Number.

No sooner had Pythagoras brought the last fingerful of honey to his bearded lips than he espied his prize student, Archytas, eagerly ascending the slope to his teacher's cave. Pythagoras sighed, daunted by the zeal of the young man.

Archytas began talking excitedly before he'd even reached the ledge. Something involving the golden ratio and a new ruler-compass method for inscribing a regular pentagon within a circle. Pythagoras let the words flow past him undigested. He found his young acolyte's modernistic, geometric constructions overly refined.

"O, why not just use trial and error till you find something that's reasonably close to cutting the circle in five?" said Pythagoras. He would have despised such a thought a year ago, but his escalating traffic with the demons of the *apeiron* had corrupted the asceticism of his taste.

Hoisting himself level with Pythagoras, Archytas gave a short, braying laugh, assuming his mentor to be joking. "Indeed. And why not jump headlong into the pit of impiety and say that integral numbers are not the basis of all things? Why not maintain that the *apeiron* is the very warp and woof of our world?"

"Will Eurythoë be coming for her lesson today?"

Taken aback by the abrupt change in topic, Archytas made a face as if he had bitten down on an olive stone. His demeanor grew stiff and somewhat remote. "My mother, the gods save her, indeed persists in her uncommon thirst for knowledge. Echoing my father Glaucas' complaints, the other wives look askance at Eurythoë's unbecoming philosophical ardor, wondering why she cannot content herself with simple domestic pursuits. But I quash all such talk by defending your virtues, both as a citizen and as a wise man."

Archytas stared grimly at his teacher. "I hope my faith in you is fully justified."

Pythagoras felt a smidgen of shame. He disguised the feeling with a peremptory manner. "Of course, of course. But you still haven't answered my question."

Archytas forced out the reply: "Yes, my mother plans to visit you in the late afternoon."

This matter settled, the two men picked up their dialogue not from Archytas' revolutionary construction, but from the point where Pythagoras' discourses had ended yesterday. As the sun rose higher, they were joined by other young scholars from Tarentum, until finally Pythagoras sat at the center of a stellated polygon of questing minds. The topic for today was Pythagoras' wonderful, geometric proof of his great theorem that in a right triangle, the square on the hypotenuse equals the sum of the squares on the sides. To illustrate his argument, Pythagoras drew a diagram in a flat patch of sand; it was his "whirling squares" image, showing a square inscribed at an angle within a larger square.

Though Pythagoras' belief in his original worldview was all but shattered, he still enjoyed the verbal puppet-show of his ideas. He taught with a craft and grace that come from long experience; he could make dry magnitudes and geometries sing like the notes of a fine musician's lyre.

When the sun was high overhead, rumbling stomachs dictated a break, and the living polygon of scholars fell apart into its component points. Taking advantage of the shade in the mouth of the cave, the town dwellers broke out food from their wallets, eagerly vying to offer Pythagoras the choicest morsels of flatbread and feta. Their teacher accepted with the stern good nature that chose no favorites.

Gourds of cool water from Pythagoras' personal spring complemented their simple fare.

"King Glaucas spoke of you again last night, master," said the sinewy, wolfish Alcibedes. Unlike the other pupils, he wore a short sword at his belt. "At dusk in the forum. He told the senators and the slow-witted priests of Apollo that you are a sorcerer. The icosahedral ball you gave Eurythoë—Glaucas terms it a magic amulet. He claims the mere sight of it caused the goats to give sour milk."

"My father is troubled," said Archytas. "He fears the people tire of his rule. The unity of our little band disturbs him. He fears you may foment a revolution, Pythagoras. Now that you've won his wife and son as pupils, who else might not follow you?"

"A tyrant's bed is most uneasy," murmured Alcibedes, staring down at his sword.

"What of the common citizens, then?" said Pythagoras. "Do they speak well of me?"

"The farmers are happy to have their fields well-surveyed," said Meno. "And the innkeepers rejoice to have so many of your students lodging in Tarentum."

"Pythagoras' knowledge of the heavens has even helped the priests in their computations of our calendar," chimed in Dascylus. "After all, was our teacher not the first to reveal the identity of the Evening Star and the Morning Star?"

"Even so, Glaucas can inflame the rabble to hate me," said Pythagoras. "At times I fear for my life."

"Perhaps Glaucas fears for his life as well," said Alcibedes. "Who knows what the future might bring? It seems unlikely that both you and he can live here forever, O Master. What if you really were to die? You should prepare us. Can you not lift the injunction of secrecy from your great teachings? We long to spread your wisdom far and wide. Indeed no man is immortal, and when you pass into the Elysian world, it will be our lot to inculcate your noble truths. Were it not better that we begin to practice at it even now?"

For the second time today, Pythagoras felt a twinge of shame. His reasons for making his teachings secret were simply that he did not want to give away that which he could sell to students. "I will ponder upon your suggestion, Alcibedes," he said slowly. "But now, my children, let us return to our studies. If some day you are to farm these plants, you must learn their foliage well."

After several more hours of vibrant discourse, Pythagoras abruptly called a halt to the day's lesson. "My faculties are waning, lads. We shall delve further into the consequences of my great theorem tomorrow."

As he watched the sturdy youths rollick down the slope toward Tarentum, Pythagoras realized he had told them only half the truth. While his intellectual powers were indeed spent for the day, the energies of his loins had reached an almost painful peak as he anticipated the arrival of Eurythoë.

Pythagoras barely had time to clean and curl his beard before he spotted Eurythoë on his side of the river, her delicate, sandal-clad feet scribing a clean curve across the rocky slopes, a curve designed to intersect the vertex of his soul.

She arrived, flushed from her hike and infinitely desirable. Black curls lay pinned by a sheen of sweat to her brow. Her bosom fluttered beneath the white fabric of her robe. A subtle musk as of some wild animal rose from her pleasing form.

Eurythoë's deep gray eyes met the gaze of the philosopher, yet her manner was skittish. Rather than immediately accept Pythagoras' embrace, as was her wont, she looked nervously back toward Tarentum.

"What troubles you, dear Eurythoë?"

"I am consumed by fear that our illicit love will be discovered. I saw a most evil omen this morn."

"What manner of omen?"

"One of the slaves returned from the market bearing a pannier of fish, and atop the wet pile lay one with a dark, muddy tail! You've often inveighed against those very creatures! *Eat not fish whose tails are black.*"

Pythagoras made a dismissive gesture. "My reference to the evil nature of such creatures was but an allegorical warning against those who draw strength from muck. Do not trouble yourself any further, Eurythoë. You didn't eat of the fish, did you? Very well then, we've nothing to fear. Let us hie ourselves to my soft, warm pile of sheepskins."

Conducting the wife of Glaucas, the mother of Archytas, into his cave, Pythagoras soon reveled in the sight of her naked charms. Quickly doffing his own clothing, Pythagoras caught her up in his embrace. As she always did, Eurythoë began their lovemaking by stroking his golden thigh.

Marvel of marvels, an extensive, irregular patch of Pythagoras' inner left thigh was some substance other than flesh. The stuff was utterly impermeable, too hard to cut with a knife or even to scratch with the noblest gem, yet it was also like the thinnest leaf of beaten metal, flexibly mimicking the architecture of his muscles and tendons and veins, the bright patch merging imperceptibly with his skin. Though the inadequacy of language forced Pythagoras to call it "adamantine gold," the thigh seemed really to be of a substance quite other than anything seen upon Earth.

The golden thigh was an uncanny scar from Pythagoras' very first dream meeting with the creatures of the *apeiron*, the thigh an ever-present reminder that the creatures were indeed more than dreams. In that first meeting the Braided Worm and the Crooked Beetle had appeared to him, the Worm, a loquacious and foully knotted creature whose form so defied all definition that Pythagoras could never determine if its component strands numbered two, or three, or four. The Worm had offered Pythagoras the magical power of the River Number, and when Pythagoras had greedily accepted the offer, the Beetle had bitten deeply into his thigh, turning a part of it into adamantine gold. The Beetle had laughingly termed the change a "memory upgrade," and then somehow the Worm had transferred the River Number into the enhanced Pythagoras. He'd woken from that dream irrevocably changed.

At first, Eurythoë had been frightened and repelled by Pythagoras' gleaming thigh. But when he told her the alteration was a sign of the gods' favor—and why not believe this?—she learned to find it erotically stimulating.

She drew her fingertips across the eerily sensitive surface of the golden thigh, and soon the dust rose from Pythagoras' mound of sheepskins as he bisected Eurythoë's triangle and became the radius to her sphere. The even and the odd blended into the One. And then, all passion slaked, the couple lay loosely embracing, smiling full into each other's eyes.

Trying, as always, to mentally encompass the wonder of Eurythoë, Pythagoras mused that she herself must embody a number form, as did every woman and man. Women were even numbers, men odd. But what a large number it would take to adequately represent Eurythoë, to capture in a net of notational dots this woman's scent, the curved surfaces of her honey-colored skin, the soothing tones of her normal speech, and her sharp cries of ecstasy.

Suddenly there was a clatter from the lip of the cave. Falling stones? Pythagoras sprang nimbly to the arched opening, feeling himself lithe and wise. A well-aimed rock whizzed past his head and shattered against the cliff beside the cave's mouth. All at once he felt himself nude, middle-aged, and absurd.

"Against the advice of your own maxim, you have poked

fire with the sword, O Pythagoras," sang a mocking voice. "All the town will hear of it."

His tormentor was an open-mouthed, fat-bellied little figure in a white toga that revealed bare, thickly tufted legs. At first glance he looked like—a vengeful fish with a black tail. Evidently he'd come to spy on Eurythoë's lovemaking. He made the insulting gesture of the fig and raced down the slope like a homing pigeon.

"Senator Pemptus!" exclaimed Eurythoë. "One of my husband's spies. O, Pythagoras, you must flee. I'll hurry down and try to salve my husband's wounded pride. But I fear the worst for you." She began weeping.

"Must I run from an innumerate, bean-eating tyrant like a common slave?" said Pythagoras. "And what of my pupils? What of our love? I'd rather remain here in my cave, aloof with my music." Pythagoras gestured at his beloved monochord, a one-stringed instrument that had taught him much. "I've not told you this, Eurythoë, but the gods have granted me certain miraculous powers in addition to my golden thigh."

Eurythoë hugged him, dried her eyes, and began trying to repair the disarray of her hair with ivory pins. She succeeded only in making it appear that she wore a lopsided bird's nest atop her head. Finally, she spoke again.

"There are too many of them, Pythagoras, and they will come for you. Humble yourself and flee. For what does anything matter if you or both of us are dead? Save yourself, and let me do what I can to salvage my own position. Think of your own maxim, Pythagoras: *Give way to the flock!*"

"You are right, my dear," said Pythagoras, quietly pulling on his robe. "*The flying dust survives the storm.* I leave on the instant. Spare me one last kiss."

Smooth lips met bearded ones, and then Eurythoë was light-footedly gone. Pythagoras dallied in the cave only long enough to pack a wallet with food. All other necessaries were kept within the confines of his skull.

Emerging into the reddening light of the westering sun, the philosopher paused for a moment's strategic reflection. Behind him, above his vantage, stretched an impassable wilderness of mountains: easy to lose pursuers there, but dangerous terrain to the hunted one as well. From those treacherous peaks he might never emerge. No, much wiser to head downhill, cross the Nessus, skirt Tarentum slyly while the citizens still organized themselves, and then light out for greener pastures. No stranger to travel, Pythagoras had sojourned far and wide, residing for extended stretches in Thebes and Babylon, not to mention Athens, Rhodes, and now the rustic backwater of Tarentum. Surely he would easily find a new home in a land where the people were more understanding of the needs of genius.

Assuming he could bypass rustic Tarentum with his skull intact.

For the first time in many months, Pythagoras descended the scree-strewn slope that led from his cave. His golden thigh throbbed, but whether from simple exertion, in warning of some evil to come, or in memory of Eurythoë's delicate touch, the savant could not say.

The Nessus was bridged by but a single structure. Though it was too distant to be quite sure, it looked as if the dregs of Tarentum might be massing there. His enemies. To avoid the brutal herd, Pythagoras would need to cross the river Nessus on his own. Though there was no convenient ford, he had no fears about traversing the flood.

On the weedy banks of the river, well upstream of the bridge, half-concealed amidst some fragrant bushes, Pythagoras halted. Summoning up the Braided Worm's number of the river and poising the form in his mind, the philosopher dangled his hand into the water.

At his touch, a pair of liquid lips as big as a man's body cohered on the surface of the gurgling waters, like bas-relief on an Assyrian temple.

"Greetings, Pythagoras!" said the Nessus, its voice like a pair of fish slapped together. "You have not visited in too long. Shall we resume our discussion of Atlantis?"

"I haven't time now, my friend. Enemies are near. Can you bear me safely across your width?"

"Gladly. Indeed, I can carry you dry for as long a distance as you like."

Pythagoras thought for a moment. "Very well, then, bear me downstream past the furthest limits of Tarentum."

"Step atop my flow."

Continually keeping the River Number in his mind, Pythagoras walked out across the top of the river and seated himself cross-legged upon the surface in midstream.

The water felt smooth and cool beneath him, a bit like a leathern cushion to the touch. The current swept him downstream towards the bridge.

Yes, just as he'd feared, a motley mob of the ignorant were gathered there, with Glaucas and Pemptus at their head. Armed with sickles, slings, pitchforks, and the occasional sword, the citizens watched gawking and gape-mouthed as the reviled philosopher surged toward them. But now Glaucas gave a high cry, and the attack began. A stone splashed into the water but one cubit from Pythagoras' chest, then another, and then a spear.

Without losing his focus upon the River Number, Pythagoras moved another of his power numbers into a fresh part of his mind. It was a Cloud Number, the gift of the Swarm of Eyes. He invoked the vast, inchoate magnitude and was instantly enveloped in a great bank of impenetrable fog. Thus cloaked from view, he got to his feet and walked to a new position upon Nessus' rushing stream. Cries of fear and anger sounded from above and missiles splashed into the river at random.

Nessus bore Pythagoras onward, hastening toward the sea. As the river and philosopher traveled along, they discoursed. "Searching your mind, I see an interesting maxim ascribed to the philosopher Heraclitus," said Nessus. "*No man steps in the same river twice.* But is not my form always the same? Do I not ever respond to the same number?"

"Yes, your essential form remains the same," answered Pythagoras. "But, as a river, your watery substance is ever-changing. Heraclitus' teaching has a subtler and more esoteric meaning as well. A man is like a river in that his substance *also* changes from day-to-day, not so rapidly as a river's, but just as ineluctably. One could even say, *No man kicks the same stone twice.* The stone may be fully the same, but the man is not the same, nor is the man-kicking stone. For a man, as for a river, all is flow. May I ask you a question now, Nessus?"

"Verily you may," said the great watery lips that rode the surface at Pythagoras' side.

"Last night I received the knowledge of a number from the Crooked Beetle," said Pythagoras. "The Beetle said this was the last of these magical magnitudes that I shall learn. If I hold it up in my mind can you study it and tell me it's meaning? I need to know how to use it. I feel I will need every arrow in my quiver for the trials to come."

Just then the river narrowed and entered a steep gorge. For the time, all philosophical enquiry was set aside in the necessity to bear Pythagoras intact past splintered branches and jagged stones. By the time they reached the calm pool beyond the final cataract, both Pythagoras and Nessus' powers had flagged. Pythagoras settled down through the water's surface to find himself standing knee-deep upon a spit of sand. It was dusk.

"Your new number is a mystery to me, O Pythagoras," said Nessus softly. His lips were as tiny as ripples. "Good luck unriddling it. I leave you here. And when you step in me again, though we are different, may our friendship be the same."

"Give my regards to King Poseidon of the sea."

"I am with him even now, as am I also with Zeus in the springs of the highest hills. It's a pity you know not the number of the Ocean. Poseidon could do much to help you."

"I daresay I'm out of Tarentum's reach already," said Pythagoras confidently. "I can settle into the next comfortable cave I find."

It was growing dark quickly. Pythagoras found himself shelter beneath a thicket and used the Tangled Tree's handy Sheepskin Number to make himself a comfortable bed. He lay there, nibbling bread and cheese from his wallet, wondering if Eurythoë were safe. Perhaps she could still visit him once he'd resettled. Presently he fell asleep.

Tonight it was the Braided Worm who addressed Pythagoras in his *apeiron* dreams. Fearfully bright, the Worm had but a few strands, surely no more than five, but these were, as always, too oddly linked to enumerate. The braid ended in a flat head at one end, with three bright eyes and a fanged mouth.

"Why haven't you started teaching of us yet, Pythagoras?" demanded the indeterminate Worm. "Why keep spreading the wishful lie that whole, finite numbers are the substance of all things? Aren't you grateful for what the *apeiron* has done for you? My River Number saved your life today."

"Yes, and it was your friend the Beetle who spoiled my leg during your very first visit, you unclean thing," muttered Pythagoras.

"It is thanks to the adamantine gold of your thigh that you have the mind power to understand numbers that approximate the unbounded essences of true things," said the Braided Worm. "The thigh is, one might say, the wax and feather wing upon which you soar."

"But like any such a wing, it can melt," whispered the Tangled Tree, which seemed to have replaced the thicket beneath which Pythagoras had bedded down. The Tangled Tree curved up through several levels of simple branchings, but at less than a man's height above the ground, it split into a disordered gibberish of uncountable forkings, followed by yet more layers of endlessly ramifying twigs. The Tree's voice was a woolly drone, with a burred edge to it. "Remember the tale of Icarus," said the Tangled Tree. "He flew too near the Sun."

Now there was a crashing noise and the Crooked Beetle forced his twittering mandibles through the chaos of the Tangled Tree. "My companions are too gentle with you, Pythagoras. Know you this: before the sun sets twice, your flesh will die. Speak well of us while you have time, for the new number I gave you will save you from utter annihilation."

The crashing of the Tangled Tree's twigs grew louder, and now the grinning Bristle Cat and the Swarm of Eyes appeared, pressing towards Pythagoras, the Bristle Cat performing its unsettling trick of turning itself inside out, changing smoothly from spiky fur to a pink, wet flesh that no human should ever have to see. The Swarm of Eyes moved like a cloud of gnats or flies, with each wheeling member of the Swarm a tiny bright Eye. Yet whenever Pythagoras stared very closely at one of the dancing Eyes, the Eye dissolved into a smaller Swarm of smaller Eyes, who were perhaps still smaller Swarms themselves—there was nothing solid at all in the Swarm and no end to its divisions, the Swarm of Eyes was *apeiron* in the very highest degree.

"Praise us before you die," chorused the five terrible forms. "And we will save you with the Beetle's number." The

Crooked Beetle gave Pythagoras an admonishing nip, and now the terrified philosopher woke up groaning. Horribly, the crashing of brush continued. It was early dawn, with mist rising up from the pool of the river nearby. More crashing and heavy breath. A growl. Lions? No, worse, it was dogs, followed by the railing tenor voice of King Glaucas.

"Keep a good lookout, citizens! The dogs smell something. I'll wager the old goat is bedded down here."

Desperately, Pythagoras invoked the Cloud Number given him by the Swarm of Eyes. This added greatly to the mist that filled this little glen, but the new dampness seemed only to heighten the sensitivity of the dogs' noses. By the time Pythagoras could fully get to his feet, the hounds were upon him, baying and slavering as if the great philosopher were a cornered fox. The men's rough, ignorant hands bound him at wrists and ankles.

The trial before the Senate and the priests of Apollo took place in the town forum that very afternoon. Pythagoras' announced crimes were sedition and blasphemy—and not adultery, for Glaucas had no wish to publicly wear the cuckold's horns. The charges averred that Pythagoras was teaching things contrary to the beliefs that underlay the established orders of heaven and earth.

"Do you deny that King Glaucas' power is divinely ordained?" demanded Pemptus, his fish-lipped mouth a self-righteous ellipse.

"Of course I deny it," said Pythagoras. "There is nothing more absurd than an aging tyrant." The only one who dared to cheer this remark was Alcibedes, standing well back in the crowd, one hand on his sword.

"And do you teach that all things are numbers and that mathematizing mortals may hope to comprehend the divine workings of the world?" asked the head priest, a bullying blockhead named Turnus.

"This is what I have ever been teaching. But—"

Pythagoras' followers were there in a mass, and now Archytas rose to his feet. "Father Glaucas, may I speak?"

Glaucas shook his head, but when Eurythoë, at his side, gave him a sharp elbow in the ribs, he sighed, "Yes, my son."

"If it be a crime to believe that numbers are all things, then execute me and these other young savants with our wise, though imperfect, teacher. All of us follow his noble precept that to understand numbers is to understand all things. Be this capital blasphemy, Glaucas, then your son too must die. Rather than persecuting the pursuit of truth, O Father, why not let Pythagoras go into exile? And we adepts of his secret teachings will be free to follow along."

The priests and senators conferred. Eager not to sow further dissension among the polis, they soon approved this notion of exile for Pythagoras and his band.

"Very well then, let them travel away and start a new colony," intoned Glaucas. He, for one, would be happy to have his young and vigorous heir far from the scene.

Thinking this to be the salvation the Crooked Beetle had promised him, Pythagoras now felt impelled to honor the requests of his *apeiron* helpers. He stood and raised his hands for silence. "Good people, I have indeed been teaching for many a year that all things are a play of little numbers. I have taught that God is 1, Man is 2, Woman is 3, Justice is 4, and Marriage is 5. And my followers know that numbers embody solid shapes as well: consider how subtly a mere eight vertices can limn a cube. My researches have revealed that there are five, and only five, regular solids to be formed by small dot patterns, and it has been my teaching that these solids form the essences of all material things." There was an approving murmur of excitement. Archytas looked startled and pleased, and even the hard-faced Alcibedes allowed himself a smile. The master was finally sharing his noble truths with all! Even the thick-headed priests of Apollo seemed intrigued by the great precepts. Pythagoras paused till silence returned, then continued.

"Yes, I have taught that Earth is the cube, Air is the octahedron, Fire the tetrahedron, Water the icosahedron, and the Cosmos the dodecahedron. Well and good." Pythagoras drew a deep breath and gathered the courage to continue. "But now I must tell you that these teachings are nursery rhymes, childish fables, the fond pratings of an old fool. The *apeiron* runs in and out of every earthly object, and, lo my little ones, the infinite even inhabits our minds." A furious hubbub threatened to drown him out. Pythagoras raised his voice to a shriek. "Everything is crooked, irrational, unlimited, *apeiron*—"

Loudest among the voices was Archytas. "Pythagoras has gone mad!"

"Kill him!" cried the crowd.

"No!" screamed Eurythoë, but Pythagoras had no firm defenders other than this single, fair voice.

"He will die on the morrow!" rang Glaucas' fruity tones.

"Behold what the *apeiron* can do!" screamed Pythagoras in desperation.

He invoked his four familiar power numbers to make a mound of Sheepskins, to set them reekingly on Fire and burn off the bonds that held him, to shroud the forum in a Cloud, and to call the River to overflow its banks and rush into the streets of Tarentum. He'd expected to use the confusion to escape, and until he found himself pinned in the arms of Pemptus and Turnus, he thought perhaps he'd succeeded. But the confusion in the forum eventually abated, and he was once more a captive on display.

"Look at him, Eurythoë and Archytas," called Pemptus,

tightening a rope around Pythagoras' neck. "Look at the dirty old goat. We'll put him under a door and crush him tomorrow. Each of us will add a stone. And I'll see to it there's no shirking."

"Well said," chortled Glaucas, appearing through the smoke and fog.

Archytas drew close. "Have you then become a sorcerer, O Master? Only to befoul the noble truths of mathematics? Nevertheless, I shall spread your earlier teachings."

"And what if my power is such that your fool of a father is unable to kill me?" demanded Pythagoras. "What then, Archytas? I have certain assurances from my *apeiron* familiars that—that—"

"That what?"

"O, Pythagoras," cried Eurythoë, her voice breaking. "Where has your madness brought you?"

Pythagoras spent a sleepless night penned in a dusty boulder-walled granary. His thoughts during the night were not of death, but rather of mathematics. He felt he was about to die with something great left undone.

Pythagoras was proud of his analysis of the five regular polyhedra, eternally grateful to the One for his discovery of his noble theorem about the right triangle, and well pleased with the philosophical frills and furbelows he'd embroidered around the properties of the smaller numbers. But something was still missing, some key consequence of his theorem of the right triangle—and he couldn't quite pin down what it was. It had, he was sure, something to do with the *apeiron*, for surely this was the reason why God had sent the mentors to him. During the very wee hours of the morn, he became absorbed in contemplating the nature of the ratio between the diagonal and the side of a square. He sat lost in thought till the crowing of the cock.

Wakeful as he was all that night, Pythagoras remained

unvisited by any of the warped denizens of the *apeiron*. But, wait, at the exact moment when the pompous Pemptus came to lead him away to his doom, he thought to detect, impossibly, the perpetually leering face of the Bristle Cat peering at him from a shadowy corner of the storeroom. The fearsome, feline features, composed of myriad thorny projections, appeared to wink at Pythagoras, who stopped dead in his tracks.

"Superstitious about a granary cat?" laughed Pemptus. "Crazy dreamer. Better to worry about something real— something like a rock." Pemptus kicked at a loose stone the size of a melon. "Bring this along for me, would you, Pythagoras? It can be the first one placed upon your door."

Pythagoras hesitated and the cat—seemingly a real cat after all—ran across his path and out the door. But how complex and richly structured the beast was, how subtle were its motions. And just as it passed from his sight, the cat seemed to perform the Bristle Cat's loathsome trick of turning itself inside out—but surely this was impossible.

"Carry the rock, you," grated Pemptus' muscular centurion.

Pythagoras kept his head high and gaze level as he was led through Tarentum, ignoring the jeering crowd. A large, open-air altar of slate, already warm from the rising sun's embrace, awaited the hapless body of the old philosopher. Thrown on his back onto this unyielding pallet, Pythagoras sought to compose his mind while a wooden door was laid upon him. Glaucas himself set the first of the stones onto Pythagoras' chest, the very stone that Pemptus had forced him to carry. The door pressed down as if Pythagoras were the pan of some insensate scale, or the conclusion of a sum whose components were the killing weights.

The citizens pressed forward, each carrying a stone, a few of them leaning close to hiss curses of execration, but surprisingly, many whispering words of comfort. The rebellious Alcibedes was missing from the line of citizens, but Eurythoë and Archytas were there, forced forward by a soldier with a drawn sword. Their stones were no larger than hens' eggs, yet they of all the weights felt the heaviest of all.

Breathing was quickly becoming an impossible task for the old man's frail chest. Letting the air out was easy, but drawing the air back in—ah, there was the bring-down, there was the drag. The sun blazed in Pythagoras' eyes, and a buzzing filled his ears. Something shiny came at him—a fat beetle, landing on his chin. The citizens filed by, still placing their rocks. The omen of a glistening insect upon the tortured man's face was so inauspicious that each of them felt impelled to look away.

The beetle gave a modulated buzz, and Pythagoras let himself imagine he could hear it as words. "Use the number I gave you, fool," the beetle seemed to say. "Focus!"

Another stone descended, followed by yet another, and that one by a third and fourth. Pythagoras felt his ribs compress and snap, pain flooding him like liquor from Hades. Into his blood-buzzing ears came the noises from the crowd of watchers: taunts and shouts and a lone female sob.

"Enough now," yodeled Glaucas, who'd been closely watching the torture from one side. "The man is broken. Remove the rocks. You three slaves over there, carry him to the riverside midden to expire. It will be fitting for Pythagoras to exhale his soul into the fumes of human waste. That should be *apeiron* enough for him."

Glaucas raised his voice to a yet higher pitch. "Let this be a warning to any who would challenge my might! I am as a god, and all must bow down before me."

Far from prostrating themselves, the citizens simply stared at Glaucas. This unpleasant execution seemed to be doing the king's popularity no good. And many were the hands that reached out to remove the rocks and door from Pythagoras.

When the weight went away, Pythagoras' punctured lungs snatched whistling breaths of sweet air. At some far remove he witnessed himself lying uncovered in the forum, saw the weeping Eurythoë and Archytas bid him farewell, and saw his bloody form tossed onto a rude cart and trundled through the streets by three slaves. He was beyond pain now, well into the tunnel to the Elysium. He was ready for the end.

Yet his progress into the final ecstasy kept being thwarted by something nipping at him, buzzing, tickling. Either it was the bug upon his face, or it was a vision of the Crooked Beetle. At this point, inside and outside were the same.

"You did well to speak for us, Pythagoras," said the bug or the Beetle. "You are a worthy man. Now use my number."

"Hhhhhow," came Pythagoras' faint sigh.

Emerging from within the Crooked Beetle's very mandibles, the Bristle Cat said, "We can't tell you what the number means, because if you don't know it yourself, you don't know yourself to know nohow. Contrariwise, if I tell you to know there's no you knowing, you know?" The Beetle pinched irritably at the smirking Cat, but the protean beast drew its head down into its body, sending a commensurately-sized pink bulge out from its rear.

The shock of Pythagoras' body landing in the dump caused his eyes to flicker open. He was fully anaesthetized and paralyzed by his body's collapse. His filmed eyes stared dully upwards. The slaves who'd had brought his corpse thither walked away, laughing at the lot of the only citizen worse off than themselves.

Pythagoras tried to inventory his pitiful condition. He lay beneath a dead tree of bare, polished wood beside a sparkling filth-choked rivulet worming through the dump. A swarm of glistening flies buzzed around his chest wounds, tasting of the fresh blood. And there was a beetle crawling on his nose; from the corner of one eye he could see it. A tufted yellow cat came ambling up, leaning over to taste, like the flies, of his hot, sticky blood.

His vision grew fainter; his heart beat as weakly and erratically as an infant drummer; his lungs drew in only the most shallow of painful draughts; his broken bones jabbed like a thousand daggers. From these incredible wounds, he would never heal. This was the end.

Pythagoras could feel his densely cultivated mind beginning to disintegrate. Strange, to imagine that such a unique individual as himself could disappear, that a being composed of such hard-won constituents could simply dissolve. His golden thigh began to throb then, as if to remind him of all the ways he differed from other mortals. Focusing on that preternatural portion of himself, Pythagoras was reminded of the great magical numbers that this memory enhancement enabled him to store. The numbers for Sheepskin, River, Fire, Cloud, and—

A great revelation struck the dying philosopher with titanic force. The fifth number form represented the quintessence of Pythagoras. Of course! Summoning all his vaunted powers of concentration and willpower, Pythagoras took mental control of the fifth number, then projected it outward from inside his dying self with explosive force—

He had a moment of dual vision. On the one hand, he was dying, moving forward through a tunnel towards an all-encompassing white light. On the other hand, he was standing in the dump, looking down at the tormented form of a poor, old man.

Pythagoras held up a vigorous, apparently normal arm before his eyes and laughed heartily. Triumph, even over death! Such were the godly rewards of his brave explorations of the *apeiron*. He took a deep breath into easily working lungs, then swung a fist to thump himself on his chest.

Much to Pythagoras' alarm and surprise, his fist merged with his torso like the obscene bodily involutions of the Bristle Cat! At that moment, a familiar voice rang out. It was an apparition of the Crooked Beetle, floating as a large, dusky ghost above the physical beetle that was still perched upon his old body's face.

"Hail, Pythagoras!" twittered the Beetle, seemingly in ecstasy over the philosopher's new body. "Welcome to life as a pure mathematical form! I encrypted you rather nicely, don't you think? I did the basic encoding that night I first bit you. And all along I've been updating the Pythagoras number to include your most recent thoughts. That's what I was doing sitting on your face just now. Keeping your number right up to the minute. You remember everything, don't you?"

Pythagoras nodded mutely and pulled his limb from his chest with a queer, unnamable sensation. Ranged around him were also ghostly forms of the Tangled Tree, the Braided Worm, the Bristle Cat, and the Swarm of Eyes. Each of them was connected by the finest of tendrils to their earthly instances here in this malodorous dump.

"Your new, numerically defined body still has only a not-quite-life," explained the Beetle. "It's unreal in the same way that your number-conjured flames are but colorful tetrahedra until being boosted into full reality by the presence of the elemental Fire within the kindling wood. Your broken old body—it contains *your* kindling."

Pythagoras looked down at his dying carcass with a feeling of revulsion. It was as uninviting as a soiled, wet toga. "You're not counseling me to don that same old mortal coil, are you?"

The Crooked Beetle spat, not a number this time, but

a viscous, dark glob that landed on Pythagoras' foot with a tingling sensation. It was a tiny, crooked copy of the Beetle itself, connected to the ghostly Beetle by another of the thin, silken strands. The new beetle stretched out its wings, waved them tentatively, and then buzzed into the air. "I don't like to explain everything," said the great Beetle.

"You need your you to be you," said the smiling Cat, rubbing against Pythagoras' ghostly leg and then passing right through it. "Be your own son and father."

"Breathe in what you expire," buzzed the Swarm of Eyes.

The Braided Worm beside the little brook swayed back and forth like a charmed snake. "Don't fail us, Pythagoras. It still remains for you to prove your greatest result—to prove that we are real."

"So bend down and breathe in your dying breath!" exhorted the Tangled Tree, gesturing with every one of its innumerable branches.

Of course. Now Pythagoras remembered the custom whereby a child would try to breathe in the last breath of a dying parent. His insubstantial body knelt at the side of his supine flesh. With eyes near-blinded by the light of eternity, he stared up at his fresh-minted body. With clear, fresh, new eyes, he stared down at his old self. Now came the dying man's final breath, the expiration, and Pythagoras' number-built, new body breathed it in.

From the viewpoint of his old self, Pythagoras felt as if he'd been yanked out of paradise. He felt grief and a kind of homesickness at not fully merging with the divine One whose hem he'd only just begun to touch. From the viewpoint of his new self, Pythagoras felt invigorated, renewed and—above all—solid and real. And then he was no longer two, but one. The infinitude of his divine soul had now fulfilled the incarnation of the number-model of his body.

Looking around the dump, Pythagoras could no longer see the ghostly images of his *apeiron* friends—and friends they truly were, not rivals or enemies. Their earthly avatars still here upon the midden remained mute: a tree, a worm of water, a cat, a swarm of flies, a beetle. Pythagoras fully felt how truly these earthly forms did embody the *apeiron*, felt more strongly than ever the undivided divinity that is present within all things, whether great or mean.

His newly-made body felt strong and sound, though not overly so. The number form was, after all, only that of an old man. But he was no longer an old man who'd been crushed to death by stones. There was one more change as well. The adamantine gold was gone from his thigh, and looking within himself, he saw that he'd lost his knowledge of the five magic numbers. He was glad.

So what to do next? Most important was to see Eurythoë. And the Braided Worm had said something very intriguing about Pythagoras having another great result to prove. Perhaps the simplest would be to go back to his cave, receive visitors as always, and continue to think about mathematics. Surely his resurrection would frighten Glaucas into leaving him alone.

But before doing anything else, Pythagoras tended to his soul's former shell. Gripping the corpse by the shins, Pythagoras bumped it across the slope of the midden and into a patch of trees. He lacked any shovel with which to dig, but he used a stick to scrape out a shallow grave, and then gathered a great heap of brush to decently cover the body. It took a long time, several hours in fact, but what did time matter to a man risen from the dead? While he worked, the rudiments of a new and wonderful theorem began coming to him. It hinged, as he'd suspected, on the ratio of a square's diagonal to its side.

His earlier theorem of the right triangle said that the

square on a diagonal is equal to the sum of the squares on the two sides. If the two sides were equal, this meant that the diagonal square was twice the magnitude of each side square. Put differently, a diagonal square and a side square were in proportion two to one. And put differently once again, the ratio of the diagonal to the side could be called the "square root of two".

For several years now, Pythagoras and his followers had sought a whole number ratio to represent this curious "square root of two." The search involved looking for squares that were in a perfect two to one ratio. Forty-nine to twenty-five was close and one hundred to forty-nine was closer, which meant the square root of two was close to the ratio 7/5 and closer to the ratio 10/7. But the match was never quite perfect, and now that he'd finally let the *apeiron* all the way into his heart, Pythagoras fully grasped that the match would never be perfect at all. There was no whole number ratio precisely equal to the square root of two.

He found himself singing a happy tune as he finished up the reverential chores of covering his corpse. Now that he fully understood what he wanted to prove, he would find a way to do it. Mulling over the distinctions between odd and even numbers, Pythagoras set out towards Tarentum. The clever Archytas could help him hone a proper proof.

At the edge of the dump, Pythagoras encountered Eurythoë, her face wet with tears. She was dressed in the black garments of mourning. For him? She didn't really see him, for she was too busy peering past him, looking for his body on the dump.

"Woman, why are you weeping?" said Pythagoras. "Whom do you seek?"

Eurythoë wiped her face with the black cloth of her veil. "Sir, if you have carried him off, tell me where you have laid him, and I will take him away."

Pythagoras spoke her name. "Eurythoë."

She turned and fully saw him at last. "Pythagoras!"

"My dear, even-souled Eurythoë. The *apeiron* has saved me. Good as new." He chuckled and skipped about, executing a little twirl.

"My dear, odd-brained Pythagoras," sang Eurythoë. "But what of your madness?"

"What madness? Believe this, woman, I'm working on a proof of the reality of the *apeiron*! It all has to do with evens and odds."

"Then I can help you! Let's go up to your cave."

"Right now? What about Glaucas and the priests?"

"Glaucas is dead," said Eurythoë, seemingly not overly saddened by having to deliver this news. "Alcibedes slew him only minutes after they carted your body away. My son Archytas is the new king, and the populace rejoices. The priests of Apollo will do as Archytas says. We already have Turnus' abject assurances." She burst out laughing. "Glaucas is the official reason why I'm wearing mourning. But, O Pythagoras, it was only for you."

"I should speak to Archytas," said Pythagoras. "About the wonderful new proof."

"We'll do that later," said Eurythoë, kissing him. "After the cave. I want to give you a proper welcome."

"Very well then," said Pythagoras. "Let's take the bridge across the river."

"No more sorcery?" said Eurythoë.

"No," said Pythagoras. "Just mathematics."

Plainly, I'm well into my second childhood, if such a stage can be defined by the return of adolescent passions. From age five to twelve, I devoured comic books by the score. But when I discovered the more "mature" allure of science fiction novels and stories, I turned away—without any real thought or regret—from my first love. Decades passed wherein I paid absolutely no attention to comics, except for collecting reprints of Will Eisner's Spirit *series.*

But just a few years ago all this changed, for psychic reasons unknown to me. I began to dip my toe into the ocean of contemporary comics, first with such "alternative" titles as Eightball, Love and Rockets, *and* Hate, *and then with the full-fledged superhero output of Marvel and* DC. *Now I'm completely immersed once again in the medium, haunting my local comics store weekly for such standouts as* X-Static *and* Greyshirt.

But this story features no superheroes, instead focusing on another four-color universe entirely. Just call me "Goofy" and give me a pair of four-fingered white gloves.

Stink Lines

Gyro Gearloose loved Ginger Barks.

Had that deeply simple sentence possessed no further clause or codicil, no qualifier or amplification, all would have been well. Love, courtship, marriage, babies, grandparent-hood, senescence, life-support, heavily monitored, institutionalized death, and the survivors left arguing about what to do with the chipped china: the old, old human progression would have flowed like hydrogen through the fuel cell of a new 2025 Wuhan Panda. No headaches, no heartaches, no troubles—

No story.

So:

Gyro Gearloose loved Ginger Barks—but *she* did not love *him*.

And that essential lack of reciprocal affection was why Gyro decided to reinvent their world in her honor.

* * *

The day on which Gyro Gearloose upended the unsuspecting world in the name of unrequited love began like any other. Gyro's bed catapulted his lanky, naked form into the soft embrace of the auto-valet's capture net. Via an overhead crane system, that talented apparatus deposited him fully dressed at the kitchen table. The multi-appendaged, radar-eyed oil-drum-on-a-unicycle that served as his chef and butler brought him breakfast: two dodo eggs with a side of mammoth hash. This repast Gyro consumed rather heedlessly, while having the old-fashioned newspaper read aloud to him by another mechanical servant shaped like a large, bespectacled, green bookworm. Then, after getting his teeth brushed, Gyro rode his unique, firecracker-powered vehicle to his office at Happy Duck Research.

Inside his quiet sanctum, Gyro's desk quickly ventured to attract his attention. "Mr. Gearloose, you have over 100 messages awaiting your input. In order of importance, they—"

"Not now," commanded Gyro, and the desk fell silent. Gyro tossed himself in a lovesick fashion onto a couch. Reaching over and behind his head to an end table, he grabbed a framed photo and brought it before his forlorn gaze. The portrait depicted a smiling woman whose delicate features summed perfection in the eye of this beholder. Of an age with Gyro, dark-haired and lithe, this temptress was none other than Ginger Barks. Shaking the frame like an antique Etch-a-Sketch to realign the picture's intelligent molecules, Gyro was rewarded with the image of a child, plainly an earlier version of Ginger. This was the waif Gyro had first fallen in love with at age five, at a time before he had even borne his current name . . . .

No one in the real world today is ever named Gyro Gearloose from the moment of birth. For one thing, a majority of the ancient Gearlooses went extinct during the Age of Reason, victims of ill-conceived phlogistonical and etheric experiments that tended to end in fatal explosions. Those scions remaining changed their surnames shortly thereafter in order to overcome a certain ditzy image. For another thing, no parents—not even gadget-besotted engineers—would name their child "Gyro" in the multicultural early-twenty-first-century USA, out of fear of having him mistaken for a Greek sandwich. No, the only universe from which one may choose to adopt the Gearloose name remains a famous comic book one. Which is precisely where our own Gyro Gearloose found his alternate appellation. Or rather, had it thrust upon him.

Little Gary Harmon was five years old in the portentous year of 2001. And whatever that year might have meant for the rest of Earth's multifarious population, for Gary it signaled massive upheavals. For 2001 was the year during which Gary's mother abandoned the ineffectual and distant Warren Harmon for the love of another woman, and, consolidating her custody of Gary, moved to Duckburg.

The town of Duckburg had until very recently been known as Los Gatos, California, an upscale hamlet on the edge of Silicon Valley. But in the year 2000, Los Gatos was purchased outright by the Disney empire, flush with cash after the success of its latest animated feature, *Disney's Golden Ass of Apuleius.* (The computer industry that formerly provided much of the area's wealth and stable tax base was churning spastically under the introduction of carbon-based buckytube circuitry, and Governor Schwarzenegger saw the sale of Los Gatos as a fine way to tauten a sagging bottom line in the state's budget.) This charming, compact town, not far from major population centers, suited Disney's plans perfectly: the corporation intended to construct a monument to one of their relatively unsung geniuses, a staff creator for much of his life who had yet managed to emerge from the bland anonymity that cloaked most Disney artists.

The cult artist Carl Barks had been born in 1901. At the turn of the century, he was still alive. And his work had more fans than ever.

Starting in the late 1940s, Barks had jolted the basic, boring, Donald Duck print universe—always a minor tentacle of the Disney octopus—with about ten zillion volts of creative energy. In hundreds of comic book adventures over the next three decades, Barks added intriguing new characters and dense back story to the formerly one-note Disney property, creating a rich Benday-dot cosmos. Aided by superior artwork, abetted by humor and a sense of adventure, Barks succeeded in placing his own unique stamp on Uncle Walt's creation. Barks' work had been reprinted and idolized now for nearly half a century. Motivated by a smidgen of benevolence and a heap of self-interest, the Disney suits had decided that Barks' centennial was the time to build the man a monument.

The Disney imagineers moved into Los Gatos. Under the terms of their purchase, they owned every property in town, which the state had first seized by eminent domain. But the generous enterprise promptly leased the buildings back to any citizens and businesses that wished to remain through the transition. Within twelve months, thousands of workers had transformed Los Gatos into a fenced-off simulacrum of Barks' Duckburg. Role-playing employees were brought in to supplement the other, non-costumed citizens, the admission booths were opened, and Duckburg was in business, after a stirring ceremony involving its humble, aged founder and a host of luminaries.

The Disney drones had even found some genuine Barkses willing to relocate to Duckburg. Harry and Norma Barks, with their young daughter Ginger, were distant relatives down on their luck and happy to move to a town where they would become instant celebrities with a new home and guaranteed income.

At the same time, the former Mrs. Jane Harmon, having reverted to her maiden name of Greer, arrived at the model community, looking for a new start. With her lover, Lorna Lish, and using money from her divorce settlement, Jane Greer set up a ceramics shop in Duckburg. (Having successfully beaten the pitifully ineffective Southern Baptist boycott, Disney was now actively and openly encouraging gay and lesbian participation in all its affairs, and so endowed Jane Greer with many generous tax breaks and incentives.)

And so it was that little Gary Greer-Lish was soon enrolled with Ginger Barks and all the other potential Junior Woodchucks in Duckburg's school.

No genius was necessary to coin Gary's nickname in this milieu. Within an hour of the first roll-call, every one of his peers was hailing him as Gyro Gearloose.

Gary's consternation, as might be imagined, was thick and weighty. Uprooted, friendless, and unfamiliar with the basis of his new community, he reacted badly at first to the nerdy nickname.

One recess period, as Gary sat disconsolately in the fragrant shade of a eucalyptus tree, one of his female classmates approached him.

"*I* think Gyro Gearloose is *cool*," Ginger Barks said, then, red-faced with embarrassment, hurried off.

That was all it took. Gary was in love.

Over the next few months, as Gary ineluctably became more intimate with the history of his chicken-headed humanoid namesake, he felt himself growing comfortable with his new unshakeable name.

Barks' Gyro *was* cool. Unfettered by marriage or convention, brilliant, carefree, and indomitable in the face of disaster, Gyro was perhaps the one citizen of classic Duckburg with complete freedom. As role models went, you could do much worse.

In subsequent years, as certain of the growing boy's own intellectual proclivities began to manifest themselves, rendering him something of a happily asocial loner, the identification with Barks' creation became complete.

So around about the time Gary Greer-Lish got his third virtual Ph.D. (he was nineteen), he answered more readily and easily to Gyro Gearloose than to his legal moniker. And a few years later, when he opened his Happy Duck Research in Duckburg with a few hundred million dollars deriving from his patents on a process that boosted the efficiency of chlorophyll by 200 percent, Gyro Gearloose *was* his legal name.

As for Ginger Barks, she had left Duckburg in their first year of high school. Her parents had eventually crumbled under the pressure of permanently being on display and had relocated to San Francisco. Cruelly, at just that period when Gyro was becoming mature enough to deepen his relationship with his one true love, she flew out of his reach. During subsequent years, despite Gyro's constant attempts at forging closer bonds, Ginger had remained seemingly uninterested in Gyro as anything more than an old childhood friend. Nowadays, in her demanding job as a reporter for the *San Francisco Examiner*, Ginger seldom even bothered to punch Gyro's address into her pocket-pal's e-mail window.

Gyro now planted a kiss on the glass front of Ginger's

picture. The glass fastidiously cleansed itself of his lip prints, otherwise Ginger's features would have been obscured by an overlay of such daily traces.

"If only I could do something that would bring Ginger back to Duckburg," Gyro wistfully said to the seemingly untenanted room. Not recognizing a command or request, his desk remained silent. "Even if only for a little while. Surely she'd soon see how much I care for her! But what could I do that would be marvelous and startling enough to attract her attention?"

There came a tugging at Gyro's pants leg. Looking down, he saw Li'l Bulb, his Helper.

Li'l Bulb was Gyro's loyal personal assistant. Approximately fifteen inches high, his form was simple: his head resembled a faceless, Edison-era, pointed light bulb sitting in a knurled chrome collar; below that, a flexible, stick-figure armature, feet encased in bulbous shoes and hands begloved. These primitive looks, however, belied Li'l Bulb's astonishing features. Inside his mock-filamentous head (opaque, with a *trompe-l'œil* holo giving the illusion of tungsten-occupied transparency), buckytube architecture granted him a processing capacity of many, many teraflops, the equivalent of several old-time supercomputers. The titanium rods of his body were packed with miniature power sources and sophisticated sensors. The one thing Li'l Bulb could not do was speak. In this day and age where practically everything talked, Gyro preferred silence in his assistant. However, Li'l Bulb's miming was surprisingly information-dense, and if necessary, he could always scribble a quick note.

Now Li'l Bulb's message was obvious. In response to Gyro's plaint, he was waving a rolled-up comic he plainly desired Gyro to read.

Gyro took the book, which was one of the many reprints of Carl Barks' drakely adventures to be found at various souvenir stands within Duckburg. Overly familiar with such fare, Gyro perused it briefly, then said, "What's the point, Helper?"

Li'l Bulb whooshed his hands as if simulating flight. He gestured in a wavery fashion as if portraying heat-distorted air. He shaped an obvious balloon above his head. He cupped his hands and then exploded them outward.

Gyro scratched his head. "Are you saying I should fly a plane to the desert and blow something up?"

Li'l Bulb slapped his indestructible glass forehead in frustration, then snatched paper and a pencil from the end table. After writing two sharp words, he handed the paper to his boss.

"'Special effects.' Hmmm." Gyro took another look at the comic. In one panel, Donald had just been drenched in perfume by an irritated Daisy. From his sodden, dejected, feathered, self-radiated, thick lines indicative of exotic pungency.

Gyro shot to his feet. "Helper, you're worth your weight in Einstein-Bose condensate! Now, fetch me my hat!"

* * *

One article of apparel the original Gyro Gearloose was never seen without was his hat. Some kind of yellow felt porkpie with a black band and curved-up brim, it remained securely atop his brown thatch through whatever chaos ensued, thanks to a handy elastic string running under his chin.

Our Gyro, no stickler for imitating the appearance of his namesake, went hatless on a day-to-day basis. The hat now being dragged across the floor by a responsive Li'l Bulb clutching its string, although outwardly identical to the original model, was in reality a special instrument devised by Gyro and used only on certain needful occasions. The crown of Gyro's hat was packed with circuitry that could interface with his thoughts via electromagnetic conduction and induction, amplifying them in radical ways and bolstering his natural creativity and genius. However, the device was neurologically enervating to a certain degree, and Gyro used it only sparingly. Besides, somehow the hat felt like cheating. Even though it was his own invention, he preferred relying only on his unassisted natural brain.

If the hat helped him win Ginger though, he'd gladly compromise any principles and sacrifice any number of gray cells.

Li'l Bulb reached Gyro's feet and wiped imaginary sweat from his brow. The inventor bent down to retrieve the hat. Placing it on his head, he snapped the string under his chin, thus activating the amplification effect. Immediately, his face assumed a loopy expression; you fully expected Gyro's eyes to spin like the cylinders on a slot machine until they came up all cherries.

In an abstracted voice, Gyro addressed the desk: "Open new spec file for our nanofab plant, production to begin immediately upon file closure." Gyro launched into a long recitation of abstruse assembly parameters, terminating the instruction string with a final "Close." He snapped the chin string again, powering off his hat, then removed it. Wearily, he slumped onto the couch, hat cradled in his lap. Li'l Bulb hopped up beside him.

"Well, Helper, would you like to hear what I've just invented?"

The automaton shook his head no.

"Really? Why not?"

Li'l Bulb snatched up his pad and pencil and scribbled a note.

"'Legal and ethical deniability.' Oh, come off it! When have I ever gotten us in trouble before?"

Holding up his left three-fingered, one-thumbed hand as if to enumerate occasions, Li'l Bulb began to count off with his right index finger. He reached five sets of four before Gyro stopped him.

"Okay, okay, but this time won't be like those. I've simply adapted an old theoretical idea for my own purposes. Have you ever heard of 'utility fog?'"

Li'l Bulb clasped his head with both hands as if in alarm.

"What's wrong with utility fog? An evenly dispersed, permanent aerosol of intelligent nanomachines about as dense as the air pollution in twentieth century LA. An ambient mist that living creatures can breathe harmlessly. Nothing alarming about that. And utility fog could really be helpful. Say your car was filled with the stuff. You'd never notice it until you got in an accident. Then—instant airbag, as the invisible machines protectively swarm and cohere between you and the dashboard!"

Furiously moving pen across the paper, Li'l Bulb finished another note.

"'Why hasn't utility fog been marketed before now if it's so wonderful?' Well, there are all those foolish EPA regulations for one thing . . . "

Li'l Bulb began to run in circles on the couch. Without warning, he leaped up onto Gyro's lap and grabbed a handful of Gyro's shirt. Frantically, the small assistant began to shake his boss.

"Helper, stop it! My mind's made up! Nothing's going to go wrong. I've programmed my utility fog to monitor GPS coordinates and remain within Duckburg city limits. And its effects will simply be certain, ah, visual enhancements. Besides, it's too late now. The assembly instructions included immediate dispersal of the first few units into the atmosphere, with self-replication thereafter."

Falling back onto the couch, Li'l Bulb lay on his back with hands folded in corpse posture across his tubular chest.

"Oh, what a melodramatic clown you are, Helper! But by this time tomorrow, when the fog reaches critical mass, you'll see that all your fears are unfounded."

Li'l Bulb's unstirring attitude and fake, flickering filament somehow managed to convey immense sarcastic doubt.

* * *

When Gyro awoke the morning after his Ginger-winning brainstorm, he first moved his arm tentatively, noting nothing unusual accompanying its passage through the air. Critical mass of utility fog had plainly not yet been reached. Before he could perform any further noninstrumented tests, the bed, sensing his change in consciousness, launched him into another day.

At the office, all was as before. Gyro dealt with many matters pertaining to the swelling fortunes of Happy Duck Research, losing track of time. It was only when his secretary knocked on his door, causing a seated Gyro to look up from various interactive displays, that the savant realized his scheme had borne strange fruit.

Each rap on Gyro's door produced an accompanying visual phenomenon. A jagged-edge, canary-yellow splotch, as substantial and coherent as a piece of floating gauze, materialized in midair near the door. Inside each splotch was printed in black the punctuated word **KNOCK!** These manifestations lasted approximately three seconds before fading to nothing.

"Come in," Gyro called.

Above his head appeared an unmistakable word balloon. A white oval roughly the size of an unfolded diaper with a dangling, curving tail functioning as source pointer, the balloon repeated Gyro's words: **Come in**.

Gyro got to his feet. "Oh, excellent." A second balloon materialized, even as the first was fading. Gyro walked quickly around the collection of intelligent particles. As solid to the eye as a sheet of vellum, the word balloon displayed its message on both sides in readable orientation.

The door to Gyro's office swung open, framing Gyro's secretary, Mina Lucente, who bore a tray from the company cafeteria. Today, to complement her Daisy-Duckish pinafore, Mina wore robin's-egg-blue pumps. As she crossed the office's tiled floor, each percussive strike of her high heels was accompanied by a spatter of purple centered around a **click** proportionately smaller than the loud **KNOCK!**

"Mr. Gearloose, I brought you some—" Mina faltered as her words appeared in quasi-tactile form above her head. Holding the tray one handed, she covered her mouth.

"Don't worry, Mina. That balloon's not issuing from you. Well, not entirely." Gyro explained what he had done, his own continuous speech flickering across the surface of a single balloon as if on a teleprompter, as the clever utility fog maximized its resources. "Now, set that tray down and go draft a press release. I'm sure we'll be getting quite a number of calls about this enchanting modification to Duckburg's environment."

As Mina was leaving, Li'l Bulb entered. Confronting Gyro with hands placed on imaginary hips, Li'l Bulb regarded his boss sternly for a moment, then reached out and snapped his fingers. The **snap** was represented as a green bubble that popped out of existence rather than faded.

Gyro handed his assistant a pen and paper, and got back this message: "You don't know how glad I am that I cannot speak."

Gyro smiled. "Oh, don't worry. The utility fog will soon respond to things other than sound. Just wait and see."

* * *

When the mayor of Duckburg stormed into Gyro's office, he found the giddy inventor testing the limits of the unasked-for civic improvement. Uttering any old gibberish that came into his head in order to keep a speech balloon alive—the Gettysburg Address, pop song lyrics, his projected Nobel acceptance speech—Gyro was attempting to discover the self-repair capacity of the utility fog. Ripping big hunks out of the floating speech display—the ragged, weightless fragments remained alive for a few hundred milliseconds in Gyro's cupped hands, their portion of print warped and distorted—Gyro watched appreciatively as new nanomachines swarmed into the damaged area to repair the hovering text balloon.

Seeing the mayor, Gyro called out gleefully, "It's just incredible! Without my hat, I can't even recall all the routines I put into these little rascals, but I must have cobbled together some really neat code!"

Already once retired, the octogenarian Mayor Floyd Ramie was not generally the excitable type. From 2005 to 2015, he had had a flourishing career with Disney in their Touchstone division, performing in such cinematic hits as *Voodoo Lounge* (2012), where he costarred with a geriatric Mick Jagger as one of a pair of doddering hippies intent on opening a Club Med franchise in Haiti upon that nation's ascension to statehood. Pensioned off to Duckburg, he had won the mayoral post in an uncontested election.

The mayor's generally benevolent and somnolent disposition, however, had been drastically frayed by an hour of watching his own speech—and that of all the frantic visitors to his office—come and go above his head. Mayor Ramie had never realized how full of awkward pauses (indicated in the speech balloons by the conventional three-dot ellipsis), stutters, fragments, and senseless interjections his own unscripted conversation was.

Now the mayor banged a fist down on Gyro's desk. His action was accompanied by a dull brown **THUMP!** causing Gyro's desk to cry "Ouch!" an exclamation that was simultaneously ballooned in a square shape, indicating machine speech.

"Goddamn it, Gearloose, what the, um, hell is going on here? What've you done? Er, does Disney know about this? Is it something they, ah, asked you to do? Why wasn't I informed first? Do you realize it took me, er, over an hour to catch up with your, um . . . press release?"

Gyro smiled. "No, Floyd, this is entirely my scheme. I thought I'd bring Duckburg a little welcome notoriety. Ticket sales have been off this year, haven't they? Ever since Rio Disney opened. Mighty hard for Uncle Scrooge to compete with all those thong-clad Carioca babes."

Watching his own just-uttered words, while simultaneously trying to formulate new ones, was inducing a kind of psychic vertigo in Mayor Ramie, introducing strange loops into his neural speech circuits. Face flushed, he groped for coherence. "Jesus, Gearloose, I can't believe you thought I believe you can't Jesus—"

At that moment the perpetually replicating utility fog crossed a new threshold, exhibiting a startling emergent property.

Mayor Ramie's head caught fire.

Wide-eyed, Gyro felt his jaw drop. The mayor, realizing by Gyro's gaze that something novel was occurring in the vicinity of his stubbornly unmodified bald pate, reached up. His hands disturbed the vaporous mock flames, but of course he felt nothing.

"What, what, what?" he spluttered.

"Oh, it's nothing. Just that your head appears to be burning up, obviously because you're angry with me. You see, I endowed my nanomachines with the ability to monitor human physiological responses, including EEG traces. They're akin to miniaturized emotion-detectors, only much more sophisticated."

With visible effort, Mayor Ramie composed himself, and his crown of flames died down. "So everything I, ah, feel is going to be made, er, objectively clear to everyone?"

"More or less. But let's face it, Floyd—you were never exactly what anyone would call 'poker-faced' before now."

Mayor Ramie seethed in silence for a few seconds, until his accusatory glare triggered a new response from the utility fog.

From the vicinity of the mayor's eyes, twin streams of tiny daggers flowed, impacting harmlessly on Gyro. The inventor's involuntary laughter was the last straw, sending Mayor Ramie storming out.

Mina Lucente entered hard upon the Mayor's departure. Chewing gum, she was accompanied by an orbital cloud of evanescent pink pearls, each encapsulating a small **snap**. "Mr. Gearloose, I'm holding off hundreds of news organizations that want to talk to you."

"Is one of them the *San Francisco Examiner*?"

"Yes."

"Tell them they'll have an exclusive interview with me if they send their reporter Ginger Barks to Duckburg."

Mina frowned. "Your old sweetheart?" A giant glossy red Valentine heart materialized over her head, then cracked into shards. "Very well, *Mr.* Gearloose!" Mina **stamped** off.

"And to think I never even suspected . . . Oh, well, it's all for the best. Things are working out exactly as I planned."

Little did Gyro suspect that he might soon have to eat his words.

Literally.

* * *

Preening in front of his office mirror, Gyro congratulated himself once again. Ginger Barks had entered Duckburg and was on her way to his office. Her enforced stroll through the living-comic book town (vehicles other than code-approved ones, such as Gyro's firecracker-mobile were prohibited within the metro-park) would surely impress her with Gyro's genius. During their interview, as he expatiated at length on his latest invention and on his boldly adventuresome future plans, he would gradually direct the conversation toward personal matters. By the end of their session, Gyro was willing to bet, he'd have a date with Ginger. After that, it was simply a matter of time before she agreed to become Mrs. Gearloose.

Gyro's door burst open, hitting the wall with an impressive orange **THWACK!** In rushed Li'l Bulb. The lively, small automaton was plainly very excited. Jumping up and down, he pointed backward out the door, then pinched the space where his nose would have been.

"What is it, Helper? Another leak at the bioremediation plant? I thought we fixed that for good."

Li'l Bulb shook his head in the negative. He began another miming, then abruptly stopped. Folding his hands across his chest, he composed himself patiently, as if to say, *You'll soon see.*

And see Gyro did. For at that moment Ginger Barks, eternal romantic icon lodged in Gyro's perpetually adolescent heart, re-entered his life. Not unaccompanied, however.

For radiating from Ginger's entire body were innumerable stink lines.

The nanomachines had outdone their past creative efforts. The stink lines they had created were inch-wide, wavery ribbons of various bilious shades: diarrhea-brown, vomit-yellow, squashed-bug-green, fresh-roadkill-purple. Extending upward from Ginger's anatomy in varying lengths, they resembled a forest of sickly, current-stirred kelp.

Gyro was dumbstruck. The look on Ginger's face did not help him to recover his voice: her beautiful countenance was contorted with anger. When she fixed her baleful gaze on Gyro, a small black storm cloud appeared over her head, discharging tiny lightning bolts and thunder **rumbles**.

"Gyro Gearloose! I assume you're responsible for all this! What the hell are these, these *attachments*?" Ginger was unmistakably displeased. "I picked them up as soon as I came into town!"

Gyro hesitated to name the display with its conventional rude tag. "They're, um—fragrance motifs! I assume you're wearing some kind of perfume . . . ?"

"Yes, of course. Calvin Klein's newest. *Compost*. It's part of his whole 'Wake Up, Gaia' line."

Advancing tentatively on his beloved, disinclined to sample any odor that could have provoked such an abundance of stink lines, Gyro essayed a delicate sniff. Not surprisingly, given Calvin's fine reputation, Ginger's perfume proved to be an attractive mélange of subtle, organic scents. However, some esoteric chemical underpinning must have provoked the utility fog's garish reaction.

"Quite nice," Gyro hastened to compliment Ginger. "You smell like a summer tomato. As for the, er, fragrance motifs, they're just a small glitch in my creation, I assure you. I have an idea! Let's talk outside. Perhaps the effect will dissipate out of doors."

Ginger's personal storm cloud vanished, and she bestowed a warm smile on her childhood friend. Gyro hoped the smile reflected personal affection and not just dreams of a Pulitzer.

"Okay! I need to learn all about what you've done here, Gyro. The whole world needs to learn! I can't believe you granted me an exclusive!"

"The least I could do for my dearest friend," Gyro dashingly said. He motioned toward the door and moved to drape an arm around Ginger's shoulders as gentlemanly guidance. But at the last moment, he hesitated. Those stink lines—

As they left the office, Gyro looked back over his shoulder.

Li'l Bulb was doubled over in silent laughter, slapping his knee.

Gyro wondered if he could possibly sneak back for a moment and kick his Helper's blank, titanium butt.

*   *   *

On this lovely sunshiny day, Duckburg was packed with tourists. Drawn by media reports detailing the unprecedented improvements to the familiar Disney attraction, visitors had swarmed in. The park employees and Duckburg's infrastructure were hard-pressed to deal with the flood of visitors. Lines had formed outside the restrooms (from which structures, Gyro was mortified to see, garish stink lines radiated in Hydran profusion), and also outside the snack stands (from which sinuous good-aroma tendrils, colored in various ice cream shades and equipped at their tips with beckoning fingers, slithered out to olfactorily entice).

"Let's stroll down Main Street," suggested Gyro. As they walked past various storefronts—including Greer-Lish Pottery, now no longer run by Gyro's two mothers, who had sold the business and retired to Ariel's Palace, a floating Disney arcology—Gyro recounted his inspiration and the method by which he had endowed vanilla reality with these Lichtensteinian bells and whistles. Ginger nodded intelligently, recording his words on her pocket-pal.

Out from an alley raced a stray cat being chased by a loose mongrel dog. The dog's **yaps** were concretized as steely BBs, while the cat's **hisses** were a spiky corona.

Several feet past the alley, on a small outdoor stage, the actress wearing the concealing outfit of duckly sorceress Magica DeSpell went through her accustomed act, threatening her bound captives, Huey, Dewey, and Louie. To the amazement of the onlookers—and most likely to her own—Magica's mystical gestures were accompanied by actual spark trails and fizzing lighting bolts.

Shortly, Gyro and his guest found themselves near one of the village's main attractions: Uncle Scrooge's Money Bin, the repository of the fabled Number One Dime. A crowd of several hundred people was gathered in the square. Gyro now had a chance to see how certain of the utility fog's processing routines fully manifested themselves. For instance: the utility fog tried not to overlap individual speech and noise balloons, if possible. Positioning a balloon ideally above the head of each speaker, the fog would only layer the balloons like multiple windows on an old-fashioned computer desktop if individuals were crowded together, such as now.

Additionally, of course, louder noises and shouts produced proportionately larger displays, which perforce interfered with smaller ones. Quickly picking up on this, children had begun screaming in order to overlay their parents' words. The consequent decibel level was almost painful.

Gyro glanced up at a clock on the town hall. "It's time for the daily raid by the Beagle Boys."

"As if I could ever forget," Ginger said. "Don't you ever

wonder sometimes, Gyro, what kind of people we would have been if we had grown up in a normal town?"

Gyro astonished himself with his boldness. "Why, I think *you're* just perfect as you are, Ginger."

Ginger smiled and said, "Thank you," with Gyro's words hanging embarrassingly in the air between them.

Right on time a gunshot rang out, accompanied by an unprecedented, leaden **BANG!** and the trio of masked and stubble-faced Beagle Boys tumbled out of the Money Bin, clutching bags of loot. But as they ran from the arriving Duckburg police, something new was in evidence.

The Beagles were surrounded by *motion lines*.

In the air behind them, the runners left day-glo jet streams, and their pumping legs were hidden in spinning-prop effects, making the robbers appear to be torsos mounted on careening wheelchairs.

Disconcerted, the Beagles ground to a stop and began to wave their arms about, as if to shoo curious, encircling bystanders away from their possibly dangerous appearance. Their arms exhibited ghost-replication: faint duplicates of their limbs traced the paths of their every movement.

Gyro turned to Ginger. The reporter with whom he was incurably in love was regarding Gyro as if he were a caged specimen of the bullet-headed Bomb Birds that Donald had encountered in "Adventure at Bomb Bird Island."

"Heh-heh, quite harmless. Over a certain velocity and under certain emotional stresses, these effects kick in, you see . . . "

Now the Beagles were arguing with each other. One began to swear, and his curse words were represented in his balloon by various censorious icons: asterisks, whirlwinds, stars, and such. A second Beagle decided that the show must go on, and he resumed running. Unfortunately, he tried to continue the argument at the same time, looking over his shoulder, and thus impacted a tree. Despite the protection of his foam costume, he fell unconscious to the ground, and a flock of twittering bluebirds began to circle his head.

"I need pictures of this!" Ginger said. "My camera's in the car."

"I'll come with you," Gyro hastily said, wondering how he would ever begin his romantic pitch under these awkward circumstances.

Together, Ginger and Gyro reached the main gated entrance to Duckburg. Departing the town limits, they headed toward one of the many parking lots. They were halfway there before Gyro noticed something.

Ginger's stink lines still attended her.

"No," Gyro unbelievingly said, "this can't be." His words were promptly ballooned.

Ginger stopped. "What's the matter?"

"The utility fog is supposed to be constrained within the perimeter of the town. No leakage."

Gyro looked back at Duckburg. A small mechanical figure was hastening through the gate toward them. In a few seconds, Li'l Bulb had caught up with his boss. The assistant carried Gyro's pocket-pal, which the inventor had forgotten while focused on impressing Ginger.

Gyro took the all-purpose device from Li'l Bulb. His assistant had already tuned the communicator to a news broadcast:

"—solar flares of unprecedented dimensions. All GPS satellites are out of commission. The system is not expected to come back online for a week. For further details, visit—"

"A week," Gyro moaned. "Without proximity constraints on their replication, the utility fog could fill the earth's whole atmosphere in a week! This is awful! What else could go wrong?"

The answer to Gyro's rhetorical question was not long

in coming. For over Ginger's head, a new kind of balloon had formed. Nubby-edged in contrast to the sharp lines of the speech capsules, its connection to its owner made not with a tail, but with a series of bubbles, its species was self-evident.

It was a thought balloon. And it contained this observation:

What a fuckup!

* * *

Gyro's weary head lay cradled in his folded arms atop his silent desk. Suspended above the woeful inventor's noggin was a thought balloon filled with colorful graphic images: Gyro strung from a noose, Gyro with his head in a guillotine, Gyro wilting under a hail of stones thrown by an angry mob of citizens.

Some such fate, it seemed, was very likely to be his at any moment. For he had failed to stop the utility fog. And that mission was the only reason he retained his freedom, instead of languishing in some Federal oubliette, awaiting *the* trial of the young century, followed, no doubt, by public tarring and feathering. Oh, the frustration, not to mention the damage to his pride! And he had come so close—

Of course, a cautious Gyro, under the earlier influence of his mind booster hat, had engineered a failsafe into the fog. A certain signal, broadcast on a certain frequency, was supposed to trigger instant shutoff in the nanodevices. And so, with minor reluctance, as soon as he verified that the fog had indeed seeped past Duckburg's city-limits, Gyro had sent that killer message. At first, all seemed well. But Gyro had not reckoned with mutations. Stray high-energy particles from the same solar flares that had decommissioned the GPS satellites had also jiggered with the quantum-sensitive nanodevices. One percent of the invisible critters ignored the shutoff command.

That proved to be plenty.

Consistent with Gyro's off-the-cuff estimate, during the past week the escaped nanomachines from Duckburg had contaminated every cubic centimeter of the globe's atmosphere up to several miles high. Despite their early near-extinction, the fecund utility fog easily filled all available niches. (Replication thereafter among the communicating, contiguous nanomachines, as programmed, slowed to replacement levels.)

Within six days, the entire globe had been Barkserized.

Not very many people were happy with this. In fact, practically no one.

The bulk of the fog's pop-ups and highlightings were surely annoying, yet easy enough to deal with. Although nobody really appreciated stink lines, for instance, signaling the inefficaciousness of their underarm deodorant, they could live with such indignities, since everyone else was subject to the same automatic insults. (In fact, one positive aspect of the silent invasion was that personal hygiene, as monitored by a partially functioning CDC in Atlanta, actually improved.) Perhaps people could even have learned to tolerate the truly ridiculous motion-lines that accompanied the intimate actions of lovemaking. (What *had* Gyro been thinking?) But the one intolerable aspect of the fog, the ultimate intrusion, was the thought balloons.

The same mind reading circuitry found in Gyro's intelligence-amplifying hat existed in distributed form among the nanodevices. And all censorship filters had been wiped. Any thought that reached a certain density of conceptualization was fair game for display, as words or pictographs. Husbands and wives, bosses and employees, salesmen and news anchors, diplomats and world leaders—all found their formerly hidden sentiments suddenly spotlighted for anyone to read. International and domestic antagonisms that would not be settled for decades instantly blossomed.

The initial effect was similar to worldwide attack by deadly antipersonnel bombs that left infrastructure intact. Streets and public buildings emptied as people huddled at home (in separate rooms for each family member) closeted with their suddenly naked thoughts. And had most of society's vital services not been fully cybernetically maintained (Li'l Bulb's cousins, anthropomorphic or not, had no thoughts of which they were ashamed), complete collapse of society would have swiftly followed this mass abandonment of the workplace.

Within a couple of days of the advent of this prosthetic telepathy, a few makeshift strategies to avoid the thought balloons had been devised. The highest levels of the world's many governments now functioned in airtight rooms whose atmospheres had been cleansed of fog by meticulous filtering. And since the dramatic yet wispy utility fog displays could be dispersed with a sufficient breeze, the few people brave enough to mingle took to carrying portable fans and blowing away their thoughts before they could be read.

During this crisis, Gyro had not been inactive of course. Spending debilitating hours under his neuron-goading hat, he strove to come up with some method of disabling the utility fog. But no easy answer presented itself. His best plan—to release killer nanodevices in sufficient numbers to eat up the fog—was instantly and loudly vetoed by every world leader. No one was willing to risk a second plague possibly worse than the first.

Today Gyro was at the end of his wits. Racked by guilt—that manifested itself as an impressive yet weightless anvil atop his shoulders—he probably would have simply quit by now, had it not been for his small band of supporters: Mina, Ginger, and Li'l Bulb. These three stalwarts had never been far from his side during the past week. Mina, seemingly recovered from her heartbreak, handled all practical details, including meals. Ginger dispensed cheer, while filing report, after objective and charitable report, to her newspaper, and thence to an expectant and angry world. Li'l Bulb helped on the technical front. Additionally, Mayor Ramie, designated the official government contact with the criminal inventor, visited often, bringing with him blustery reassurances and encouragement, along with invariably innocuous thought balloons that testified to his essentially empty mind. (Already, there was talk of running him for governor of California.)

There came a visible and audible knock at the door. How long ago it seemed, thought Gyro weakly, that first knock of Mina's proving his ill-omened brainstorm a reality. Gyro raised his weighty head, and the ever-present anvil recalibrated its location on his shoulders.

"Come in."

Ginger Barks had lost her stink lines. Too busy to go home and get her perfume, yet not neglecting revivifying showers in the Happy Duck Research gym facilities, she no longer triggered the utility fog's repulsive iconography. Holding up incredibly well under the pressure, she actually looked more radiant by the day. Gyro loved her more than ever, yet had never felt her to be further out of his reach.

After that first harsh thought had escaped her in the parking lot, Ginger had been very careful to keep her displayed inner sentiments scrupulously neutral. This control *could* be achieved, but only by stringent acts of will of which most people found themselves incapable. Prior practice with some form of meditation appeared to help, and Ginger had indeed been practicing Tibetan visualization techniques for many years, ever since interviewing the elderly Richard Gere in his retirement home in liberated Tibet.

The thought balloon above Ginger's head now conveyed her pity for Gyro; a pity more hurtful than scorn: *Poor guy! He looks like he's on his last legs. This can't go on much longer . . .*

Gyro pretended not to have seen this thought. (Already, etiquette involving keeping one's gaze low was developing. Yet this tactic did not solve what was perhaps the thought balloons' worst feature, which was often not being able to see your own. Gyro understood some people now never left sight of an arrangement of paired mirrors that would allow them to monitor their thoughts continuously.) Essaying a weak smile, he tried to put a positive spin on things.

"Well, Ginger, I'm planning to go under the hat again within the next hour. I expect this will be the turning point. At some point the solution has to come, you know—"

Ginger closed the door behind her and crossed the room. Unexpectedly, she sat on Gyro's lap. Ignoring his insubstantial anvil, she put her arms around his neck. "Gyro, don't fake it for me. Do you know what you really thought just then? 'She'll hate me if I fail.' I won't hate you, Gyro! How could I? I've known you since we were children, and you've never been anything but kind to me. But this insistence on being the brightest, on being infallible—ever since elementary school, it's made you almost unapproachable. I never felt I'd be good enough for someone who held himself to such impossibly high standards."

Gyro relished Ginger's comforting touch. He felt simultaneously chastised and reinvigorated. "Well, you certainly see now that I'm not infallible, and so do I. As for being the brightest—sometimes I think my Helper is smarter than me!"

"You're just human, in other words."

"Uh, very," Gyro warily agreed, sensing certain physiological responses to Ginger's weight in his lap. Then she leaned down for a kiss.

For the next twenty minutes, after the couple moved from chair to couch, their thought balloons fused and displayed a frisky scene only slightly more suitable for immature viewers than the physical reality of their entanglement.

As they were dressing, rather shamefacedly keeping their eyes away from their now separate postcoital thoughts, another knock sounded. Before Gyro could call out permission to enter, the door swung open. Dragging Gyro's thinking hat, in trudged Li'l Bulb.

The usually cheerful autonomous automaton seemed preoccupied, as if struggling with some important decision. Every line of his sexless frame expressed inner tumult. He brought the hat to Gyro, regarded the two humans thoughtfully for a moment, then went to a small, locked cupboard with doors suited to his height. Keying them open, he revealed a shrine.

"Why, Helper, what is this? I never knew—"

Ignoring his boss, Li'l Bulb kneeled down before a triptych displaying three portraits: Isaac Asimov, Alan Turing, and Hal 9000. In front of the triptych sat a model of the first printed circuit. Bowing his head, Li'l Bulb prayed silently for a minute or so. In response, the utility fog constructed a halo around his pointy bulb head. Finally rising, Li'l Bulb gestured to Gyro to don the hat, and the man did so. Then Li'l Bulb motioned for a hand up. Perched on Gyro's anvilless, sex-soothed shoulder, Li'l Bulb opened up a port in the hat. He took off one glove, and it was instantly apparent that the port was meant to receive the four fingers of the assistant. Li'l Bulb jacked in and nodded.

Gyro snapped his chin string.

Instantly, Li'l Bulb stiffened as if electrocuted! Real smoke began to rise from his ridged collar! Meanwhile, Gyro's face was undergoing contortions worthy of an exorcism. Ginger, horrified, dared not interfere.

With a conclusive, concussive **POOF!** both the hat and Li'l Bulb shorted out. The automaton toppled from his perch, swinging lifelessly from his still-socketed fingers.

With great reverence, Gyro removed his hat with one hand, cupping Li'l Bulb's body in the other.

Above Gyro's head now flared a giant, antique light bulb, signifying a Really Big Idea.

"I never even thought to try such a thing. He linked all his idiosyncratic processing power with the hat's," Gyro explained, "even though he knew the two operating systems were ultimately and fatally incompatible. But it worked. I know now how to deal with the utility fog. It's trivial."

Ginger poked Li'l Bulb gently with one finger. "And now your friend is gone for good?"

Gyro smiled. "Of course not. I'll just dig out one of his spare bodies and reboot him from this morning's backup. The little bugger could never resist milking humans for all the pathos he could get."

Ginger flung her arms around Gyro. "You did it then! You and Li'l Bulb! I've got to run and file my story now! Don't go anywhere!"

"I'll wait here forever for you, Ginger, if you tell me to."

"Oh, it won't be that long!"

On her way out, Ginger stopped in the doorway, turned—and blew Gyro a kiss.

The larger-than-life, wet, glossy red lips flapped across the room and plastered themselves on Gyro's cheek with a **smack!**

There were *some* things about this catastrophe he was going to miss.

* * *

The pride of the official Disney spaceship fleet appeared to hail straight from the Tomorrowland of seventy-five years ago, a finned rocket styled by Werner von Braun, fit only to top some antique writing trophy. But its looks were as deceiving as those of Li'l Bulb. Its fantasy shell housed the latest in space-faring equipment and drives, and the ship saw regular use ferrying rich, pampered tourists to Disney attractions as distant as Minnie's Mars, Horace Horsecollar's Helios, or Bucky Bug's Belter Bar.

Now, however, the retro-looking, fully provisioned craft was about to blast off on an Earth-saving flight carrying only a single passenger.

Mayor Floyd Ramie of Duckburg.

A safe distance away from the soon-to-be-unleashed rocket flames, Gyro stood with his two friends, Ginger and Li'l Bulb. This last-named, calf-high individual wore a miniature Chinese coolie hat atop his pointy, ultraglass head, strictly as a fashion nod toward the hot Florida sun—an orb now obscured, but one which everyone hoped would soon reappear, once the massed utility fog from all corners of the globe ceased to form a dynamically maintained white roof above their heads.

Rebooted into a new body with no memory of his last few hours, Gyro's Helper had steadfastly refused to admit he might have sacrificed himself for his boss in another incarnation, even when presented with the sight of his own corpse. Furiously scribbling, he finished his first postdeath note and passed it to Gyro.

With amusement, Gyro read aloud, "'Even Holy Asimov never perpetrated such a maudlin tearjerker! Give it up!' Well, I think you protest a trifle too much, Helper. But if you want to pretend that you have no feelings for me, that's fine. I know what I know."

Li'l Bulb thumbed his blank nose at his boss, then left

the room. In the week since, the feisty mannikin had quite consistently carried out his duties with an air of blasé servitude that only made Gyro smile.

Quickly following his revelation about dealing with the rogue fog, Gyro had summoned Mayor Ramie to his office. When the bland and blustery fellow arrived, Gyro was happy to see that his accompanying thought balloon—despite the ongoing life-or-death crisis—reflected the man's typical vacuity, consisting mostly of an empty white canvas with some children's primer figures—Dick, Jane, and Spot—romping about.

"Mayor Ramie, how would you like to earn all the credit for ridding Earth of my accidental plague? I'm sure that a grateful global populace would let you name your reward afterward."

A puzzled expression occluded the Mayor's features, and his thought balloon changed to a depiction of a shyster trying to sell the Brooklyn Bridge to a rube. "Will I, ah, be, er, alive afterwards to enjoy my reward?"

"Of course. The one catch is that you'll have to stay in orbit for a year first."

Mayor Ramie pondered this proposal momentarily, his exteriorized thoughts symbolically represented by a slate with the equation $2 + 2 = ?$ chalked on it. Finally he consented, saying, "It's only because I trust you personally, Gyro."

Genuinely touched, Gyro clapped a hand on the mayor's shoulder. The utility fog produced a synthetic puff of dust and a couple of moths, as if the mayor's clothes had been hanging in a closet for decades.

With the mayor's consent secured, Gyro got busy with his simple plan, a basic variation on the Pied Piper fable.

Above all, the fog was cerebrotropic, flocking to individual loci of thought. All Gyro had to do was make one amplified point source of thought that outshone all others. So as not to interfere with this fog-seductive broadcast, the human bait should possess very few of his own thoughts to project.

Floyd Ramie matched that description to the tenth decimal place.

With Li'l Bulb's help, Gyro quickly cobbled together a new version of his thinking cap, one that simply radiated an irresistible come-hither to the fog. Once all the principals were assembled at Disney's Florida launching site, Mayor Ramie had been hustled aboard the ship wearing the activated cap. The instant results were impressive.

All the fog in the immediate vicinity began to collect above the rocket, forming a thought balloon as large as a dirigible. This massive balloon depicted nothing but two gigantic words:

COME HERE!

The urge to swarm now radiated outward from one nanodevice to another. Even as they gravitated toward the impulse, they passed the baton of command backward to more distant fellows. In a week's time, every iota of utility fog from around the planet had collected here or died trying. In their amalgamated mass, they now formed a flat sheet spreading above many square miles centered around the rocket. Thick as clouds, the fog allowed a level of illumination equivalent to a stormy day.

Standing at the distant mission control, Gyro felt immense satisfaction. The solution was so elegant it almost made him forget his initial stupidity. Nothing remained except to send Mayor Ramie into space, taking the utility fog with him.

"I guess it's time," Gyro announced.

Ginger stopped dictating her latest dispatch into her pocket-pal long enough to squeeze Gyro's hand. "I'm proud of you, Gyro. You never gave up."

"Maybe that quality of mine has its drawbacks. Never giving up on you was what caused this whole mess in the first place."

"Oh, Gyro, what woman wouldn't be flattered that someone loved her enough to risk the end of civilization as we know it to win her?"

Li'l Bulb corkscrewed his finger at the level of his temple and turned away in disgust. Gyro and Ginger kissed. Then, using his own pocket-pal, Gyro triggered the launch.

The inventor had expected the rocket to pierce the semi-living cloud, soar ahead, and then pull the fog behind it. But he had forgotten the cloud's self-positioning routines. Seeking to maintain a stable distance from the rocket, the cloud lifted first above the needle-nosed ship as soon as it sensed movement. As the rocket climbed, the cloud went with it as a cloak, as if it were an enormous, message-imprinted, fluted, silk handkerchief caught on the prow of the rocket.

Soon the rocket and its companion dwindled to a dot. Cheers erupted from happy bystanders. Ginger held up her communication device so that Gyro could make a public statement.

"Citizens of Earth, I apologize profusely for the past few harrowing weeks. Rest assured that the utility fog, lacking raw materials for replication in the vacuum of space, will all die within a year's time. There will be no further repercussions from this invention of mine."

But of course in between the moment when the fleet of aliens announced their proximity and their actual arrival in the solar system, Gyro had had plenty of time to revise his opinions about the wisdom of mounting a gigantic welcome mat in orbit.

Cognitive dissonance is a wonderful gift. On the one hand, I'm a rational skeptic concerning UFOs and other X-Files phenomena. On the other hand, I'm inclined to accept reincarnation and daily miracles as a given. ("Anyone who doesn't believe in miracles isn't a realist," as Ben-Gurion opined.) In this story, the miracle-lover wins out.

But does that outcome render this story fantasy or science fiction?

Working for the U

Wrath is anger of a superior quality and degree, appropriate to exalted characters and momentous occasions.

I was no exalted character, nor could I believe the hyperbole of my superiors and construe this latest alarum to be a truly momentous occasion. As far as I could discern, this was just another day of working for the U.

But by gum, was I wrathful anyhow!

To coin a non sequitur: in the midst of light, I was in deafness. Blind also to the ambient noise, thanks to a temporary neural rerouting.

Alien hands and instruments, I knew, probed painlessly at me, like mice at the remnants of a banquet. Nothing much I could do but abide the familiar treatment. Patience, after all, is the ability to appear meek until an uncommon revenge is possible.

Finally my employers were finished with me. For the moment.

They popped my eyes back in, screwed on my ears, zipped shut my 1,001 scars, and then turned the rusty key in the lock of my senses.

I climbed nonchalantly down off the operating table and began to get dressed. The Big Grays and Little Grays who had been attending me melted away, ascending with grasshopper leaps or diving like sylphs, out of the weight field that still anchored me and across instrument-cluttered air and into the luminous corridors radiating in every direction from the surface of the huge spherical room.

The Teaball, I called it. I was standing on an invisible gravity-supplying plate of force at its center.

Once I would have deemed such a scene the height of impossibility. But the acceptance of outrageous unlikelihoods is directly proportional to one's own powers of lying. And after nearly a century of practice, I had become a most expert liar.

Muttering imprecations all the while like a politician denied his suck at the public teat, I stuck my left leg into the rubbery one-piece garment that would holo-project the image of a G-man's forbidding black suit once its circuitry was engaged. I got my right leg in, then began pulling the covering up. It was like donning a full-body French letter, and I felt like a Turkish eunuch assisting at an Ottoman orgy.

As I struggled with the slithery skin, the Captain came into the Teaball, levitating head first down an upper tube, then spinning in mid-course to land beside me feet first. I ignored him while I finished dressing. Whatever he had to say could wait.

Cap'n Carl knew or sensed that my anger extended to him, despite our usual friendship (a ship big enough to carry two in fair weather, but only one in foul), so he didn't interrupt my suiting up. He just stood there calmly, smoothing his neat beard in that really irritating manner he had, at once superficial and portentous, earthbound and superior, rather like a Brahman sage pondering his income tax return.

When I was finished, I deigned to address him.

"What is it now, Carl? Last minute, typically inconsiderate additions to the mission? Perhaps you wish me to eviscerate a herd of hapless cattle in my spare time? Is our commissary in need of fresh lights and livers? Or shall I lay down several smallish crop circles here and there? I'm fully up to date on the Higher Druidical runes. Maybe I should just suborn a few influential plutocrats? Do we need a new source of radium?"

Cap'n Carl was not amused. "Ach! You are too hard on me, Ambrose! You know that I merely pilot the ship and supervise onboard activities. And that is madhouse enough for me! No, your terrestrial duties are dictated by others. The tightbeam from the relay on Planet X carries your instructions directly from the Pleiadian Radiant Ones stationed at Wolf 359. There can be no argument with them. It was they, not I, who interrupted your R&R and scheduled you for early maintenance in preparation for this latest assignment. Take up your grievances with them, if you wish."

Mention of my cancelled R&R irked, as I had been enjoying a splendid carnal session with a minx of an aviatrix named Amelia. (Ah, Amelia! She was proof enough that woman is a feline beast of prey, having only a rudimentary susceptibility to domestication.)

"I feel only contempt for the Pleiadian Radiant Ones, contempt being defined as—"

Carl broke into my edifying discourse with typical Swiss pedantry. "Yes, yes, after all this time together I am overly familiar with all your witticisms. 'Contempt is the feeling of a prudent man for an enemy who is too formidable safely to be opposed.' Such knee-jerk verbal reactions are manifestations of a maladaptation to your inescapable situation, and it does you no ultimate good, Ambrose. Better to compose your mind to the limits of this strange life we all share, and thus achieve some inner happiness."

I was just about to offer a scathing definition of happiness (an agreeable sensation arising from contemplating the misery of another) when the Virgin Mary rocketed up from below us like a bat out of Heaven. Landing on the platform—I began to find it a bit crowded with so much contiguous wisdom and holiness—the Mother of Christ began to rant like a costermonger's wife.

"Where are My rose petals, My Son damn it! I'm supposed to manifest Myself in New Jersey in exactly five minutes to a crowd of believers, and there isn't rose petal one on this My Son-buggered excuse for a ship! Is this the kind of treatment you routinely accord an archetype of My stature, Captain Jung?"

"Madonna—" Cap'n Carl began, only to be immediately swatted down with hurricane-like force.

"*Don't* call *Me* by that *name*! How many times do I have to remind you that I no longer wish to share a sobriquet with that little whore! The *nerve* of that *bitch*! Why, if I weren't Mercy Incarnate, I'd cover that cheap, trashy imposter's ass with boils the size of her empty head!"

Cap'n Carl adopted his best diplomatic airs (diplomacy, of course, being the art of lying for one's country—in this case our alien Pleiadian lieges). I was really enjoying seeing him put on the spot like this. My wrath had in fact been replaced by a tolerant glee at watching someone squirm under greater responsibilities than mine (responsibility being, if one was adept, a detachable burden easily shifted to the shoulders of God, Fate, Fortune, Luck or one's neighbors).

"Ach, of course," continued Cap'n Carl in his pandering of the Virgin, "such presumption from a mere mortal is deplorable. But as for your rose petals, Mother of Mankind, it is entirely the fault of the soldiers—"

The Virgin Mary huffed. "Soldiers? What soldiers? And how could soldiers be concerned with *My* rose petals?"

"You are aware that the U carries onboard all the century's missing-in-action ex-combatants commonly supposed to be held by enemy forces for decades after the cessation of their respective conflicts, are you not?"

"Well, yes, My Omniscience had gathered something to that effect—"

"One of their assignments has been gathering the requisite floral components of your earthly manifestations. The lads seem to enjoy what might strike some as a decidedly non martial activity. The subliminal connection between death and flowers, poppies and Flanders fields, and all that—"

Not to be diverted, the Virgin drew Herself up to Her full impressive height and, with stony mien, frostily demanded, "And why have they not fulfilled their duties in time for My latest appearance?"

"They are on strike. Herr Hoffa has been organizing them. We are counting on Judge Crater to mediate a settlement—"

Before the Virgin could reply to this, we were hit by an Ontological Lacuna. I spotted the Miasma of Unbeing halfway across the Teaball, propagating like a wave of nothingness toward us as it raced through the fabric of the U, destroying like Shiva and rebuilding like Vishnu in its own wake. There was nothing we could do to brace ourselves or resist it, no way to temper its queasy-making passage, so I did not bother to warn the two interlocutors sharing the platform with me of its swift approach.

Sometimes ignorance is the better part of valor.

Like a sadistic catechist, the OL, as it engulfed us, revealed existence once again to be "a transient, horrible, fantastic dream/Wherein is nothing yet all things seem." I felt as if I were a hanged man imagining he yet breathed and was free. Simple oblivion by contrast would have been purest Nirvana.

When our molecules had reluctantly reassembled themselves, Cap'n Carl and the Virgin were suitably chastened, their dispute forgotten. The Virgin murmured something about being willing to make Her Own rose petals by miracle just this once, and left. Cap'n Carl turned his attention to me.

"Ambrose, do you need any further persuasion of the importance of your mission? These Lacunae are increasing in their frequency and duration. If you and the other field operatives do not deal with the disbelievers who are at the root of the calamity, all of us aboard the U will soon perish forever!"

"I never asked to play with the toy of immortality, Carl."

"No, granted. But neither have you yet abjured it."

With an air of negligence I was far from feeling, I flicked on the circuitry in my rubbery integument and was immediately swathed in an imposing, authoritarian disguise, complete with the outward image of mirrored sunglasses, which from my perspective was a heads-up data display floating in midair.

"Oh, very well, Carl. I was getting itchy from too much pleasure anyway. It's only the least hateful form of dejection, after all. I assume there's a waiting Spindle coded to me?"

"Yes, of course." Cap'n Carl sighed mournfully, like a ne'er-do-well nephew hearing the testamentary sternness of a dead, rich uncle. "I am exceedingly grateful for your cooperation, as I have an unusual number of crises to handle here. The simmering dispute between the Atlantean and Lemurian factions of the crew alone . . . " Cap'n Carl trailed off, realizing my lack of interest. "Well, anyhow, I hope you succeed Ambrose. For all our sakes."

"Hope is only desire and expectation rolled into one, Carl," I said, and then leapt upward.

On my vector across the Teaball, I passed Elvis heading the other way, plainly intent on giving Cap'n Carl what for.

"Not only am Ah out o' Moon Pies," the King peevishly

explained to me in transit, "but that las' batch of abducted li'l girl runaways was wearing *synthetic* undies 'steada cotton ones!"

Another case of the synonymity of "famous" with "conspicuously miserable."

* * *

The thing I really despised about the ride from the Mothership in orbit to landfall on Earth—whether in a Spindle or a Saucer, a Globe or Will o' the Wisp, a Cigar or Disk—was the trip's interminable and senseless duration. All the landing vessels on the U had been programmed to perform seemingly impossible inertialess, aerobatic maneuvers once within the atmosphere, simply to give human authorities, seated at their primitive radar consoles, the screaming fantods and skull-splitting megrims. The descent to the surface of my old home could have been accomplished in about sixty seconds. However, I had to spend a good half hour or more immured in the Spartan craft, while it—with its radar transparency, electromagnetic emissions and albedo shifting across the spectrum—buzzed military and civilian population centers around half the globe.

Shielded from any hints of acceleration or pressures, I passed the time reading Jerry Salinger's newest novel, a tragicomedy of drugs and sex, conformity and rebellion at a New England prep school entitled *Their Parents' Hell*. I'm proud to say I personally spotted the worth of that boy early on, and he had only gotten better since he began writing strictly for the U.

My Spindle finally landed by night with feathery grace in the middle of some scraggly woods, outside a major city on the eastern seaboard of the United States. Emerging from my chrysalis like a veritable babe (a misshapen creature of no particular age, sex, or condition, chiefly remarkable for the violence of the sympathies and antipathies it excites in others), I oriented myself with the GPS unit buried in my skull and proceeded to hike to the nearest highway.

Once there I had little trouble securing transportation.

From a hundred yards away, aiming my combustion-suppression device, I shut down the engine of a likely vehicle, then trotted up to the car as it coasted to a stop by the side of the road. As the cursing driver emerged, I employed another simple hand-held unit to commandeer his mind and nervous system from several yards distant. Once again behind the wheel of his revivified auto, my pet zombie drove me faithfully cityward. After release, he would revert to his normal mental state of unwarranted and dim-witted assumptions about the divinely mandated beneficence of the universe toward humanity, with nothing but an inexplicable bout of amnesia to enliven his dotage and anecdotes with which he would certainly bore his grandchildren.

I employed the driving time fruitfully, studying the projected information on my assigned quarry.

Randi Gardner was the head of the local chapter of the Society for the Investigation of the Paranormal. A determined skeptic and debunker, he was frequently encountered in print and on daytime television broadcasts as a tediously sane foil to the claims of the more alluring occult hoaxers.

Had he remained content to concentrate his scorn on faith healers and crystal-mongers, Mr. Gardner would have likely escaped the attentions of the U. But of late he had begun to focus on our abductees, questioning their veracity, subjecting them and their stories to ridicule, penetrative pessimism and the essence of his distilled, hundred-proof criticism.

In short, Mr. Gardner was one of those responsible for propagating the Ontological Lacunae that threatened to rend the very fabric of the U.

And as such, he had to be dealt with.

Gardner's house was set on a tree-shrouded acre or two in a tony neighborhood that reminded me of where the gluttonous gentry had congregated in my old San Francisco days. Its lighted windows revealed the bachelor Gardner to be in a position to accept callers. Standing on his front step, I summoned the house's master as if he were a servant, by means of his electric bell, an invention of the devil only slightly less disagreeable than the telephone and lexicographers.

Gardner appeared shortly, a largish fellow with every hair licked into place like an arrogant cat. He regarded me suspiciously for a moment, then laughed.

"An actual 'man in black!' If my enemies can't do any better than you, I'll have to consider my life's work done. Now, if you'll excuse me—" He made as if to close the door, but I obtruded my foot like a Bible salesman.

"Mr. Gardner, I've come a long way just to have a few words with you. Perhaps you'll have the courtesy to hear me out."

Gardner succumbed to politeness, that most acceptable form of hypocrisy. "Oh, very well then! Speak your piece, make your threats. But I warn you now, I won't be swayed. If you think I'm going to abandon my crusade to restore some common sense to this day and age of delusionary beliefs, you'll soon find yourself wrong."

I admired Gardner's steadfastness and candor, his affirmation of the tangible over the numinous. I had once been that way myself, enthusiastic in the cause of debunking. But enthusiasm is a distemper of youth, and working for the U had shown me that there were indeed more things in the world than my old philosophy had ever contained.

"Have you ever, Mr. Gardner, considered the power of human wishes to reify the image of their desires? We see it around us in its simplest form so often that we take it for granted. For instance, I shape a mental whim to consume an apple. This incorporeal dream-picture soon becomes reality, as I extend my hand, grasp the fruit, and bite its crispy flesh. Given such a transformation of mind-stuff to real world actions, is it not entirely possible that even more vivid conceptions, if fervidly enough held, might come into being?"

Gardner was puzzled by the unexpected tack of my rhetoric. "What are you saying? Surely you don't maintain that humanity has willed such phenomena as UFOs into actual being? That's absurd!"

I shrugged with Gallic disdain. "Absurdity is only a statement manifestly inconsistent with one's own opinion, Mr. Gardner. Just consider for a moment. All the witches and ogres and fairies of mankind's youth, whose desirable existence was attested to by innumerable firsthand accounts— Whereto have they vanished? And why were UFOs born at such a critical postwar junction and not before? Could it not be that they arose to fill a gap in humanity's psychic bowels? Such at least was the conjecture of at least one respected psychologist—"

"Oh, don't give me that Jungian bullshit about the collective unconscious, Mr. Whoever-you-are! Flying saucers filled with archetypes and the cast-off superstitions of the ages! I've heard more than enough!"

Gardner ejected my foot forcibly and slammed the door in my face with a negativity that I was certain had been felt aboard the U as another existential quavering.

"Bierce is the name," I said quietly to the oaken portal. "And education is my game."

Sweet words had had their chance. It was now time to compel Gardner's attention, using the eloquence of power. My client was about to experience what I liked to refer to as "whangdepootenawah," the Ojibway term for an unexpected affliction that strikes hard.

My onboard comm circuits raised the U. Keyhoe, Mantell, and Palmer were manning the boards tonight, it being downtime for Mack, Hynek, and Valle.

"Bierce here. Patch me into Area 51." When I had been put through, I gave my coordinates and ordered up a batch of Foo Fighters.

I had just enough time to withdraw to a discreet distance, insuring my bodily safety, and then the zippy little crafts were soundlessly present, arriving more speedily than even the Blue Book's prearranged "findings."

After surrounding Gardner's few acres with a space-time discontinuity to insure we wouldn't be disturbed, they vaporized the entire upper story of Gardner's residence with quantum-bond unlocking beams, faster than an architect could pick your pocket, leaving the house's interior exposed to the open air. I heard an anguished wail of disbelief from the gentleman inside. It increased in intensity as he was raised up by a lurid pink tractor-beam and deposited on his lawn.

I walked up to the shaking disbeliever. "Care to change your mind, Mr. Gardner?"

Give the man credit, he braced himself and threw down the foolhardy gauntlet of his skepticism. "You'll have to do better than showing me some secret Air Force technology from the black budget before I relent!"

"My pleasure, sir."

Well, I reckoned it was time to pick up the pace considerably.

I brought down a troop of exceedingly noisome yeti from the U and let the females have their way with Gardner while the males hooted and bestowed liberal pinches. I averted my eyes from the calamity (as always, a more than commonly plain and unmistakable reminder that the affairs of this life are not of our own ordering), but was still treated to an alarming variety of yelps, grunts, and squeals.

When I had sent the yeti back aloft, I turned to Gardner. Reeking of Himalayan musk, the poor man was left speechless, but with a glint of disbelief still evident in his eyes. So I let the Goatsucker chase him around the bubble for a time, taking liberal nips out of his arse. Next I collapsed the security bubble and had the Foo Fighters lift us out to the mystic omphalos known to the hoi polloi as the Bermuda Triangle. Summoning Nessie all the way from Loch Ness, I gave Gardner the ride of his lifetime.

While he was enjoying the serpentine antics of Nessie, I raised up a skeleton-festooned pirate ship and asked the U for a couple of helpers. When they arrived, I put a suitably costumed Barney and Betty Hill in charge and left instructions for them to take Gardner on a little "shake down" cruise when he got back. During that interval I spent some time aboard one of the Foo Fighters having an enlarging conversation with Phil Klass on the arcane customs of Magonia and Counter-Earth.

Then I brought Gardner back to his home.

He looked like one of Pancho Villa's interrogation victims. Dripping wet, clad only in the rags of his clothing, blood trickling down his buttocks, seaweed entwined in his hair, the tail of a small fish sticking out of the waistband of his underwear, and the finger bone of a skeleton protruding from one ear, Gardner was trying to mouth something. I lowered my ear to his lips and heard, "Nuh-nuh-no. Still . . . don't . . . believe . . . "

"Tsk, tsk, Mr. Gardner. You remind me of one of my editors who could never see the pertinence of my arguments. Your inaccessibility to the truth, as manifest by the splendor and stress of our advocacy, is the very definition of obstinacy. Now, let me see—what do I have left to show you . . . ? I have it! If you'll be patient for just a moment longer."

Gardner moaned and closed his eyes. I let him rest for the minute or so it took my ultimate persuaders to arrive.

Sensing the presence of someone new, Gardner opened one eyelid the merest crack. But even that glimpse was too much. He screamed like a virgin who had just tried to pet a dissolute and intemperately lusty corniphallic mythic quadruped. Stiffening like a board, he lapsed into catatonia.

I turned to thank my helpers. "Whitley, ET—good job. I'll see you back aboard the U."

ET lit up his mute moronic finger, and naked Whitley sociably waggled his permanently installed rectal probe, like a friendly leper at a Newport cotillion.

When the man and the extraterrestrial had departed, I had the Foo Fighters rebuild Gardner's house from stored templates and place the cleaned and healed man in his own bed. I seriously doubted that tomorrow's dawn would witness the resumption of his old career.

I hitched another ride back to my Spindle, congratulating myself on a job well-done. I had helped insure my own and my compatriots' continued more-than-mortal, less-than-heavenly existence for some indefinite future span. Not a bad night's work. Especially for a wraith who was little more than a bad case of spiritual jaundice and a collection of verbal tics.

Much to my surprise, I found one of my U-ish coworkers waiting for me at the Spindle. A fellow ink-stained wretch, no less, yet one of the more companionable ghosts (we ghosts being outward and visible signs of an inward fear).

"Ah, Berick, good to see you! What brings you here?"

Traven shook my hand tentatively, and I instantly recognized him as the reluctant bearer of bad tidings. "New instructions, I fear, Ambrose. We have not yet earned our rest. The U needs two experienced operatives to hold some hands at the White House. It seems the president's grown quite nervous. He just saw the videotape of an overly imaginative Hollywood film that has him worried we might be planning something similar to his domicile . . . . "

I thought of refusing for a moment, of staging my personal insurrection (fated by definition to be an unsuccessful revolution), but soon thought better of it. With a weary nod, I assented. "Ah, Berick, once again we pay the price of our experience."

"Which you always maintained was a wisdom that enabled us only to recognize as an undesirable old acquaintance the folly that we had already embraced."

I smiled. "You're as bad a line-stealer as Cap'n Carl, you old rascal. Well, I suppose there's no point in delaying."

And so we climbed into the Spindle and went back to working for the U.

A few years ago the World Fantasy Convention returned to Providence, the site of the very first such affair. I attended, although I generally can take or leave such gatherings, simply because the con was in my backyard, so to speak. At dinner one evening in a local Chinese restaurant, I was seated a few seats over from Erin Kennedy, the teenaged daughter of editor and publisher Ann Kennedy. I quickly discovered that Erin liked the music of the Cure, as did I. And suddenly something clicked.

I had long wanted to write a story riffing on the Cure's brand of Goth, but nothing concrete had ever presented itself to me as the basis for a plot. But within seconds of talking to Erin, I had the whole story, based on her as protagonist, firmly in mind.

Thanks again, Erin, for the loan of your alternate-world self.

Doing The Unstuck

1. IN BETWEEN DAYS

Ten times larger-than-life and twice as sobering, Robert Smith's visage brooded down from the ceiling of Erin Merkin's bedroom. Perched on a shadowy staircase, the lead vocalist and lyricist for the British band called the Cure had been captured by the camera in an implacably Gothic moment. His gamin features, layered in white and black makeup, if juxtaposed next to the face of one of his spiritual ancestors—Poe or Shelley, perhaps—would have caused those infamous mopes to be viewed as positively Pollyanna-ish. Smith wore enough mascara and liner around his sad eyes to impersonate a raccoon, and his lips were lacquered in a red so dark as to appear black.

Most astonishing and compelling, however, was Smith's hair. A wild pouf dyed black, Smith's hairdo appeared less a deliberate look than the result of a lightning strike or unwise tampering with a fuse box. Radiating in every direction like a nest of snakes, the singer's spiky elflocks projected such a dynamic image that they practically assumed a separate identity.

From the giant poster pasted to the ceiling, this postmodern Rimbaud known as Robert Smith glowered down with the classically alluring despair so attractive to sensitive and disaffected youth (a despair best captured in Smith's own line, "Yesterday I got so old I felt like I could die") upon the lone inhabitant of this suburban adolescent's tidy bedroom, typical save for its Gothic clutter: Erin Merkin.

Hopelessly fourteen, Erin lay as if rigidly pinned on her back laterally across her daytime-made-up bed, her clothes and demeanor offering a startling contrast to the frilly pink counterpane. From her bureau-top CD player, set to an endless repeat of a single track, the melancholy Mr. Smith warbled "To Wish Impossible Things" over and over, bathing the young girl in waves of weltschmerz.

Completely kitted out in light-devouring black, from monstrously large boots to loose multi-pocketed cargo pants and on up to a voluminous long-sleeved T-shirt (advertising a brand of very long nails not sold at hardware stores), Erin was instantly recognizable as a stout-hearted acolyte of Mr. Smith and company. A tackle box's worth of plastic and metal fixtures serving as jewelry—embedded into flesh or simply hanging loose—completed her outfit.

The only anomaly in Erin's chosen appearance was her hair. Chin-length, fine and supple, and colored like glossy-wet autumn oak leaves, her coif more suited a folk singer or hippie communard than a club-hopping night-gaunt.

Erin's own thoughts must have been focused on this

same disfiguring incongruity, for her pale, pretty, round face suddenly contorted in a fierce scowl, elevating her silver nose-stud nearly an inch, and she reached up both hands to tug at her hair.

Emitting a rough growl, Erin sought to yank her hair out by its roots, but with an admirable healthy tenacity, it resisted her best efforts. Finally admitting defeat, Erin released her innocently offensive hair and dug one hand into a lumpy thigh pocket. The hand—its chewed nails painted a gruesome shade sold under the name "Ghetto Grit"—emerged clutching a small cellphone. Erin prodded its buttons with displaced furiousness.

"Hello, Elise? Yeah, it's me. No, she wouldn't let me. I hate her! I don't care if she is my mother. She doesn't understand me, and she never will! Yeah, well, you're lucky. Listen, meet me at the boardwalk. Homework? Are you a total pus-bucket or what? Okay, see you there."

Erin repocketed the phone and stood up. Snatching a backpack from a hook (the pack's fabric plastered with stickers), Erin clomped out, her boots raising a din as if every last British POW were marching defiantly across the Bridge on the River Kwai.

From his coign, the implacable Robert Smith surveyed the empty room, his dour expression syncing most portentously with the unattended CD player's pronouncement, "The stars are dimmed by clouds and tears, and all I wish is gone away."

2. *STANDING ON A BEACH*

The boardwalk stretched empty under a November sun pale as cottage cheese. The arcades and vendor stalls running parallel to the boardwalk along its western edge wore protective plywood cladding across their doors and windows, against the coming winter. The unpopulated beach beyond the railings immediately to the east, its lifeguard towers now stored away in nearby sheds, assumed a primeval cast, as if the patient shore and questing sea had stolidly consorted just so for millennia without human intervention.

The stomping walk with which Erin had departed her bedroom had abated in fury, acquiring a more resigned and leaden tone. She moved her weighty boots in a desultory manner, gradually approaching a bench that faced the sea. She dropped down, slinging her pack beside her onto the slatted seat. For a minute or so, she gazed pensively toward the horizon. Then, a chill wind caused her to shiver and dig in her knapsack. From it she removed a leather vest adorned with emblems and pins. After donning this ineffective garment over her long-sleeved shirt, she continued to root through her bag, coming up with a pack of bidis and a lighter. Soon the maritime-scented air was overlaid with a sweet herbal perfume.

Erin puffed meditatively for a time, apparently heedless of her surroundings, until without apparent cue she lifted her pack of Indian cigarettes out of her lap, upward and backwards over her shoulder.

"Thanks."

Elise had arrived, strolling up directly behind Erin. Now the second girl took a bidi and also lit up, before swinging around to share the bench with her friend.

Elise Bamonte evinced an obvious spiritual sisterhood with Erin. The restricted palette of her wardrobe bespoke a shared allegiance to all things Goth. But Elise completed the regulation look with a tangle of bottle-black, pink-streaked hair perched above her longish, plain face like an untidy gull's nest on a cliff.

Erin cast a covetous glance at her friend's hair, then stubbed out her cigarette and flicked the butt away.

"My *god*, I can't *stand* it! Look at your *hair*! It's *so* awe-some!"

Elise primped, proud of her finest feature. "It hasn't seen a comb in six months now."

Erin batted at the silky drapery of her own hair. "What I wouldn't give to get rid of *this* mess. But *she* won't let me!"

"Tell me why again?"

"My father. She keeps reminding me of how much he 'adored' my hair. I can change anything else about my looks but that. Jesus, I loved the guy too, and I'm really sad he's dead. But it's like I'm walking around with his *tombstone* on my head for two years now."

"Bummer. What if you just went ahead and did it any-way?"

"She'd probably scream and cry and wail so much I'd feel like shit. Then who knows? Maybe she'd kick me out, send me to live with Aunt Gladys. I sure don't want that. I like my Mom most of the time, and I like my home too. But I can't stand this dictator shit."

Elise finished her smoke. "What about running away?"

Erin vented a dismissive snort. "Where to? I don't want to end up some skanky ancient thirty-year-old slut in a *bus* depot with like dozens of *heroin* needles sticking out of me!"

"I don't know what to say then. Charlotte sometimes—"

"Oh, the hell with Charlotte! She's a spoiled, rich bitch. No, I've got to face it—I'm stuck for good right where I am."

Elise obligingly changed the subject. For half an hour the girls talked about school, about boys and teachers and cliques. They traded information about new brands of nail polish. And they discussed items of musical interest, such as the possibility that the Cure might go on tour and play an unannounced free concert at the local civic center, where

Elise and Erin would be invited from the front-row audience to come onstage.

But eventually, as the sun began to sink lower behind the friends' backs, Elise announced that she had to go, since her mother would be serving her favorite meal soon: nachos and ramen.

"That's cool," Erin replied with forced insouciance. "I'm just going to hang here a little longer."

Elise soon dwindled down the short streets leading back to town. The growing cold prodding her now, Erin stood and descended several steps to the sand. Assuming a woeful look of supreme martyrdom, she began to scuff along the beach, her clodhoppers sending explosive gouts of sand aloft, dragging her knapsack by its straps like some bohemian Christopher Robin pulling a drunken Pooh by one stuffed leg.

3. *FROM THE EDGE OF THE DEEP GREEN SEA*

The eastern sky above the ocean began to purple; like some lost platoon, a swath of afternoon blue in the celestial west fought to sustain itself against the scarlet sunset on one flank and the encroaching Tyrian shades sweeping in from the other.

Erin halted her aimless trudging, about half a mile from the amusement center, at an undeveloped spot where only dunes bordered the beach. Here was a site to match her hopelessness: meaningless, barren, windswept, unwired. She faced out to the uncaring waters.

Like a sudden eruption of whiteheads, the strongest stars had begun to pimple the night's complexion. As Erin watched, one errant light detached itself and began to fall.

Wide-eyed, the girl observed the falling star grow larger and larger. Its vivid nearby passage through the atmosphere was soon traced by a corona of flame. A sizzling and crackling noise accompanied its wild flight.

And then the star fell into the sea with a surprisingly small splash, several hundred yards offshore.

Erin wistfully addressed the sunken luminary. "Wow! Does this mean I get a wish? I forgot to make one while you were falling though, Mr. Star. Still, what have I got to lose? Okay, here goes—I wish, I wish—I wish to get unstuck!"

Dropping to the sand in an easy half-lotus posture, Erin resolved to await any possible results of her spontaneous appeal to cosmic magic.

Her appeal was answered in about twenty minutes.

From the surf crawled an unnatural entity Erin could only partially perceive in the waning light. It appeared to have a myriad of small, candy-striped legs emanating from a body resembling a mass of sodden seaweed.

Erin jumped up and slowly began to back away.

The creature crawled up to the wrack at the waterline and stopped. Then, in a reassuringly cute canine manner, it shook itself free of water.

Immediately Erin beheld a miracle: before her stood Robert Smith's living hair.

The creature now resembled a fright wig with innumerable small tentacles on its underside. Whatever body to which the hair and crawly feet were attached was practically one-dimensional, a thin scalp. No sensory organs showed. But whatever the creature lacked in substantial torso, it made up for in pelt. Its black, spiky Medusan tumult of hair could have outfitted both Mr. and Mrs. Robert Smith with enough to spare for an heir.

Instinctively reassured by such a delightful appearance, Erin inched closer to the sea creature.

"Here, little guy, here I am. Can I pet you?"

Erin extended her hand. The creature quivered playfully in response.

Then in a flash it leaped onto her arm, scuttled up to the top of her head, and clamped down with every last delicate yet exceedingly sharp leg.

4. WHY CAN'T I BE YOU?

For a microsecond or three, Erin felt as if a million hungry children were digging into her skull with blunt spoons. She tried to scream, but only a gargled cacophony emerged. Her vision cycled through a kaleidoscope of weird psychedelic effects, and her ears filled with oscillating sourceless squeals. The stud in her nose seemed to flame white-hot. Muscles twitched up and down her body like a bowl of earthworms goosed by electric current, and her mouth filled with a banquet of tastes, known and unknown.

Then normality resumed. All pain vanished. Her senses reported familiar surroundings: sand, sky, stars, and sea; the swoosh of cold wind and scent of drying kelp.

And the creature who had attacked her? Gone, or still resting on her seemingly unburdened skull?

Tentatively, Erin reached up to the level of her chin. With uncommon gratitude, she touched her despised, long, sleek hair—

But at the instant she did so, all her hair was retracted upward, like a snapped roller shade or slurped spaghetti!

"Eeek!" Erin stifled her squeals after the first one. Very carefully, as if balancing a weightless book on her head, she bent down to retrieve her pack. From within, she removed a makeup mirror.

There was just enough radiance from the dusky sky and city street lamp spillover for her to see herself faintly.

Call her Robert Smith's female clone. An extravagant mass of dark twisted hair topped Erin's skull.

As she studied herself incredulously in the small glass, she saw a tendril of hair extend itself downward. The hair coiled around the mirror and angled the compact to its satisfaction.

"Yes, that's better. Thank you for the loan of your eyes and cranium. Quite a nice fit."

The voice possessed a self-assured genderless vibrancy and seemed to emanate impossibly from a spot only an inch away from Erin's ears.

"Who—who's talking?"

"It is I, your new friend."

"Are you using telepathy on me?"

"Not as conventionally defined. I do have access to your neurological states, but reading them directly is awkward and time-consuming. However, I can tap and interpret your nerve impulses just before they reach your vocal mechanisms, in effect 'hearing' you speak. Then, I supply my responses directly to your auditory inputs. Much easier than trying to tamper with the complexities of your cortex."

"So no one but me can hear you?"

"Correct."

Erin pocketed her mirror and covered her ears with her hands. She mimed the words "say something" without actually speaking.

"A very clever test of my statements. I can see you possess a sharp intelligence, Erin."

Erin dropped her hands. "Thanks—I guess. That's what all my teachers say just before they flunk me. Wait a minute—how did you know my name?"

"As I said, I have access to your brain and its contents."

"This is too creepy. If you were a guy, I'd freak. But since you're just some kind of cuddly alien like ET, I suppose I can handle it. Do *you* have a name?"

"You may call me Caterpillar."

"Cool! Did you know—"

"—that is the title of a song by your favorite musical group? Yes, of course."

Erin was beginning to relax a bit. The situation was improbable and spooky, but countless movies, videogames, and television shows had prepared her for just such a visit. So far, there had been no bad fallout from her contact with this creature. All she had gotten was the hairdo for which she had perpetually longed.

That thought raised another. "What happened to my real hair?"

"I ingested it, to replenish myself after my arduous crawl to land. I assumed you would not require your original hair for cosmetic purposes as long as we were bonded."

That last word gave Erin a chill. "Are you going to use me like a puppet or something now?"

"Not unless I have to in the course of my mission."

"And what might that be?"

"I intend to Europaform your planet."

5. JUPITER CRASH

This last statement from Caterpillar did not reassure Erin. "What do you mean? You're gonna make the whole world look like Europe? Will we all have to listen to French accordion music or German polkas? What about the food? I am *not* eating snails!"

Caterpillar's voice grew irritated. "You are confused. I am referring to my home world, Europa, one of the moons of Jupiter."

"You're planning to give Earth some kind of make over so it looks like your moon? Why?"

"Perhaps you recall several years ago the collision of Comet Shoemaker-Levy with our primary?"

"Hel-*lo*! Do I look like some kind of poindexter to you?

Why would I *ever* have paid any attention to such a thing when I was like ten years old and still playing with *Barbie* dolls?"

"Allow me to provide a video summary then."

A vivid waking dream instantly filled Erin's vision, as if a movie screen had been pasted to her eyeballs. Her vantage was a point in near orbit around the titanic, mottled globe of Jupiter. As she stared in fascination at the immense, fantastic landscape of the gas giant, Comet Shoemaker-Levy flashed into the scene, shortly thereafter impacting cataclysmically with the big planet.

Control of her vision returned. "Wow! Some fireworks!"

"Indeed. My race became very alarmed at this event. Despite living beneath two miles of ice on a separate globe, we realized that we were not safe from any future such events. We needed to develop a second habitat for our kind. But the choice of your world was also determined by an additional factor."

"What was that?"

"We became aware through monitored radio broadcasts that your national space agency was developing plans to send a probe to our world, to drill through our holy ceiling of protective ice and penetrate our happy seas. This we could not allow. So I was sent alone in a one-way interplanetary ice-pod to effect the sterilization of your planet."

Erin could not repress a guffaw. "Not to put you down, Caterpillar, but how is a lone talking rag mop going to conquer a whole world? Especially when you're attached to me? Do you have any idea how powerless teenage girls like me are in this country?"

"Powerless? Did you not render the Backstreet Boys millionaires?"

"*Eeyeuw*! Believe me, I had *nothing* to do with *that*!"

"No matter. My plan will soon become apparent, once we reach your house, which I intend to use as my world-converting headquarters."

Erin crossed her arms defiantly across her chest. "And what if I just plant myself here and won't budge?"

"Alas, that is when I find myself with the unpleasant necessity of taking control of your motor functions."

And with that statement, Erin found herself trotting confidently across the beach much against her will, heading straight for home.

"Oh, no! Stop right now!"

"Am I overtaxing your body?"

"No, but I hate running! It's like gym class—you get all *sweaty*!"

"Perspiration is good. I will extend portions of myself to absorb it for my sustenance if you permit."

"No, no! I'll sweat, I'll sweat!"

6. FASCINATION STREET

While she helplessly jogged home, Erin was treated to another personal screening of an educational filmstrip. This time the experience included multisensory stimulation as well. It was frightening to realize that she was galloping blind and deaf through the however lightly trafficked night streets of her town. But Erin had to assume Caterpillar knew what it was doing.

Erin was a swimmer in the lightless, tasty, echoic seas of Europa. Despite the lack of sunshine, she could somehow perceive a wild ecology in full color. Teeming with garish and bizarre alien life-forms, both mobile and sessile, dotted with smoking volcanic-vent oases, the homeworld of Caterpillar seemed a cheerful industrious place. Erin witnessed many of Caterpillar's fellows swim by. A few moved independently with a scalp-flexing maneuver, but most rode a variety of host creatures, from long, sleek, shark-like beings to bloated floaters. Erin assumed that the other caterpillars controlled their mounts just as she herself was now being ridden.

Closer and closer to a heavenly dome—dimly sensed at first, then more and more vivid—Erin swam, the pleasantly warm waters sluicing by. Finally the jagged, faintly luminescent underside of the miles of ice that enclosed the Europan biosphere loomed above her. Erin felt her soul fill with a deep religious appreciation of this miracle shield that allowed her world to exist. It felt like attending Christmas and Easter services rolled into one.

Europa vanished, and apprehension of her immediate surroundings returned. She was almost home.

"You see now why we could never allow earthlings to sacrilegiously penetrate our icy mantle. And once your own planet is encased in a similar crust, any of your species lucky enough to adapt and survive will certainly thank us for allowing you to share such a blessing."

"We're a very ungrateful bunch of bastards."

"No matter. We are highly altruistic enough to compensate for your bad manners."

Erin came to a stop on her doorstep.

"If I restore control to you, will you promise not to run away?"

Erin sighed. "All right. I don't have anywhere else to go anyway. I'm certainly not going to walk into a police station and announce that my hair wants to be taken to our leader."

"I do not care about your leaders. They are irrelevant."

Erin chuckled. "You're here only an hour and already you sound like talk radio."

"We have learned much from your unwise profligate broadcasting."

The front door swung open, and Erin's mother stood framed within.

A bit taller still than her rebellious adolescent offspring, Anne Merkin shared Erin's stubborn round face, engraved with age-accumulated worry lines. Her gray-streaked hair was bound up in a banana clip, a few tendrils escaping. Did they stir with impossible sympathy toward Erin's new do? No, it was only the play of shadows.

Dressed in robe and slippers, Anne wore an expression that any parent would have recognized instantly: a blend of concern, anger, and puzzlement.

"*What* are you doing out at this hour, young lady? And why didn't you— My god, what have you done to your hair!"

"Mom, can we not have this discussion in the front yard, please?"

Anne Merkin grabbed her daughter by the shoulder and pulled her inside. The slam of the door was followed by the start of a rant.

"You look like a savage! Your father must be rolling in his grave! To think of all the care and love we've both lavished on you. But you don't appreciate anything, do you? I've never seen a more ungrateful child! Well, this is the last straw! I'm calling your Aunt Gladys right now!"

"Who is Aunt Gladys?"

"She's my mother's sister, a real bitch. She lives way out in the country. I'll probably be locked in my bedroom there for a week. But they'll probably try to shave my 'hair' off first."

Erin's second scalp crawled in revulsion. "This cannot be!"

Anne Merkin was dialing the phone. "Quit your mumbling, young lady!"

A long extrusion of Erin's new hair shot out and wrapped itself around Anne Merkin's neck.

"Urk!"

"Don't choke her, Caterpillar! You'll kill her!"

Like a stack of poker chips flicked with a finger, Anne Merkin dropped unconscious to the linoleum at the same time that Caterpillar replied, "I merely needed to discommode her long enough to gain control of her sleep centers. Those circuits are locked in a feedback loop now, and she will remain unaware until I choose to awaken her."

Erin's hair reeled itself in. The dangling phone played a message of operator annoyance, and Erin absentmindedly recradled it. She moved to her mother's side, arranging her limbs more naturally. Fetching a pillow and afghan from the parlor, she made the sleeper as comfortable as possible. Caterpillar did not interfere until she was finished.

"Very well. Now we must get to work."

7. *JUMPING SOMEONE ELSE'S TRAIN*

The time was now after midnight. Quiet as the interval between tracks on a CD, the neighborhood—including of course Anne Merkin—slept peacefully, unaware of the coming planetary doom birthing beneath Erin's fingers.

Erin's hands had apparently developed skills and a mind of their own. She found herself watching in bemusement as they began to do the kind of things that gear-head boys liked to do with cars. With several tools no more complex than a kitchen knife, a pair of tweezers, a Gameboy, and, ironically, a hand-held hair dryer, Erin's hands began to assemble a strange mechanism.

First she watched her familiar digits, each chewed nail enameled in flaking Ghetto Grit, deconstruct the Merkins' television, radio, VCR, microwave, and Waterpik into a junk heap of parts spread across the parlor floor. Then she marveled as Caterpillar, using her personal limbs like waldoes, began to put the components together according to distinctly nonhuman rules. Erin had never imagined that the nozzle of a Waterpik might possibly funnel microwaves, but such seemed to be Caterpillar's intent.

After the first hour of this painstaking work, Erin began to grow bored and uncomfortable.

"Hey, Caterpiggle! Can't I change the way I'm sitting? My legs feel like they're gonna fall off!"

"Sorry. Allow me to reconfigure your badly engineered circulatory channels and remove all discomfort."

Without shifting position, Erin suddenly felt wonderful. "Gee, thanks!" This attention to her commandeered body raised a parallel question in her mind. "How come you can survive in our atmosphere? Why aren't you flopping around like a fish out of water?"

"My race is basically anaerobic. Our metabolisms can get by without oxygen, although we can toggle into several other modes as well. I must admit, though, that the dryness of your atmosphere is distressing to me."

"Are you asking me to go soak my head?"

"Later, perhaps. Now the work must continue."

Half a dismal hour passed. Erin found herself pondering another puzzling question. "Do you guys have machines and stuff like this on Europa? I didn't see any in your home movies."

"No, we are a nontechnological culture, employing direct mental control of universal forces. You see, the cosmic roiling in the space-time continuum created by the electromagnetic-gravitic plasma dance amongst Jupiter and its satellites allows us to access certain energies directly. We naturally evolved to manipulate forces of which you lower orders have little conception. Here on your cold planet, however, I have to resort to cruder methods, plucked directly from your memories."

"What are you talking about? I don't know any of this electronics shit."

"So you believe."

Erin was left to ponder the implications of this statement while Caterpillar continued his work. Eventually, she found herself dozing off in a natural manner, despite her busy eyes remaining wide open in order to continue guiding her darting hands.

Several hours had slipped by when she regained awareness. Her hands were cradling the Gameboy, which was cabled to the softly glowing asymmetrical mess of jiggered parts. The screen of the video game displayed a welter of scrolling alien icons.

"I need several more components not available in your domicile. We shall have to visit a military base."

This bland statement was the most insane thing Erin had heard since Caterpillar had attached itself to her, and its absurdity set her off.

"Are you absolutely bugshit? I'd be shot on sight!"

Caterpillar remained unperturbed. "I think otherwise. You see, in the course of my investigations of your mentality, I have discovered certain latent, untapped potentials in your brain that will make our task fairly straightforward. It seems that your race, in partial compensation for your unfortunate choice of birthplaces, has evolved so as to be able to take spontaneous and irregular advantage of certain loopholes among the physical laws. Nonlocal actions, extratemporal sensing, and other seemingly freakish abilities not available to more sophisticated beings like me are open to your race. I simply propose to put these talents under my direct and precise control."

"I still don't see what all this guff means for me."

"Only this. Please concentrate on the nearest military base you know of."

Obligingly, Erin summoned up a picture of Fort Vandermeer, where her Dad had once done his National Guard duty. She pictured the main parade grounds where she had once strolled, hand-in-hand, with her father.

Pre-dawn illumination tinged the frosty sky above the barracks. Gravel crunched under Erin's boots as she pivoted incredulously. The only figure in sight was a guard at the gate facing quite rationally outward, toward potential invaders. In the chilly silence, Erin distinctly heard the guard cough twice.

"Holy—"

Caterpillar cut her off. "Quiet! Now, I would adjudge that windowless structure a warehouse—"

The interior of the barnlike shed was quite dark. But suddenly Erin found that she could see, if only in black-and-white.

Caterpillar directed the girl up and down a number of aisles. Soon, her arms were loaded with hardware.

The next second she again stood in her parlor. Gratefully, she dumped her burdens to the floor.

Picking up a GPS unit with Erin's hands, Caterpillar said, "The fastenings on this unit are nonstandard. Let us visit a hardware store."

Having done so well with her first jump, the prospect of teleporting a second time seemed more agreeable to Erin. "Could we maybe stop for some food too? There's no chocolate in the house at all!"

Erin paid close attention to what Caterpillar did next with her mind.

8. THE LOVECATS

Fueled by a dozen Kit Kat bars liberated from the locked but hardly impregnable-to-teleporters grocery store, Erin labored long hours under Caterpillar's behest. As the morning progressed, sunlight gradually flooding the parlor and revealing all the weirdness with a level of detail that the night had half-concealed, Erin could feel herself growing sweatier and grosser by the minute. Caterpillar's unceasing construction of its looming Doomsday Device required Erin to be in constant motion: climbing up and down chairs, crawling under projecting shelves of circuits, bending into odd-shaped cavities. Combined with the jog home from the beach, this activity left her grottier than young Patti Smith's armpits. Adolescent musk rose off her in powerful waves. Almost as strong as the desire to get clean was the craving for a bidi.

"Caterpillar, I need a break!"

"Are you experiencing any aches?"

Erin inventoried her muscles. Curiously, they did not feel fatigued. "No. But I have to take a shower before I make myself faint!"

"I too would like to immerse myself in the second-rate yet potentially refreshing waters of your world. But its conversion to Europan parameters must be initiated first. My whole race is depending on me."

"Yeah, well, I never signed up for this little chore."

"Did you not extend the gullible hand of interplanetary friendship to me on the beach and invite me onboard?"

Erin paused. "Well, maybe I kinda did . . . . But that was before I knew about your evil plans!"

"What do you care about the fate of your globe? Do not attempt to persuade me of your nonexistent charity toward all mankind. Recall that I have access to your memories. You often wished the world would explode and end your so-called 'suffering.'"

"I—I was just being melodramatic! I didn't mean anybody any real harm! I just got pissed when narrow-minded jerks said stupid things. Like during the Gulf War when I was little, and all anyone could talk about was killing an Arab!"

"Nonetheless, you should be glad that the pitiful charade of human existence is about to be transmogrified."

Erin tried to teleport out of her house to the police station, but nothing happened. Apparently, the function remained under Caterpillar's control. Instead, she found herself stepping will-lessly back from the alien machine. The Gameboy was still cabled to the bigger contraption, and now Erin's fingers danced across the controls, causing a parade of portentous icons to march across the display.

"Now the door to the Funhouse is open."

A liquid platinum lambency filled one irregular cavity of the machine, and the next second something popped out.

The creature that emerged resembled ball lightning or a swamp-gas will-o-the-wisp, a sparky, fuzzy roil of energy—except that it appeared to possess infinite depths filled with churning, hazy images. Erin thought she could see a kind of Cheshire Cat face surface, melt, and then surface again, time after time. Erin sensed a kind of playful curiosity, a joy and élan radiate from the vital creature. As if reciprocating her attention, the being began to "purr" on some subliminal yet detectable level.

"What—what is it?"

"This is an intelligent creature composed entirely of what your scientists have just recently begun to call 'funny energy.' It originates out of the very substrate of the universe, from below the Planck level. We have often usefully employed them as assistants, for they are able to directly manipulate matter at the quantum level."

Suddenly a second creature—Erin found herself thinking of them as "Lovecats"—blipped into the parlor. This Lovecat did not linger with the original, but shot straight through the house's walls without damaging them!

Now a steady stream of Lovecats began to emerge, all

darting away in different directions. Only the first, the Master Lovecat, remained behind.

"He will serve as a relay between the machine and his flock," Caterpillar said.

"What are they going to do?"

"I have set them multiple tasks. First they are going to increase the albedo—the reflectivity—of your polar ice caps. This will start the chilling of your globe, as more and more solar radiance is returned to space. Then the Lovecats, as you name them, will attend to other changes involving carbon sequestering and such. Your damaged climate is already balanced on a needle, and only needs a slight push to plunge into the deepest Ice Age ever seen. In only a few years, your globe will be entirely frozen, a new Europa suitable for colonization by my kind. I estimate that your civilization will take approximately six months to collapse. As I suggested earlier, however, a few humans might make the transition to the new world, if they adopt the habits and capabilities of certain marine mammals."

Now Erin felt so awful about what she had helped unleash, even her own lack of bodily hygiene or addict's clove-cravings paled in comparison.

9. *WILD MOOD SWINGS*

Throughout the long morning and into the afternoon, an endless procession of bristly, crackling, weightless Lovecats emerged from the Doomsday Machine. All Erin could do was watch in muted horror as the agents of Earth's freeze-out zipped off to fulfill Caterpillar's wicked commands. The alien seemed not to care about rest or sustenance or comfort, for either itself or its mount, but instead remained focused on the smooth workings of its gateway to the basement boiler room of the cosmos, the Funhouse.

Erin's mind raced in tight circles. How could she escape?

How could she save her planet? Would the new Ice Age possibly spare an England sustained in warmth by the Gulf Stream, and thus leave habitable the home of the adorable Robert Smith, the clone of whose hair she now sported? And finally, what was this looming planetary catastrophe going to do to her virginal love life?

Around 3:00 in the afternoon came a knock at the front door.

"Do not respond," Caterpillar warned.

"Erin, hello! It's me, Elise! Why weren't you at school today?"

"She's got a key," Erin told Caterpillar. But this intelligence came to late to save her friend.

The door swung open directly onto the parlor. Elise stepped inside, spotted Erin, and exclaimed, "Wow, look at your hair!" before promptly vanishing.

Ten seconds later came an identical knocking on the door, which had mysteriously closed itself.

"Erin, hello! It's me, Elise! Why weren't you at school today?"

Elise entered the house, spoke her ultimate line—"Wow, look at your hair!"—and disappeared again. Ten more seconds ticked by, and the entire scenario replayed once more.

"What have you done to Elise, you monster!"

"I have rolled up her entire existence into this short sequence of events, then set her adrift from the continuum. She is like a hoop rolling through a landscape of time, surfacing at regular intervals forever."

"Erin, hello! It's me, Elise! Why weren't you at school today? Wow, look at your hair!"

"Erin, hello! It's me, Elise! Why weren't you at school today? Wow, look at your hair!"

"Erin—"

"Oh, this is awful! You have to set her free! Look, the neighbors will soon spot something wrong and call the cops."

"No, they will not. They will think you girls are simply playing around, as foolish young females frequently do. In any case, the changes engineered by the Lovecats will become irreversible within the next few hours. In fact, so confident of my success am I, that I believe I will now take advantage of your offer to soak your head."

Caterpillar marched Erin past her sleeping mother, out of earshot of Elise's ceaseless litany, and into the bathroom. There, the alien compelled her to strip. Beneath Erin's black garb she wore a lace-trimmed camisole and white cotton panties, the latter garment bearing the image of Badtz-Maru, the enigmatic penguin friend of Hello Kitty. Seen by Erin in the mirror, the gloomy bird seemed to proclaim, *Finally, Earth will become a world fit for penguins!*

Completely naked the next minute, Erin was forced to contemplate herself in the full-length mirror, a task she generally avoided. Oh, God, why couldn't she be built like Xena? Maybe then she'd be able to save the world . . . .

Caterpillar disdained to close the shower curtain before setting only the cold water gushing from the lower tap. The twist of a valve set the frigid spray pouring out the shower nozzle directly onto her head. For a brief moment, Erin felt encased in ice. Then she experienced the bitterly cold flow as pure pleasure.

"Ah, if only there were more sulphur in this pale fluid, I would be completely at home!"

Erin decided to make the best of this experience and get clean. On a hanging wire rack stood several plastic bottles: shampoo, crème rinse, pre-rinse, after-rinse, and half-a-dozen other hair condiments. Although Erin had hated her old locks, she had taken scrupulous care of them. No sense being grotty just to spite her mom. Now she reached instinctively for a bottle, but found her hand halted.

"What are those?"

"Just soaps."

"Ah, cleansing agents. We do not have these on Europa. Very well. Proceed."

Erin squirted her alien hair full of pearly, aromatic liquid and began to work it in.

A strange feeling of disorientation passed through her. Then Caterpillar began to chant.

"Oh, the bliss! Oh, the joy! Sweet heavenly scents! Marvelous compounds! My veins thrill with ambrosia! More, more, more!"

Like a crazed beautician, Erin dosed Caterpillar with six kinds of hair preparations. His chanting turned to ecstatic gibberish.

Experimentally, Erin reached out and turned off the water. Nothing stopped her. She stepped freely from the tub. Caterpillar continued to moan and croon. Erin grabbed a spray can of mousse and covered Caterpillar with it, sealing the intoxicating chemicals beneath a layer of stiffening goo, much as Caterpillar had wanted to cordon off Earth.

Regarding herself in the mirror, Erin saw, on one level of perception, a teenaged living mess: skin blue and goose-pimpled, hair crusted over.

But on another level, Xena herself looked back.

In its delirium, Caterpillar had plundered her memories and emerged with a snatch of a Cure song. Now the alien sang over and over, in its androgynous contralto, a snatch of Smithian lyrics:

"Show me, show me, show me how you do that trick! The one that makes me scream, 'She's sick!' And I promise you, I promise that I'll run away with you!"

266

Erin smiled. "Oh, don't you worry, Mr. Badass Sea Slug. I'll show you a trick or two!"

10. GONE!

The Master Lovecat wasn't a bad guy at all once you got to know him. Frisky and curious, amorally cooperative, the energy creature, summoned from the warp and weft of the plenum, wanted nothing more than to please anyone who exhibited a token friendship by inviting Lovecats up the scales of the multiverse into the macroverse.

It had taken Erin more than an hour to establish efficient communications with Lovecat Number One. (She still wasn't sure whether the scattered horde of beings shared one identity or many.) She certainly wasn't aided by the background roar of raving nonsense Caterpillar kept chattering into her auditory nerves. Strange physical sensations—itches, bad tastes, and dizziness—plagued her as well. But by mentally tweaking her newly talented brain (Erin pictured the operation as adjusting slider controls on a boom box), she managed to lower the buzz and random stimuli from the alien, but not completely eliminate it. That was just as well, she figured, since she had to keep monitoring the Europan to make sure of its intoxication levels.

By sheer persistence, Erin had eventually broken through the language barrier to send and receive information to and from the Master Lovecat. Not that language was precisely the word. Unlike Caterpillar, the Lovecat seemed to communicate by pictures and feelings and gestaltic lumps. Talking to it was more like trying to manage a directed dream. But after many frustrating minutes, during which Erin counseled herself not to freak because like all of Earth was counting on her, she finally felt that the two of them understood each other.

So, taking a deep breath, Erin ordered the Master Lovecat to reverse the climatological changes initiated by Caterpillar.

Done, she thought she heard/felt/remembered.

Erin expelled a gust of held air. "Whew!"

"Erin, hello! It's me, Elise! Why weren't you at school today? Wow, look at your hair!"

"Erin, hello! It's me, Elise! Why weren't you at school today? Wow, look at your hair!"

"Erin—"

Continually cycling through time, popping in and out of Erin's perceptions like a skipping film, Elise had been an annoying, subliminal midge-drone, while Erin concentrated on saving mankind's ungrateful and ignorant, but irreplaceable ass. Now, however, Erin felt she could spare a moment to rescue her friend.

Digging mental fingers into an unnatural n-dimensional knot she sensed around the front door, Erin untied Elise's contorted lifeline.

"Erin! Where are your clothes!"

Clothes? Who could bother with clothes now? Did Xena stop fighting if she busted a bra strap?

"I'll explain later." Erin suddenly considered the plight of the third human in the room. She teleported over to her mother, touched her shoulder, probed inside, and woke up Anne Merkin.

Mrs. Merkin gazed up at the ceiling. Her brain seemed to be lagging behind her eyes. "How did I get here?"

"No time to talk now! I've got to fix my hair's little red wagon so we're never bothered by it again!"

Erin transmitted the concept of a soft, warm blanket to the Master Lovecat, who was busy reabsorbing all his scattered task-finished minions back into himself.

Protect me, she pleaded.

She stepped sidewise across 480 million miles of space.

11. *HOT HOT HOT!!!*

Jupiter's glow reflected colorfully from Erin's nose jewelry, like Christmas lights in a silver ornament. Cocooned in a glowing, transparent nimbus, the Master Lovecat hovering at her shoulder, the nude girl regarded Europa, the snowball home of the aggressive caterpillars.

Atop her head, the mousse-encapsulated, balsam-besotted alien laboriously seemed to take cognizance of its altered surroundings.

"Where—are—we? Home? How—?"

"Shut up! I'm going to make sure you guys never mess with my world again!"

"No! What—what are you planning?"

"Oh, you'll see!"

Erin felt Caterpillar strive to regain control of her mind. But she was too strong for it now, at least in its attenuated state. The alien was reduced to pleading.

"Please! Visit my world! You'll see then. We don't deserve whatever doom you intend!"

"All right! But no funny stuff!"

Erin reappeared under miles of Europan ice. Her eyes adjusted themselves to the level of illumination. Here in reality was the watery world she had seen from Caterpillar's mental filmstrip.

Within minutes, she was surrounded by many of Caterpillar's peers all mounted on their various steeds. They could not speak to her directly, but she sensed their unease and abject surrender. They were more pathetic than a bunch of middle schoolers.

"Oh, damn! What a bunch of lameoids! All right, you've convinced me! Here, you can join your friends!"

Erin psychically transported Caterpillar off her head—Ow! those sharp feet!—out of her protective force-shell and into the welcoming sea. The water dissolved the hallucinatory rinses and shampoos off Caterpillar, and through some fading quantum thread of connection, she heard the alien's familiar, nasty voice exclaim, "We'll be back! And when you don't have the Lovecats with you—!"

Erin smiled. "Right." Then she popped out into space again, close to Europa, where, with a little generous help from the Lovecats, she pushed the satellite out of its orbit, just as effortlessly as her father had once impelled her on a swing.

The titanic splash the moon made in Jupiter's atmosphere, photographed by a startled but quick-thinking astronomer at the controls of the Hubble telescope, was destined to become the best-selling poster of the next five decades.

12. JUST LIKE HEAVEN

Erin's chestnut-colored hair hung long and lush to the shoulders of her new black leather jacket. At 8:00 P.M. on a beautiful summer Friday night, she stood in an extensively winding line with Elise outside their hometown civic center. The two girls could barely control themselves. Puffing on bidis, bouncing with anticipation, and breaking into spontaneous broad smiles, they advanced slowly with the other ticket holders. To pass the time, they debated possible set lists.

"'Friday I'm in Love!'"

"'Mint Car!'"

"'Wendy Time!'"

"'Pictures of You!'"

"'Close to Me!'"

Once inside the auditorium, they rushed to their reserved front-row-center seats. Even the grungy techies moving equipment around on the impossibly close stage looked to their eyes like the glamorous priests of an exotic cult.

"Oh, Erin! It's like a dream come true! Remember this winter, when you were feeling so down, and you like went mental and destroyed all your appliances and ripped out your hair and started sleepwalking around naked until you snapped out of it? Who would've ever guessed that a few months later we'd be sitting right here? It just goes to show that whenever you think you're stuck, something will come along to unstick you!"

"You are so right, Elise!"

The lights went down, and the opening act came on. Elise whispered, "Do you think we'll get to go onstage? That would be the ultimate!"

"I can't say," Erin replied, and she really couldn't.

She had pulled a lot of tricks to get the Cure here and secure these tickets. Teleporting into the record company's offices and jiggering their computers had been the easiest part of it. But for the moment, she was finished with trickery.

If she did get called up tonight to stand onstage in front of thousands of admiring eyes with her favorite band in the world, it was going to be strictly because of who she was!

Tales of absentminded or obstreperous saints form a minor canon in fantasy literature, from the works of Anatole France to James Branch Cabell. This contribution of mine is the closest I've ever come to employing my long-abandoned upbringing as a Roman Catholic in my fiction.

This story first appeared in England, in an anthology edited by the redoubtable Mike Ashley. In that peculiar country, the term "mathematics" is shortened to "maths." But we both agreed that "Maths Takes A Holiday" destroyed all the desirable allusiveness to "Death Takes a Holiday." So much to the confusion of the British audience, my story appeared with its original title.

My thanks to Rudy Rucker for help with some of the more abstruse mathematical concepts herein.

Math Takes a Holiday

Lucas Latulippe pitied the religious physicists and mystical biologists, the prayerful chemists and godly geologists of his acquaintance. As a mathematician who also chanced by a fervent and unexpected midlife conversion to be a practicing Catholic, Lucas felt extreme sadness when he contemplated the plight of his fellows in the scientific community who sought to reconcile their spiritual beliefs with the tenets of their secular professions. The Creation versus the Big Bang, the Garden of Eden versus Darwinism, the Flood versus plate tectonics. What a mind-wrenching clash of diametrically opposed values, images, priorities, and forces these valiant men and women faced every day! To embrace the rigorous cosmos of Einstein, Hawking, and Wilson without letting go of the numinous plenum of Augustine, Mohammed, or Krishna— An impossible task on which one could waste much valuable mental energy better spent formulating theorems.

Lucas owed his unique peace of mind and consequent productivity entirely to his youthful choice of discipline. When his epiphanical conversion had ineluctably struck him—one cool autumn day while daydreamily crossing the campus and witnessing a dove alight on the chapel steeple—Lucas had faced no interior conflicts. His newfound faith offered no impediments to his practice of theoretical mathematics, nor did his academic pursuits interfere with his worship.

That was the beauty of the kind of rarefied math Lucas practiced. It was completely divorced from practical implications, had no bearing on the workings of the universe, and thus held no potential for conflict with the received wisdom of the Church. Oh, certainly the other, less refined sciences used math to embody and clarify their own findings, contaminating the glorious legacy of Pythagoras and Euclid to a certain degree. Lucas would not deny, for instance, the famous observation that a simple little equation underlay the hard-edged reality of the atomic bomb. But admitting this much was like saying that a few of the same glorious words employed by C.S. Lewis could be utilized in the instruction sheet for assembling a playground swing set.

Blessed with such an ethereal conception of his discipline, Lucas enjoyed an ease of worship that he was certain scientists of any other ilk could not experience. He attended Mass daily with a clean conscience and undisturbed soul. In the parish church not far from his office (attended mostly by Hispanic immigrants with whom Lucas exchanged few words), he was able to feel an unconstrained and untainted relationship with God, Whom Lucas actually dared to think of as the Supreme Mathematician.

Lucas Latulippe pitied his peers. He prayed daily they could all someday experience the raw glory of mathematics.

"Dear God, please allow my mocking colleagues to witness the transcendental glory of Thy sovereign mathematical Holy Spirit—"

But despite his deep faith, he never really expected that one day his prayers would be answered.

* * *

For some unfathomable reason of His Own, at this exact noninstant of the eternal, unbegun Now that filled Heaven from one infinite end to the other, God had chosen to manifest Himself as a Sequoia Tree, albeit the largest Sequoia ever to exist. The crown of this enormous redwood standing in for the ineffable Face of the Creator soared into the heavenly clouds—galaxies?—far out of sight of the two human figures standing at its gnarly base rooted not in soil, but in the very stuff of celestial hyperexistence.

Despite the immeasurable distance separating the two auditors and the invisible foliage of the God Tree—from which Crown as from a Burning Bush one might reasonably assume any Voice ought to issue—the words of God resounded quite plainly in the ears of the man and woman standing tensely at the Tree's base.

"Do I have to send both of you to your Mansions, or will you cease this bickering instantly?"

The dark-eyed woman continued to glare at the man, who glared just as fixedly back with a gaze of piercing blue. Their enmity seemed implacable, until an ominous quaking of the numinous stratum beneath their bare feet conveyed to them the actual measure of God's rising displeasure. The tension and anger then dissolved from their postures, and they turned partially away from each other, pretending to adjust their identical white robes or study the unvarying quilt of uncreated Ur-stuff on which they stood.

"That's much better," God commended. "Now you're both acting like real Saints."

The young woman shook her black, wavy hair and smiled, an expression that lent her rather coarse and Mediterranean features an alarming, rather than reassuring, cast. Her long flowing samite robe failed to conceal a not unattractive figure.

"Some of us never forgot the humility we exhibited in life. But those who lorded it over peasants back on Earth seem to have become even more haughty once beatified."

Beneath furry brows, the eyes of the older male Saint threatened to combust. His magnificent, almost Assyrian beard seemed to writhe as if alive. "You willful daughter of Eve! Disobedient toward your mortal father in life, you continue to disrespect your Eternal Father after death!"

"Dioscorus, my earthly father—just in case you've forgotten, Hubert—was a disreputable pagan who had his pious Christian daughter beheaded. Should I have honored such a parent?"

"You are deliberately obscuring my point, Barbara. I am merely arguing for a proper chain of command and obedience—"

"Because you're descended from the kings of Toulouse! And because you were once a bishop!"

"What of it? I'm proud to have been Bishop of Maestricht and Liege!"

"Certainly, certainly, a wonderful item on your CV. But you were once married as well, don't forget!"

Saint Hubert coughed nervously. "The Church had different policies back in my time—"

Saint Barbara crossed her arms triumphantly across

her chest. "On the other hand, I am still a virgin. A virgin *and* a martyr!"

Stiffening his pride, Saint Hubert countered, "I was tutored by Saint Lambert himself!"

Barbara snorted. "I learned my precepts at Origen's knee!"

"I was vouchsafed a vision—a cross appeared between the horns of the stag I hunted!"

"I experienced a miraculous transport from my tower prison to a mountaintop!"

"As Bishop, I converted almost the whole of Belgium!"

"I was one of the Fourteen Holy Helpers! You probably prayed to me!"

"You—you insolent young pup!"

"Young pup? I was born four centuries before you!"

"Where's your historicity, though? Not a single documented proof of your actual existence. Why, you're positively mythical!"

"Mythical! You dirty old huntsman, I'll show you what a sock from a mythical Saint feels like—"

"ENOUGH!" God's thundering command froze the Saints just at the point of coming to blows. Chastised, they separated and attended circumspectly to God's further speech, His Utterances tinged with a rustling of Sequoia foliage.

"Now, pay attention. I summoned you before Me, Hubert, because I had a new assignment for you. Conversely, Barbara, you intruded yourself. What claim do you make upon My Audience?"

Barbara sniffed like a frustrated teenager. "It's not fair. We're both Patron Saints of Mathematicians, but You're always giving Hubert the best missions. Pardon me, Lord, but it strikes me that Heaven might have a, shall we say, glass ceiling?"

The Sequoia shivered nervously. "Please, Saint Barbara, do not raise this touchy issue. I have spent the past mortal century trying to remedy this perceived imbalance between the sexes in My Church, and I don't need to have My Works undone by hasty accusations. Why, how many appearances of the Virgin have I authorized this year alone—? But why am I humoring you thus? I do not have to justify My Ways. This is one of My favorite Privileges. Now, tell Me what objections you have to your recent assignment."

Saint Barbara placed her hands on her hips. "I've been watching over the same fellow for several years now, and I'm sick of his face. I need a change."

God paused in that endearing, fake way He had, as if consulting a file. "Hmmm, one Rudy Rucker. Yes, you've done an admirable job of reforming him. He's truly treading the path of righteousness now. But wouldn't you like to hang in there until he wins the Nobel Prize in 2012?"

"No, I wouldn't. The last time I visited this Rucker character, he pinched my arse so hard I was black-and-blue for days!"

Saint Hubert muttered, "Virgin—ha!"

"Well," God continued, "I suppose I could transfer his care to Saint Francis de Sales, under Francis' remit for writers, since that's what Rucker's Nobel Prize will be awarded for . . . . Consider it done! Now, are you arguing that you should take over Hubert's new task?"

Saint Barbara seemed a trifle discomposed at her easy victory and disinclined to ask for too much. "Not take it over, exactly. Perhaps we could share?"

Saint Hubert nearly shouted. "Share my mission! With this little chit? How she ever got to be patron of mathematics anyway, I'll never know."

"I have as much mathematical ability as you, Hubert."

"You commissioned one measly tower window as a

mortal patroness of architecture, and that qualifies you? In my day—"

"QUIET!" God ordered. "My Mind is made up. Both of you will answer the prayers of My faithful servant by name of—ah, I have it right here—Lucas Latulippe. Go now, and manifest My inscrutable Being."

The Sequoia popped out of existence without apprehendable transition, leaving the two Saints face-to-face.

Hubert sighed wearily. "Thy Will be done. Shall we take a chariot pulled by some cherubim?"

"If you're too tired. But on such a beautiful day, I prefer to walk."

Saint Barbara set off across the pastures of Heaven, and Hubert gamely followed.

"Why I didn't pot that cursed holy stag with an arrow when I had a chance—"

* * *

Pisky Wispaway weighed a muffin short of 300 pounds. Old family photographs (from idyllic days in Piscataway, New Jersey) testified to her early existence as an indubitably trim child of elfin features who must have evoked many a smile from adoring adults when queried as to her name. Unfortunately, the whimsical legal name bestowed on her by her parents sat less endearingly on the fatty shoulders of the dean of the astronomy department at Lucas Latulippe's university. Yet so good-hearted was Pisky—so relatively reconciled to her sad status as campus butt of all sniggering fat jokes was she—that she never winced when called upon to introduce herself, even insisting to just-met acquaintances, "Call me Pisky, please." With bouncing, curly, auburn hair of which she was inordinately proud, clad in one of her many billowing, colorful, tent dresses and several yards of costume jewelry necklaces, Pisky could often be seen sailing across the quad like some massive galleon pregnant with cargo from the Far East.

Today Pisky sailed into Lucas' office, catching him behind his desk. A big smile bisected her round face, causing her eyes to nearly disappear within the crinkled flesh surrounding them.

"You're coming to our party this afternoon, aren't you, Lucas? For our new professor, remember? Dr. Garnett."

Lucas liked Pisky well enough as a distant colleague. She was an intelligent and affable individual. But he had come to intensely dislike her increasingly frequent visits to his office, often on the slightest of pretexts. He suspected that certain romantic inclinations underlay these pop-ins, feelings he did not now feel capable of reciprocating. Moreover, she so filled Lucas' small quarters that he invariably felt suffocated, especially when trapped behind his desk, away from the window. Not a sizable fellow himself, Lucas simply could not compete for spatial domination with the oversized woman.

Anxious now to empty his office of Pisky's bulk, Lucas nonetheless felt compelled to prolong the conversation by asking, "Will Hulme be there?"

"Why, of course Owen will be there. He's our senior professor."

"I don't know if I will attend then. You realize of course that we don't get along—"

Pisky brushed Lucas' objections aside with a wave of one hammy beringed hand. "You just have to ignore Owen when he tries to get a rise out of you. That's what all the rest of us do. He's prickly with everyone, you know. 'Brilliant but prickly,' that's just how *New Scientist* characterized him."

Lucas squirmed in his chair, finding it hard to breathe. Was Pisky actually using up all the air in the room? "I comprehend those personality defects, Pisky, and I would be perfectly willing to overlook Hulme's barbs if they didn't always concern my faith. That's one topic where I cannot let his insults slide off me. He's not just demeaning me, you know, but two millennia of holy men and women."

Pisky decided to rest one oxen-like haunch on Lucas' desktop, overlooking his instinctive shrinking away. The casters of Lucas' chair hit the wall, and he was forced to end his retreat. Pisky leaned forward to convey the intimacy of her request.

"We need your stimulating presence at this party, Lucas. I promise you that I'll personally intervene if Owen steps over the bounds of good manners. Please, won't you promise to come?"

"Yes, yes, certainly. I'll be there!"

Pisky regained her feet with surprising grace and ease, considering her tonnage, and moved toward the door. "I'll see you this afternoon in Crowther Lounge then."

After Pisky had left, Lucas directed his eyes to the crucifix hanging across the room. He tried to compose a small prayer of thanks for his restored solitude, but his mind was diverted by the sight of the agonized Christ's distended rib cage.

When was the last time Pisky had seen her own ribs? Lucas found himself helplessly wondering.

* * *

Crowther Lounge sported the usual mix of unappealing chairs and couches marked by threadbare armrests and stained stuffingless cushions resembling the defective hemoglobin of sickle cell sufferers in shape. On a Formica-topped folding table, an assortment of novelty crackers and unnatural cheeses occupied plastic silver trays. Jug wine in assorted surreal shades begged to be decanted into plastic cups, tasted once, then surreptitiously poured into the sickly potted plants scattered around the room on the traffic-grooved carpet.

When Lucas arrived, the soiree was already in full swing. The faculty of the astronomy department, supplemented by volunteers from allied divisions, busily besieged both the refreshments and the famous Dr. Ferron Grainger Garnett, the university's latest star hire. Garnett had achieved a measure of media prominence with his BBC- and PBS-broadcast television special: *When Bad Universes Happen to Good Sapients.* Mixing pop psychology with cosmology, shallow philosophy with the many-worlds school of physics, the series had appalled Lucas. Naturally, it had been a smash.

As soon as Lucas entered the lounge, Pisky spotted him and began to wave. Sighing helplessly, Lucas moved through the crowd to within a tolerable distance of his large friend.

"Oh, Lucas, you must meet Dr. Garnett! Here, let me introduce you."

Pisky gripped his elbow and forcibly maneuvered herself and Lucas through the crush around the superstar astronomer. Once within the inner circle, Lucas was horrified to realize that his nemesis, Owen Hulme, stood directly at Garnett's right hand. Moreover, Hulme's aggressively sparkling wife, Britta, flanked Garnett much too familiarly on the newcomer's left.

For a brief moment before anyone registered Pisky and her victim, Lucas sized up the trio. Stocky and bulldoggish, Owen Hulme had chosen to offset his monkishly bald pate with a fierce, dark beard. Lean and whippetlike, his wife Britta overtopped him by a good six inches, half of her advantage inherent in a magnificent teased crown of blonde hair. Lucas could not help but think of the couple as minor caricatures from a *Tintin* comic. (Lucas had confessed this sin of uncharitableness more than once, but kept sinning helplessly every time he saw the pair.) Ferron Grainger Garnett, on the other hand, possessing the rugged virility of a Burt Lancaster or Spencer Tracy, seemingly ordered up from Central Casting to fill the role of a manly astronomer.

"Dr. Garnett," Pisky enthused, "meet my dear colleague, Lucas Latulippe. Lucas holds the Ashley Chair in the mathematics department. He's the university's prime candidate for a Fields Medal, if ever we had one."

Embarrassed by the praise, Lucas extended his hand too precipitously, nearly jostling Garnett's drink. Managing to connect after some fumbling, Lucas sought to deprecate his accomplishments.

"Hardly, hardly. Just a few minor papers concerning n-dimensional manifolds appearing in the odd journal here and there."

"I think I've seen your work footnoted," said Garnett pleasantly enough. "In a paper by Tipler perhaps?"

This conventional scientific compliment on Lucas' quotability index failed to please the mathematician. The last thing he desired was to have his pristine work find practical application in the far-out theories of some cosmic snake oil salesman. Nevertheless, Lucas bit his tongue and offered a demure acknowledgment of the supposed honor.

A red-faced Owen Hulme had been glaring at Lucas throughout the exchange. Now the brusque, compact fellow slugged back his wine, thrust his face forward, and said, "Lucas is our resident mystic. A regular saint, in fact. Claims numbers come direct from God, or some such bosh. Or is it the Pope who delivers your axioms?"

A smoldering rage, kindled by the mere sight of Hulme, now threatened to flame up within Lucas' bosom. He battled to control himself. "Professor Hulme's words conceal, as usual, a seed of truth within a husk of hyperbole. My private faith, centered in the earthly representative of God, known as the bishop of Rome, does increase my reverence toward my vocation. And I plead guilty to having claimed that mathematics offers proof of a divine basis for creation. I think perhaps in the best of all possible worlds, we would all feel this synergy between our work and our devotional impulses."

Britta Hulme contributed her thoughts now. "My hairdresser, Simon, has started practicing Santeria. He claims that the goddess of the sea, Yomama, or some such silly name, guides him when he gives shampoos."

Garnett tried to smooth over the nearly visible tension with a chuckle and a platitude. "Well, all religions have their share of wisdom now, don't they?"

Lucas' disgust expanded exponentially, and he blurted out his true feelings. "That is the kind of spineless guff that leads to indulgence in the worst sort of pagan nonsense. Witches, astrology, and druids!"

Hulme said, "You should talk, Latulippe! Your beliefs verge on the Kaballah!"

"The Kaballah! Why I never—"

Pisky intervened. "Lucas, I'm sure Owen meant nothing critical against your beliefs or against the Jewish religion either. Why, look—you don't even have a drink! Come with me and I'll get you a glass of vino."

Lucas allowed himself to be steered away. Hulme could not resist a parting shot. "Has your Pope burned any astronomers lately, flower boy?"

Turning back to offer an indignant reply—something along the lines of John Paul's graceful millennial *mea culpa*—Lucas found himself yanked so violently by Pisky that he lost the opportunity.

At the refreshment display Pisky apologized profusely, but in whispers. Calming down somewhat, Lucas accepted her apology but insisted on making an immediate departure.

Outside, Lucas unchained his Vespa from a bike rack and donned his safety helmet. Unable to afford both a car and accompanying monthly garage fees, Lucas had hit upon this type of motor scooter as the ideal mode of transportation for his daily short-range needs, having witnessed the utility of the little motorbike on Roman streets during a pilgrimage to the Vatican.

Halfway to his apartment, Lucas pulled up outside his church. Father Miguel Obispo, refilling the fount with holy water, greeted Lucas kindly. Distracted, Lucas nodded rather too curtly and proceeded to the Communion rail nearby the altar. He kneeled and fervently began to reiterate his daily prayer for chastisement of unbelievers.

Midway down the sunbeam road between Heaven and Earth, Saint Hubert turned to Saint Barbara and said, "Persistent fellow, isn't he? Doesn't he know we're already on our way?"

"Did you ask the Bird to announce us?"

"Why, no, I thought you did."

Saint Barbara huffed. "Forgetful old coot!"

"You juvenile hussy!"

The rest of the trip passed in frosty silence.

* * *

The morning after the disastrous astronomy department party, Lucas Latulippe woke up to his birring alarm feeling positively sanctified. That spontaneous detour for prayer had settled his soul. He couldn't recall ever feeling so hale and hearty, in both mind and body, this early in the morning. Why, he felt almost as if the Rapture had occurred while he slept. Still lying in bed with his gaze fixed on the familiar stippled ceiling, he patted himself tentatively through the coverlets. His bodily sensations seemed within the normal range for mortal existence, and no Last Trump sounded from outside, so he reluctantly concluded that he had better get up and start his normal routine.

After a visit to the bathroom, Lucas, belting his dressing gown about him, headed to the kitchen. Oddly enough, he could smell fresh coffee. Had he left the coffee machine on overnight? And what was that radiance spilling out of the room? Had he forgotten to turn off the overhead light as well? Usually he was meticulous about such things—

An elderly, bearded man, somewhat grouchy-looking, and a youngish woman of definite vivacity, both strangers to Lucas, occupied two seats at his small kitchen table. Each wore a flowing, silken, ivory robe terminating just above their bare feet. Each cupped hands around a mug of steaming coffee, gratefully, and even a trifle greedily, inhaling the aroma. And each sported a floating halo dispensing several thousand candlepower.

"Won't you join us, Lucas?" the woman agreeably said.

"Pull up a chair, son," the man advised.

Like an obedient zombie, Lucas did as he was bade. The man poured him a cup of coffee, and the woman asked, "Sugar? Cream?"

"Nuh—neither," Lucas stammered.

The woman lifted her cup and drank eagerly. After setting it down, she said, "Ah, that was blessed! It's a shame there's no coffee in Heaven."

The gowned man had duplicated his partner's actions and now agreed with her sentiments. "A beverage reserved for Earth and hell, unfortunately."

"Who—who are you two?"

"Oh, I'm so sorry," the woman apologized. "Allow me to make the proper introductions. I'm Saint Barbara, and my friend is Saint Hubert. We've come in answer to your prayers. We're the two patron saints of mathematicians. But I suspect an intelligent worshipper such as yourself knew that already."

The awe and reverence Lucas had been experiencing now began to be subsumed by a natural suspicion and paranoia tinged with anger. "Saints, are you?" Lucas half arose and swished his hand between the unsupported halos and the tops of the intruders' heads. "A nice effect, but I'm not taken in so easily by a simple hologram. Who sent you to play such a mean-spirited trick? Was it Owen Hulme? Of course, who else would stoop to such an irreligious prank?"

The man who had been introduced as Saint Hubert showed some irritation. "We know nothing of this Hulme fellow. We're obeying God's direct instructions. You requested, as I recall, that your mocking colleagues be allowed to witness the transcendental glory of Thy sovereign mathematical Holy Spirit."

Lucas grew deeply confused. "How could you know the contents of my prayers?"

Saint Barbara expressed some impatience of her own. "Hubert *explained* it quite sufficiently to you. God heard your prayers and sent us down to satisfy them."

Lucas cradled his head in his hands. "I don't know what to believe. Could you at least turn those halos, or holograms, or whatever they are down a trifle? They're giving me a splitting headache."

"Oh, sorry."

"Certainly, no problem."

Once the halos had dimmed, Lucas looked up again. "Hubert, Hubert—I don't ever remember reading about a Saint Hubert. Barbara, now, though, I recall your story. Quite dramatic. Your father had your head chopped off, didn't he?"

Saint Barbara smirked at her partner. "Yes, he did. And then he held it up for everyone to see, just like this."

Saint Barbara grabbed a handful of her own thick hair at the crest of her skull and lifted her entire grinning head off the sudden stump of her neck, separating the two at an indiscernible wound. An enormous quantity of blood gouted out, splattering across the table into Lucas' lap.

Lucas' own head, still attached to his body, shot backward in horror and hit the wall. He slumped unconscious to the floor.

"If there's one type of person I detest most heartily," Hubert peevishly said, "it's a showy martyr."

Barbara's head, speaking in gory isolation, was a disconcerting sight even to Hubert. "Showy, maybe. Convincing, definitely."

* * *

When Lucas awoke for the second time that morning, he felt more damned than exalted. His head ached, and he was disinclined to open his eyes. Perhaps his earlier nightmare would prove consequenceless if he just lay here—

"You'll feel much better if you sit up and drink your coffee," Saint Barbara said.

Lucas groaned and opened his eyes. He had been carried to his parlor couch. No trace of blood remained on his pristine clothing. The visiting Saints flanked him solicitously.

As if reading his thoughts, Hubert volunteered, "I apologize for my partner's shock tactics. Your kitchen is spotless again. I even emptied the filter basket on the coffee maker."

Lucas sat up with a groan and accepted the mug of coffee. "If I acknowledge your sainthood, could you please make my headache go away?"

"Only with some aspirin," Barbara said. "We can't really perform healing miracles, you see. That's not our provenance. We have to stick to mathematical miracles. Each saint has his or her own area of expertise."

"No healing of lepers. No raising the dead," Hubert

affirmed. He paused thoughtfully. "Multiplying fishes. We can do that, since it involves math. Wouldn't that qualify as something of a biological miracle? I wonder if we'd be trespassing on anyone's territory there?"

Barbara waved off this quibble. "There's overlap, certainly. But I don't think He would mind."

"I appreciate hagiology as much as the next person, but if one of you could get me those aspirin now please—"

After two cups of coffee and aspirin, Lucas felt considerably better. Growing accustomed to the reality of his celestial visitors, Lucas found his curiosity and interest growing. "Mathematical miracles, you say? Exactly what would those be like?"

Hubert answered, "Oh, basically the practical realization of any abstruse mathematical proof or theorem or concept. For instance, why don't you get up and try walking into the kitchen?"

Lucas stood, took a single step—

—and found himself instantly two rooms distant. He turned to confront the gleeful Saints in the doorway.

"How did you do that?"

Hubert answered smugly. "I simply gave you momentary access to a few of the higher dimensions you're always speculating so blithely about. Hardly broke a sweat."

An enormous sense of the possibilities inherent in having two mathematical Saints apparently ready to do his bidding in the campaign to enlighten his pagan enemies suddenly burst over Lucas, and he smiled broadly. He suddenly felt like he imagined the unburnt Joan of Arc must have.

"Am I the only one who can see you two?"

"We will manifest to whomever you please," Barbara said.

Lucas chafed his hands together like a silent film miser ready to foreclose on a mortgage. "Excellent. Let me get dressed, and then I'll ride into the university. You can meet me in my office."

"We can transport you there instantly," Hubert offered.

"No, no, I can't waste God's gifts on trivialities. Save your sacred powers for the reformation of the unbelievers."

Lucas departed to shower (despite being clean, he couldn't quite shake the memory of his earlier bloodbath) and dress in street clothes. When he had closed the bathroom door behind him, Barbara said to Hubert, "What a charming fellow. Really sweet and cute too. And he's so much more considerate than my last client. I don't know how many times I had to transport *him* to campus when he was running late."

* * *

Rather than utilize his favored bike rack, Lucas parked his Vespa, dropping the kickstand but not chaining the bike, outside the Blackwood Building that housed the astronomy department. He looked over his shoulder at the empty air and asked in a low voice, "Hubert, Barbara—are you there?"

His skin pringled as if with a wash of holy radiation, and Hubert's voice issued from a fluctuating crack in space. "We're right behind you, lad. Consider yourself shielded in godly armor."

Reassured by his invisible choir, Lucas strode boldly into the building and straight for the office of Owen Hulme. Fluorescent light shone through the frosted glass inset into the designated door, and Lucas heard muted voices from inside. He knocked boldly on the door and was answered with a gruff, "Come in!"

Bracing his shoulders, Lucas entered the lion's den like angel-guarded Daniel.

Hulme occupied his desk chair while Dr. Garnett sat in the single visitor's seat. The two men evinced differing reactions to Lucas' appearance. Garnett expressed mute embarrassment, as if recollecting Lucas' humiliation at the reception, tinged with a general air of disinterest, while Hulme actually let loose with an involuntary bestial growl.

"What brings you here today, Latulippe? Unless you intend to make a full apology for your disgraceful behavior yesterday, you might as well turn straight around and hie yourself back to your private miniature Vatican."

Feeling his cheeks redden, Lucas nonetheless spoke boldly. "Far from intending to apologize, I have come here today to throw your impious folly back into your hairy face, Hulme! Prepare to meet the messengers of an angry God. Barbara! Hubert! Reveal yourselves!"

The two barefoot Saints popped into existence at floor level, flanking Lucas.

"Yes, God was indeed angry the last time we saw Him," Hubert volunteered, reaching up to adjust his canted quasar-bright halo. "But we two were the focus of His wrath, not these gentlemen."

Barbara rudely admonished her partner. "Shush, you old fool!"

The astronomers had startled slightly at the miraculous visitation, but soon regained their coolly rational, dismissive attitudes. Hulme in fact seemed more irritated than stunned.

"Very impressive, Latulippe. Just like a third-rate mystery play. But unless you get these two shabby conjurors and yourself out of my office immediately, I will have to call campus security."

Lucas trembled with indignation. "You dare to mock God's chosen representatives? What will it take to convince you that your whole materialistic life is founded on a lie?"

Hulme did not deign to answer, but instead punched buttons on his phone, receiver already held to his ear. "Hello, security? This is Professor Hulme. Please send over a squad car to deal with some intruders—"

Lucas felt the situation spiraling out of his control. What had gone wrong? No one was following his plan. These unbelievers appeared unfazed by saintly auras. Earlier, Lucas had imagined this moment as his invincible triumph. But nobody seemed to know their lines in the script he had mentally written. Desperate to regain the upper hand, Lucas shouted a command:

"Barbara, stop him!"

The phone receiver clattered to the desktop, although Hulme's hand still remained closed. And although the man's mouth continued to move beneath his beard, no sounds issued. Something seemed wrong about Hulme's whole appearance in fact. He seemed flattened, subject to ripples racing across a body rendered insubstantial. And when Hulme turned sideways to look imploringly at Dr. Garnett, the astronomer disappeared completely.

Lucas instantly realized what Saint Barbara had done. "You've reduced him to two dimensions!"

Barbara exhibited an immodest pride. "Euclidean, my dear Watson. The quickest and neatest solution to your request."

The thinner-than-paper Hulme was vaporing about the office in a dither, appearing and disappearing randomly as he alternately displayed his remaining visible dimensions or accidentally angled them away from the observers. Meanwhile, Garnett had shot to his feet in alarm.

"I don't know what you've done to Owen, you popish madman! But I won't let you get away!"

Garnett lunged at Lucas, who darted one side in a narrow escape. "Hubert, help!"

The newest addition to the astronomy faculty suddenly

flopped to the rug, unable to stand. His limbs had been replaced with smaller, complete copies of his entire body. Where his hands and feet should have been, Garnett now boasted scaled-down versions of his own head. And the limbs of these bizarre appendages consisted of even smaller bodies, and so on and so on till Lucas' eyes glazed over.

A chittering noise of the infinite heads all complaining at once overlaid the macro-assaults coming from the original Garnett mouth. Lucas sagged down into Hulme's chair. Hulme would certainly not need it, for the flat professor had accidentally slipped into a closed desk drawer through a slit.

"You've fractalized him?" Lucas wearily asked. "Rendered him self-similar?"

Hubert grinned. "Precisely. A little something I picked up while peering over Mandelbrot's shoulder one day."

Lucas heard a siren. Hopelessly, he opened the drawer into which Hulme had vanished. The papery savant shot out like a jack-in-the-box, causing Lucas to surge wildly to his feet.

At that moment Britta Hulme gaily strode into her husband's office, spotting her transformed husband in a moment of deceptive substantiality.

"Ready for an early lunch, dear? We need to hurry if I'm not to keep Simon waiting—"

The filmy ghost of her husband silently beseeched his wife for help. His weird anxiety finally registered on the dense woman.

"Are you feeling all right, dear?"

The sight of Owen shaking his head in the negative was not something Lucas would have chosen to view or retain in memory. The professor's head seemed to snap in and out of existence as it rotated through one plane after another.

For nausea-inducing properties, the display rivaled Saint Barbara's earlier demonstration of her past misfortunes with an executioner's axe.

Britta screamed with operatic violence. Lucas opened his mouth to reassure her, but she screamed again. And again. And again—

Her fourth scream possessed less volume. The next even less.

Britta was shrinking. Dwindling while retaining her perfect proportions, her voice dopplering to insignificance, she passed the size of a child, cat, mouse, bee, midge, and then utterly vanished.

"I assumed you'd want her silenced," Saint Barbara matter-of-factly explained. "So I recalled some interesting corollaries in a paper by Stephen Smale from the *Journal of Nonlinear Dynamics* about strange attractors with a flow line sink leading down to the Planck level—"

Before the loquacious Saint could finish her explanation, various exclamations from the gathering crowd of horrified people at the office door interrupted her.

Lucas was covered in a stinking sweat. His mind roiled like the surface of a fractal sea. "We have to get out of here," he husked.

Pleasant sunshine fell upon Lucas and the two Saints, and a mild breeze played with Lucas' damp hair and ruffled the saintly robes. Higher-dimensional transit had its definite advantages during emergencies.

However, they were not yet out of the woods. Having parked alongside his Vespa, the campus security squad car was just disgorging its officers.

The lead cop resembled the cult film director, John Waters, except possessed of a mean scowl. "Where's the trouble, sir?"

"Up—upstairs."

The other rent-a-cops studied the two Saints suspiciously for a moment, until Lucas mastered himself enough to offer a pretext for their uncouth looks. "My, ah, my visiting friends are old hippies, officer. They teach at, um, Berkeley. West Coast, Mother Earth, nature worship, all that bosh. Those halos? You know the light sticks kids use at raves? Of course. You understand, I'm sure."

The cops grunted and raced off toward the growing, noisy disturbance inside Blackwood. At the outer entrance of the building, they met the immovable bulk of Pisky Wispaway, clad in a hideously checkered, tentlike shift. A brief, Robin-Hood-meets-Little-John-on-the-log-bridge struggle for passage occurred, from which Pisky emerged victorious. She waddled as fast as she could toward Lucas, her costume jewelry rattling like a bead curtain in a hurricane.

Before his large lady friend could arrive, Lucas turned to the Saints.

"Can you undo what you did to those three people?"

"Of course," Barbara said.

"I really don't know if we should obey his orders any more," Hubert quibbled. "After that awful lie he told the police. Old hippies indeed!"

Lucas fought not to yell. "It was only a venial sin! I'll confess it as soon as I can and do whatever penance the priest assigns!"

"Well, in that case then—"

Barbara sounded a practical note. "You realize that as soon as your opponents are restored to normality, they'll accuse you of all sorts of horrid things. It'll be just like the nasty scene when my father heard about my conversion."

"I know, I know, but I'll deal with that somehow. Just put them right."

The Saints nodded to each other, blinked once, and then chorused, "Done."

Pisky now joined the trio. Her flushed face showed nothing but sympathy and concern for Lucas, mingled with some natural curiosity directed toward his strange companions.

"Oh, Lucas, whatever is the matter? Did you and Owen get into a fight?"

"Yes, I fear we did, Pisky. I simply showed up on his doorstep with proof of the surety of his eternal damnation unless he repented, and he reacted badly. I confess that I was forced to defend myself."

"How dreadful! Lucas, I was so worried about you! I've been thinking over all my deep feelings for you all night long, and I just want you to know how much I admire your principles. You can do no wrong in my eyes. I'm so proud of you for standing up to Owen!"

Pisky gripped Lucas' arm and leaned her bulk against him. He experienced a claustrophobic sensation akin to what the Princess' pea beneath a thousand mattresses might have felt. Grateful enough for Pisky's declaration of alliance, he nonetheless gently sought to extricate himself.

"Ah, well, yes, thank you, Pisky. I did not emerge victorious alone, of course. I had the help of these two Saints. Allow me to introduce Saint Barbara and Saint Hubert, Heaven's mathematical experts."

Hubert took Pisky's hand and kissed it genteelly like the courtier he once had been. "Charmed, madame. Your voice reminds me of Empress Theodora's."

Barbara returned no handshake, but only a somewhat frosty verbal greeting, smoothing her robes across her trim waist rather ostentatiously. Lucas thought to detect a certain flattering jealousy in his female protector, but could not concentrate now on what otherwise might be a stimulating opportunity.

Such pleasantries, however strained, instantly terminated the next moment, as the Hulmes and Professor Garnett appeared on the steps of the Blackwood Building, backed by a force of concerned bystanders.

"There they are, officer! Arrest them!"

Lucas hopped upon his Vespa and cranked its motor into sputtering life. "Pisky, we'll continue our interesting discussion later. I have to flee immediately, until I can figure out how to clear myself of these ridiculous charges."

"I'll come with you, Lucas!"

Before the mathematician could protest, Pisky hoisted her skirts and swung her leg over the passenger seat of the tiny machine, engulfing it. The Vespa sank down so far upon its rear tire that the front wheel almost rose from the ground, in partial mimicry of the Lone Ranger's steed.

"Pisky, please—"

"Go, Lucas, go—they're running toward us!"

Lucas goosed the throttle, and the protesting, over-burdened bike moved at a pace barely faster than a jog. The Saints, in fact, easily kept abreast on foot, without super-natural exertions.

"This is no good!" Lucas wailed. "Hubert, Barbara—can't you get us away any faster?"

"Where would you like to go?"

"I don't know! I just want us to fly off!"

The Saints fell back and put their heads together to whisper as they ambled. Lucas caught snatches of their dialogue:

"—cosmological constants—"

"—numerical in nature—"

"—don't believe we'd be contravening—"

Their pursuers had almost caught up when the Saints finished their intense discussion. Hubert began to lecture. "You are aware, perhaps, of the universal force designated 'Lambda'—"

Lucas could actually hear Owen Hulme's angry growls amidst the crowd noise. "Whatever you're going to do, for God's sake just do it!"

Why was the ground falling swiftly away from beneath the Vespa? Had the Saints opened up a crevasse in the earth? Had Lucas been gulled all along? Were Barbara and Hubert actually demons, perhaps, finally taking their tormented victims down to hell? Lucas felt no sensation of falling though, smelled no brimstone. Instead, he realized that he was ascending, rising into the air. The ground remained fixed.

The Vespa was flying, its front wheel pointed toward the sun.

Pisky was squeezing Lucas so hard around his midriff that he could barely breathe. "I didn't believe, I didn't believe! But now I do, now I do!"

Lucas turned to look downward over his shoulder. The agitated mob had come to a dead stop, their upturned faces fixed in slack-jawed amazement on the buoyant bike and its incredulous riders sailing into the sky, the levitating Saints alongside like pilot fish.

Before they got much higher, Lucas heard a guy on the ground say, "Hey, I can see right up the broad's robe! She's buck naked underneath it!"

Barbara's face darkened. "Why, you ill-mannered spawn of a toad! Let's see how you like your guts twisted into a Mobius strip—"

"No, don't!" Lucas ordered, and Barbara obeyed, although she continued to grumble.

As the bike soared higher and farther away without mishap, Lucas gradually relaxed, as did Pisky. His natural scientific curiosity reasserted itself enough to have him ask, "How does this flight qualify as a mathematical miracle?"

Hubert appeared proud of their accomplishment. "Our first step consisted of suspending the commutative and

associative laws for tensor operators. Once quantum iner-
tias failed to group, we next altered the numerical value of
Lambda—the force that controls the expansion of the universe—in a small pocket around you, resulting in directed
antigravity. The whole cosmos is based on just six numbers,
you know. N, E, Omega, Lambda, D, and Q. Now, take Q
for instance—"

"I appreciate the beauty of the theory, Hubert. But
where are we headed?"

"That is entirely up to you, sir. I suppose we could perch
out of sight atop a cloud. It's what we Saints are commonly
thought to do, after all."

Now Pisky spoke. "Oh, Lucas, they really are Saints!
I thought you were just joking. How wonderful! And to sit
on a cloud and look down on the earth—I've dreamed of
such a romantic thing since I was just a little girl back in
Piscataway."

Lucas sighed and gave his consent. The Vespa speeded
up, and before too long pierced the lowermost cloud layer.
On the far side, the bike halted above the fluffy sun-glazed
and shadowed terrain, a pasture of purple and gold.

"Step off," Barbara said.

Lucas regarded the feisty Saint warily. Would she play a
deadly trick on him for thwarting her revenge on the Peeping
Tom? Yet what choice did he have but to trust her?

Pisky settled his doubts by dismounting first. She sunk
into the clouds up to her ankles, but no further.

"A slight local alteration in the values of N and E—"
Hubert began.

Now standing on the cloud stuff, Lucas walked to the
nearest edge, accompanied by Pisky. They tentatively looked
over at the patchwork earth, a quilt of browns and greens
stitched by roads.

"It's so beautiful," Pisky cooed.

Saint Barbara snorted. "Anything gets old after a millennia or two. Even love, I suspect—though I couldn't say for sure," the female Saint wistfully concluded.

Pisky fervently grabbed Lucas' hand. "Oh, I don't know about that. I'd like enough time to find out, though."

Lucas gently disengaged himself. Such idle talk would be pleasant enough, if all else were well. But his current troubles filled his mind to such a degree that he could spare no attention for Pisky's romantic babble. And yet some subtle hook in her speech lured his thoughts along possible lines of salvation.

Inspiration struck Lucas. "Time! Of course! Can you two somehow—"

Hubert sighed. "Here it comes again. Reverse time? Naturally. Strictly a mathematical phenomenon. Actually, that old dodge is the way we get out of most fixes."

"I can't tell you how bored I am with that tiresome tactic," Saint Barbara complained. "If only mortals had a little more imagination. Now what if we altered the sun's radiational output—"

"No! I don't care about imaginative solutions! I just want my old life back. But I need to keep my memories of all this, so that I never let my pride and piety get the better of me again."

"Easy enough. Okay, get ready—"

Pisky surprised everyone by intervening. "Stop! I don't care if I have to lose all memories of this glorious moment in order to help Lucas. But could I ask one favor of you?" The big woman bashfully looked down and kicked a divot of cloud. "Could you make me skinny? Even if only for a minute? Please?"

The Saints conferred again.

"—reverse Banach-Tarski—"

"conformal mapping into the lemniscate—"

Saint Barbara turned to address the other woman with a certain condescending sympathy. "All right, dearie, just close your eyes."

The transformation of Pisky Wispaway pulled an involuntary grunt from Lucas. Her figure seemed to implode in an organized fashion, while the checkerboard pattern of her dress morphed to a horseshoe-crab-shaped pattern out of a Saupe and Pietgen textbook. Stripped mathemagically of nearly 200 pounds, she also lost her oversized altered dress and undergarments, which slipped off to pool around her feet, leaving her clad only in strings of beads. A most attractive daughter of Eve, the newly svelte, naked Pisky hurled herself into Lucas' arms. He surprised himself by clutching her eagerly.

The Saints affectionately regarded the pair of mortals.

"Get ready for time reversal," Hubert said.

Barbara leaned in to kiss Lucas' cheek. "You were one of my nicest clients."

"Speak kindly of us to God in your prayers," Hubert said. "We can always use another letter of recommendation to our Employer."

In a blink, the mortals disappeared.

Hubert turned to Barbara. "Well, another assignment satisfactorily completed."

"I thought this one turned out much better than that botch you made of Fermat's Last Theorem. 'No room in the margin' indeed."

Hubert sniffed. "And what of your little cold-fusion debacle?"

Barbara winced. "I've improved over time." She offered her arm for an escort back to Heaven, and the linked Saints walked away over the cloud tops.

"That, I believe," Hubert offered, "is God's plan."

*　*　*

Lucas Latulippe envied his conflicted peers. The war in their bosoms between faith and skepticism allowed them to pursue their scientific careers with a certain useful level of doubt in both arenas. Unlike Lucas, they were not always warily looking over their shoulders, nervous about the possibility of inconveniently real miracles.

But after several years of freedom from saintly intervention, Lucas had learned to tamp down his unease. Frequent prayers beseeching God to provide an uneventful daily existence helped. And of course, having a beautiful, slim, loving wife like Pisky would make any man's life quite happy.

And after all, they were the only couple they knew whose marriage had literally been made in Heaven.

Please picture this entire story as an animated cartoon drawn by the lowbrow artist supreme, Robert Williams. And, yes, it was as much fun to write as it hopefully is to read.

Neutrino Drag

I know why the sun doesn't work the way the scientists think it should.

Me and a guy who called himself Spacedog fucked it up back in 1951, racing our roadsters in a match of Cosmic Chicken out in space, closer'n Mercury to hell itself.

I never told a soul about that last grudge match between me and Spacedog. Who'd've believed me? Spacedog never returned to Earth, you see, to back up my story. And no one else was there to witness our race anyhow, except Stella Star Eyes. And she never says anything anytime, not even after fifty years with me.

But now that I'm an old, old guy likely to hit the Big Wall of Death and visit the Devil's pit stop soon, I figure I might as well try to tell the whole story the exact way it happened. Just in case Spacedog's car ever maybe starts eating up the sun or something worse.

* * *

I got demobbed in '46, went back home to San Diego and opened up a welding shop with the few thousand dollars I had saved and with the skills the Army had generously given me in exchange for nearly getting my ass shot up in a dozen European theaters from Anzio to Berlin. Palomar Customizing, Obdulio Benitez, proprietor, that was me. I managed to get some steady, good-paying work right out of the holeshot, converting Caddies and Lincolns to hearses for the local funeral trade. The grim joke involved in this arrangement didn't escape me, since I still woke up more nights than not, drenched in sweat and yelling, memories of shellfire and blood all too vivid. If any of a hundred Nazi bullets had veered an inch, I would have already taken my own ride in a hearse—assuming any part of me had survived to get bagged—and never been here building the corpse wagons.

One of the first helpers I hired at my shop was this high school kid, Joaquin Arnett.

You heard me right, Joaquin Arnett, the legendary leader of the Bean Bandits, that mongrel pack of barrio-born hot rodders who started out by tearing up the California racing world like Aztecs blew through captives, and then went on to grab national honors from scores of classier white-bread teams across the nation. By the time he retired from racing in the sixties, Joaquin had racked up more trophies and records than almost any other driver, and fathered two sons to carry on his dream.

But back in the late forties, all that was still in the future. I hired a wiry, smiling, wired kid with skin a little lighter than my own, a kid with no rep yet, but just a mania for cars and racing.

Joaquin got his start picking up discarded car parts—coils and magnetos—and fixing them. He had taught himself to drive at age nine. By the time he got to my shop, he'd been bending iron on his own for several years, making chassis after chassis out of scrap and dropping flatheads in front, fat skins in back, and deuce bodies on top. Once he got his hands on my shop's equipment, he burst past all the old barriers that had stopped him from making his dreams really come true. The railjobs and diggers he began to turn out in his off-hours were faster and hotter than anything else on the streets or tracks.

Joaquin had been driving for the Road Runners and

the Southern California Roadster Club since 1948. But when 1951 rolled around, he decided he wanted to start his own team. He recruited a bunch of childhood buddies—Carlos Ramirez, Andrew Ortega, Harold Miller, Billy Glavin, Mike Nagem, plus maybe twenty others—and they became the Bean Bandits, a name that picked up on the taunts of "Beaners!" they heard all the time and made the slur into a badge of ethnic pride.

When Joaquin first came to work for me, I was driving a real pig, something the legendary little old lady from Pasadena would've turned her nose up at. An unmodified '32 Packard I had picked up cheap before the war, which had subsequently sat on its rims in my parents' garage for five years while I was overseas. I plain didn't care much about cars at that point. They were just transportation, something to get me and Herminia—Herminia Ramirez, a distant cousin of Carlos'—around town on a date.

But working side by side with Joaquin, watching the fun he had putting his rods together, was contagious. The customizing and racing bugs bit me on the ass, one on each cheek, and never let go. Soon on weekends and nights I was elbow-deep in the guts of a '40 Oldsmobile, patching in a Cadillac engine that was way too much power for the streets, but was just right for the dry lakes.

The Bean Bandits, you see, raced the cars they created at a couple of places. Paradise Mesa, the old airfield outside the city, that was our home track, and the dry lakebeds of El Mirage and Muroc. There the drivers could cut loose without worrying about citizens or cops or traffic lights, focusing on pure speed.

When I started running my new Olds—painted glossy pumpkin orange with black flames, and its name, *El Tigre*, lettered beautifully across both front fenders—first in trials with the Bean Bandits and then against drivers from other clubs, I found that my nightmares started to go away. Not completely, but enough. That sweet deal alone would have hooked me on racing forever, if all the other parts of it—the sound, the speed, the thrills, the glory—hadn't done the trick already.

The real excitement started when we discovered nitro. That was nitromethane, a gasoline alternative that did for engines what the sight of Wile E. Coyote did for the Road Runner. At first, we thought nitro was more volatile than it actually was, and we carried it to meets in big carboys swaddled in rags. "Stand back! This could blow any second!" Scared the shit out of the competition, until they got hip to nitro too. And eventually, when we discovered the shitty things pure nitro did to our engines, we began to cut it fifty-fifty with regular fuel. Still, plenty of extra kick remained, and nitro let us get closer and closer to the magic number of 150 MPH with every improvement we made.

I remember Joaquin boasting to me one day, "Papa Obie, soon enough we're gonna be as fast as them damn new UFO things people are talking about."

'Course, I didn't think twice about his figure of speech till I got into space myself.

I don't feel like I was ever a real card-carrying member of the Bean Bandits. I never wore one of their shirts with their silly cartoon on it—a Mexican jumping bean with sombrero, mask, and wheels—and I never lined up at the Christmas Tree with them in any for-the-book races, just the unofficial drags. The main thing that kept me out of the club—in my own mind anyhow—was my age.

When I left the service I was already twenty-six years old, and by 1951, I had crossed that big red line into my thirties. Joaquin and all his buddies were a lot younger than me. They liked to tease me, calling me "Papa Obie" and names like that. Not that they ever discriminated against anyone, on any basis. Mostly Hispanics, the Bandits had members who were Anglo, Lebanese, Japanese, and Filipino. They would've taken me on in a heartbeat. But my concerns weren't the same as theirs. They had nothing in mind but kicks. I had a business to run and was thinking in a vague way about marrying Herminia and settling down.

Still, I hung out with the Bandits a lot and never felt like they held me at arm's length. Practically every weekend in 1951, you could find me behind the wheel of *El Tigre*, hauling ass down three dusty miles of dry lake bottom trial after trial, the nitro fumes making my eyes water and nose burn, smiling when I beat someone, scowling when I got beaten, and already planning refinements to my car.

Yeah, that was my routine and my pleasure all right, and at the time, I even thought it might last forever.

Until Spacedog and Stella Star Eyes showed up.

* * *

That Saturday afternoon at Paradise Mesa, the sun seemed to burn hotter than I'd ever known it to shine before, even in California. I had gone through about six cans of Nesbitt's Orange Drink between noon and 3:00, a few gulps used to wash down the tortillas we had bought at our favorite stand on the Pacific Coast Highway on our way up here.

At that moment, Herminia and I were sitting on the edge of one of the empty trailers used to transport the more outrageous hot rods that couldn't pass for grocery getters, trying to get a little shade from a canvas tarp stretched above us on poles. We were the only ones facing the entrance to the drag strip. Everyone else had their heads under hoods or their eyes on the race underway between Joaquin and some guy from Pomona. Joaquin was running his '29 Model A with the Mercury engine, and the driver from Pomona was behind the wheel of a chopped and channeled Willys.

307

That was when this car like nothing I had ever seen before pulled in.

This rod was newer than color TV. It looked like Raymond Loewy might've designed it fifty years from now for the 1999 World's Fair. Low and streamlined and frenched to the max, matte silver in color, its window glass somehow all smoky so that you couldn't see inside, this car skimmed along on skinny tires colored an improbable gold, making less noise than Esther Williams underwater, but managing to convey the impression of some kind of deep power barely within the driver's control.

I had gotten to my feet without consciously planning to stand, tossing my last cone-topped can of soda, still half-full, onto the ground. Herminia was less impressed and just kept slurping her Nesbitt's up through a straw.

I now think that might have been the instant things started to go wrong between us. Not when I finally made a play for Stella, and she responded, but when Herminia didn't register the magnificence of that incredible car.

This Buck Rogers car pulled up a few yards away from me, and then doors opened, one on each side.

And those damn doors just seemed to disappear! All I could think was that they had slid into the body of the car faster than my eye could follow, like pocket doors in a house.

The driver stepped out first, followed on the other side by the passenger.

From the driver's side unfolded this lanky joker well over six feet tall. He wore a wild Hawaiian shirt with a pattern of flowers and ukuleles and surfboards and palm trees that seemed to form hazy secret images where they overlapped and intersected. The shirt hung loose over a pair of lime green poplin trousers. Huaraches revealed his bare feet, but sunglasses concealed his eyes. He had Mitch Miller facial hair—Big Sur bohemian mustache and unconnected chin spinach—but his head was otherwise hairless, either shaved or naturally bald. And then there was the matter of his skin.

I've always heard people say that someone had an "olive" complexion, and usually what they mean is that the person they're talking about is dago-dark. But in this case, it was really true. All the skin I could see on this guy was a muted dusky green, kinda like dusty eucalyptus leaves.

While I was still trying to get my mind around both the guy and his car, I caught sight of his passenger.

Back in the Army, I used to truly dig this girlie cartoon the thoughtful brass produced for us dogfaces. Ack-Ack Amy was the name of the character, and the artist—I made a point of remembering his name—was Bill Ward. Man, could he draw stacked babes! Even on paper, Ack-Ack Amy seemed so physical—although I doubt there had ever been any real gal built like her—that you could almost feel her in your arms. Especially if it was a lonely night in your foxhole.

Back home, I ran into Ward's stuff again. He was doing this funnybook where the gal was named Torchy, and he had only gotten better at drawing. Torchy was Ack-Ack Amy times ten, more woman than any six regular gals rolled together.

The woman who got out of the strange car could have been Torchy's va-va-voom fashion model sister.

Her hair was chin-length, colored platinum, with a flip. Milk-white skin contrasted with her boyfriend's jade tint. Her nose was pert, her lips lush and lively, and her jaw line was honed finer than the cylinders in a Ferrari. Thinking back, I certainly didn't notice anything funny about her eyes from that distance. Mostly because I was so knocked out by her body. That body—oh, man! She had firm, out-thrusting boobs like the nosecones on a Nike missile, a rack that

Jane Russell would've have killed for, and they were barely concealed under a blue angora sweater that molded itself to every braless curve. (The sweater was long-sleeved, but she wasn't sweating that I could see, even in that heat.) Pink toreador pants lacquered her sassy rump and killer legs, and a pair of strappy high heels in crocodile leather raised her almost as tall as her companion.

My heart was threatening to throw a rod. Herminia finally noticed my reaction and immediately got huffy. She sneered at the newcomers, especially the woman, said, "*Que puta!*" then returned to her soda, slurping up the last of it with exaggerated rudeness.

I covered the distance between me and the strangers in about five long bounds.

Once I got up close to them, I noticed three odd things.

The shell of the car was cast all in one piece and was too thin to hold any concealed doors. It also didn't look like any metal I had ever seen, more like plastic.

The man's bare head featured concentric circles of bumps on his skull, just under his scalp, like somebody had buried a form-fitting, waffle iron grid underneath his skin.

And the woman's eyes held no pupils. In place of the expected little human black circles stepped down against the hard sunlight, her irises were centered with sparkling, irregular, golden starbursts.

Before I could ask anything about any of these abnormal features, the man stuck out his hand for a shake. I took his paw, and although his grip was strong, his hand felt all wrong, like it had been broken and reassembled funny. Then he spoke.

"Zzzip, *guten*, chirp, *bon*, zzzt, hallo! Name Space, skrk, *chien*, zzz, *perro*, no, zeep, dog! Name Spacedog is. Here to, zzzt, race I am."

The guy's crazy speech was studded with pauses and wrong words. Weird noises—buzzes and clicks and grinding sounds, some of them almost mechanical in nature—alternated with the language. He reminded me of a bad splice job between a tape of an argument in the UN cafeteria and one of that new UNIVAC machine at work. But I can't continue to imitate him exactly for the rest of this story, although I can hear his voice just as clearly today as I did fifty years ago. Just remember that every time I report Spacedog's conversation—some of which I only puzzled out years after he had vanished—all those quirks were part of it.

"Well," I said, trying to maintain my cool, "you came to the right place." I was dying to get a look under the nonexistent hood of his car. And the furtive glimpses of his dashboard, which I was snagging through the open door, were driving me insane! There were more dials and knobs and buttons and toggles on that panel than any car had a right to feature. And some startling missing parts: no steering wheel or pedals!

But all thoughts of engines vanished when I realized Spacedog's girlfriend had come around to our side of the car. And now she stood close enough to me for my breath to stir the fuzzy fibers of her sweater.

"Obdulio Benitez," I said and put out my sweaty, trembling hand. She took it with her small, dry palm and delicate fingers and smiled brilliantly, but said nothing.

Spacedog spoke for her. "This Stella is. Crypto-speciated quasi-conjugal adjunct. Exteriorized anima and inseminatory receptacle."

I couldn't make heads nor tails out of this description, but my brain wasn't working properly just then. I felt like a million buzzing bees had flowed through that ultrafemale handshake and now swarmed in my veins.

Stella continued to broadly smile without speaking. I couldn't manage to get out a single word myself.

Very reluctantly, I released Stella's hand and tried to focus on Spacedog.

By this time, all the other Bandits and competitors and spectators had come over to see who these visitors were. Excited murmurs and exclamations filled the air at the unexplained mirage of the weird car and its occupants. All the guys were putting themselves in danger of severe whiplash, jerking their heads back-and-forth between Stella and the car, while the women huddled in a tight knot of suspicion and jealousy, growling and hissing like wet cats. I beamed what I hoped was a reassuring glance at Herminia, but she didn't accept it. In her midriff-knotted shirt and Big Yank jeans, she suddenly looked bumpkinish, compared to Stella's sophistication, like Daisy Mae next to Stupefyin' Jones, with me, some poor wetback Little Abner caught in the middle.

Finally Joaquin shouldered to the front of the crowd. Doffing his helmet—a football player's old leather one he had stuffed with asbestos pads—my little buddy said boldly, "So, *amigo*, you're probably here to drag."

"Yes! Probability one! Speed-racing most assuredly Spacedog's goal is! Burn longchain molecules! Haul gluteus! Scorch the planetary surface! Bad to the osteoclasts! Eat my particulates, uniformed societal guardian!"

I could sense that everyone here wanted to ask Spacedog about his green skin. But this was exactly the one question nobody in the Bandits would ever voice. After all the prejudice we had experienced, and our unwritten club law of no bias against any race, we just couldn't make an exception now, no matter how strange the guy's coloration was. Spacedog had perhaps come among the only bunch of racers in the whole country who would never broach the topic of his origins.

And today I wonder just how accidental that arrival was.

The closest Joaquin could come to the topic was a mild, "So, where you from?"

Spacedog hesitated a moment, then answered, "Etruria. Small node of Europa. Earth continent, not satellite. Stella and Spacedog Etruscans are. Speak only old tongue between ourselves."

Here Spacedog unloaded a few sentences of wild lingo that sounded like nothing I had ever heard in Italy. Stella made no reply. All the listeners nodded wisely, mostly willing to accept his unlikely explanation.

"No racing in Etruria. Must to California for kicks come."

Joaquin made his decision then, speaking for all the Bandits. "Well, *pachuco*, Paradise Mesa is racing central in this neighborhood. Let's see what you and your crate can do."

Spacedog clapped his hands together like a five year old at the circus. "Most uptaking! Stella, alongside kindly Oblong Benzedrine, please wait."

I didn't know what was harder to believe: my good luck in being nominated as Stella's companion, or what I saw next.

Spacedog hopped into his car and picked up a stretchy helmet like a thick bathing cap. The cordless device was studded with shiny contacts on the inside—contacts that matched the bumps on his head. He snugged on the helmet, and suddenly disappeared from view: the mysterious car doors had rematerialized out of nowhere.

Quiet as smoke, the Flash Gordon car then wheeled off as the crowd parted for it, angling across the lakebed toward the rude Christmas Tree lights that marked the starting line. By the time all the spectators were properly arrayed, Joaquin had pulled up in his own car.

Joaquin hazed his hides while getting into position, sending up smoke from his tires and exhausting mind-blowing billows of nitro fumes. Very cool and intimidating. But Spacedog, invisible behind his smoked glass, didn't choose to play up his own engine power at all.

The lights worked down to green, and the cars were off.

Spacedog crossed the finish line before Joaquin had covered a third of the distance. Nobody even got Spacedog's elapsed time. The guys with the stopwatches just couldn't react fast enough.

Joaquin came to a stop halfway down the track in an admission of total defeat I had never before seen.

I turned my head to gauge the reaction of Stella, standing close by my side.

Although she continued to smile, the starry-eyed woman showed no extra emotion, as if the outcome had never been in doubt. She just radiated a kind of animal acceptance of whatever occurred.

Within the next minute, the two drivers had returned to the starting line. Spacedog disappeared his door and emerged from his car.

"Victory! Spacedog *uber todo*! More race! More race!"

Well, that was a challenge none of us could refuse.

Over the rest of that afternoon, as the sun sank and reddened, we threw everything we had against Spacedog and his super car. Or, to use the nickname that the crowd was now chanting, "UFO! UFO!" Useless, all useless, like lobbing softballs to Micky Mantle.

When it was my turn to pit *El Tigre* against the UFO, my heart was in my throat, despite the certainty of failure. What if by some fluke I was the one to beat him? What would Stella—I mean, Herminia—think of that?

Needless to say, I didn't beat him.

Finally, after Spacedog had whipped our collective ass six ways from San Diego, we called it a day and broke out the *cerveza*. Spacedog made a funny face when he first tasted the beer, as if he had never before encountered such a drink. But soon he was downing cans of Blatz like a soldier just home from Korea.

After suitable lubrication, Joaquin broached the question uppermost in all our minds.

"What's that car run on, 'dog?"

"Neutrinos."

"You mean nitro?"

"Yes, nitro. Excuse tongue of inadvertent falsity, please."

Joaquin pondered that revelation for a while, then said, "Custom engine?"

"Spacedog himself engine grow."

We all had a laugh over that and quit pestering Spacedog. We all figured we'd have a good, long look at his engine before too long.

Especially once we had made him the newest member of the Bean Bandits, a solemn ceremony we duly enacted a half hour later.

One arm around Stella's wasp waist, Spacedog raised his beer in a toast when we were done.

"Liquid token of future conquests hoisted! Leguminous reivers hegemony established is!"

We all cheered, though we weren't quite sure what we were endorsing.

* * *

Well, the exploits of the Bean Bandits during the next few months of that long-ago year of 1951 should have been engraved in gold for future generations. But instead, hardly any records were kept. That was just how we thought and how we did—or didn't do—things in those days. Who had time to write stuff down or even snap a few pictures? There was always another tire to change or mill to rebore. Nobody knew that the kicks we were having would someday become the stuff of legend. We just lived for the moment, for the roar of the engines and satisfaction of leaving your opponents in the dust.

So that's why, search until you're blue, you won't find any pictures of Spacedog and his four-wheeled UFO. Which is not to say you can't get a lot of the surviving old-timers to talk about him. Nobody who was around then is likely to have forgotten the scorched path he cut through the California racing world. Anybody who ever saw that car of his soundlessly accelerate faster'n a Soviet MIG would never forget their jaw-dropping reaction.

Up and down the state, we raced against a dozen clubs and blew all their doors off. The Bandits had been hot shit before Spacedog, but now we were unbeatable. Soon, we knew, we'd have to go further afield for competition. Probably first out to Bonneville Flats, then off to some of the prestige southern tracks. (Though how a bunch of beaners would fare down in the Jim Crow South was something we hadn't considered.)

Everybody in the club was ecstatic all the time, especially Joaquin. To be on top of the racing world, that was all he had ever wanted. It didn't matter that he wasn't personally behind the wheel of the top car. As long as Spacedog was a bona fide Bean Bandit, Joaquin could bask in the shared glory.

As for Spacedog himself, I've never seen anyone so hepped-up all the time. You'd think he was earning a million dollars per win. I remember one time after we won every heat against a crew from Long Beach, Spacedog drank twelve cans of Pabst Blue Ribbon and stood atop the roof of his car reciting some kind of Etruscan poetry that sounded like a vacuum cleaner fighting against ten coyotes and losing.

And me, I felt pretty good too. But in my case, it wasn't the racing that made me happy. It was having Stella Star Eyes hanging on my arm.

I never knew whether Spacedog really wanted me personally to watch his girl, or if my good fortune was just an arbitrary thing. Did he pick me for some special reason, like because I was the oldest, most responsible-seeming guy in the Bandits, with a steady girl of my own? Or would the privilege and duty of minding Stella during the races have gone to any guy who Spacedog happened to meet first?

This question bothered me a little from time to time, but mostly got lost in the sensual overload whenever I was side by side with Stella. Race after race I squired her around, fetching her drinks, finding her the best vantage for viewing Spacedog's triumphs. Standing within inches of her, I became lost in the heavenly geography of her knockout body, my mind turning all hazy with dreamy lust. Something about her silence magnified the sheer animal attraction of her incredible physique. Whenever it came time for me to climb into *El Tigre* and run my own races, I practically had to tear myself away from her.

It was difficult, but for all those months I never acted on my desires. The code said not to steal the girl of another Bandit. And if Stella was feeling anything for me, I never saw any evidence of such feelings.

Stella was always polite and aboveboard. She never gave me any come-ons or randy signals, never flirted or teased. Of course her lack of speech had lots to do with the maintenance of her proper behavior, as well as mine. Kind of hard to hit on someone if they can't answer your pickup line. But of course words aren't everything, or even the main thing in such matters, and I was pretty sure even by her body language that she felt entirely neutral toward me.

As for Herminia—well, things had cooled off considerably between us. She didn't come to meets anymore, and we only saw each other about once a week, usually for a movie and burger and a kiss goodnight at her doorstep. Her cousin Carlos asked me what was wrong between us, and I couldn't really explain. Hell, it wasn't like I was even cheating on her. I was just keeping the foreign girlfriend of one of my fellow club members company during the time he was busy racing.

I don't know how long I would have gone on in this crazy white knight, blue balls way without making a play for Stella. But matters were taken out of my control one day when something really quite simple happened.

Spacedog's UFO ran out of fuel.

* * *

All the Bean Bandits had traveled out to Paradise Mesa for a race against some guys from Bakersfield. Spacedog and Stella were slated to arrive separately from the rest of us. From what we could learn from the secretive, twisty-talking, green-faced Bandit, he and Stella didn't live in San Diego proper, but somewhere on its outskirts. Where, exactly, no one had ever learned. That was just one of the lesser mysteries surrounding Spacedog and his woman. But because we wanted to respect and humor our winningest member, we didn't push it.

The sleek UFO hummed through the gates on its golden tires. All the Bandits and the hometown crowd raised a rousing cheer at the sight of the unbeatable dragster, and a shiver of despair passed like a chill breeze through the Bakersfield boys.

But then the unexpected happened. The miracle car, which had never even burped or stuttered before, seemed to ripple and shimmer in a wave of unreality, as if plunged into an oven made of mirrors. Then it rolled feebly to a halt halfway to the starting line.

The doors did their vanishing trick, and Spacedog hurtled out, followed more calmly by Stella. The man's face beneath his omnipresent sunglasses and rubber helmet was two shades greener than normal, and in his hands he clutched a black cylinder a little bigger than a beer can. He hustled toward us, yelling wildly in Etruscan. As he came close, I could see that the cylinder had a hairline crack jaggedly running down its length.

Spacedog got a hold of himself enough to switch to his peculiar brand of English.

"Cataclysmic tertiary release! Subatomic bombardment! Unprecedented, anomalous, undetected! All fuel lost! How Spacedog race now?!? Racing Spacedog's life is!"

We had never actually got a chance to inspect Spacedog's engine all these months. One thing or another always intervened, and he seemed reluctant to give us a look. Another matter we didn't push. The sight of this tiny removable fuel chamber was the most detail we had gotten so far about the workings of his super car.

Joaquin clapped a comradely arm around Spacedog, little young guy acting like a father to the older, bigger man. "Calm down, calm down, *chico*! Let me see that."

Spacedog hopelessly tendered the cylinder to Joaquin, who inspected it and glibly said, "Hell, we'll have this crack welded in a few seconds, then we'll refill it with nitro. Where's the intake valve?"

Looking as if he wanted to tear out his nonexistent hair, Spacedog wailed, "Nitro, nitro! Your nitro not my fuel is! Not nitro, neutrinos! All those once handily contained now blasted spherically above and through your planet and racing away toward Oort Cloud."

Nobody knew what the hell he was talking about. Joaquin persisted anyhow.

"Suppose we weld this here chamber—"

"Noncoherent heat to fix eleven-dimensional gravitic storage modulator? Why not just big rock apply!"

"No need to get huffy, 'dog. Don't you have a spare?"

Spacedog instantly went placid, faster than any normal person would've. "*Verdad*! *Mais oui*! Back at mother— Back home! Fully charged with particles of powertude!"

"No problem then. We'll just have someone drive you there to pick it up, and you'll be back to racing before you can say 'Jack the Bear.'"

"*Nein*! Spacedog alone must go. No accompaniment needed or possible. Perimeters of defensive illusion not breached must be!"

"Oh . . . kay. Who has a street machine they can lend Spacedog?"

"He can take *El Tigre*." The words were out of my mouth before I knew they were coming.

"Oblong! *Mi companero*! Spacedog your primitive pride and joy will kindly treat. Back in the shortest span!"

Joaquin shook my hand and said, "Thanks, Papa Obie. I know you don't let just anyone drive your buggy. But we need Spacedog to win today."

"Sure. No sweat." I followed Spacedog toward my car and handed him the keys. He slipped easily behind the wheel, toyed with the shift and pedals, and then cranked the engine.

"You sure you're good with driving this kind of car? It doesn't work by helmet, you know . . . "

"Downloading scripts even as we speak. Finished! Haptic prompts all in place! *Adios, mon frère!*"

He roared off then in a cloud of dust, faster than Korean Commies retreating before MacArthur's troops.

When the air cleared, I saw Stella left alone in the crowd.

I hurried to her side.

I don't think Spacedog meant to leave her behind. In fact, in retrospect, I know he didn't. But he was just so jazzed about racing that he forgot all about his woman. It's an oversight not a few hot rodders have made.

Stella was showing more emotion than I had ever seen her display before, but unfortunately, it wasn't the good kind. Her usual smile had been replaced by a fretful grimace. She was kind of twitchy all over, and her jagged unnatural pupils were changing shape and size like the neon chaser lights at Googie's.

"Hey, Stella, what's the matter? Don't worry, the old Spacedog will be back soon. And he actually looked like he knew how to drive my car, so he probably won't get in no accidents. Don't worry about nothing. You need a drink? Come with me, and we'll grab a couple of cold sodas."

I walked the jittery woman over to where I knew a cooler of drinks waited, on the far side of one of the car trailers. The races had already begun, and everybody who wasn't tinkering with their machines or driving was busy watching. Stella and I were totally alone for the first time since we had met, and Spacedog was accelerating away from us.

I bent over, fishing for two bottles of pop from the cracked ice. "You like grapefruit? All I see here is Squirt."

When I straightened up with the drinks and turned to face Stella, I nearly died.

She still wore her blue angora sweater, but she had stripped off her pants. Her bush blazed as platinum as her hairdo.

Now she lunged at the waistband of my trousers, and I dropped both bottles to fend her off.

"Stella, no! We can't! Not here!"

She wouldn't listen. Her hands fastened on my pants and popped the top button. The sound of my zipper unladdering sounded louder to me than the engines a few hundred yards away.

Stella leaped up and wrapped her legs around my waist, and suddenly there was no more possibility of resistance. I was harder than Egyptian algebra, all the stifled lust of several months coming to a head.

I grabbed her boobs as she wriggled her pelvis to fit me into her wet heat, and despite my enthusiasm and hers, I nearly wilted.

That was no sweater Stella always wore. Her torso was covered in blue fur. I had twin handfuls of shaggy tit, like grabbing a combination of Lily St. Cyr and Lambchop.

But underneath the short fur, they were still the most incredible boobs I had ever handled.

I pivoted to brace Stella's back against the side of the trailer, and in less time than it takes to tell, we finished the hottest, wildest, most surprising knee-trembler I had ever dared to imagine. She never made a sound the whole while.

No one caught us. When it was over and I had stopped panting, we dressed again and rejoined the crowd.

Spacedog returned from his mission in under an hour. With the replacement fuel source installed in his car, he rejoined the field and proceeded to whomp Bakersfield ass.

Finally, around sunset, he came triumphantly to where Stella and I waited for him. But as soon as he got within a few feet of us, Spacedog somehow knew. He threw his arms toward the sky and wailed.

"Ruined! Polluted! The imprinting of my gyno-symbiote all shattered! Now either Oblong or Spacedog must die!"

* * *

Behind the wheel of *El Tigre*, heading south out of San Diego toward Ensenada in early darkness, following the taillights of Spacedog's sleek UFO down the highway, I felt a crazy mess of emotions. Shame, fear, pride, anger, and happiness—I could hardly begin to sort out my feelings. Sure I had betrayed a friend. But I hadn't made the first move. His girl had jumped my bones. And what a jumping! But was she responsible for her own actions? Was Stella simple-minded? Had I taken advantage of a beautiful moron? And what part of Italy grew girls with blue fur and starry eyes?

I tried to dismiss all these confusing questions by concentrating on the road. I didn't know where we were going, but I was honor-bound to go there.

Back at Paradise Mesa, the Bean Bandits had held an impromptu court to decide how the affair between me and Spacedog would play out. (I confessed everything up front. Stella, natch, stayed silent through the whole debate.) Spacedog, as the affronted party, had gotten to call the tune.

"I this *cabron* challenge! Cosmic Chicken the trial!"

Joaquin wore a sad and solemn look. "I don't know about that, 'dog. Playing chicken usually ends up with someone getting killed. We don't want any heat from the cops. That would spell the end of the Bandits."

"No worry. Not here ritual of the Chicken enacted. Distant place, only Oblong and Spacedog present, no witnesses."

"Well, whatever's gotta be." Joaquin gripped both our hands. "May the best Bandit win."

I didn't relish playing Chicken with Spacedog, especially at night. But I owed him something for my betrayal of his trust, and this was the method of payment he had chosen.

Halfway to Ensenada, in the middle of nowhere without a sign of civilization around, Spacedog flipped on his turn signal, then pulled a left off-road. His headlights, then mine, illuminated an empty field.

Empty for the first second or two of our arrival. Then a giant lighted hatch opened in mid-air about twenty feet above us. From the lower edge of the hatch, a corrugated ramp extruded itself to the turf, and Spacedog drove straight up it and into sheer impossibility. *El Tigre* was right behind him, but the car must have been driving itself, since my brain was frozen in disbelief.

We came to a halt inside a vast vaulted hanger, full of strange machineries and stranger smells and a couple of smallish spindle-shaped craft that looked like the Air Force's worst nightmares.

I climbed out of my car to join Spacedog and Stella.

"This thing is a spaceship! A *real* UFO! You two aren't from Italy at all! You're aliens!"

"*Verdad*, traitorous *companero* of yore. Now must you the limits of your primitive worldview finally acknowledge. But surely Bandits one and all already knew as much."

I considered Spacedog's words. "I guess we all did. But we just didn't want to admit it. So long as you were winning races for us, it didn't matter."

"Understood. And I too the boat did not wish to rock. Too much fun I was having! Spacedog not welcome on home world any longer. Too oddball, too flippy, too wild! Only racing with new friends my sole *raison yo soy*. This big secret, not to be broadcast. But you not ever return will, so consequence of my telling nil."

"Let me off this thing, Spacedog! I didn't agree to this!"

"Too late. Observe."

Some kind of deluxe TV screen on a nearby wall flared into life. The whole stinking Earth, small as a cloud-wrapped, custom blue gearshift knob, barely registered in a lower corner of the star-filled image.

"Where are we heading?"

"To the hottest track around. Your primary."

"Primary what?"

"Your sun, your sun!"

I slumped back against my car. "We're going to play Chicken against the sun?"

"Correct."

"Would you at least tell me why we have to do this?"

Spacedog indicated the hangdog Stella, who looked as if she were suffering from the worst kind of hangover combined with a bad case of the flu. "My exteriorized anima you have psychosomatically contaminated. No longer bonded to me alone, but now partly to you she is. With the death of one of us, she whole will restored be."

There was a lot more talk about entangled muon pairs and hormonal tipping points and morphic resonance and quantum brain structures and the various telepathic alien animals from which Stella had been constructed, and how she had panicked once Spacedog's mentality passed out of contact, and how she had fastened on me as his replacement. But I wasn't paying any attention, because all I could focus on was Spacedog's eyes.

He had removed his sunglasses to reveal some kind of chrome robot eyeballs in place of natural ones. Now he levered up the hood of my car, and his eyeballs telescoped out of his green face on flexible stalks to examine hidden parts of my engine.

"Impossible to retrofit. Must dissolve and grow new one."

He went to a cabinet and found what appeared to be a spray can and a silver egg. He sprayed *El Tigre*'s engine, on which I had labored so many hours, and the whole thing just crumbled into sand. Then he dropped the egg into the empty space, sprayed that from the same can—only after twisting the nozzle—and closed the hood.

"New power plant ready by time we Mercury pass. Now to control room for much-needed sustenance."

We three rode some kind of antigravity chute up to the bridge. A ring of TVs showed a dozen different outer space views that sent my brain deeper into a tizzy. The view that really flipped me out was the one that displayed our sun. That raging furnace swelled even as I watched and soon filled the whole screen. Then the magnification dropped a notch, and the hell spot was small again. But the whole cycle just kept repeating: swell, diminish, swell, diminish— At this rate we'd be there in no time.

Spacedog and I sat down in some kind of chairs that squirmed around to accommodate our butts. Stella moved half-heartedly about, assembling some kind of space food. I guess I ate, but I don't really remember. Nobody said anything until Spacedog spoke. His manic manner had faded to a thoughtful cast.

"Resistance to Stella by any hominid inseminator futile is, Oblong. This I admit. Also my complicity and unforesightedness in leaving her behind under your exclusive care. And yet our duel in the sun must still take place. Regrets profound, *lo siento mucho, pero que sera, sera.*"

"Likewise, I'm sure."

In no time, Mercury hurtled by us like a forlorn piece of grit under the wheels of a dragster. When the spaceship finally stopped, Spacedog told me were just one million miles from the sun.

326

On the TV down in the hanger, the sun boiled and lashed like an insane beast. Giant prominences erupted, whipped the vacuum, and then collapsed back into the white-hot speckled chaos of the surface. Heaving clouds of colored gases shimmied like Gypsy Rose Lee. The scene was like looking into Satan's flaming asshole itself.

I drew my terrified eyes away to focus on the new engine under the hood of *El Tigre*. A featureless, irregular, silver blob, the mechanism floated, unattached to any drive train or controls.

"This neutrinos eats. Not from small container source used on Earth, but taking from ambient flux put out by sun. Think of ramscoop on hood of your car. Power from neutrinos used to warp space-time geodesics and propel vehicle. Much higher speeds reached out here."

"And how do I control it? I don't have head bumps to run a helmet like you."

"Neutrino drive now interfaced to your standard controls. Pedals, steering wheel, shift."

"So, I assume we both race toward the sun till one of us burns up?"

"Not so. Contest over too soon if heat a factor. Protective fields surrounding your car absolutely resistant to temperatures of over ten billion Kelvins. Sun only one million tops."

"Then what's the danger?"

"Gravity. Drive not powerful enough to overcome sun's pull. Too close, and trapped forever you are, lost in the turbulence of convection zone. Death when limited oxygen supply in car runs out. Quite painless, actually, with unique scenic surroundings."

"So the first one to chicken out actually survives and wins Stella."

"Yes. But then victor also number one coward fake hot rodder, full of *merde*, and must forever live with undying shame."

I considered for a moment. The alien logic was all twisted, with the "chicken" getting the girl. But then the matter of honor hit home. My mind ran back to the war, when I had nearly bought the farm a score of times, sticking my head up out of the foxhole to snap off a few rounds, rather than be thought a coward. Maybe Spacedog's logic wasn't so twisted after all.

"With any luck, both of us'll die. Let's rumble."

Stella had been left back on the bridge. I climbed behind the wheel of *El Tigre* and noticed a small TV screen that looked like it had somehow been grafted right onto my dash. The tiny TV lit up, showing Spacedog in the cockpit of UFO.

"Shields on," Spacedog said, and instantly our two vehicles were surrounded by glowing transparent bubbles of force.

"Actual photons not permitted to truly pass through shields to your eyes. Exterior conditions reconstructed based on information hitting shields, then result displayed on inside of bubble. Sophisticated simulation, all virtual but highly accurate."

The hull hatch opened, air puffed away, and the car we called the UFO zipped out. Tentatively I pressed the accelerator, and *El Tigre* responded like a charm.

Outside the big ship, we aimed our noses at the raving furnace of the sun. A virtual set of Christmas Tree lights appeared on the inner surface of my shields and began to work down to green.

I didn't wait, but tromped down when they turned yellow, shooting ahead of Spacedog.

Even if I had to cheat, this was one race between us I was going to win. Or lose, depending on your point of view.

All the fear and resignation and dismay I had felt inside the ship had been burned away by the awesome sight of the sun and realization of the unique chance I had been given.

No one on Earth had ever pulled a drag like this, a neutrino drag. Behind the wheel of the most souped-up car ever, I was blasting down God's own blacktop, toward certain glorious death and a place in racing legend.

Assuming Spacedog was honorable enough to report back to the Bandits.

"You'd better tell Joaquin and everyone else about me winning!" I yelled at the TV screen.

"Factual impossibility! Spacedog to perish here! You chicken out will!"

I looked out my side window and saw that Spacedog had pulled up even with me. "Never!" I yelled, and then shifted up.

I noticed then that my speedometer had been recalibrated—into fractions of light speed, according to the new label—and that I was hitting point oh one.

This race was going to be over pretty damn fast.

"Entering fringes of photosphere now, coward! Turn back!"

Although my cockpit was cool, I was sweating buckets. The enormous tendrils of the sun coiled around us in slow-motion horror, arcs of fire big enough to swallow the whole Earth.

I put *El Tigre* in third gear.

"I your shadow am! Cars equal, no outrunning each other!"

"Then join me in hell, Spacedog!"

And at that instant, some force yanked my nose ninety

degrees off course. I spun my wheel uselessly, screamed and swore, but all to no avail.

"Ha-ha! Spacedog wins! I satisfied die! Oblong, listen! Ounce for ounce, the human body hotter than the sun burns!"

And with those enigmatic words, he flew on straight for the heart of the star.

El Tigre exited the photosphere at right angles to its entrance path. And there was the big ship, guiding me back inside along some kind of invisible attraction beam.

Stella had pulled me out of the death race.

Me, not Spacedog.

She entered the hanger once it had filled with air again. I climbed out of *El Tigre*, exhausted and numb.

But when I saw her restored to her old, vivacious, ultra-Torchy magnificence, I just couldn't feel down.

She came into my arms, and we made love right there, her gorgeous ass resting on the flames painted across *El Tigre*'s fender.

* * *

We sunk the spaceship—including *El Tigre*, the one item that really hurt me to lose—in the Pacific, a mile offshore, more by accident than on purpose. Stella kind of knew how to pilot it, but not really. The swim nearly killed us, and I guess we were lucky to escape alive. We made our way back to San Diego and the old scene: my business, the Bandits, a very frosty Herminia. We tried to fit back into the old routines, but it just didn't work out. I had lost my taste for drag racing and working as a plain old mechanic on cars just didn't make sense any longer. Besides, although Joaquin and the Bandits never said anything outright, I knew they all thought I had killed Spacedog to get his girl.

And of course, in a way I had.

Stella and I moved to San Francisco and opened up a coffee shop. We called it "The Garage," and decorated it with fake posters and lame souvenirs no real hot rodder would have ever approved of. But Stella drew customers like money draws lawyers, and we did well.

I didn't have any regrets about surviving. I knew I had been prepared to run that solar race to the deadly finish line, and that only Stella's intervention had stopped me.

But what I did worry a little bit about, on and off, was the fate of Spacedog's UFO.

After some thought, I figured that the power plant inside the protective force field was still sucking down neutrinos, and that Spacedog's suffocated corpse was hauling ass in tight orbit around and around the sun, or was maybe even stuck at the center, doing Lord knows what to the way the sun worked.

When the astronomy guys began talking in the sixties about the sun not making enough neutrinos to fit their theories, I knew my hunch was right.

But what can I do? All this took place fifty years ago, and Earth's still around, right? A little hotter on the average, sure, but everyone agrees that's due to all the chemicals in the atmosphere, not the changing sun. It's just that I want to tell someone, so that the information survives after I'm gone. I can't count on Stella carrying the knowledge forward. Oh, sure, she hasn't aged one iota in five decades, and she'll probably be around for another century or two. (You should see the envious looks I get from guys as she pushes my wheelchair down the street. I hope she fixes on a nice young fellow when I kick the bucket.) But in all that time, she's still never said a word. I don't think she's got the kind of intelligence that needs or uses speech. So I can't rely on her.

And I can almost hear Spacedog say, "*Verdad, companero*! Every racer ultimately all alone is!"

—*The author would like to acknowledge Leah Kerr's* Driving Me Wild *(Juno Books, 2000) as an important source of information on the history of hot rodding.*

It's not often that a writer can come up with a fantasy motif that's never been thought of before. Vampires, were-wolves, unicorns, wicked stepmothers, magic rings, cursed talismans, enchanted castles— The stock in trade of modern fantasy novels consists of immemorial tropes that were old when Grimm and Anderson began to catalog them. But with this story, I believe I conjured up something never before crystallized.

We are all familiar with the notion of three wishes—or an infinite ability (granted by a genie, perhaps) to make whatever we mentally desire come true. But what if we had to share such a power? What if only by mutual agreement between two people could a wish come true? The potential for humorous conflicts of interest immediately struck me. And this notion, it seems to me, has never before been explored.

Originally I intended to provide a magical explanation for such a linked power. But in the end, I opted for some sci-entific mumbo-jumbo, which I now fear might have obscured the lineage of this story. Trust me—you're really reading a fairy tale.

What Goes up a Chimney? Smoke!

Dr. Beverly Cleaver was a beautiful, ill-mannered mush-mouth, annoying in the extreme. Far from being a matter of mere opinion, this quadruple characterization was verifiable by scientifically impartial observation.

Her beauty: all the male employees of Mesoscale Engi-neering tended to cluster around her like dendrites around a synapse, vying to run her personal errands, offering their latest findings for her approval as if gloriously pristine research results were frivolous, smelly bouquets.

Her ill manners: Dr. Beverly Cleaver, that martinet, never politely requested, never cajoled, never teased. She barked, she demanded, she issued orders like some termagant game show hostess.

Her mush-mouthedness: born and raised in Bucksnort, Tennessee, Dr. Beverly Cleaver contorted the English language in painful ways. When demanding high precision, for instance, she asked not for "five nines" performance, but some alien measure of exactitude known as "fy-ive nans."

Her annoyingness: admittedly, this quality was the most subjective. Obviously all her admirers at Mesoscale Engineering would beg to disagree. Many employees—and the firm's financial backers—felt she was a competent, creative administrator, able to produce results—and profits—with a minimum of friction.

But not Josh Stickley. Josh found the unpredictable yet inevitable intrusions of Dr. Beverly Cleaver into his lab—billed hypocritically as "progress chats"—irritating and frustrating. Every time the woman showed up, Josh's experiments had a way of developing inexplicable glitches, exhibiting transient phenomena that took days to track down and rectify. The point had been reached where just the unique staccato sound of her approaching footsteps was enough to cause Josh to flub some vital adjustment or measurement.

Realizing he could not openly undermine his nemesis, Josh had tried to take her image down a peg or two by some mildly subversive tactics. Around the water cooler, he had initially begun referring to her as "Beaver Cleaver." But reference to this mild-mannered, pre-adolescent television icon had failed to resonate with his fellows, and so Josh changed her nickname to "Clever Beaver." This somewhat misogynistic moniker stuck immediately—Josh heard many references to his boss under this nickname—but had the opposite of the intended effect, humanizing her in the eyes of others and making her even sexier.

Frustrated, Josh admitted a temporary defeat and ceased his covert campaign against the beautiful, ill-mannered, annoying mushmouth. Instead, he focused even more intently on his current research, with an eye toward future glory.

True, any patentable discoveries he made would become the property of Mesoscale Engineering, and he would not benefit financially (aside from any potential bonuses granted purely at the whim of the corporation). But if he could achieve what he dreamed of—

Well, a Nobel Prize would be fair compensation for all the years of abuse at the hands of the Clever Beaver.

* * *

That Tuesday evening found Josh running mice. The test he had devised for his furry subjects exhibited an admirable simplicity, although its goal was not immediately discernible to an outsider. A complex maze—its partitions reconfigurable after each run—featured a food reward at its center. Into this labyrinth Josh would place one of two mice, and time the success of the animals. Once the first mouse found the treat, Josh would remove it, sterilize the maze to eliminate murine scent trails, and then allow the second mouse (heretofore isolated in another room) to attempt the identical maze. After the second mouse had penetrated the center, Josh would compare their trial times. Then he would rearrange the interior of the puzzle, sterilize, and run the mice separately again.

Beyond all the random variations in times due to mouse vitality, mouse skills, time of day, and maze complexity, Josh was searching for one trend: he hoped the second mouse would run the maze faster than the first, as if somehow possessed of superior knowledge of its pattern.

But after statistical filtering of the data, Josh remained disappointed. The second mouse never did any better than its predecessor, even when he switched their roles.

This trial was the seventy-seventh of the day, and Josh had steadily grown more weary and impatient, despairing of any desirable results. He cajoled the mice in no uncertain terms.

"C'mon, you damn cheeseheads! Send and receive, send and receive!"

"Send and receive, Dr. Stickley?"

Holding Mouse A in his hand, Josh reacted so badly to the unexpected voice that he nearly squished his subject. Striving to regain his composure, he very deliberately returned the mouse to its cage, then slowly turned.

Sneakers. The Clever Beaver wore a pair of pink Nikes, the better to silently steal up on her employees.

Tracking his gaze, Dr. Beverly Cleaver mush-mouthed in a way that forced Josh to pay close attention in order to understand her. "I'm dressed to go home, Dr. Stickley. It's 7:00 PM. While I appreciate your dedication, I wonder if it wouldn't be better for y'all to get some rest. You seem rather distraught."

Tiredness made Josh lower his guard. "True, I'm not seeing the results I hoped for. But any day now—"

The Clever Beaver signaled her disbelief with an annoyingly dramatic sigh. "Dr. Stickley—don't you think it's about time to abandon this particular improbable quest of yours? After all, engineered telepathy— Really, it's hardly likely you'll succeed now, after so many failures, isn't it? If you hadn't been well along in your research when I took over the administration of Mesoscale, I never would have approved even the continuation of such a project. And now, sixteen months into my tenure, I'm beginning to think we should just pull the plug on this futile line of investigation."

Josh panicked. "But, but, really, I don't use many resources. Just a little time with the circuit boys, drafting schematics for the meso-ifrits. Then just an hour or so on the assembly line, cranking out the mifrits themselves. The doses required for my test subjects are so small, really. After that, it's just me and the mice! And the theory— The theory is very sound! Consciousness is a quantum phenomenon, mediated by cerebral Penrose microtubules. Once my mifrits are injected and attach themselves to the neural reticulum, they cause subatomic resonations entrained with synaptic activity, sub-Planckian information waves that should be perceivable by other hosted mifrits elsewhere, regardless of spatial constraints."

"'Should be,' but obviously are not. And your methodology stinks! How can you expect *mice* to communicate with y'all, or otherwise conclusively exhibit the experience you are trying to stimulate?"

"No, you don't understand! I just need to vary the resonance amplitude—"

"Dr. Stickley, please don't embarrass both of us with abject begging. I'm afraid my mind is made up. When the Board convenes next week, you'll receive a hearing. But your lack of results inevitably dooms your project. Don't worry, though. We'll find other interesting work for you. There's one highly practical and potentially very profitable project that could use a man of your skills."

"Not—"

"Yes. Dr. Oakeshott's work to perfect self-renewing, anti-shower-scum tile-cleaning mifrits."

After that final insult, Dr. Cleaver pivoted with a small squeak of rubber on industrial flooring and strode off triumphantly.

* * *

The homes of some unspoused scientists might very well be marvels of interior design and spotless to boot. But Josh's domicile was most definitely not one of these hypothetical showplaces. Empty pizza boxes consorted with dirty shirts; a pile of videotapes formed a Gothic ogive with an equal stack of journals; a heap of unread junk mail carpeted the top of the dining room table.

Josh drained his fifth beer and let the bottle fall to the rug. Sprawled across his shabby sofa, he looked hopelessly at the blurry clock. Ten at night, and he still wasn't drunk enough to pass out. How was he ever to forget his dire predicament for the night? God, if only he could stomach hard liquor! Then all his problems would be solved . . . .

Just as he haltingly arose to fetch with distaste another beer from the fridge, his doorbell rang.

Stumbling across the room, Josh opened the door.

There stood four identical women. Josh blinked frantically, passing a hand across his face. No, his visitors were only two identical women. And he knew them well.

Evadne and Siboney Pilchard lived directly across the street from Josh. Twenty-four years old, the identical twins possessed flaming red hair, precisely plotted curves, and dark-speckled green eyes resembling kiwi-fruit slices. When Josh had first moved into his home, the sisters had been bike-riding twelve year olds. In the intervening years, they had entered onto quite familiar terms with their oddball, bachelor neighbor, maturing from playing fiendish pranks on Josh to using him as a shoulder to cry on when their parents died in a freak oil-pipeline explosion while photographing a herd of wildebeests during an African wildlife tour.

In all that time, Josh had never figured out a way to distinguish between Evadne and Siboney, either as girls or women. From day-to-day they dressed identically, and, still in their relative youth, bore no unique wrinklings or scars to use as identifiers. The isotropic nature of their personalities further confounded the issue. In the end, Josh had simply abandoned all hope of slapping a definitive name on either of them. And unlike those twins who demanded respect for their individuality, the Pilchards seemed to relish the confusion their xeroxed status caused.

"Oh, Josh," one Pilchard said, "you've got to hide us!"

"Please, please, please," the other said. "It's a matter of life and death!"

"Sure," Josh slurred, "c'mon in."

The twins hustled indoors and quickly drew the drapes on the windows facing the street.

"It's those awful Pawkeys."

"Ed and Sid."

"We made the mistake of answering our phone after 9:00."

"And there they were!"

"They said they were coming by to take us out for a drink."

"And saying 'no' was not an option."

"So we just ran."

Josh tried to wrap his buzzing brain around the conversation. "Do I even know these people?"

Evadne and Siboney huffed in a peeved manner.

"We told you all about them!"

"We met them at a mixer for twins."

"When we foolishly gave them our names, they freaked."

"'We have the same initials,' they said."

"'E.S.P.'"

"As if that made us fated to go out with them."

"Awful, awful brothers."

"Shaped like avocados."

"With very similar skin."

"Balding, dressed in pure polyester."

"Used-car salesmen!"

"And now they won't leave us alone!"

Josh felt bad for his pretty neighbors. The portrait of ignorant harassment they painted was embarrassing to the whole male gender. He swept the sofa free of debris and gestured to the seat.

"Here, sit down and relax. Wanna beer?"

"Sure."

"What do you have?"

Josh bent down, almost losing his balance utterly in the process, and retrieved an empty bottle. "This stuff."

"Narragansett?"

"We've never heard of it. But how bad can it be?"

"Great. Goes down smooth." Josh went to the kitchen and returned with three brown bottles. "Howdy, neighbor—neighbors—have a 'Gansett!"

The women sipped their beers, seemed not too repulsed, and then looked with concern at their host.

"Josh, what's the matter?"

"We know you don't get this drunk every night."

"We would have seen all the empty bottles in the recycling bin."

"Oh, it's just my damn job." Josh recounted his troubles at work. The sisters expressed voluble sympathy, but had no inspiration on how to circumvent Clever Beaver.

"If only I could get some solid results," Josh mournfully intoned. "Then she'd have to let my project alone!"

Both sisters spoke simultaneously then, each dulcet voice overlaying the other precisely, forming one doubled voice.

"Mean bosses suck the worst!"

Following this pronouncement came an odd ritual. The women hooked their little fingers together and recited a rhyme:

"What goes up a chimney? Smoke! May your wish and my wish never be broke!"

A conception as bright and stunning as a solar plume erupted out of Josh's alcohol-soaked gray matter. "Identical brains," he muttered. "They already resonate the same—"

From left and right, the women poked him in the ribs.

"Speak up!"

"Talk sense!"

Josh felt a sudden flush of guilt at the Machiavellian train of thought subsequent to his revelation. Leaning awkwardly across one of the women and thus provoking giggles from both, he fumbled for the television remote on a side table, found it, and powered on the set, all in order to distract his guests.

"Let's see what's on E.S.P.—I mean, ESPN."

* * *

The team responsible for laying down and reifying the mifrit circuitry were familiar with Josh's eccentric designs. They actually found his requests a challenge to their skills. But this time he had plainly ventured over some nebulous border into a gray zone of spooky weirdness.

"These designs aren't compatible with mouse brain architecture," said Joe Grillo, scratching his bald head. "In fact, if I didn't know better, I say they exhibited many complementarities with human wetware."

"Listen," Josh urged, "you guys are just supposed to

follow my instructions, not question the direction of my research."

"I know, I know. But what about the size of these doses? It's just not right. The amounts tally with a mass of approximately 120 pounds—"

Josh smote his own forehead with the heels of both palms. "What the hell do I have to do to get you to perform your damn job?"

"Okay, okay, no need to get nasty. But I'm warning you, Stickley. Today's Friday, and Clever Beaver will get the weekly reports on our production when we close down the line at 3:00 PM this afternoon. When she sees the specs for your job, she's gonna go apeshit. Miss Scarlett O'Hara will be all over you like boll weevils on cotton."

"Not till Monday. And by then I'll be world famous. You'll be able to charge the tabloids hundreds of thousands of dollars for the story of how you helped me."

"Right. And on Monday my wife will wake up looking like Uma Thurman. I'll give you your mifrits, Stickley, but all the responsibility is on your shoulders, not mine."

"That's fair. I owe you big time, Grillo."

Josh spent the hours until he could claim his new mifrits running over the timeline of his scheme.

Dr. Beverly Cleaver would not read the damning production report until Monday. That gave him all weekend to obtain the incontrovertible proof that his invention worked. Siboney and Evadne had already agreed to come to dinner at his house tonight. He had secured the illegal drugs he needed to render them temporarily unconscious—just a handful of roofies from one of the disreputable young mullet-haired guys down in packing and shipping. (Here Josh showed enough guilty conscience to wince internally at this cruel deception, so unlike him. Yet the demands of science and his personal survival demanded even such treachery against his friends.) Once the twins awoke, Josh would explain the immense favor he had done them and begin running some double-blind experiments designed to elicit the evidence of their new telepathy.

After that, only contacting the news media remained. And he was certain that Evadne and Siboney would appreciate their new celebrity status and any attendant riches. How satisfying, after all, could their present daily grind as nail technicians at the Venus in Furs Beauty Salon be?

A knock at his lab door caused Josh to jump. But the visitor was only an interdepartmental courier bearing two vials of invisible, self-replenishing brain rearrangers, packed in dry ice.

Josh grabbed two clean hypodermics and headed home.

A stop at the local market provided all the ingredients for lasagna, Josh's one reliable dish. Salad fixings, bread, wine (a strong zinfandel to conceal any taste of roofies), and might as well forget any dessert, since his guests would be comatose by then.

When the doorbell rang at 7:00, Josh had a beautiful table laid. He had cleaned up the worst of the bachelor detritus, lit candles, and put an easy-listening jazz CD on the deck.

Evadne and Siboney traipsed in gaily. Tonight the twins wore blue silk pantsuits that nicely brought out their fair skin and carroty hair, and some modest gold jewelry.

"Oh, Mr. Stickley, what a devilish ambiance!"

"If we didn't know better, we might think you were out to seduce us!"

"Nonsense, nonsense. Just intent on sharing a nice meal with two good friends. Let's have some shrimp first, with a little white wine. Later, of course, with the pasta, we'll have to switch to the red."

* * *

Josh dabbed at the second needle puncture in female flesh with a bit of gauze soaked in rubbing alcohol. The women had been arranged comfortably on the wide sofa, heels to heads, like human bookends, and gave every evidence of enjoying an easy, light, chemical sleep. By the time the women awoke in the morning, the mifrits would have penetrated their blood-brain barriers and distributed themselves along their Penrose network.

Sighing, Josh objectively tried to assess his deed. True, the Pilchard sisters had not volunteered for this experiment, but the honor he was conferring on them certainly more than made up for any slight ethical transgressions.

With a turbulent mind, Josh went to bed. Of course he could not sleep, and so spent the long hours till first light rehearsing the acceptance speech he would give at Stockholm.

The day dawned with a promising splendor. Josh shaved, brushed his teeth, showered, and dressed in casual clothes. For the umpteenth time, he shuffled the deck of Rhine-symbol cards that he intended to use in the upcoming trials, and then went to the kitchen to prepare some coffee.

The smell of the brew aroused tentative rustlings and feminine groans from the parlor. A few moments later, the kitchen table hosted the still dazed, but apparently quite healthy Pilchard sisters.

"Oh, my God, what happened to us?"

"We're so sorry, Josh. All that wine—"

"Did we actually pass out? How mortifying!"

Josh set down mugs before his guests. They each sugared and creamed their coffee identically, then sipped with real appreciation. Brightening a bit and recovering their normal aplomb, they seemed inclined to flirt.

"We hope you didn't take advantage of us."

"No hanky-panky."

"Not that under other conditions we wouldn't be—"

Josh interrupted before any romantic nonsense could arise to complicate his scientific quest. "It's not your fault, ladies, none of it. You see, I was completely responsible for your early sleep."

Siboney and Evadne narrowed their green eyes, then spoke together: "What do you mean?" So disturbed by his words were they that they neglected their little superstitious ritual attendant on synchronized utterances.

Josh explained all. His speech started off boldly, but as the frowns and grimaces of his audience deepened, he began to falter, till at last he tapered off into silence.

"That's the only reason you invited us to dinner last night?"

"To use us as guinea pigs?"

"What a horrible thing to do!"

"And your evil stupid scheme didn't even work!"

Cowering, Josh risked a question. "How can you be sure?"

"Because we're still isolated inside our own heads."

"Don't you think we'd recognize any actual transfer of thoughts, something clearer than our usual intuitive connection as twins?"

"Your theory is garbage!"

"Your invention is crap!"

Then, as one: "Oh, how we wish we had a gun!"

The boom of the shot rang out like thunder in the close confines of the kitchen, setting Josh's ears ringing as gunpowder fumes filled his nostrils. The scientist had re-flexively closed his eyes at the report, and now reluctantly opened them, aware only that he had not been hit.

One of the women gripped an enormous smoking pistol. She stared at it in a dumbfounded manner for a moment, then dropped it.

"We wish we were safe at home!"

Evadne and Siboney vanished.

Josh hesitated only a moment, then dashed out of the house and across the street. Standing on the Pilchard porch, he banged on the door.

"Let me in! Siboney, Evadne, I think I know what's happening to you!"

The door cracked a hairline.

"How can we possibly trust you?"

"You don't have to trust me! Just listen and judge for yourselves."

The door swung open, and Josh entered. He barely registered the neat decor, the Ikea-style furnishings the Pilchards favored. Before the frightened women could hurl any of a hundred questions at him, he offered his theory.

"My mifrits weren't impotent! They just didn't have the effect I predicted. Here's what I think is going on. Your linked brains are now interacting directly with the quantum level of the space-time continuum. For the first time since the dawn of consciousness, paired mentalities are imposing a unique torsion on the cosmos. When you both conceive of a desire, you alter local probabilities in a Heisenbergian manner to allow your will to be enacted. Or maybe you branch the entire universe onto a timeline where your wish is already a *fait accompli*. I can't be sure, but it's definitely one of those options. Listen, let me try something. Erm, there's no polite way to ask this, but—which one are you?"

Josh pointed to the twin on his left.

"Siboney."

"Siboney, try to wish for something your sister doesn't want. If that's possible."

"Um, okay. We—"

"No, not 'we!' Say 'I.' C'mon, you can do it!"

"Uh, uh—I wish for a rum raisin, butterscotch smoothie."

"Ugh, gross!" Evadne said.

The trio waited patiently, but no frosty drink appeared.

"Now you, Evadne."

"I wish for a videotape of Mel Gibsons' new movie that's still in the theaters!"

Siboney scowled. "That jerk?"

No tape materialized.

Josh was exultant. "It's proven then! Your minds *are* communicating after a fashion. It's just not on the conscious level. This connection will allow us to attempt all sorts of interesting experiments—"

The Pilchard twins erupted.

"Experiments!"

"Just to prove your crazy theories?"

"And earn you a Nobel Prize?"

"You've already turned us into freaks!"

"Monsters!"

"I-dream-of-Jeannies!"

Josh sought to soothe them. "Now, now, consider the pluses—"

"Shut *up*! We wish you were *dead*!"

* * *

Being dead was not apprehendable while one was actually experiencing the condition. Only in retrospect did Josh retain or recapture or recreate a sense of black duration, of infinite encapsulization, of bright omnipresence. But once his flow of living thoughts resumed, he instantly knew that down deep he would harbor this dreadfully alluring memory of the afterworld all his life.

As long or short as that might prove to be.

The trembling of his eyelids and the rise and fall of his chest triggered a most unexpected response from his killers. Josh found himself smothered with kisses. He opened his eyes to find the sisters kneeling beside him on the floor.

"Oh, you're alive! Thank God!"

"We're so sorry, Josh! We didn't really mean that last wish!"

"No, we just said the first thing that came into our heads."

"It was only an expression of anger."

"Temporary anger."

"But we're not angry any more."

"No, not at all. We forgive you, you see."

"That's why we wished you alive again."

"When you died, we realized something vital."

"We love you!"

Josh sat up. "Both of you?"

"Yes, of course."

"We've always loved you; we realize now. Ever since we were little."

Gaining his feet took all Josh's strength. The affirmation of love from Evadne and Siboney had rendered him even more weak-kneed than having been dead.

"And—and this is not a problem?"

"What?"

"Two of you and one of me?"

"Not with us."

"We always do everything together."

Josh sat weakly down. "Well, ladies, I'm—I'm flattered.

I've always found you two quite attractive and charming. And I suspect that my feelings, if I ever gave them rein, might qualify as love. But consider the social consequences!"

At that moment, the doorbell rang.

The women moved to the door's peephole and took turns squinting. Their expressions registered annoyance that morphed all too swiftly to a kind of predatory glee that alarmed Josh more than anything else that had happened so far today.

"It's those Pawkeys."

"We told them not to bother looking for us this morning."

"But they obviously didn't believe us."

"They wanted us to go to a classic car festival with them."

"Well, now they'll learn that they should have taken our 'no' seriously."

Before Josh could caution the women against involving anyone else in this unfolding affair, the door had swung open, and the Pawkeys had crossed the threshold.

As previously described by the sisters, their suitors were most unprepossessing. Josh estimated they were younger than he, but already prematurely bald, with bad comb-overs and NFL mustaches circa 1975 vainly seeking to compensate. The outfits they had chosen for a relaxing Saturday were matching nylon tracksuits in a hideous shade of mauve. Their dumpy physiques were not offset by blotchy complexions.

Ed and Sid's initial smarmy bonhomie dissolved upon sighting Josh. They slitted their eyes in a gesture of hostility.

"Who's this chump?"

"What's he doing here so bright and early?"

"Are you girls playing us for suckers?"

"He's not coming along with us, whoever the hell he is."

Siboney and Evadne were plainly enjoying everyone's discomfort. Performing elaborate hair-fluffings of their titian tresses and batting their eyes, they seemingly sought to placate the Pawkeys. But Josh suspected the unwelcome visitors were merely being set up for the kill.

"Oh, he's only a neighbor."

"Josh Stickley."

"He just came over here to pick our brains."

"But he didn't get very far."

The Pawkeys seemed mollified. They brushed their hands across their greasy strand-camouflaged scalps.

"Well, that's all right then."

"So, are you girls ready to come out with us?"

"Those getups are kinda formal though."

"Looks more like you're ready for a night out on the town."

The Pilchards smiled wholesomely.

"That's because we slept over at Josh's last night."

"We've all just tumbled out of bed."

Now the Pawkeys gaped like catfish in a creel.

"This—this is an goddamn insult!"

"You can't treat us like this."

"We're not your lapdogs!"

Josh winced, for he now saw what was coming.

"Oh, aren't you?"

"We wish the Pawkeys were *peekapoos*!"

Instantly, two small, shaggy, hybrid dogs blinked up from the carpet. Panting, casting their heads about dazedly, they began to nervously whine. Siboney and Evadne bent down to pick up a pet apiece.

And that's when Josh noticed that each dog bore a small bald spot on its crown.

This surreal confirmation of the dogs' real identities suddenly brought home all the terror of the day more vividly than even declarations of love or his own death.

Josh bolted and ran for home.

* * *

What to do, what to do! Josh had no idea of how to regain control of his unwise experiment. He had been a fool, he realized, ever to plunge ahead so recklessly with this untried technology. He had screwed up his own career, derailed the peaceful existences of two friends—women who, he now knew, loved him and with whom he might have had some rewarding, if untraditional, future—and deprived the world of a pair of used-car salesmen. Okay, so maybe that last charge against him could be written off. But still, nothing except chaos had arisen from his attempt at playing God.

Dithering in his living room, Josh frantically sought a scheme to put things right. He was most troubled by the capricious behavior of the Pilchard sisters. Were their personalities being warped by some unforeseen neural side effect of the mifrits, turning them into dangerous egomaniacs? Or were the women just exulting as any mortal might in the sudden access of such unlimited power? Would they eventually calm down and listen to reason? How long would they hold any quite justifiable grudges against him?

Oh, Lord, the situation was hopeless!

And it was all the fault of Clever Beaver. Josh suddenly reverted to hatred of his boss as his last bastion of certainty. If not for her harsh threats to kill his project, he would never have been driven to this extreme. Yes, in the final analysis, only Dr. Beverly Cleaver bore the ultimate responsibility for this unholy mess.

Josh threw himself on the sofa and began to sob.

"There, there, don't cry."

"Here, pet Ed or Sid for a while. They're so silky. Keeping a dog lowers your blood pressure, you know."

"It's scientifically proven."

Carrying their lapdogs, Evadne and Siboney had materialized on either side of Josh. Their hair had been wished into elaborate coiffures. They each displayed millions of dollars of jewelry upon their persons. And they wore haute couture outfits snatched direct from some Milan runway.

"Don't—don't kill me again—please—"

"Kill you?"

"Why would we ever do that?"

"We already told you we love you."

"And we're having so much fun with our new powers now."

"It just took some getting used to."

"But now we're so happy you injected us with your little beasties."

Josh wiped his dribbling nose on his sleeve. "You—you are?"

"Really, we are."

"Here, let us express our gratitude."

"We wish Josh was *really, really hung*."

Josh shot to his feet. He clutched at his unnaturally bulging crotch. Stuttering a stream of nonsense syllables, he found himself embarrassed into speechlessness.

"Now we're going to show you how to enjoy our present to you."

The bonging of the doorbell sounded like a welcome intrusion from another universe. Frantically Josh leapt for the door, hindered somewhat by the unwonted bulk of his foreign appurtenances.

Dr. Beverly Cleaver radiated hostility the way the Large Hadron Collider spewed particles.

"Okay, Dr. Stickley, this is the end of the road! I don't

know what y'all're up to, but I read the reports from the mifrit production section this morning and saw your latest attempt to circumvent my directives! I intend to reclaim the property of Mesoscale Engineering and put an end to any crazy schemes of yours."

Dr. Cleaver bulled past Josh before he could stop her. She came to a halt before the unexpected sight of the Pilchard sisters, sitting cool and unruffled as hit men on the couch.

"Who's this loudmouth, Josh?"

"She's very pretty."

"Are you two having an affair?"

Josh held his head; it seemed to weigh a hundred pounds. "No, no, she's my boss. Clever Beaver—"

Too late, Josh realized he had spoken the nickname aloud.

"What!" Dr. Cleaver screeched. "How dare you—"

Blessed silence descended.

For certainly, the animal known scientifically as *Castor fiber canadensis* had never been known to speak.

Dr. Beverly Cleaver thumped her broad paddle of a tail in a rhythm of frustration. The Pilchards set down Ed and Sid, who began to chase the beaver around the room, yipping and snarling. They all three disappeared out the open door, putting on a show the staid neighborhood had surely never before seen.

So much for Dr. Cleaver denouncing Josh before the Board of Mesoscale Engineering.

"Now that that annoying interruption is fixed, let's have that fun we promised you."

Josh instantaneously found himself with Siboney and Evadne in what he assumed was their bedroom. In the next second, they were all naked.

"Do you think we should give him a second one maybe?"

"There are two of us after all."

Josh huddled around his groin. "No, no, one's enough!"

"All right, all right, don't freak out on us."

Josh's mind worked in overdrive. How could he escape a future of endless servitude—however sensually pleasant—under the willful minds of the two women—

Two women. *Two* women!

Josh forced himself to straighten up and smile. He placed an arm around the waist of each sister and drew them close.

"Siboney, Evadne, I've never done anything like this before. Do you think you could make it a little easier for me? Just for our first time?"

"How?"

"Well, what if you two, um, merged? Physically became one. Just temporarily, of course! Isn't it something you've always dreamed of experiencing anyhow? No more painful division into two beings, just unity. If you were a single woman, I could really concentrate on showing you a good time. And neither one of you would have to wait their turn."

"What would you call us?"

"Oh, I don't know. Siva?"

"That's cute!"

"We'll do it!"

The next eyeblink brought the merger: a single sister stood before him.

Josh braced himself for the possible failure of his plan. "Ah, Siva, before we start, could we have, uh, some champagne?"

"Sure, why not? We wish for a bottle of champagne!"

Nothing happened. Siva pouted and wished again. No results.

"You—you tricked us! It took two of us to make things happen!"

"That's right! And now you're just a normal human again!"

In his triumph, Josh spared a moment's thought for Sid, Ed, and Clever Beaver. But he was already contemplating restoring them to their original appearances, via a more tractable set of twins—men this time—injected with his mifrits.

Putting aside her anger, Siva Pilchard wrapped herself around Josh. "Well, at least *something's* left over from this crazy morning. Something *big!*"

Several hours later, Josh fell into a deep sleep. Siva Pilchard remained awake for a few minutes longer however.

Long enough to say, "We wish Josh forgets everything that happened last night and this morning. We wish he remembers only that he's always loved the one and only Siva Pilchard."

For one subliminal moment, there was a flash of two women, not one on the bed.

Josh twitched as the new knowledge overlaid his memories.

Then Siva linked the little finger of her left hand with the little finger of her right and said, "What goes up a chimney? Smoke! May your wish and my wish never be broke!"

The keen-witted critic Nick Gevers opined that this story represented a case of sour grapes. With a trip to Mars unlikely in my own lifetime, I was seeking to undermine the fantasy trips to the Red Planet that had provided so much pleasure to SF readers in the past. Well, I confess to no such heinous motives. Like any natural-born satirist, I was simply seeking humor in the disjuncture between the "naïve" style of Weinbaum's original "A Martian Odyssey" and the postmodern way we conceive humans behave. Of course, in their daily doings and behaviors, our ancestors were no less sophisticated than us. It's only that the conventions of older periods often sanitized certain actions before they reached print. Someday, I'm sure, my story—if it's lucky enough to survive as long as Weinbaum's has—will look stilted and simple-minded.

But for now, I still think it rocks.

A Martian Theodicy

> *"Mars is a queer little world."*
> —Stanley G. Weinbaum, "A Martian Odyssey"

"Remember, men," Captain Harrison sternly advised, "we don't kill Dick Jarvis unless he forces our hand. Understood?"

In response to the Captain's mortal admonition, Karl Putz, the engineer on mankind's second mission to Mars, spat derisively out the open airlock of their ship, the *Ares II*. His saliva landed on the dusty terracotta soil of the Red Planet, instantly attracting a score of the walking native grass blades that roamed at random around their landing site.

"*Ja, ja*, agreed. But mine hand is damn near forced already, for truth."

Frenchy Leroy, crack biologist, absentmindedly fondled

the butt of his own holstered radium pistol, as he watched the ambulatory grass blades surround and absorb the blob of his roughshod comrade's spit. Shivering, the dapper doctor said, "Zis world, she makes me itch. Too many strangenesses by far."

"Frenchy, you didn't signify your assent to my command."

Leroy ceased rubbing his gunbutt and waved his hand dismissively. "*Oui, oui,* I will not slaughter zee traitor like zee *cochon* he is, until you permit it, *mon capitaine.* Despite all zee grief he has caused us personally, despite zee five years of stagnation in the conquest of zee solar system, which can be laid directly at his renegade feet, he is still a human being deserving of civilized justice under zee League of Nations protocols."

"So we hope," Captain Harrison grimly said.

The three men stood at the head of the ship's extruded duralloy ramp in moody silence, breathing the thin but sufficient air of the alien world into their Himalayan-conditioned lungs, pondering the dangerous, uncertain, and even repugnant mission they were about to undertake. After a brief time spent in meditation and reminiscence, they were startled from their reverie by the arrival of the fourth crew member, who blithely allowed the screen door of the port to slam behind her.

"Hi, boys!" Fancy Long gaily exclaimed. The gorgeous blonde star of the *Yerba Mate* televid show filled out her regulation uniform in ways the solemn designers back at Space Command in Zurich could never have envisioned. Her lithe dancer's limbs carrying her even more frolicsomely in the reduced gravity, her trained singer's voice sounding elfishly attenuated in the lesser atmosphere of Earth's ruddy neighbor, Fancy Long was the brightest sight in millions of miles, and her advent cheered the men considerably.

Leroy took her hand and kissed it. "Ah, *Mademoiselle* Long, you discover us drearily engrossed in our responsibilities. Please forgive our manifold discourtesies."

Putz clicked his heels and saluted. "*Fraulein*, you are a testament to der bright Aryan spirit of adventure."

Captain Harrison blushed faintly at the way the ultra-vulcanized, vacuum-proof rubber fabric molded the woman's form. "Ahem, Miss Long—Fancy—we were just discussing the outlines of our mission—"

Fancy batted her eyelashes and fluffed her Mars-bouncy hair. "Why so glum, then? We're finally going to rescue Dick from this awful fix he's gotten himself into, after five whole years! You should all be happy at the prospect of seeing your old shipmate again! Goodness knows, as his girlfriend, I'm terribly thrilled to think we'll be together again after so long!"

The men made no response to Fancy's bright chatter, and she became worried.

"What's wrong? Is there some new development you're not sharing with me? Have you had bad news from Dick over the radio? Or from Earth? Is the globe at war again? Have the Han Chinese broken out of the League blockade?"

Captain Harrison stroked his chiseled chin and spoke slowly, carefully choosing his words. "No, no, Miss Long, fortunately neither of your suppositions is correct. Earth continues to be blessed with peace—thanks to the cooperation of our wise leaders—and the last communication we had from Dick Jarvis left us assured that his, ah, situation remains stable. But you see, there are certain, um, facts about Dick's continued, unplanned presence on Mars that neither you nor any other civilians have ever been made aware of."

Fancy's pretty face expressed absolute confusion. "Why, whatever do you mean, Captain?"

Harrison tried to approach the uncomfortable subject from an angle. "Did you ever wonder, Miss Long, why you of all people were selected for this rescue mission, rather than, say, another scientist or even some practiced adventurer, such as Lowell Thomas or Richard Halliburton?"

Plainly this thought had never occurred to Fancy. "No, I can't say I ever wondered about it. Maybe I assumed that my fame had something to do with my selection. You know, good publicity for Space Command—"

Putz interrupted with Teutonic impatience. "You vere chosen, *madchen*, as a tool, a possible lever vee could use to pry dot swine Jarvis out of his foul nest."

Fancy began to weep. "Oh, I don't understand! Why are you all so mean all of a sudden? What did poor Dick ever do to any of you, except get abducted by the rotten old Martians?"

Captain Harrison coughed, tugged at his collar braids, and then said, "Miss Long, your fiancé was not kidnapped by the Martians. He deserted. And he nearly doomed us before he left. Let me fill you in on the secret aspects of our first mission to Mars."

* * *

In short order, Captain Harrison recounted the bizarre adventures the crew of the original *Ares* had undergone, particularly Dick Jarvis.

During a recon mission in one of the two small flyers carried by the mother ship, Dick Jarvis had crash-landed in the wastelands of Thyle, 800 miles from base camp, victim of his drive's defective atomic tubes. Uninjured, he had gamely set out to walk home, burdened with massive amounts of supplies made relatively light in the Red Planet's lesser gravity.

Before too long, he encountered one of Mars' more intelligent life forms, the ostrich-like sapient Jarvis came to call Tweel. Rescuing Tweel from a hypnotic carnivore, Jarvis had earned a friend for life. Together the two sentient beings began to traverse the hostile territory separating the human from the warmth and comfort of his own kind. The loquacious and helpful Tweel considerately kept his pace to the human's, restraining his 150-foot jumps that ended beak-first in the rusty sands.

After encountering a strange, immortal, silicon life form that secreted bricks as part of its lifecycle, the two friends avoided yet another dream-beast—this time with Tweel rescuing Jarvis from a hallucination of Fancy Long herself—before finally coming upon a city of eight-limbed barrel beings engaged in odd ritualistic construction duties. Tweel and Jarvis had wandered into the labyrinthine tunnels and chambers of the technologically sophisticated barrel creatures, ultimately becoming lost. Stealing a crystal talisman from the heretofore oblivious creatures, Jarvis incurred their wrath, just before man and Mars-bird broke through once more to the surface. Staging an Alamo-like last stand on the crimson sands, Tweel and Jarvis were on the point of being overwhelmed when a long-searching Putz dropped down with his own flyer and rescued Jarvis. In the confusion, Tweel took off on his own, leaving Dick Jarvis inconsolable at the loss of his new alien friend.

* * *

"But this contradicts everything the public was told!" Fancy interrupted. "The whole world listened to your debriefing over all the televid networks with shock and sympathy! You reported that shortly after setting down on Mars, the first *Ares* was attacked without provocation by a horde of angry natives who damaged its propulsion tubes. We all know that Dick was captured when the vile creatures shot down his avenging scout ship. Then the rest of you brave adventurers, after laborious repairs, limped back home, to rouse Earth and mount a rescue mission."

"If only it were so," Captain Harrison mused, "the world

would be a nobler place. But the authorities at Space Command and the League deemed the truth of our first expedition too volatile and shameful for general dissemination. We fabricated a cover story that we felt would encourage public support for a second mission. But allow me to continue with a summary of the actual events.

"That first night when Dick Jarvis safely lay in his bunk again, he apparently went mad. All that afternoon he had been fixated on that weird, glowing, egg-shaped crystal he had stolen from the barrel beasts. He had previously told us how the crystal had cured an old wart on his left thumb when he touched it, and how the mystery stone had also eased the pain in his battered nose. We all speculated for a while about the curative properties of gamma rays. But when we asked to handle the miraculous object, he refused us! He clutched the alien bauble tightly and a horrible expression of greed, fear, and contempt flowed over his features as he defied us, with the crystal pressed to his brow like a radiant leech!"

Fancy shuddered at the image. "Poor Dick," she whispered. Harrison patted her shoulder in sympathy before resuming.

"'No, you can't have my treasure!' he hissed. 'You're all too ignorant of Mars. You don't deserve to handle it! None of you have been out there on foot like I was! I suffered for this! Immured behind your machines, you know nothing! It was different for Tweel and me. Tweel! Only Tweel knows! Tweel, where are you, Tweel? Save me!'"

Frenchy Leroy intervened in the Captain's account. "In a blink, zat madman makes zee beeline for zee lock! Thank zee Lord, we have put zee latch upon zee screen door previously!"

"Vee had to wrestle him down," Putz said, "und jab him vit a sedative."

"Unfortunately," Captain Harrison said, "the sedative

we used was not sufficient to counter his raging, jewel-influenced metabolism for long. Around midnight, while we all slept, Dick awoke. We had not bothered tying him very securely, and he escaped his bonds. He slipped out, hijacked our remaining scout ship, and took off. Awaking, we mourned and cursed this desertion. But it was only during a routine inspection the next day that we discovered your boyfriend's cruel parting gift."

A few tears trickled down engineer Putz's cheeks. "Mine beautiful, beautiful tubes! Der *schweinhund* had scoured dem vit common kitchen grease from our galley! Bacon drippings and Crisco smeared all over dose delicate rockets! Somehow he knew dot der organics vould foul dem beyond repair! Six months vee labored, first to discover a deposit of dohenium, den to excavate, smelt, refine, and shape der material into new linings."

Captain Harrison proudly nodded at the heroic past exploits of his sturdy crew. "Even Doheny himself, that mad American who perfected the atomic blast, could not have done better."

Leroy spoke. "But zee new tubes were not perfect. We could not risk zee high-energy burns zat had brought us so swiftly to Mars. We had to crawl home on a slower ballistic. And once all zee Brie and Beaujolais ran out, it was hell!"

Captain Harrison added yet more infamy to Dick Jarvis' name, causing Fancy to quietly weep anew.

"Of course we tried to raise Jarvis on the scout ship's radio and convince him to return and help us. The return of the scout would have made our repairs so much easier. But when he deigned to speak with us, all we could get from him were insane rants. Apparently, he had managed to hook up again with his beloved feather duster, Tweel. Together, they had taken over the city of the barrel beasts, setting themselves up as despots with the aid of the healing crystal. But that wasn't the worst of it. Jarvis would rave for hours about the God of Mars. Somehow he had learned of the myth of this pagan deity through Tweel. Now he had some crazy plan for making contact with this superior being."

Putz patted his pistol. "I vill make contact vit dis God of Mars, all right. Right after vee settle Jarvis' hash."

Drying her eyes with a frilly hanky she removed from the hip pocket of her rubber coverall, Fancy put a bold and optimistic face on their mission. "I understand the situation more clearly now. I'll do everything in my power to convince Dick to abandon his megalomaniacal delusions and return with us to Earth for professional help from Zurich's best alienists." Fancy straightened her back and saluted winsomely. "You can count on me, Captain."

His stern mien brightening, Harrison returned the salute crisply, then said, "What are waiting for then, crew? Let's go corral our lost sheep!"

* * *

Several hours into their flight, as they soared across the barren, canal-slashed sands of the Red Planet, their underbelly film cameras recording every inch of the journey for rapt appreciation by the televid audience of Earth upon their return, the four people crammed into the small scout ship shared a certain apprehensive silence. Out the cockpit windscreen clearly loomed the strange object that had cast the quartet into this blue funk. The anomalous fixed feature on the landscape had seemed to rise monolithically above the horizon as they rocketed around the curve of the globe. After several hours of supersonic flight, the enigmatic object had swelled to fill most of their forward-facing window.

"At first I thought it was some sort of natural bluff or mesa," Captain Harrison said, "although no such geographical feature appears on our maps. But now it's apparent that we're viewing some kind of construct. A monumental curving wall or tower larger than anything ever seen on Earth."

"Der lesser gravity permits extraordinary architectural feats," Putz said. "But how could Jarvis have accomplished so much in only five years?"

"Don't forget," Leroy said, "once he became zee Napoleon of zee barrel beasts, he must have had all zair resources at his disposal."

"And most importantly," Fancy said, "despite his madness, he's still a human, the top-dog species in the solar system. And Dick was always a 110-percent he-man."

Putz snorted, Leroy rolled his eyes ceilingward, and Harrison politely coughed.

"What?" Fancy demanded. "What's the matter with you all? What are you trying to imply?"

"Miss Long," Harrison gently said, "I don't know how to break this to you, but your fiancé exhibited certain deviant tendencies to us on the first trip. Apparently, his libido, ah, flowed in wider channels than that of your normal man."

"Dot's putting it mildly," Putz chimed in. "Remember ven you accused him of being in love vit dot Tveel, und he said, 'So vot, I love you too!'"

Fancy's face flushed nearly as red as the terrain below, and she uttered a stout defense of Dick Jarvis. "That's impossible! I'm sure you're all just misinterpreting some innocent banter. Dick has physically proven his passionate love for women to me many times!"

Leroy smoothed his own Lothario's mustache. "No doubt, *Ma'm'selle*. But trust a Frenchmen in such matters: men who walk both sides of zee street of Eros are more common zen you might imagine."

Fancy snittily replied, "Well, I can't imagine what you need *me* for then. Surely one of you nancy boys could appeal to Dick's raging hormones as well as I could!"

Leroy was unruffled by Fancy's insult. "Perhaps, *cheri*. But why not have backup as well? Dick Jarvis has not seen a human woman in five years. Your presence might very well tip the scales in our favor."

No rebuttal to this cynical view occurred to Fancy, so she fell silent. Meanwhile, the men clustered about their instruments, intently examining the landscape ahead.

"Der optiscope under highest magnification has picked up der city of der barrel beasts," Putz announced. "It is sitting right at der base of der construction."

"Any idea yet of exactly how big that wall is?"

"*Nein*! I have no sense of der proper scale yet, since I do not know der size of der city."

Harrison smacked a fist into his palm in frustration. "Damn! If only the eggheads back home had perfected that radar gizmo they were yakking about before we left!"

"Vhen I rescued der traitor last time, der surface part of der city occupied only a few hectares dotted vit mounds made from dried mud. But mine guess is that it has expanded considerably since den."

Within half an hour, their craft overflew the perimeter of the nonhuman city, and they could see that the newest buildings were sizable brick edifices. Now the still-distant yet dominating wall balefully loomed over them, its top unseen, more like one of Mars' two moons suddenly brought close than any artificial thing. In the labyrinthine streets below, the wiry-legged quadripedal barrel beasts raced about on obscure errands, their upper four limbs engaged in carrying enigmatic objects or pushing their famous wheelbarrows so vividly described by Jarvis.

"Vhere should vee set down, Captain?"

"Try to find the original center of this cursed place. We'll have to assume Jarvis never bothered to move his HQ from its initial location."

Ten further minutes of flight carried them to the unchanged aboriginal portion of the city, a dusty clearing spotted with crumbling tumuli and the occasional scuttling barrel creature. Careful not to injure any of the natives, Putz deftly set the scout ship down between two of the mounds, right next to the weather-corroded hull of the stolen scout from the first mission.

"I'm glad the *Ares II* is safely distant from here," Harrison said. "No sense in giving Jarvis a second chance at fouling our tubes! Well, men—Fancy—let's establish contact with these queer fellows!"

Once the ramp was extruded, the nervous humans descended at a deliberately dignified pace. A creature like a vertical oil drum with a ring of eyes all the way around its circumference awaited them at the foot of the ramp, its four unencumbered appendages snakily wavering, its four lower extremities firmly planted on the ground.

Recalling how these aliens had once learned to parrot a single phrase Jarvis had once used, Harrison raised an open palm and said, "We are friends—ouch!"

The diaphragm at the top of the living drum vibrated in perfect replication of human speech.

"Please do not say 'ouch' unless you are actually feeling pain, Captain Harrison. That particular yokelish expression has become anathema among us, a reminder of our early nescience. Now come with me, please. The high priest Jarvis awaits you."

* * *

No attempt was made either to coerce them or remove their weapons, so the humans warily accompanied their tubular guide, entering the hidden belowground city through the entrance of one of the mounds and embarking down a slanting, well-lighted, temperate corridor.

Captain Harrison made proper introductions to the barrel man and then asked, "Do you have a name?"

"Stanley."

"Well, Stanley, perhaps you can tell us what this enormous construction outside is all about."

"I think the high priest himself would prefer to explain."

"Very well. We certainly have a lot of questions for Dick Jarvis."

"*Ja*, dot's for sure. Und he'd better have some damn good answers!"

Deeper and deeper under the surface they descended, twisting and spiraling past inexplicable mechanisms and scenes of antlike activity. Captain Harrison kept careful record of their trail, employing compass, pencil, and graph paper, so as to avoid getting lost as Jarvis had on his first visit. Leroy and Putz maintained a watchful defense of Fancy, who, to her credit under the trying circumstances, exhibited a calm and level head beneath her blonde curls.

Finally they passed into a large domed room fit for a throne. But instead of any such formal seat, a welter of leathery pillows and exotic fabrics, seemingly more organically formed than artificial, filled the center of the hall.

Sprawled across the cushions in tangled intimacy, like some evil Oriental potentate and concubine (as depicted on the nightly televid news), lay Dick Jarvis and his native bird-friend, Tweel.

Jarvis wore a kind of Robinson-Crusoe-on-Mars get-up, native hides from some anonymous species roughly tailored into trews and vest. Beneath these new clothes, tattered remnants of his old undergarments remained. On his feet, clumsy sandals; on his head, a crude cap. A five-year-old beard draped his chest. Strapped to his brow with leather thongs like some barbaric fillet, the radioactive crystal talisman that the barrel beasts worshipped glowed like a third eye.

Tweel, the sentient ostrich—thin legs with four-toed feet, rubbery neck, four-fingered hands, tiny head with eighteen-inch, vaguely prehensile beak, plump body in which was secreted his powerful brain—that companion who had lured the human away from his very race, looked somewhat the worse for the passage of time as well. His mottled gray-blue feathers had lost their sheen, and a faintly dissolute droop to his neck conveyed some world-weary ennui, or exhaustion from attempting a task nearly too great for mortal strength.

Dick Jarvis registered the newcomers with only faint animation, as if drugged, his heavy-lidded eyes widening slightly and a small smile twitching his chapped lips. He removed his arm from where it had been slung around the feathered shoulders of his equally sluggish companion and clumsily forced himself to his feet. He lumbered across the stretch of pillows and extended his hand. Captain Harrison gingerly shook it, and then hastily let it go.

Jarvis spoke, and the visitors were washed by his oddly spiced, not unpleasant breath. "Ah, my old friends! You'll have to excuse Tweel and me, we were just indulging ourselves in a little recreational inebriation after a day's hard labors." Jarvis removed a small canister from his pocket, uncapped it, and poured some nearly weightless silicaceous BBs into his palm. He snorted them, exhaled with a deep satisfaction, and then seemed to gain new vigor.

Appalled, Harrison demanded, "What are those exotic grains, Dick? Can you be certain they're safe?"

"Surely you recall my description of the spores discharged by the brick-laying pyramid creature I encountered? Well, we have enough of those beings here in the city now to fill all the zoos of Earth, and they produce more spores than we need for breeding purposes. I discovered their pharmaceutical properties strictly by accident one day, but you can bet that Tweel and I have made good use of the surplus since!"

Leroy expressed the shock they all felt. "*Mon Dieu*, man! You are snuffling up zee eggs of a non carbon-based life form!"

At Jarvis' mention of his name, Tweel had levered himself up on his stalky legs and sidled down to stand beside the human renegade. After five years of tutoring, the Martian bird's rubbery forebeak articulated human speech quite well now, in a reedy tenor.

"Cool your jets, Pierre. I bet you mugs all swill down the hooch easy enough."

The quartet from the *Ares II* gaped in astonishment at being thus reprimanded in slang by a sentient struthiod and received a further shock when Jarvis seconded the bird.

"If you've come all this way just to lay a Carrie Nation spiel on me, you might as well go home now. Tweel and I don't need your hypocritical do-gooding. We're on a mission from God."

Harrison tried to smooth the waters. "We're not interested in criticizing your mode of living, Dick. I imagine that isolation and deprivation have bred some sloppy habits that we can help you kick. But we do need to know why you abandoned us so precipitously five years ago—nearly condemning us by your mean-spirited sabotage to join your exile—and what you've been up to since."

"Fair enough. I can sum up all my activities since we parted in a single phrase: the Tower of Babel."

* * *

The stunned silence that greeted this insane declaration was shattered by the harsh voice of the ship's engineer.

"Vot nonsense is dis!" the short-tempered Putz bellowed.

Possessed of an unflappable calm, Jarvis easily replied, "No nonsense of any kind, Karl. I am in contact with the God of Mars, who dwells on the satellite Deimos. Tweel and I are engaged in a project to bring us closer to Him, so that we may more fully receive his divine instructions."

"I haff had enough—" said Putz, making a move for his sidearm. But Harrison restrained him and said, "Let us hear Dick out, Karl."

Jarvis had not blinked at the threat, and now continued his strange story with easy equanimity, lightly touching the crystal indenting his brow as he spoke.

"When I first came into possession of this gem, I began to receive the most bizarre mental impressions, as if some superior being were trying to contact me via telepathy. At first I thought I was going mad! Evidently you all did too, forcing you to dope me and loosely secure me to my bunk. But during that fateful night, as the information began to sort itself out and my overworked brain began to make some partial accommodations, I realized the veracity of my experience, and what I must do.

"In a nutshell, here is what I learned.

"Millions of years ago, extrasolar visitors of surpassing intelligence and moral probity—call them gods, for by our standards they were—established outposts on both Luna and Deimos. They seeded the two prehistoric planets around which the satellites orbited—in both cases, home at this time only to brutish beasts—with thousands of these artificial gemstones, endowing the baubles with curative powers to insure that any intelligent individual yet to develop would cherish them upon discovery. The crystals also had another function, that of communicator with the undying guardian entity left behind on the moon of each world. When utilized by an individual of the appropriate mental development and receptivity, the crystal would unload its story into him.

"And he would be assigned a task.

"The construction of a tower at least one mile high.

"The accomplishment of this feat—a marvel of engineering and social skills—would signal the fitness of his race for the ultimate transcendence. The God left behind would initiate the uplifting of the native race to a level close to His Own, and that race would afterwards join the intergalactic community.

"Mankind had its chance. The biblical legend of the Tower of Babel is pure fact. But the biblical tower was not shattered by an imaginary Jehovah, angry at man's hubris. Rather, after work on the project was abandoned by an impious citizenry, the God of Luna turned his back on mankind. That is the true meaning of the Old Testament allegory. Nowadays, all of Earth's gems are lost. But Mars still has a chance for its own epiphany, and I intend to be the instrument of that salvation."

Jarvis finished his peroration with a valedictory air and awaited a response.

His four auditors stood gape-mouthed in disbelief. At last Fancy Long spoke, causing Jarvis to take real cognizance of her for the first time.

"Oh, Dick, you sound nuttier than Father Coughlin and Aimee Semple McPherson combined! Surely you can't believe all that bushwa!"

"Fancy—is that really you? I thought you were just an afterimage from a dream-beast session. What are you doing here?"

"I'm a real flesh-and-blood girl, Dick! Your girl, if you want her! And I'm here to try to talk some sense into you."

Tweel edged closer to Jarvis, plucking at the human's rude shirt with his odd hand. "Don't listen to her, Dick. Don't listen to any of them. They want you to fail, just like your predecessor on Earth failed. They're from the devil."

Jarvis passed a hand across his face, seemingly confused. "I—I don't know what to say right now. I need some air." But then, without exterior cause, the exile straightened decisively, as if receiving an inner prompting. "Let me show you the tower. Surely you'll sense the reality of the situation then. Stanley!"

The attentive cylindrical Jeeves responded, "Yes, high priest?"

"Arrange transport for us immediately!"

Somehow Stanley communicated invisibly with his fellows, perhaps via radio waves, and in a short time, six more barrel beasts arrived, each pushing a kind of rickshaw.

"Please, be seated," Jarvis graciously commanded. And after everyone had complied, the train set off.

* * *

The rickshaws popped out onto the surface miles away, at a busy construction site. The sun was well past its meridian, and already the bone-penetrating chill of the Martian night could be warily anticipated. This far from the shelter of the scout craft, the humans would be reliant on the good will of Dick Jarvis, Tweel, and their uncanny subjects in order to survive the night.

Clustering uneasily around Jarvis and Tweel, the Earth people found their attention inevitably drawn to the incredible wall only a few hundred yards away. This close, its known curvature was masked. Looking heavenward, the humans could gain no sight of its top. The structure was compounded of nothing more substantial than small bricks in an infinity of courses.

Dick Jarvis proudly regarded his accomplishment, like some Pharaoh ogling his pyramid.

"Ten miles in diameter at the base here, tapering as she ascends. And after a mere five years, she's already half a mile high. The outer wall has two integral helical ramps, the clockwise one for upward traffic, the other for down. You should see the intersections; it's like a barrel-beast ballet. If there are any collisions, we just push the victims over the edge. Ground crews clean up that debris. Sometimes they get hit by the falling trash and have to get swept away themselves! Let me show you one of the brick lines."

Jarvis conducted them across the bustling grounds, across which innumerable barrel beasts pushed wheelbarrows both empty and full. They came upon a long row of lumpy, rugose creatures anchored in the sand, paralleled by a slowly but efficiently moving procession of cylindrical workers and their wheeled hods. Now Tweel took over the lecture.

"When Dick and I discovered the first of these creatures, we noted that it produced one brick internally for its monumental carapace approximately every ten minutes. We were able to stimulate this rate of brick-creation considerably. Now each creature makes one brick every ninety seconds. By precisely staggering their startup times, we contrive an assembly line such that a barreloid can fill its empty wheelbarrow with 100 bricks simply by walking down the line at a moderate pace. Observe."

The process was just as described: the first featureless, gray creature moored in the soil reached down its gullet with its lone arm, extracted a brick and laid it in the empty barrow poised to intercept it. The brick carrier moved on a few paces to the next living kiln and garnered a second brick. And so on for 100 instances. Once its barrow was loaded to capacity, the barrel beast raced away to the foot of the ascending ramp. Meanwhile, staggered ninety seconds after one barrel beast came another.

Dick Jarvis beamed. "All the components of the system work around the clock. And when they wear out, we just bring young, fresh units onto the line. Our breeding programs are tremendously efficient. You know how the brick makers reproduce—those loco-coco BBs! But perhaps you forgot what I learned years ago about the barreloids. Stanley, come here!"

The loyal factotum approached, and Jarvis searched its body for a moment before finding what he wanted. "Look here! A bud! These things reproduce like Brussel sprouts!" Jarvis pinched the immature offspring nodule on Stanley's hide, twisted, and off it came. He popped it into his mouth, chewed, and swallowed. "And they taste pretty much like Brussel sprouts too. That's how I've survived so well!"

Captain Harrison stammered out a horrified response shared by one and all. "Guh-guh-good Lord, Dick! But this is monstrous! You've perverted the sacred principles of Henry Ford into a kind of nightmarish slave society even Edgar Rice Burroughs himself couldn't envision! And all in the service of a mystical delusion!"

Tweel stepped forward, his close-set avian eyes hard as the tower's bricks. "You must not criticize the high priest."

The muzzle of Putz's gun centered on Jarvis' stomach. "Vee vill continue dis fascinating discussion back on der ship. Get your hands in der air, Dick, and do as I—"

Putz ceased speaking and looked down at himself in horror.

Tweel's light, feathery body seemed glued to Putz's torso, while from the engineer's back protruded the gore-smeared beak and head of the javelin-deadly ostrich.

* * *

Pierced front to back through heart, lungs, and other essential organs, Putz dropped his gun, burbled, and collapsed to the unforgiving sands in a welter of blood. Tweel adroitly withdrew his deadly head and neck before becoming pinned down and hopped backward from the corpse. The bird opened the leather pouch he wore about his long neck, withdrew a square of cloth, and began to fastidiously clean himself of the evidence of the hideous murder.

Before any of Putz's comrades could come to succor him in his dying moments, they found themselves pinioned by several of the barrel beasts summoned by Stanley. Fancy, Leroy, and Captain Harrison struggled in vain against the tendrils enwrapping them.

Dick Jarvis exhibited no emotion other than a faint distaste. "Too bad for Karl, but he brought it on himself. Tweel is my brother. We guard each other's back. And nothing must be allowed to interfere with our holy tower."

Tweel had finished his finicky ablutions. "Quite correct, Dick."

"What are you going to do with us now, you madman?" demanded a shaken but defiant Captain Harrison.

"You and Leroy will be locked up. But you won't mind, since your jailer will be pleasant company. As for Fancy, I think Tweel and I will entertain her ourselves."

At this unwelcome announcement, the lady under discussion fainted dead away, prevented from falling only by the embrace of her barreloid captor. Without further ado, all three captives were lifted off their feet and carried away at high speed, while Jarvis and Tweel followed in their rickshaws.

Down, down, down they went, to a dim dungeon level of the city. The barrel beasts unceremoniously thrust Captain Harrison and Frenchy Leroy into a small cell, which, oddly enough, boasted neither a door nor bars. Seated in his carriage in the corridor, Jarvis spoke.

"I'm certain you recall my description of the carnivorous dream-creature from which I first rescued Tweel. A nest of ropy limbs and a slavering maw, able to project hallucinations that lure its victims to their doom. Well, you two men start with the advantage of knowing that what you face is a deadly illusion. But even so, we will see how long you are able to resist the beckoning allure of the telepathic monster!"

Jarvis reached out to press a button inset beside the doorway, and the rear wall of the cubicle began to slide upward, revealing the hideous pedal extremities of the captive dream-devil. Harrison and Leroy backed up into the farthest corners of the cell as the first burgeoning fingers of the seductive mesmeric impulses reached them, conjuring up private visions of longing.

Laughing insanely, Jarvis signaled departure for the rest of his entourage.

* * *

Fancy Long awoke in a warm, pleasantly scented bed, keeping her eyes closed for a moment just to savor the comforting sensations. What a nightmare she had had! No doubt she would open her eyes to see the familiar outlines of the cabin of the *Ares II*. No, make that her Hollywood hacienda. She was home in the Los Angeles hills, and tomorrow she would go shopping at all her favorite stores—

"Fancy, my dear, you cannot know how many times I have dreamed of this moment."

Fancy shrieked, and her eyelids flew upward like snapped roller-shades.

Naked except for a pair of ragged Earth briefs, Dick Jarvis had considerately shaved off his long beard and scrubbed himself clean of Martian grit. For one brief moment, Fancy could almost believe that her old suitor stood before her, and that they occupied a suite in the Waldorf. But then her eyes fastened on the cursed jewel bound to his brow, and she knew herself in the direst of straits.

Jarvis cooed to her in what he must have assumed was a reassuring tone, but which had the opposite effect. "Oh, my tame dream-beast could always provide a simulacrum of you obedient to my every command, for my erotic enjoyment. But having the real, tangible woman here—that is a paradise beyond compare. And to be able to share with my brother—!"

Horrified, Fancy turned her head to find Tweel's head resting on a pillow only inches from hers.

"I am most anxious to observe the mechanics of human mating. Perhaps I might even be able to assist at some point, although from what I am given to understand by Dick, my private anatomy is most unsuitable."

Fancy willed herself to lose consciousness, but apparently she had used up her fainting resources during Putz's murder. The most she could do was close her eyes, grit her teeth, and pretend that she lay upon the casting couch of the least loathsome televid producer.

The next interval was always to remain a merciful blur in Fancy's memory, a period of a thousand mingled sensual impressions, some of them not unpleasant, some of them approaching pain, with the former perhaps more disturbing than the latter. The roving hands, the twining legs, the feather-seated probing appendage, the rubbery prehensile beak— No, best to draw a curtain over it all.

When Fancy's personality finally reassembled itself into a coherent whole, the naked woman found both her sated assailants fast asleep beside her. Taking stock of the chamber, Fancy noted a small shrine of terrestrial possessions maintained by Jarvis: a framed 3-D portrait of Fancy herself, an empty can of coffee, a radio set—and a standard-issue Space Command .45 pistol.

Praying fervently, Fancy slid slowly out from between man and bird without waking them. She moved on tiptoe to the shrine, took the pistol in hand—

"What are you doing, Miss Long?"

Standing up, Tweel confronted her impassively from the rumpled bedclothes.

No thoughts passed through Fancy's mind before she fired, blowing off Tweel's tiny head.

Naturally the shot awoke Dick Jarvis, who instantly sized up the situation. The man uttered a wild ululation of grief and flung himself upon the writhing Tweel, whose midriff-concealed brain strove to deal with the pain of decapitation and loss of sensory organs. Jarvis grabbed a bit of cloth to fashion a tourniquet for Tweel's bleeding stump, and at that exact moment Fancy dived in to rip the jewel from his forehead.

The evil crystal came away with a harsh tearing sound, and Jarvis bellowed, then collapsed. Still nude, Fancy dashed from the room.

Encountering a lone barrel beast in the corridors, Fancy flashed the gemstone at it and commanded, "Take me to the other humans!"

Wrapping her voluptuous form in its neutral, dry embrace, the alien promptly complied.

Harrison and Leroy had cast themselves upon the floor of their cell in an effort to crawl to freedom. Their bloodied fingertips testified to their determined striving to counter the compulsion to submit to the slavering dream-beast. But otherwise, they proved unharmed as Fancy lowered the shielding wall, freeing them from the ill effects of the telepathic carnivore.

Gaining his feet, Captain Harrison sized up Fancy's condition and swiftly realized she had made the ultimate sacrifice for their rescue. He bravely saluted her, then took command.

"Back to the scout! Once we're onboard the *Ares*, we'll even the score!"

* * *

The leaderless, disorganized barreloids could offer no interference to the human attack. It took hours and hours of steady play of the inexhaustible Doheny jets at several points along the base of the tower to weaken it sufficiently to trigger its collapse. But when half a mile of masonry finally came down, the results repaid their efforts with a cataclysm equal to several N-bombs, effectively vaporizing the city of the barrel beasts, including the unfortunately abandoned corpse of Putz, and—presumably—Dick Jarvis and his avian catamite, Tweel.

In orbit around the ruddy world, preparing for the long trip home, the survivors of the second Terran mission to Mars exhibited a sober demeanor consonant with their horrible experiences. Finally Fancy broke the introspective funk.

"You don't suppose there was any sense in Dick's madness, do you? Could there be representatives of an intergalactic civilization on Luna and Deimos, virtual gods?"

Captain Harrison stroked his chiseled chin thoughtfully before replying. "If we ever find them, a few N-bombs should settle their hash. What nerve, interfering with human destiny!"

Fancy made no reply, but merely considered the small crystal souvenir stashed among her personal luggage. Not that she would ever use it, after seeing what the gem had done to poor Dick. But diamonds *were* a girl's best friend.

Now here's *a story that is indeed as deliberately cynical as I could make it. The anthology that this story first appeared in—*Redshift, *edited by Al Sarrontonio—established as its* raison d'être *the publication of shocking or taboo pieces. I sought to meet the mandate.*

What could be more sacred than these spontaneous displays of sorrow that nowadays appear at every national tragedy? If I could kick the shit out of this sacred cow, I'd really be pushing the envelope, I thought.

A few weeks after Redshift *appeared, the* Onion—*that wonderful journal of twisted humor—tackled the whole topic, in a quarter of the space I took, and was even funnier.*

So it goes.

Weeping Walls

"I *want* those fucking *teddy* bears, and I want them *yesterday!*"

Lisa Dutch bellowed into the telephone as if denouncing Trotsky in front of Stalin. Tectonic emotions threatened to fracture the perfect makeup landscaping the compact features of her astoundingly innocent yet vaguely insane face. Eruptions of sweat beaded the corn silk-fine blonde hairs layered alongside her delicate ears.

Seeking her attention, Jake Pasha was waving a folded newspaper under Lisa's charmingly pert nose and toothpaste-blue eyes, and this impudence from her assistant infuriated her even more. She glared at Jake like a wrathful goddess, Kali in a Donna Karan suit, but—aside from swatting the paper away—she chose to vent her evil temper only on the hapless vendor holding down the other end of her conversation.

"Listen, shithead! You promised me those goddamn

bears for early last week, and they're not here *yet*. Do you have any *idea* how many orders I'm holding up for those bears? I run a time-sensitive business here. We're talking thousands of bereaved husbands and wives, mourning parents, and red-eyed grandparents, all hanging fire. They can't process their *grief* thanks to your goddamn *incompetence*. Not to mention the fucking kids! You can't find your *nose*? Are you fucking *crazy*? Oh, the *bears'* noses! Well, I don't care if you draw the goddamn noses on by hand with a fucking pen! Just get me those motherfucking bears!"

Lisa smashed the phone into its plastic cradle, where fractures revealed a history of such stresses. Now she was free to concentrate on her assistant.

"Unless you stop shoving that paper into my face this instant, Jake, I will tear you a brand new asshole. And while your boyfriends might well enjoy that feature, I guarantee that it will make wearing your thong at the beach an utter impossibility."

Jake stepped warily back from Lisa's desk and nervously brushed a fall of wheat-colored hair off his broad brow. "My God, Lisa, you don't have to be such a frightening bitch with me! I'm already scared every morning when I walk through the door of this madhouse! Anyway, I was just trying to do my job."

Lisa visibly composed herself, her stormy expression ceding to a professional mask of good-natured calm. She forced out an apology that evidently tasted sour.

"I'm sorry. But these vendors drive me nuts. Our whole business relies on them, and they're nothing but a bunch of sleazy asswipes. Balloons, stuffed animals, flowers, wreaths, banners, candles, sun catchers—you'd think the people who sold such things would be nice, maybe New Agey people. But they're not. You know who the most upfront guys are? The construction guys. Not enough manners to fill a thimble, but if they can't deliver a wall, they let you know right away. They don't string you along like these other pricks."

"Be that as it may, dear, you've got something a tad more crucial to worry about now." Jake flourished the newspaper in a less aggressive manner, and Lisa took it from him. Folded back to the business section, the paper glibly offered its salient headline:

WEEPING WALLS TO FACE FIRST COMPETITOR

Lisa scanned the article with growing rage that wiped away her mask once again. Reaching the end, she exclaimed, "Those scum-sucking bastards! They've ripped off all our trademark features. 'Sadness Fences' my sweet white ass! Even their name's actionable. Our lawyers will be all over them like ticks on a Connecticut camper by this afternoon."

Jake took the paper back. "I don't know, Lisa. I get a bad feeling over this one. Did you see who's backing them?"

"That Aussie-Korean group, Panomniflex. So what? You're scared of a conglomerate whose name sounds like a butt-toning machine?"

"That's a lot of money and power to go up against—"

"I don't give a fuck! We have legal precedence on our side. I invented this whole concept five years ago. Everyone knows that. Before me and Weeping Walls, this industry didn't even exist. Grief was left to fucking amateurs!"

"Granted. But you had to expect competition sooner or later."

"Maybe you're right. Maybe we've been getting complacent. This could be good for us. Get us to kick things up a notch."

"How?"

"I don't know. But I'll think of something. Meanwhile,

I've got to keep all the plates spinning. What's next on my schedule?"

Jake consulted his Palm Pilot XII. "There's a new wall going up right here in town an hour from now. Did you want to attend the opening ceremonies?"

"What's the occasion?"

"Employee shooting yesterday at the downtown post office."

"That's handy. How many dead?"

"Three."

"Sure, I'll go. With that low number of deaths the media coverage should be thin. I don't think I could handle the stress from the aftermath of a full-scale massacre today. Plus, it's nearby, and I haven't been to one of our openings in a month, since that school yard slaughter."

"We could certainly plan your appearances better if we could only remove the random factor from our business—"

Lisa stood up, smoothing her skirt. "No need for you to be cynical too, Jake. I've got that angle completely covered."

Following his superior out of her office, Jake asked, "What's Danny doing these days?"

Lisa sighed. "Same as always. Sacrificing himself for his art. It gets mighty old, Jake."

"Is he making any money yet?"

"Not so you could notice."

"Any luck convincing him to come to work here?"

"Not likely. He swears he'd kill himself first. He'd have to get pretty desperate. Or else I'd have to offer him some unbelievable deal."

"You two are such opposites, I'm amazed you're still together."

"I am a pistol in the sack, honey. And Danny's hung more impressively than Abe Lincoln's assassins."

"Oh, I don't doubt any of that for one blessed minute, sugar."

*   *   *

"Could I hear from the kazoos again, please?"

Danny Simmons, his gangly limbs poised awkwardly as if he were only minding them temporarily until their real owner returned, sat in the front row of the shabby theater, directing his motley troupe on the bare stage. He addressed a quartet of actors situated stage-left and clad like harlequins, standing with kazoos poised at their lips. Before the kazoo players could comply with the polite request, however, Danny was interrupted by a large-bosomed young woman, hair colored like autumn acorns, seated several rows back.

"Danny, I've forgotten my cue."

The mild-faced skinny director turned slowly in his seat and said, "You come in when Lester says, 'The planet's dying!' Carol."

"He's going to call me by my real name? I thought I was playing Gaia."

A long-suffering look washed over Danny's lagomorphic features. "No, Carol. He'll only say, 'The planet's dying!'"

"And then I stand up and face the audience—"

"Correct."

"—and rip open my shirt—"

"Right."

"—and I say—I say—"

"Your line is 'Gaia lactates no more for cuckoos born of hominid greed!'"

Carol's painful expression mimicked that of a pressure-wracked semifinalist in a nationally televised sixth-grade spelling bee. "'Gaia lacks tits for greedy—' Oh, Danny, it's no use!"

"Carol, just calm down. You have another two whole days to practice. I'm sure you'll be fine."

"I've got the shirt-ripping part down pat. Do you want to see?"

The males on stage leaned forward eagerly. Danny yelled, "No, no, don't!" but he was much too late.

The rehearsal didn't resume for a confused fifteen minutes spent chasing popped shirt-buttons and draping blankets solicitously around Carol's chilly shoulders.

Hardly had the drama—script and music by Danny Simmons, directed and produced by Danny Simmons—gotten once more well underway when another interruption intervened.

One of the set-building crew rocketed onstage, hammer in her hand. "Hey, Danny, there's a guy from the electric company fooling around outside at the meter!"

At that instant, the theater was plunged into darkness. Yelps and shrieks filled the musty air. Feet scuffled in panic across the boards, and the sound of a body tumbling down the three stairs leading from the stage was succeeded by grunts and curses.

Eventually Danny Simmons and his troupe found themselves all out in the day-lit lobby. There awaited the theater's landlord, a short irascible fellow who resembled a gnome sired by Rumplestiltskin on one of Cinderella's ugly stepsisters.

"Haul ass out of here, you losers. Your freeloading days are over."

Danny fought back tears of frustration. "But Mr. Semple, we open on Friday! We'll pay all the back rent with the first night's receipts!"

"Not likely, pal. I finally caught a rehearsal of this lamebrained farce yesterday. I was sitting in the back for the whole damn incomprehensible five acts. No one's going to lay down a plugged nickel to see this shit." Semple paused to ogle the straining safety pin that labored to hold Carol's shirtfront closed. "You do have a couple of good assets, but you can't count on them for everything. No, I figure it's better to cut my losses right now. Clear this place immediately so's I can padlock it, and my boys will pile your stuff on the sidewalk."

Defeated, the spiritless actors began to shuffle out of the building, and Danny shamefacedly followed them. Out on the sidewalk, he turned to face the confusingly abstract poster for their show hanging by the ticket office:

GAIA'S DAY OFF

PRESENTED BY THE DERRIDADAISTS

The sight of the poster seemed to hearten him. He turned to rally his friends.

"Gang, I won't let these fatcat bastards break us up! Whatever it takes, I vow the Derridadaists will go on!"

"I am *so* glad," Carol cheerfully offered, "that I have some extra time to practice my speech!"

* * *

"All mourners wearing an official wristband may now step forward."

Dewlapped Governor Wittlestoop, suited in enough expensive charcoal wool fabric to clothe a dozen orphans, despite the hot September sunlight beating down, backed away from the microphone and lowered his fat rump onto a creaking folding chair barely up to sustaining its load. Next to the governor on the hastily erected platform sat Lisa Dutch, knees clamped together, legs primly crossed at the ankles in what Jake Pasha—lingering now obediently close by—often referred to as "the boardroom virgin" pose.

387

Lisa patted the governor's hand. Maintaining her frozen official expression of soberly condoling vicarious grief, she murmured, "Did you get the latest envelope okay?"

Similarly covert, Wittlestoop replied, "It's already in the bank."

"Good. Because I seem to be facing some new challenges, and I don't want to have to worry about protecting my ass in my own backyard."

"Nothing to fear. Weeping Walls has been awfully good to this state, and the state will respond in kind."

"Since when did you and the state become synonymous?"

"I believe it was at the start of my fifth term. By the way, I admired your anecdote today about the relatives you lost in the Oklahoma City bombing and how that inspired you years later to found your company. You had the crowd in tears. Tell me confidentially—any of that horseshit true?"

"Only the part about me having relatives."

Notes of dirgelike classical music sprinkled the air. Among the groundlings, a wavery line had formed: those members of the sniffling audience with the requisite wristbands had arrayed themselves in an orderly fashion across the post office parking lot where the memorial service for the recently slain was being held. The head of the line terminated at a row of large black plastic bins, much like oversize composters. Beside the bins stood several employees from Weeping Walls, looking in their black habiliments like postmodern undertakers, save for the bright red ww logo stitched in Gothic cursive on their coats.

Now the first mourner was silently and gently urged by a solicitous yet controlling Weeping Walls employee to make her choice of sympathy-token. The mourner, a red-eyed widow, selected a bouquet of daisies from one of a score of water buckets held on a waist-high iron stand. The Weeping Walls usher now led the woman expeditiously toward the wall itself.

Erected only hours ago, the fresh planks of the official Weeping Wall, branded subtly with the ww logo, still emanated a piney freshness. At regular intervals staples secured dangling plastic ties similar to a policeman's instant handcuffs or an electrician's cable-bundling straps. The usher brought the first woman and her bouquet to the leftmost, uppermost tie and helped her secure the flowers with a ratcheting plastic zip. Then he led the sobbing woman away as efficiently as an Oscar-ceremonies handler, rejoining his fellow workers to process another person.

Once the mechanized ritual was underway, it proceeded as smoothly as a robotic Japanese assembly line. From the bins, mourners plucked various tokens of their public grief: pastel teddy bears, miniature sports gear emblazoned with the logos of all the major franchises, religious icons from a dozen faiths, sentimental greeting cards inscribed with such all-purpose designations as "Beloved Son" and "Dearest Daughter." One by one, the bereaved friends, neighbors, and relatives—anyone, really, who had paid the appropriate fee to Weeping Walls (family discounts available)—placed their stereotyped fetishes on the official wall and returned to their seats.

Under the cheerful sun, Lisa watched the whole affair with traces of pride and glee struggling to break through her artificial funereal demeanor like blackbirds out of a pie. Then her attention was snagged by an anomalous audience member: some nerdy guy scribbling notes with a stylus on his PDA.

Lisa leaned toward Governor Wittlestoop. "See the guy taking notes? Is he a local reporter I don't recognize?"

Wittlestoop squinted. "No. And he's not accredited national media either. I've never seen him before."

Lisa determinedly got to her feet. All eyes were focused on the ceremony, and no one noticed her swift descent from the stage. Coming up behind the scribbler, Lisa remained practically invisible. She seated herself behind the suspicious fellow and craned for a view over his shoulder.

The screen of the man's handy machine was scrolling his notes as he entered them: *Offer more choices of victim memorial. Favorite foods of dec'd? Finger food only. Maybe cookies? Call SnackWell's. Sadness Fences line of candy?*

Her face savage, Lisa stood. She grabbed the man's folding chair and tipped him out of it. He stumbled forward, caught himself, and turned to face Lisa with a frightened look.

"You fucking little spy! Give me that!" Lisa grappled with the man for his PDA, but he held tight. Empty chairs tumbled like jackstraws as they struggled. Suddenly Lisa relinquished her grip. The spy straightened up, smiling and seemingly victorious. Lisa cocked her well-muscled, Nautilus-toned arm and socked him across the jaw. The guy went down.

Chaos was now in full sway, screams and shouts and frenzied dashes for cover, as if the post office shooter himself had suddenly returned. Lisa spiked the PDA with the heel of her pump and ground it into the asphalt.

Digital cameras had converged on Lisa from the start of the fight and continued to feed images of her reddened face and disarrayed hair to various news outlets. The governor's entourage of state troopers finally descended on Lisa and her victim. The spy had regained his feet and, nursing his jaw, sought revenge.

"Arrest her, officers! She assaulted me for no reason!"

The troopers turned to Governor Wittlestoop for direction. The governor nodded his head at the spy, and the troopers dragged him off.

Lisa sought desperately to explain her actions to the

appalled crowd and invisible media audience. "He was, he was—"

Jake had joined her and, under pretext of comforting her, whispered close to her ear. Lisa brightened.

"He was a Satanist!"

* * *

"Panomniflex continues to deny all allegations of satanic activity by any of its subsidiaries or their employees. Nevertheless, several senators are insisting on a full investigation—"

The well-coiffed CNN talking head inhabiting the small all-purpose monitor on the kitchen counter appeared primed to drone on all night. But Lisa moused him out of existence with her left hand, then carried the dark amber drink in her right hand up to her plum-glossed lips.

"Nice save, Leese."

Danny stood by the sink, peeling potatoes. He sought to create one single long peel from each and was generally succeeding.

Lisa drained her glass. "Thanks, but I can't take all the credit. Jake doesn't know it yet, but he's in for a fat bonus."

Danny sighed. "The productions I could mount if only I had an assistant as competent as Jake! The kind of people who will work like dogs week after week for no pay generally don't come equipped with a lot of, ah—call it smarts? But of course, that's all moot now, with the death of our show."

Lisa refilled her glass from a bottle of scotch, spritzed it, and added fresh rocks, before turning to Danny. "I might have made a nice recovery today, but this move will hardly stop Sadness Fences from trying to eat my lunch. It's only a temporary embarrassment for them. And I just can't figure out yet how to undercut them! Oh, shit—let's talk about your day again, I'm sick of mine. Tell me once more why you won't just take a loan from me to pay off your debts?"

Danny paused from rinsing vegetables to sip from a small glass of white wine. "We agreed that the loan you made to us last year so that we could stage *Motherfoucaults!* would be the last. If the Derridadaists can't find other backers interested in avant-garde theater, then I'm just running a vanity operation. And I don't want that."

"What are you going to do now?"

"Finish making our supper. After that, I simply don't know. I want to keep the troupe together, but not at the expense of my artistic pride."

Lisa kicked off her shoes. "Artistic pride! Tell me about it! That's what hurts me the worst, you know—that these Sadness Fences bastards are buggering my brainchild."

"A disturbing image, Leese, however apt. Do you want mesclun or spinach in your salad?"

"Spinach. Gotta keep the old punching arm in shape."

After supper, the big flatscreen in the den displayed *Entertainment Hourly* to the couch-cushioned, cuddling Danny and Lisa.

Seated at his minimalist desk, hair and teeth platonically perfect, as if fashioned by space aliens as a probe, the determinedly somber yet oddly effusive host launched into a report of the latest hourly sensation.

"Wynton Marsalis led his own jazz funeral today through the streets of Celebration, Florida. Diagnosed last month with that nasty new incurable strain of terminal oral herpes, the plucky horn man quickly opted to go out in style. Taking advantage of last year's Supreme Court decision in *Flynt v. United States Government,* legalizing assisted suicide and other forms of voluntary euthanasia, Marsalis received a special slow-acting lethal injection at the start of the cortege's route. Propped up in his coffin, he was able to enjoy nearly the whole procession, which included innumerable celebrity mourners. Panomniflex even loaned out their animatronic Louis Armstrong to lead the solemn yet oddly joyous wake."

The screen cut to footage of the event: in front of a team of horses, the robotic Louis Armstrong clunked along with stilted steps, mimicking horn-playing while prerecorded music issued from its belly. The human participants enacted their roles more fluidly, weeping, laughing, tossing Mardi Gras beads, and giving each other high-fives. Upright on his wheeled bier, a glassy-eyed Marsalis waved to the watching crowds with steadily diminishing gusto.

Danny clucked his tongue. "What a production. Debord was so right. Our society is nothing but spectacle. I wonder if they paid those so-called mourners scale—"

Lisa's shriek nearly blew Danny's closest eardrum out. "This is it! This is the future of Weeping Walls!" She threw herself onto Danny and frantically began unbuckling his belt with one hand while pawing at his crotch with the other.

"Leese, hold on! One minute, please! What's *with* you?"

"You've got to *fuck* me like you've never fucked me *before*!"

"But why?"

"I want to engrave the minute I realized I was a god-damn genius onto my brain cells forever!"

* * *

"Carol—I mean, Zapmama to Deconstructor. Target in sight."

The message crackled from the walkie-talkie hung at Danny's belt. Danny snatched up the small device and replied.

"Deconstructor to Zapmama. Is your weapon ready?"

"I think so."

"Well, make sure. We can't risk a screwup on our first kill."

"Let me ask Gordon. Gordon, is this what I pull—?"

A blast of rifle fire filled the neighborhood's air and was simultaneously replicated in miniature by the communicator's speaker. From his perch of command atop the flat roof of a ten-story office building, Danny could see small figures struggling to control the balky weapon. At last the automatic rifle ceased firing.

"Dan—I mean, Deconstructor?"

Danny sighed deeply. "Deconstructor to Zapmama. Go ahead."

"My gun works fine."

"Acquire target and await the signal. Over."

Reslinging his walkie-talkie, Danny walked over to the cameraman sharing the roof with him.

"Can we edit out those early shots?"

"No problem, chief."

A bank of jury-rigged monitors showed not only this camera's perspective, but also the views from other cameras emplaced on the ground. All the lenses were focused on a waddling bus, which bore on its side the legend JERUSALEM TOURS. The bus was nosing into a broad intersection full of traffic and pedestrians. Suddenly, the cars in front and back of the bus seemed to explode. Curiously, no deadly, jagged debris flew, nor did any shockwaves propagate. Only melodramatic plumes of smoke poured from the gimmicked vehicles.

The explosion brought out the hidden attackers. Dressed in burnooses and ragged desert-camouflage gear, the very picture of martyr-mad Arabs, they opened fire on the trapped bus. Window glass shattered into a crystal rain, holes pinged open in the bus' chassis, and the passengers slumped in contorted postures. One of the terrorists threw a grenade, and the bus rocked like a low-rider's jalopy. Blood began to waterfall out the door.

The assault lasted only ninety seconds, but seemed to go on forever. Mesmerized, Danny nearly forgot his own role. He fumbled with his walkie-talkie and yelled, "Cut! Cut!"

The shooting immediately ceased. Danny hastened down to the street.

A line of ambulances had materialized, directed by a few bored cops. The bus door opened, and the nonchalant driver awkwardly jumped out, anxious to avoid spotting his shoes with the synthetic blood in the stairwell. The medics entered the damaged bus—seen up close, a twenty-year-old antique obviously rescued from the scrap-heap and repainted—and began to emerge with the victims on sarcophagus-shaped carry-boards.

None of the dead people exhibited any wounds. Mostly elderly, with a smattering of young adults and even a teenager or two, they all appeared to have passed away peacefully. Many of them had final smiles clinging to their lifeless faces. As the victims were loaded onto the ambulances, the bystanders to the attack watched and commented with mournful pride.

"Uncle Albert went out just the way he imagined."

"I thought Aunt Ruth would flinch, but she never did."

"I saw Harold wave just before the end!"

Danny crunched across the pebbles of safety glass to where the elated mock-terrorists clumped. Spotting him, they shouted and hooted and applauded their director. Congratulations were exchanged all around.

"Did those charges go off okay, Danny?" an earnest techie asked.

"Just fine."

"I triggered the squibs a little late," another confessed.

"Next time will be perfect, I'm sure."

Stretching her terrorist's shirt to undemocratic proportions, a gloomy Carol approached. "I'm awfully sorry about that screwup earlier, Danny. Even though they were only blanks, I could have frightened the bus away!"

Danny silently regarded Carol while he tried to parse her logic. "You do know all this was fake, don't you, Carol?"

Carol reared back indignantly. "Of course I do! I've never even been to Jerusalem!"

All the ambulances had departed. A DPW truck arrived and discharged workers who began brooming up the glass. A large tow truck engaged the derelict bus and begun to winch its front wheels up. A car and several vehicles blazoned with the modified WW logo (now reading WW&FE) pulled up, and Lisa and Jake emerged from the lead vehicle.

Clad in a tasteful and modest navy shift, the owner of Weeping Walls took swift strides over to her husband, pecked his cheek, and then turned to address the crowd.

"Thank you, friends, for participating so enthusiastically in the inaugural performance by Fantasy Exits. I'm sure all your loved ones appreciated your attendance today, as we ushered them off this earth in the manner they selected. Incidentally, your DVD mementos will be available within the next three days. As for those of you who have pre registered to commemorate the departure of your loved ones during the accompanying Weeping Walls ceremony, you may now line up in the space indicated by the temporary stanchions."

As the spectators began to herd, Lisa spoke to her crew in lower tones. "Okay, people, let's shake our butts! Our permits only run until 2:00."

In a short time, the standard Weeping Walls arrangement was set up—the prefab wall itself going up quickly on a leased stretch of sidewalk where prearranged postholes awaited—and the friends and relatives of the chemically slaughtered bus riders were being processed through their relatively restrained and somewhat shell-shocked grief.

Lisa and Danny moved off to one side, away from their respective employees.

Lisa's eyes flashed like the display on an IRS auditor's calculator. "Not bad, not bad at all. Fifteen hundred dollars per staged suicide, times sixty, plus the standard Weeping Walls fees from the survivors. A nice piece of change. Even after paying your crew and mine good money, there's plenty left for you and me, babe."

Danny pulled at his chin. "I appreciate having steady employment for my people, Leese. But I continue to be troubled by the ethics of this hyperreal simulation—"

"Ethics? What ethics? These losers were going to off themselves with or without us. We didn't push them into anything. All we did was provide them with a fantasy exit—a trademarked term already, by the way. They sign the consent and waiver forms, get the hot juice in their veins, and then sail away into their fondest dreams of public crash-and-burn. We're like the goddamn Make-A-Wish Foundation, only we follow through with our clients right up to the end."

"Okay, granted. Nobody forced these people into our simulation. But some of these scenarios you've got me writing—I just don't know—"

"Aren't your guys up to some real acting?"

Danny grew affronted. "The Derridadaists can handle anything you throw at them!"

Lisa smiled in the manner of a gingerbread-house-ensconced witch with two children safely baking in her oven and a third chowing down out in the fattening pen. "Good, good, because I plan to ride this pony to the bank just as fast and hard as I ride you."

* * *

"I think you'd better have a look at the deckchairs, Lisa."

Jake Pasha stood tentatively at the door to Lisa's office.

His boss had one phone pinched between her neck and bunched shoulder, and held another in her right hand, while she guided a mouse with her left.

Lisa wrapped up her conversations with both callers and toggled shut several windows before turning to Jake.

"This had better be important."

"I think it is."

Jake made a beckoning motion, and a worker in paint-splattered overalls carried in an old-fashioned wood and canvas deckchair. A legend on its side proclaimed it PROPERTY OF WHYTE STAR LINES TITANICK.

"They're all like this," Jake complained.

Surprisingly, Lisa did not explode, but remained serene. "Oh, I guess I didn't get around to telling you. As I might have predicted, the bastards at Panomniflex wouldn't lease the rights to use the real name, so I figured we'd get around them this way. They've still got a hair the size of hawser up their asses since we pulled this end-run around their pathetic Sadness Fences. Have you seen the price of *their* stock lately? Their shareholders have to use a ladder to kiss a slug's ass. And I hear they're switching to *chainlink* to cut costs."

"But won't our customers complain about the inaccuracy?"

"Duh! Our *customers*, Jake, will be a bunch of romantic *idiots* just minutes away from a watery *grave*. If it makes you any happier, we'll just hit them with the hemlock cocktail before they even board our tub, instead of after. They'll be too woozy to recognize their own face in a mirror, never mind spotting a frigging historical fuck up. Just make sure you round up enough dockside wheelchairs, okay? And don't forget the GPS transponders for the clients. We don't want to lose any of the stiffs once the ship goes down."

"What about the relatives, though? Won't they see the error in their souvenir videos and complain?"

"Those fucking vultures! Most of them are so happy to see their enfeebled parents and aunts and uncles going out in a blaze of glory that they couldn't care less about historical accuracy. Remember, Jake—we're selling fantasy here, not something like a TV docudrama that has to adhere to some rigorous standards."

Jake dismissed the worker with the historically dubious deckchair and closed the door before speaking further.

"Is Danny still talking about pulling out?"

Lisa frowned. "Not for the past couple of days. But I can still sense he's not exactly a happy camper."

"Did you apologize to him about Bonnie and Clyde?"

"Yes, Dear Abby, I apologized—even though it wasn't my fucking fault! Who knew that both of our suicides were junkies, and that the juice would take longer to work on their dope-tolerant bodies? So a blood-gushing Bonnie and Clyde kept staggering around yelling 'Ouch!' after seeming to be hit by about a million bullets and ruined his precious script! God, he is *such* a fucking perfectionist!"

"He's an artist," Jake said.

"My Christ, what do I hear? Are you hot for him now? I wish I'd never told you about his fucking massive cock."

Jake quelled his irritation. "That's not it at all. I just sympathize with his ambitions."

Lisa stood up huffily. "All right. If it'll make you feel any better, I'll pay Danny a visit right now, in the middle of my busy workday, just to show I'm a caring kind of bitch."

"He *is* essential to our continued success, after all."

"Don't kid yourself, sweetie. The only essential one is me."

* * *

"It's just no use, Carol. I can't convince myself that helping people melodramatically die is art."

Perched on the corner of Danny's desk like a concupiscent Kewpie, Carol frowned with earnest empathy. "But Danny, what we're doing—it's so, it's so—conceptual!"

Danny dismissed this palliative jargon. "Oh, sure, that's what I've kept telling myself, for three long months. We were pushing the envelope on performance art, subverting cultural expectations, jamming the news machine, highlighting the hypocrisy of the funeral industry. Lord knows, I've tried a dozen formulations of the same excuse. But it all rings hollow to me. I just can't continue with this Fantasy Exit crap anymore. I thought I could sell out, but I was wrong."

"But, Danny, for the first time in years, we all have regular work in our chosen artistic field. And we're making good money too."

"That was never what the Derridadaists stood for, Carol! We could have all gone into commercials, for Christ's sake, if steady employment was all we cared about. No, I founded our troupe in order to perform cutting-edge, avant-garde theater. And now we're merely enacting the most banal scenarios, clichéd skits out of Hollywood's musty vaults, predigested for suicidal Philistines. And this latest one is the final straw. The *Titanic*! If only that damn remake hadn't come out last year. DiCaprio was bad enough in his day, but that little Skywalker adolescent—" Danny shivered and mimed nausea. "Uuurrrggg!"

Carol seemed ready to cry. "It's me, isn't it? My performances have sucked! Just say it, Danny, I can take it."

Danny stood to pat Carol's shoulder. "No, no, you've been great."

Carol began to sniffle. "Even when I fell off my horse during the Jesse James bit?"

"Sure. We just cut away from you."

"How about when I knocked down all those buildings before you could even start the San Francisco earthquake?"

"They were going to go down sooner or later, Carol."

"And that accident during the Great Chicago Fire—?"

"Insurance covered everything, Carol."

Carol squealed and hurled herself into Danny's arms. "Oh, you're just the best director anyone could ever ask for!"

Danny gently disentangled Carol's limbs from his and began to pace the office. "How to tell Lisa though? That's what stops me. She has such a temper. I know she loves me—at least I'm pretty sure she does—but the business comes first with her. Oh, Carol, what can I do?"

"Well, I know one thing that generally helps in such situations."

"And what might that be?"

"A boob job."

"Carol, no, please, stop right now. Button yourself right back up."

"I know what I'm doing, Danny. You've been so good to me, and now it's my turn to help you. Just sit down—there, that's better. Now let me get this zipper and this snap and this clasp— No, don't move, I've got plenty of room to kneel right here. There, doesn't that feel good? Oh, I've never seen one that was long enough to pop right out of the top of the groove like that!"

"Oh! Lisa!"

"I don't mind, Danny, you can call me by her name if it helps."

"No! She's right here!"

From the doorway, Lisa said, "She's already cast, you bastard. And you're supposed to use the fucking couch I bought you!"

* * *

"Hit that glacier with more Windex!"

Techies on movable scaffolds, looking likes bugs on a windshield, responded to the bullhorned instructions by assiduously polishing the floating Perspex glacier now anchored in the harbor. On the dock, a cavalcade of wheelchairs held the semistupefied, terminally ill, paying customers slated to go down with the fabled luxury liner (an old tugboat with a scaled-down prow and bridge attached that reproduced the famous vessel's foreparts). A host of lesser craft held camera and retrieval crews. Near a warehouse, a standard Weeping Wall and appurtenances awaited the end of the maritime disaster reenactment. Over the whole scene, the January sun shed a frosty light.

Lisa busily moved among the WW&FE employees, issuing orders. To the captain of the tug, she reminded, "Remember, get out past the twelve-mile limit before you sink her." Finally, she turned to her husband.

Danny stood contritely by, his heart and mind obviously elsewhere. But when Lisa rounded on him, he snapped to attention.

"Leese, before I set out on this final charade, I just want to say how grateful I am that you're allowing me to bow out of this whole enterprise. I just couldn't swallow it anymore."

"I'm sure that's what your girlfriend was just about to say when I barged in."

"Leese, please! I explained all about that."

Lisa laughed, and it sounded like ice floes clinking together. "Oh, I'm not angry anymore. I just couldn't resist a little dig. What a rack! She makes me look like Olive Oyl. Tell me—did it feel like getting your dick stuck in the sofa cushions?"

Danny made to turn away, but Lisa stopped him. "Okay, I went over the line there. Sorry. But look—I had something made up for you just to show I still care."

Lisa received from the hovering Jake a modern orange life-vest.

"This is a special vest, Danny, just for you. Look, it's even got your name on it."

"Why, thanks, Leese."

"Let's see how it fits you."

"Gee, do I have to put it on now?"

"Yes, you have to put it on now."

Danny donned the vest, and Lisa snugged the straps tight, like a conscientious mother adjusting her toddler for kindergarten.

"It's very heavy. What's in it? Lead?"

"Not exactly. Oh, look—they're loading the wheelchairs now. You'd better get onboard."

Danny aimed a kiss at Lisa's lips, but she offered only her cheek. Danny walked away. At the top of the gangplank, he turned and waved, bulky in his life-saving gear.

Within minutes the whole armada was steaming out to sea, including the iceberg, now stripped of its scaffolding and under tow by a second tug.

When the fleet disappeared from sight, Lisa said, "Well, that's that."

And then she slowly walked to the Weeping Wall, selected a hot pink teddy bear, and hung it tenderly, her eyes dry as teddy's buttons.

This story was inspired by two back-to-back articles in New Scientist, *my favorite science magazine. Both concerned the new field of "consciousness theory," which tries—sometimes vainly, sometimes successfully—to figure out how the human mind works. Susan Blackmore—memorialized below in the name of a public square—is one of the most radical of the thinkers associated with this exciting new endeavor. Her notion that all we call "self" is a fiction ties in wonderfully with my Buddhist inclinations.*

Now if I could just get this fictional character known as "me" to handle all the scut work in our life and leave all the good times to the real Paul!

Seeing Is Believing

Ron Fewsmith was about to rob a bank.

Armed only with a color Palm Pilot.

In person, not virtually.

Pausing momentarily outside the heavy glass doors of Merchants' Trust, Fewsmith mentally ticked off the steps in his plan again. Recollections from a hundred heist films interrupted, racing across his cinemaphile's brain. But as customers bustled past him, intent on doing their business this bright Monday morning, Fewsmith broke his reverie, realizing he shouldn't dawdle too long in this spot, lest he attract attention. Still, he hesitated a moment longer, highlighting the stages of his scheme.

He felt confident about all aspects involving the human element. Long months of diligent experimentation had left him confident that no individual in the bank would offer him any resistance, so long as he held firmly to his little Digital Assistant and remained free to deploy it. In fact, events should transpire so smoothly that no employee of the bank should realize that a robbery was even in progress. Only reconciliation of the day's transactions later that night would reveal a shortage of cash. And by then Fewsmith would be safely home, untraceable.

No, his only risk lay in the security cameras. The cameras made him sweat. There was no way that he could alter the images recorded by these monitors. Hence his disguise and adopted persona.

Fewsmith wore a large handlebar mustache reminiscent of one a nineteenth-century pugilist might have favored. Colored contacts altered his eyes. His clothing betokened some recent immigrant to these shores, perhaps a rube from the Balkans or outermost Albania. And his burlesque accent had been practiced for days.

Thus armed and accoutered Fewsmith felt, on the whole, confident of success. So: no more hesitation over this highly practical debut of his invention. Into the bank!

After joining the short line of customers standing more or less patiently in the chute of velvet ropes, Fewsmith quickly advanced to lead position. When called by the next available teller, Fewsmith put on a big smile and boldly strode forward.

The teller—a young pimple-faced fellow wearing a clip-on tie—instinctively smiled back. "How can I help you, sir?"

Fewsmith removed a sheaf of tattered foreign currency from his pocket and plopped it on the counter. "You change?"

"Oh, I'm sorry, sir, you'll have to see one of our customer-service reps for that."

"No understand. Please to use translator."

Fewsmith proffered the Palm Pilot, and the clerk reluctantly took it. "Is this like some kind of computer dictionary? What do I do?"

"Push button here."

The teller depressed the indicated control.

Instantly a series of whirling alien glyphs, phantasmagorical in their variety and motions, flooded the color screen. When these icons cleared, they were followed by a compressed digital movie, flickering at a subliminal rate. Fewsmith had carefully crafted the loop out of snippets from an old industrial training film that depicted stacks of cash being removed from a drawer and passed through a teller's slot.

The clerk seemed staggered for a millisecond by this mini-movie, but quickly recovered, his faculties apparently undisturbed. "I'm sorry, sir, but this screen's blank. Your machine must be broken."

Handing the device back, the teller reached into his cash drawer and removed a half-dozen fat stacks of banded cash. His hands seemed to be operating independently of his consciousness, as if two separate personalities shared his brain and body. The effect was disconcerting even to Fewsmith, who had witnessed it before.

Passing the money to Fewsmith, the teller said, "Thank you, sir. Have a nice day."

Fewsmith deposited both the bait money and US cash in capacious coat pockets. "Tenk *you.*"

Fewsmith nodded to the armed security guard on the way out, ready with a second digital movie, tailored for just such a situation and safely stored in the terabyte memory of the PDA, to show the guard if necessary. But the rent-a-cop suspected nothing and merely nodded politely back.

Outside the bank, Fewsmith walked several blocks to an alley. He discarded his mustache in a dumpster, found the change of clothes he had hidden there and swiftly donned them. He transferred the money to new pockets. The Albanian costume joined the mustache in the trash. He retrieved his car another few blocks on and headed home.

Triumph! Willadean would be most proud of him! Perhaps she would even finally consent to go to bed with him.

And if not—well, Fewsmith tremulously admitted a harsh yet welcome truth to himself for the first time. If Willadean continued to play hard to get, he now knew for sure that he could have her against her will, or any woman he wanted.

"Tenk you very much!"

*　*　*

Stingo Strine tilted back the PawSox cap atop his balding head and scratched his gleaming pate. He studied the imploring, hopeful, anxious face of the president of Merchants' Trust, a corpulent fellow named Shawn Hockaday. The immaculately besuited fat man looked as if he were on the verge of tears. Strine felt a deep urge to help the poor guy. But at the moment, he felt as baffled as the executive himself obviously did.

"Play the tape again, please," Strine urged in a desperate bid for inspiration.

Hockaday thumbed the remote control, and both Strine and he concentrated on the screen of the small TV in the president's office.

The camera perspective was from high over the shoulder of the teller at his station. The black-and-white images were remarkably crisp. All events unfolded in plain sight. Nonetheless, they remained as baffling as ever.

The mustached man lent his PDA to the clerk, who studied it for only a moment before returning it, along with approximately $150,000 in unmarked, undye-packed bills. Then the customer left and the teller calmly went about his business.

The tape ended, and Hockaday turned to Strine. "It was a simple holdup note on the PDA screen, wasn't it? That's what it had to be."

"Well, you know, that's exactly what I thought at first. Some new high-tech twist on the oldest routine imaginable. But a simple note demanding dough doesn't explain the rest of it."

Strine referred to the fate of the hapless teller, who had immediately been suspected of collusion with the thief. Upon discovery of his malfeasance, he had been hauled shaking and stammering into police interrogation. Steadfastly denying all wrongdoing or even knowledge thereof, the kid had consented not only to a polygraph test, but also to a course of sodium pentothal. Both approaches had been conclusive.

As far as the teller knew, nothing unusual had occurred that day. No robbery, no foreign customer. When shown the tape of his actions, he had fainted. Revived and white-faced, he looked as if he had walked into his apartment and discovered his doppelganger screwing his girlfriend.

"Any luck on enlarging the screen of the PDA so we could read it?" Strine asked.

"None. The face of the device was blocked by Mr. Fergus' body."

Strine stood up with barely contained irritation. The absurd face of the robber, his baffling actions—both immensely irked him. How had this guy done it? In fact, *what* had he even done? This situation was more frustrating than the Buckner Tunnel. Not since the botched rotator-cuff surgery that had ended his professional career had he felt so powerless.

Strine hated to look uncertain in front of a client, especially one this important. Strine's caseload had been pretty pitiful these past six months and scoring big here could garner him lots more business.

Generally, Strine avoided openly hypothesizing before a client. But in this case, frustration forced the words out of him.

"Maybe the PDA was chemically tainted with some kind of knockout drug or hallucinogen. But the perp didn't wear gloves. And what kind of drug has those effects? Leaving someone awake, making him act against his will, then wiping his memory? Could it be hypnotism? It didn't look like any hypnotism I've ever seen. And it was over too fast."

"Mr. Strine, we summoned you because we felt we needed more coverage than the authorities could provide. But if you feel the dimensions of this investigation are beyond you, perhaps we should call in a larger agency."

"No! Give me a fair shot at it. I've only just come on the case. If I don't have something solid to report in twenty-four hours, then you can yank me off it."

"Very well then. I'll be awaiting your first report."

Strine was ushered genteelly out the back door. Out on the street, he belabored his brain.

Who could he consult about this? What kind of expert? A hacker? But there had been nothing extraordinary about the PDA, no online mumbo-jumbo. No, the answer had to lie in what Fergus had seen on the screen—

What Fergus had *seen*. Now Strine knew whom he had to visit.

If only Professor Parrish Maxfield would talk to him after that very unfortunate date on which Strine had taken her.

* * *

Willadean Lawes gleefully riffled the stack of cash as Ron Fewsmith looked on with hopeful adoration, an adoration tinged, however, with no small impatience.

Her lustrous tawny hair—a mop as big as a muskrat—swirled as Willadean tossed a handful of bills into the air with a shout. She failed to note her boyfriend's subliminal impatience; or, if noted, she could not be bothered to cater to the emotion. The sight of more money than she had ever before beheld utterly captivated her. To think that little Willadean, whom all the good folks of Pine Mountain, Georgia had looked down on as white trash, now had enough money to buy the best house back home in her native town. Well, maybe not the old Bishop mansion, but at least a house better than the drafty shack in which she had been born and raised.

And this was just the start! From here on out, Ron and Willadean were on Easy Street. They'd soon be deeper in cash and all the good things of life than a mudbug in muck. Finally Willadean Lawes would have what she deserved. And when Willadean rolled back into Pine Mountain, dressed in designer clothes and sitting pretty behind the wheel of a big new Cadillac, she'd just like to see Sherri Bishop try to look down her nose at her. Why, Willadean's sneer would be big as a doublewide trailer!

Fewsmith reached across the table and gently stroked Willadean's wrist. "Dearest, what do you say? How about a little reward for your daring bank robber?"

Leaning across the table, Willadean gave her beau a peck on the cheek. His disappointment rivaled her glee.

"Willadean—" Fewsmith stridently began.

"Oh, hush now, Ron. You know I ain't letting you into my pants until after we're married. And there won't be no marriage until we are on a totally solid financial footing. That's why we need to start thinking about making our big score, and soon."

Fewsmith's hand menacingly strayed toward his holstered Palm Pilot, but Willadean only leered in supreme confidence.

"Now don't go thinking you're gonna start sending instructions to my ol' Executive Structure that easily. It's a neat trick you've discovered, but it only works if the victim ain't ready for it. All's I've gotta do is shut my eyes or look away, and your gimmick is useless. And don't think I didn't see you uploading all those porno loops into that gadget, thinking to imprint me with 'em. Lord, I never knew anyone could make plain ol' sex as complicated as those folks did! But you'll just have to restrain yourself a little longer. Grub up some rocks in the pasture or chop some logs for woodpile. That always worked for my Daddy after Momma passed on, God bless her soul."

Fewsmith looked disconcerted. "Pasture? Woodpile? I live in a condominium, Willadean!"

"No matter, you get my drift."

Fewsmith's face assumed a devious expression. "What if I use the Level One Bypasser on some other woman then? Would you be angry with me?"

Willadean experienced a deep satisfaction at this proposal. Having Fewsmith despunked by someone else would be a relief. So long as the unlucky bitch didn't set her claws into Willadean's gravy train. But she was crafty enough not to show her true feelings. Frowning, she said, "Well, I don't know. I'd be awfully jealous at first. But I suppose every man's entitled to a little tomcatting before he gets hitched."

Smiling broadly, Fewsmith said, "It's settled then. I promise you I'll be extremely careful, Willadean. I'll use all the proper protection. You have nothing to fear in the way of venereal repercussions."

Willadean paused a moment to consider her own variegated past love life, then said, "That's mighty thoughtful of you, Ron." Then, despite her initial lack of interest in the topic, she became intrigued by the notion of Ron Fewsmith attempting to seduce some strange woman, even with the aid of his Consciousness Bypassing Device. Hard to imagine any sexual bravado from this joker, even armed with his digital seducer. Why, when she had latched onto him in that yuppie bar a year ago, she damn near had to drag him out from under his barstool.

"You just gonna walk up to some gal on the street and zap her?"

"Far from it. I have a certain, ah, conquest in mind. Someone who's seen fit to deride my scientific abilities in the past. My only regret is that she won't retain any memory of the proof that my theories were correct all along."

* * *

Professor Parrish Maxfield had a run in her stockings, a long hideous laddering from ankle to hemline (and that border hovered well above her knees), visible from across a large room, and the sartorial blemish couldn't have surfaced at a worse time. Not only had she been scheduled that morning to deliver an important presentation to the board of directors of Memetic Solutions, but now the infuriating yet attractive Stingo Strine had shown up on her office doorstep. His humble attitude, literally cap in hand, failed to mollify Parrish. Not only was she irritable from the massed gazes of the board members on her legs rather than on her Power Point slides, but the memory of her first and only date with Strine still rankled.

Last summer, Parrish had promised to take her nephew Horace to a weekend Pawtucket Red Sox game. The PawSox were the farm team for the Boston Sox and usually put on a good show.

Prior to the game, Horace had cajoled her into angling for an autograph from the PawSox's pitcher, one Stingo Strine. The popular Strine was attempting a comeback after complicated shoulder surgery, a comeback that would soon prove impossible. But on that day he was still cocky and confident.

Horace had led his aunt to the lowest tier of stadium

seats. From this vantage, fans could dangle balls and pens down via plastic pails on ropes to the players as they entered onto the field. Spotting Strine, Horace had begun yelling the pitcher's name and jagging his lure like an overanxious fisherman.

Strine had been ready to walk past the offered baseball until he looked up and spotted Parrish. Smiling broadly, he took the ball and scribbled something across it, then trotted out onto the field.

Gleefully, Horace hauled up his prize. He studied the ball, and a confused expression clouded his face.

"Auntie Parrish, what's this mean?"

Parrish took the ball. Strine had indeed autographed it. But he had also included the comment, "Pitchers do it until they get relief," and his phone number.

After her indignation had faded, Parrish inexplicably found herself experiencing a growing interest in this arrogant ballplayer. Did he think he was propositioning a married woman? Did he care? His performance that day, pitching several respectable innings despite obvious pain, also intrigued her.

After returning Horace to his parents, Parrish called the number on the ball.

The next weekend, Strine arrived at her house in a vintage Mustang. He wouldn't tell her where they were going. With good reason, for their destination proved to be a strip club named Captains Curvaceous, "popular with all the hip guys on the team."

The evening went downhill from there, culminating in a short wrestling match in the Mustang that made Parrish feel as if she had somehow vaulted back to 1965.

Several calls afterward from Strine had earned him nothing but the blast of receiver smashing into cradle.

And now here he stood, suitably hangdog and repentant. But intrinsically changed? Parrish had her doubts.

Before she could order him out, Strine launched into an obviously well-rehearsed speech.

"Professor Maxfield, I just want you to know that I'm here for professional reasons, not personal ones. But before I get into the nature of my visit, I'd just like to apologize for my treatment of you last year. I was under a lot of stress then, physical and emotional, and I was hooked on pain meds too. I realize that's not an excuse, but I just wanted you to know where my head was at then. It was a crummy place to be, and you stepped right into it. But things have changed for me since then."

"Oh, yeah? How? Did you get traded to a Little League team?"

Strine winced. "No, I left the game entirely. I finally admitted to myself that my pitching career was over, without ever getting to the majors. It was real hard to let go of a childhood dream, but I think I'm better off now."

Parrish felt bad, despite her ire. Maybe she had misjudged this guy. "So, what are you doing now?"

Strine put his cap back on and took out a business card. Parrish took it, read it, and was stunned.

"Private investigator?"

"It was my uncle's firm. He took me in fulltime last year just before he retired. I used to help him during the off-season, so I had a pretty good grasp of the business."

"And a case now brings you here to me?"

Strine pulled up a chair and earnestly leaned forward. He recounted the whole story of the Merchant's Trust robbery, concluding, "So the only thing I could come up with is, this guy's using some radical, unknown kind of mind-control device. And then I remembered that was your field."

Indeed, during various nervous moments of that awful evening Parrish had babbled about her research. She was surprised that any of her words had penetrated against the competing assaults of lap dances and jello wrestling by bimbos with more silicone in them than a Home Depot caulking aisle. It was a miracle that Strine had remembered her end of the conversation, such as it was.

"Well, I wouldn't call what we do here at Memetic Solutions 'mind-control.' Although we are studying the way various ideas can colonize people's minds. But, yes, there are certain applications . . . " Despite her resolve not to get involved with any aspect of Strine's life, Parrish found herself becoming professionally interested. "Summarize for me again what the robber did."

"He convinced an innocent, honest kid to steal from his employer and then forget all about it. It was almost like he temporarily stole the kid's consciousness or bypassed it entirely."

Parrish frowned. "Bypass— No, it couldn't be—"

"What? Tell me! You onto something?"

Parrish stood up and began to pace. She turned to confront Strine with a demand.

"Tell me—what do you know about modern theories of consciousness?"

"About as much as you know about pitching."

"Well, let me see if I can bring you up to speed. One of the most radical new theories about how our brains work maintains that the self you imagine to be in control of your mind—the structure you might think of as your ego or consciousness—is simply a shallow mask over much deeper processes. And it is these processes that determine our behaviors."

Strine scowled. "You're telling me we're all zombies or puppets? I don't buy that."

"Oh, but in a way, we are. That is, if you insist on identifying only with these facades. But if you chose to displace your sense of self deeper—well then, there's no problem."

"So you say."

Parrish felt rhetorical fire building, her typical reaction to encountering disagreement. "Look, any seemingly reasoned actions you take, any ideas or opinions or conclusions you formulate, any likes or dislikes you characterize as quintessentially 'you'— None of these actually originate in the outer levels of your brain. None of them are a result of the supposedly rational chains of reasoning you can observe, which are in reality always constructed after the fact. They all flow from the depths upward. Even sensory impressions are not permitted to be acknowledged by the mask of consciousness unless the lower levels first select them and pass them on—a process called 'outing.'"

Strine's face reflected the contortions he was going through while trying to internalize this reordering of existence. "What about free will then?"

"Oh, you've still got free will. It just doesn't reside where you imagined it did."

Strine pondered this, then finally said, "It's like the Wizard of Oz."

"Huh?"

"You remember. Everyone thinks Oz is this big glowing head. But Oz is really a little guy pulling levers in a hidden booth."

"Almost exactly! But now imagine that the glowing head has some semblance of fake autonomy and believes that it's really running things. 'Pay no attention to the man behind the curtain,' the head says on its own and believes it! We call this face of Oz 'Level One,' the aspect of your mind that imagines it runs things. Level One is a two-dimensional skin, without actual free will. Level *Two* is analogous to the subconscious, the deep three-dimensional realm where all the important things get hashed out. And the Central Executive Structure is the intermediary between them, the mechanism that selects what will be outed. Level One simply performs and believes whatever the Central Executive Structure sends it. And Level One has no direct access to the workings of Level Two."

Strine lifted his cap and brushed a hand across his bald strip. Parrish thought the humble gesture rather charming.

"Man, this is your job, to sit here all day and think up this weird stuff? And I thought my business was oddball. How can you hope to get anything marketable out of this kind of blue-sky stuff?"

"Well, admittedly, the hypothesis I just outlined has stalled at the theoretical level. I myself have moved on to other areas of research. But there was one guy here who just wouldn't let go of this paradigm. A real fanatic. He kept pushing and pushing, claiming that he was learning the 'protocols' of the Central Executive Structure and the 'grammar' of Level Two. He said his goal was to insert orders into Level Two, which would then be transmitted through the CES and manifest as programmed actions in the subject. He actually got some intriguing results. But he refused to take new direction from the board, and eventually he got fired."

Standing excitedly, Strine said, "A mad scientist with a grudge. That's perfect! What's his name?"

Before Parrish could answer, her intercom bleeped.

"Dr. Maxfield, Ron Fewsmith is here to see you."

* * *

Adjusting the drape of his jacket, Fewsmith opened the familiar door to Dr. Maxfield's office. He pictured himself as the quiet yet deadly protagonist of the Coen Brothers' *The Man Who Wasn't There*, going to his fateful interview with his wife's lover. How often had he passed through this door, eager to share his latest findings with his beautiful coworker, only to be shot down like a love-struck duck falling for a decoy? For that's what Maxfield was: a cold, hard, wooden imitation of the woman he needed her to be. She had derided both his timid overtures of undying love and his scientific discoveries alike. Thank goodness he had fallen in with Willadean, strict though she was! At least Willadean cared for him! True, the difference between the two women was like the difference between Veronica Lake and Christina Ricci. But now the invincible Professor Maxfield would pay for years of insults with her glamorous body, which luckily did not share the hardened nature of her mind. A mind completely amenable, however, to whatever Fewsmith chose to insert within it.

But there was no sense in appearing slovenly, even though Maxfield would retain no memory of his visit. He did not want to endure her contempt even for one embarrassing minute that would later be wiped from her mental record.

Fewsmith strode boldly into the dragon's den. But he was brought up short by the unexpected presence of another person, standing at some remove from Maxfield and her desk. The stranger was a largish, hulking, low-browed type. Obviously not a fellow scientist, but probably one of the janitors here to replace a light bulb. Or, at a stretch, a phone technician perhaps. Although the man held no tools— No matter, he'd be easy to dismiss.

"Hello, Parrish. It's good to see you again."

"I don't wish I could say the same, Ron. What do you want?"

"I'm here to share something of vast importance with you, Parrish. A discovery so enormous that it will revolution-ize life as we know it. But I can only tell you in private."

"No can do, Ron. You can spill anything you want to tell me in front of my colleague here, Professor Strine."

Fewsmith narrowed his eyes on the stranger. Was that ridiculous cap he wore advertising a *sports team*? "*Professor* Strine? Really? I don't believe I've ever seen any of your papers before in the customary journals."

The fellow glared back. "I only publish in, ah, foreign ones."

The man was a buffoon. Fewsmith had no idea what connection Strine bore to Parrish Maxfield, but he was plainly a trivial nuisance. Strine would be easily disposed of once Maxfield had gotten her dose of erotic instructions. "Oh, that explains it then. Pardon me. Very well, I'll be happy to let both of you in on my discovery. You first, Parrish. Just take a look here."

Fewsmith unlimbered his PDA and held it in front of Maxfield's eyes. He triggered the sequence intended specifically for her, and in one short, compressed burst, the visual commands raced past her sight and penetrated her Level Two.

Fewsmith stepped back and keyed up the general-purpose immobilizing sequence he had once intended to use on the bank guard. "Now it's your turn, Professor Strine."

But Strine did not react as expected. Instead, he leaped upon Fewsmith and began struggling for control of the Palm Pilot. The two men clumsily careened around the office, tumbling over chairs and dislodging books from the bookcase, until Strine finally wrested away the PDA. Sweating, frightened, and disheveled, Fewsmith staggered back against the outer door, fumbling for the handle. Grinning nastily, Strine advanced on him.

But then a long low moan interrupted, and both men found their attention drawn to Dr. Parrish Maxfield.

She had stripped off all her clothes and stood writhing and fondling herself like Pamela Anderson at a satyrs' convention.

Strine froze, and the naked professor hurled herself upon the detective, the closest male available, in order to satisfy the script she was running.

Fewsmith used the opportunity to escape. He dashed out past the startled receptionist, fully expecting Strine to collar him at any moment. But the man never appeared, and, out in the parking lot, Fewsmith slowed, panting. He could safely assume that his pursuer had his hands full.

After all, those routines he had scripted—sexual exercises whose delights Strine was even now usurping from their rightful recipient!—were enough to keep any man busy.

Even if the lucky, damnable bastard was trying to escape them!

* * *

The only suitable covering to cloak a naked woman available at Memetic Solutions proved to be a large, silver Mylar sheet from one of the animal testing labs, where semiotic simians passed primitive memes back and forth in controlled circumstances.

Wrapped up like a baked potato in foil, Professor Parrish Maxfield sat on an office chair next to her pile of ripped and unsalvageable clothing. Her disarrayed hair framed an angry face. Her legs were crossed at the knees, and one anomalously shod foot, suspended in mid-air, bobbed with furious impatience.

Strine admired her composure. He doubted that had their roles been reversed, he could have shown such sangfroid.

Battling the amorous advances of the professor had taken all of Strine's efforts. Luckily, the office door had slammed behind Fewsmith on his hasty way out, and no curious coworker had intervened to witness the tussle.

Dominated by the script Fewsmith had uploaded to her Central Executive Structure, Parrish had wrestled Strine to the floor. There, oblivious to his clothed state and lack of cooperation, she had enacted a variety of sexual situations, one posture after another, her face simulating all the requisite emotions and reactions, the appropriate repertoire of sounds and encouragements issuing from her lips. All Strine could do was to hold her tight and constrain her wild bucking so that she did not harm herself.

Needless to say, wrestling with a naked woman—particularly one about whom he had earlier fantasized—caused no small degree of excitement in Strine's own pelvic region, despite the bizarre and unwarranted nature of the attempted copulation. Before too long, Strine's pants could have illustrated the tent pages from the REI catalog.

Thankfully, once Parrish reached the end of the enforced simulation, her instant confusion and lack of immediate memories, her distress at suddenly finding herself naked—all these created an environment that helped Strine conceal his problem until it had subsided.

Strine had initially said, "Everything's okay. Don't worry. It was Fewsmith, but I stopped him. Wait here."

With a half-assed excuse, he had convinced the curious but respectful receptionist of the urgent need for a covering of some sort, and, once the blanket was found, darted back into Parrish's office. She wrapped herself up, and Strine explained everything to her.

Parrish's last memory ended with the receptionist announcing Fewsmith's arrival. So far as Parrish knew, the man had never even entered her office.

As the full implications of what she had just undergone hit her, Parrish Maxfield moved from a flushed embarrassment to rage.

"That bastard! He planned to use me like some kind of

mindless sex toy! Well, there's no question now. I'm coming with you when you go after him."

"Hold on now a minute. This could be very dangerous. I don't think you realize—"

"Dangerous? How could that little twerp be dangerous? We've got his gadget, don't we?"

"Sure. But he must have another or can get one fast. It's just a Palm Pilot after all. It's these files that are deadly, and I'm sure he's got backups of those."

"Hand that over."

Strine gave Parrish the PDA. She jabbed at its buttons. "Don't!"

"I'm just bringing up the directory. Hmmm . . . These file names are pretty cryptic. 'Marching,' 'Surrender,' 'Handover . . . ' Hard to tell what they do."

Something bothered Strine. "How can he construct and review these hypnotic routines without being affected by them himself?"

Parrish powered off the Palm Pilot and handed it back. "Oh, that's simple. If he's really discovered the language of the subconscious, then he must have learned about some command strings, such as one that informs the CES to disregard whatever follows. Kind of like stop and start and skip codons in DNA and protein replication."

"Um, if you say so. But still, I don't feel you should, ah, expose yourself any further to this guy's crazy nastiness."

"Ridiculous! I'm a big girl, and now I have my own score to settle with Mr. Fewsmith. Besides, I can provide backup for you."

Strine considered. He was hardly averse to spending more time in the company of Professor Parrish Maxfield.

"Okay. What's our next step then?"

"First we get Fewsmith's address from human resources. Then we'll need to stop by my apartment for some clothes."

Parrish toggled the receptionist and within minutes had the information they needed.

"Um, do you want me to go to your place and bring the clothes back here?"

"That would waste time. I don't care what people will think when they see me like this. Do you?"

Strine grinned broadly. "Actually, I'd be flattered to be connected to your current condition, as long as you were smiling about it."

Parrish tried to look sober, but failed. Her wry grin made Strine desire her all the more. "Don't get any funny ideas. This is strictly a business arrangement."

"Right." Strine reminded himself that many business arrangements in which he had been involved had ended up in one or both parties getting screwed.

The young receptionist's hands stopped midglide above her keyboard, and her eyes behind her funky glasses widened to dramatic dimensions. Holding her head high, Parrish strode by her with a curt, "I'm taking the rest of the day off, Enid."

Half suspecting another attack by Fewsmith, Strine protectively hovered over Parrish until they were safely in his car.

"Got rid of the Mustang, I see."

"It's garaged. I use it on the weekends. But it's too conspicuous for stakeouts and tailing people."

"Still, an old Buick with body rot isn't much of a babe magnet."

Strine sighed. "It came with the firm. My uncle— Jesus, I don't know what kind of sex maniac you take me for! Just because I tried to get in your pants once."

"Twice, counting today."

Strine grew angry. "Listen, honey, a different kind of

guy would have jumped your bones while you were out of it without a qualm."

Parrish looked contrite. "That's true. I apologize. I guess I'm a little more distraught about what happened than I wanted to admit."

"Okay. Apology accepted."

"By the way—did you just use the word 'qualm?'"

"What's the matter? Can't a ballplayer—an ex-ball-player—have a literate vocabulary?"

"Sure. But 'qualm?'"

"How about 'the aginbite of inwit' then?"

"Oh, a Joyce scholar in juvenile headgear!"

Strine shrugged off the jab. "Being on the road most of the summer means you read a lot."

Parrish seemed done with teasing. She said nothing, but continued to study Strine until he actually grew uneasy.

Once Parrish had dressed again, they headed across town to Fewsmith's last-known home.

On the way, Strine wanted to talk some more about this whole new way of regarding human awareness.

"Despite everything I've seen, I just can't quite believe our brains work the way you and Fewsmith claim they do. Like now, when I'm talking with you. How can some shallow mechanical construct be formulating all this speech?"

"It's not. Your Level One is just relaying rapidly formed sentences that have been outed by the CES from your Level Two region."

"I just can't buy that."

"That's because one of the most vital artifacts of Level Two is a belief in the primacy of Level One, as a kind of public face for daily interactions. Look, where did you get that word 'qualm' a minute ago? Was it a conscious choice? Could you have predicted even a millisecond ahead of time that you'd use that word? No, of course not. As Professor Jeffrey Grey says, 'Consciousness occurs too late to affect the outcomes of the mental processes it's apparently linked to.' Simply put, the Level One persona you imagine to be in charge is nothing more than a monomolecular film over the depths of your mind. Let me ask you this: who's driving?"

"Huh?"

"Who's driving the car right now while you're talking with me? Are you consciously steering and using the brake and accelerator? Or are subconscious routines handling everything, well below your Level One awareness?"

"But that's just training and habit and, and—"

Strine's brain—every level—began to hurt. He stopped talking before he made it worse.

They parked a block away from Fewsmith's building. Without any concierge, the premises offered little barrier to Strine's expert skills: he awaited the entry of a resident and slipped in behind the unsuspecting fellow. Soon he and Parrish stood in front of Fewsmith's apartment door.

"What now?" Parrish whispered.

Strine placed an ear to the door. "I don't think anyone's home. I'm going in. You willing to break the law?"

"Against this jerk? Of course."

The interior of Fewsmith's home—and it was definitely his, as revealed by some junk mail on a tabletop—was in wild disarray, revealing a hasty exit, possibly permanent. Dresser drawers had been left open, and a suitcase with a broken zipper lay discarded.

"He's split. Damn it! *Now* how do we find him?"

Parrish held up a frilly slip. "Can you believe that creep was actually living with a *woman*? What did he want with *me* then? Just revenge?"

"Maybe his regular girlfriend couldn't conduct science-type pillow talk with him."

"Yeah, right, like that routine he zapped me with even included foreplay."

Strine kicked angrily at the abandoned suitcase. "If only we could read those files without being forced to enact them! They might give us a clue. Say, maybe I could put myself through them, and you could take notes and try to guess what each one represented . . . ?"

Parrish pondered this suggestion. "No, too iffy. How could we be sure what real-world action was represented by some odd set of calisthenics? And what if some routines were meant to inflict harm on the subject or on others? No, we need to be able to review the routines harmlessly, just as Fewsmith does— Wait a minute! I know someone who might be able to do just that!"

"Let's go then!"

On the way to the car Strine asked, "Who is this person? Another scientist?"

"No, she's my guru, Kundalini Glastonbury."

This time it was Strine's turn to stare at Parrish.

*   *   *

Busy daydreaming about her new life to come back in Pine Mountain—she had just shocked all the mousy women at the church social with her chic clothes and big-city ways for the hundredth time—Willadean was unprepared for the alarming entrance of her frustrated lover-in-name-only.

Fewsmith's mild face was reddened with consternation and exertion. His flyaway hair resembled a badly groomed shih-tzu's. He was huffing and puffing and it took him a few seconds to get his words out.

"They know it's me! They know it's me!"

Willadean jumped up, instantly tense and infuriated. "Who knows about you? Out with it, peckerhead! What happened?"

Fewsmith recounted the fiasco in Parrish Maxfield's office. Willadean relaxed just a little when he finished his tale.

"Okay, let's look at this objectively like. You show this scientist gal your little computer screen, and she gets all sexed-up and goes into heat. Then the stranger starts brawling with you. Maybe he was just jealous you turned on his nerd girlfriend. How's any of this connect you to the bank job? Your old flame ain't gonna remember nothing, and the guy who whomped you don't know you from Adam's uncle."

"But why did he jump me so fast? Maxfield hadn't even had time to react to the instructions, but he was on me! It was as if he recognized what I was doing. That's the only explanation. The cops have already been to visit them, seeking their help, and they were warned in advance of what I could do."

Willadean glowered. "You know, you just might be right for once. Okay, we can't take any chances. We're gonna have to go for the big score right now. Screw any more planning! Luckily we've still got a few hours until the armored car pickup at 5:00. Meanwhile, we pack up a few things right away, load our car, and cruise around till 5:00, killing time. Once we have the dough, we hit the road with no one the wiser. Are you sure the guards pick up a million dollars every day?"

Fewsmith seemed to be regaining a little composure. "At least." He went to his desk on which, sat a PC, unlocked a desk drawer, and removed a second Palm Pilot. He cabled it into the bigger machine. "You start packing. I need to download a few routines. It's all prime material, derived from several exemplary films, including a segment from one very fatal thriller for anyone who crosses us this time. In fact, I just hope that guy who was in Maxfield's office shows up again! I'll settle his hash!"

Willadean patted the scrawny shoulders of her meal ticket. "That's the way to talk, tiger. But don't forget my part just cause you've got a hard-on to get your revenge. Where's that tape I need?"

Fewsmith dug out a standard videotape cassette. "Here you go."

"And this is gonna work just as good as your dinky computer thing?"

An exasperated sigh gave evidence that Fewsmith's temper was still not in equilibrium. "Of course! I take control of people through their visual systems. It doesn't matter how the instructions are delivered. They could come through a *flipbook* if you could flip the pages fast enough! No, there's nothing to worry about on that end. But are you sure you can get into the control room?"

Willadean bumped Fewsmith with her bountiful hip, almost sending him staggering. "Didn't I spend a couple of months already cozying up to this bird? He's already let me in once while he was alone on duty, and we tore us off a— I mean, we had us some smooching."

Fewsmith looked forlorn. "Willadean, if I thought you were giving your favors out left and right to everyone but me—"

Enveloping the smaller man in her capacious bosom, Willadean said, "Aw, honey, you're so cute when you're jealous."

And so goddamn annoying, she thought.

* * *

Parrish felt a little guilty intruding on Kundalini Glastonbury at this hour. Glastonbury conducted a lunchtime session of astral travel instruction for busy office workers who couldn't attend her nighttime classes. Then, from 1:00 to 2:00, the guru locked her classroom door and took her own vegan lunch, followed by a session of meditation and pranayama breathing to get herself centered for the rest of her equally busy afternoon. And now here Parrish blew in, interrupting her spiritual guide's only private time. But such impoliteness couldn't be helped if they were to catch Fewsmith before the renegade memetician could subject anyone else to his mind games.

On the drive over, Strine had quizzed Parrish with genuine curiosity about her outré spiritual practices. He seemed baffled at the seeming incongruity with her scientific side. Finally, Parrish had gotten exasperated.

"Listen, nothing says science has all the answers about the universe. Haven't you ever heard of 'hidden variables?'"

"No. What are those?"

"The postulated rules of the universe that exist down below any level we can observe, and which would explain all the seeming inconsistencies of modern physics and other disciplines. I'm a firm believer in them. And my teacher helps me access that side of existence."

Strine snorted. "Fairies. Elves. And I thought ballplayers were superstitious."

Parrish folded her arms across her chest. "All we care about now is results, not how we get them. At least give Kundalini a chance."

"Wasn't that a John Lennon song?"

"Jerk!"

It took Glastonbury several minutes to respond to their insistent knocking. But at last she appeared, a petite woman, with a mop of tight blonde curls and startling eyes like chips of Arizona sky, wearing a worn green leotard that had plainly seen many a backbend.

Seeing only Strine at first, Glastonbury scowled. "Mister, this had better be the number one crisis of the last ten kalpas—" But when Parrish stepped forward, the bristling yogini softened.

"Kundalini, I'm sorry to interrupt your private time, but we desperately need your help."

"Come in, dear, come in."

Glastonbury was brought up to speed in only minutes. Unlike Strine, she easily accepted Parrish's paradigm of human mentality as conforming to facts she already knew under another guise.

"I think I can handle these deviant instructional blasts," the small woman said with utmost confidence. "They're just like intrusions by Tibetan *dons* into the *alaya* level of consciousness." Not for the first time, Parrish found herself wondering just how old Glastonbury was. "I'll disconnect my mind from my body entirely. The routines might run internally, but they won't make it past my temporary barrier. But tell me this: what am I looking for?"

Strine, who had been impolitely rolling his eyes at this talk, said, "Except for his vindictiveness against Ms. Maxfield, Fewsmith seems mainly motivated by money. So we're after something like the trick he pulled at the bank, something involving cash or other valuables."

"Very well. Just give me about five minutes to prepare myself. Then you can start showing me the movies."

Glastonbury did not assume a full lotus, but rather reclined on her back on the floor, her muscles going slack.

"The corpse position," Parrish whispered.

After allowing the stipulated time to pass, Parrish positioned herself to hold the PDA above Glastonbury's open eyes. Then, one by one, she launched the various mental-subversion files.

Aside from a few minor twitches, Glastonbury exhibited no effects from watching the preemptive commands.

Apparently her Level Two and CES had been completely snipped out of the motor loop.

"Jesus," Strine said, "I never would've thought it possible—"

Parrish paused long enough to spare her partner a gloating smile.

Finally the directory was exhausted. Parrish handed the demonic device back to Strine, and he stuck it in a back pocket. The investigators sat back for several minutes while Glastonbury came out of her suspension.

"Whew! I feel like I just had a three-day workout with Mr. Iyengar's evil twin! This technology is absolutely perverted, Parrish. I trust you'll make sure it does not spread."

"Yes, mahatma."

"C'mon, c'mon! Any leads? Do you recall anything that could help us?"

Glastonbury fixed a penetrating gaze on Strine and said, "Before I gaze into my crystal ball, you must cross the gypsy's palm with silver."

Strine had his wallet out but stopped when the two women began to giggle. Chagrined, he repocketed his cash and finally joined them in laughter.

When they had finished chuckling, Glastonbury said, "There's one image that seems relevant. I saw people pointing to a giant television screen mounted on a building. Then the screen began showing them what to do. Money was involved somehow. But the rest of the details are hazy. My Level Two isn't much more forthcoming than yours, I'm afraid, after those unnatural assaults."

"Giant television on a building . . . Not the stadium then—that screen's freestanding. It's got to be that big screen unit down in Blackmore Square. It's the only one in town. Let's go!"

Glastonbury made a bow to usher them out that Parrish returned.

Give Strine credit: he tried to copy the elegant gestures of the women, despite ending up, thought Parrish, looking rather like a bobble-head dashboard figurine.

* * *

Waiting nervously a few feet away from the parked Wells Fargo truck in Blackmore Square, Ron Fewsmith examined the bandages wrapping his left hand. Bulkier than required by any unswollen appendage, the wrappings concealed his deadly Palm Pilot, leaving the screen exposed. Wary of flashing his instrument of coercion—surely the police would be watching for just such a move after the bank heist—Fewsmith had conceived of this concealment. Additionally, the sympathy generated by the sight of the bandages should help focus the attention of his victims on the display.

Fewsmith felt confident of his ultimate success, despite his jitters. Had he not selected coercive routines from among the work of the finest auteurs? A shouted command from the old *Superman* TV show; some images from the sci-fi masterpiece *Strange Days*; crowd scenes from *Cotton Comes to Harlem*— What more would he need? Once Willadean succeeded in launching these subversive images upon the giant flatscreen mounted on the Berkeley Building—the mosaic of panels was now occupied by the feed from CNN—a carefully planned chaos would erupt, during which time Fewsmith would hijack the entire contents of the armored car, easily a million or more in unmarked cash. He and Willadean would rendezvous at their vehicle, then make good their escape.

Images of a naked, supplicating Willadean—fabricated solely from Fewsmith's imagination—swarmed his vision, distracting him for a moment from his fixity of purpose. If at this advanced stage of their relationship she still refused to let him have his way with her, then she'd find herself dumped on the side of the highway. Let her even go revengefully to the authorities and try to strike a plea bargain, if she wished. Fewsmith had nothing to fear. With his invention, he could become invisible at will. All he needed to do was immerse himself in some pleasant Mexican village, say, then program all the inhabitants to deny his very existence when questioned. He could live like a potentate—with his own harem—on the proceeds of this day's robbery, not to mention any future conquests.

A far cry from the humble and demeaning researcher's existence.

Recalling his old life led Fewsmith to relive his humiliating experience in Parrish Maxfield's office. He looked about the busy square for that hulking cretin who had assaulted him. Pedestrians thronged the sidewalks, nothing more than dismissible programmable robots, and traffic flowed in complicated patterns through the five-way nexus. No sight of that aggressive jerk though. But Fewsmith remained vigilant.

Two guards trundled out a bag-laden trolley from the bank door beside which Fewsmith stood. The other two guards stationed by the rear of the Wells Fargo truck instantly came alert, weapons poised.

At the same moment several bystanders shouted, "Look!" Fewsmith knew then that Willadean had succeeded in getting her tape to play.

Fewsmith felt particularly proud of the sequence of commands now cycling over and over on the big TV. First he had included the comic-book-hero command to yell "Look!" and point at the screen. This insured that as soon as a few people were enraptured, the rest would quickly follow, obeying their natural instincts to obey a pointing finger.

But the next set of commands was a stroke of genius.

All around Fewsmith people began to take out their wallets and open their purses and throw their cash into the air.

Cars screeched to a halt. The few citizens not captured by Fewsmith's video began to dive after the flying dollars. As more people entered Blackmore Square, they either became captivated by the money-throwing instructions or naturally fell to scooping up cash.

Within moments, the scene resembled the arrival of UN food trucks at a refugee camp. Any police now arriving would have their hands full.

The four Wells Fargo guards were well trained, huddling protectively around their trolley and refusing to look anywhere except around themselves at eye-level. But they hadn't counted on the nature of the second assault.

Fewsmith triggered a blood squib in his bandages. Moaning in mock pain, he stumbled toward the uniformed men.

"My hand, my hand! Someone crushed my hand!"

The guards naturally looked down at Fewsmith's bloody hand. There they viewed a vivid, shifting collage of scenes from *Groundhog Day*, *The Underneath*, *The Newton Boys*, and even that awful remake of *Dog Day Afternoon*, *Swordfish*. They instantly stiffened.

Fewsmith said, "Follow me." Two guards began to push the trolley, while the other two marched ahead like slave automatons to clear a path.

Fewsmith chortled once his car came into sight. Parked several blocks away in an alley that conveniently led out of the traffic congestion, the getaway vehicle was just as he had left it.

And there stood his woman by the car.

"Willadean," Fewsmith called out.

The woman turned.

Parrish Maxfield.

* * *

Strine drove like hell's own perpetually summoned firemen toward Blackmore Square, just six blocks away. Already, early confusing reports of trouble there had erupted from the car radio.

"We've got to stop the dissemination of the blipvert first," Strine said. "Then we can try to nab Fewsmith."

"Blipvert?"

"Sure, that's what these things are. Don't you remember Max Headroom?"

"Max whosis?"

Strine narrowed his eyes for a moment upon Dr. Parrish Maxfield before he had to wildly swerve to avoid a taxi stalled in their lane.

"What were you doing about fifteen years ago?"

"I was twelve and busy building molecular models with Legos."

"You're that young?"

"You're that old?"

"Forget it then. Just wait in the car while I go up to the control room. Good thing I was able to reach my uncle. He got the security codes and location of the place from a buddy in the agency that installed their alarm system."

"I'll do no such thing. I'm going after Fewsmith myself. I owe that bastard a good kick in the balls."

Strine thought his head would explode. "You will not! It's too dangerous!"

"Who the hell are you? My nanny? Besides, I've got the

perfect defense against Ronnie and his primitive toy. Now, if he had learned to program Level Two and the CES via sonics or haptics, we'd be in trouble. He would have been able to take over someone with a sound or touch. Hmmm, I wonder if prior instances of this discovery formed the basis for a few legends? The Sirens, the Old Man of the Sea—"

"Forget all that. Besides, what kind of defense can you have? You have to look at him to nab him, and then he's got you."

Parrish patted her purse. "Don't you worry your little Level One about me. My secret weapon's safe in here."

Abandoning any attempts to convince the stubborn memetician of the foolishness of her plans, Strine concentrated on getting them as close as possible to the civic uproar in Blackmore Square. When they finally had to ditch their car, they were only a block away.

Strine began to trot toward the Berkeley Building, Parrish gamely following along.

"Don't look up!"

"Do you take me for an idiot?"

Darting around the mad masses of money-flingers and money-graspers, avoiding rogue cars in motion whose drivers had decided to take to the sidewalks, the pair ended up at the door of the Berkeley Building.

"There's Fewsmith!" exclaimed Parrish, pointing across the turbulent street scene. "He's got some kind of entourage pushing a trolley, and he's moving slow. I'll recognize his getaway car when I see it, and I think if I anticipate his vector, I can beat him to it without him seeing me."

"No, don't," Strine said. But Parrish had already hot-footed off.

Strine hesitated a second, thinking to follow her. But the insanity in the square and the possibility of casualties determined his course of action, and he raced inside the building.

* * *

Safe behind the locked door of the control room, the unsuspecting, horny technician knocked out cold upon the floor, Willadean Lawes surveyed the scene outside the tenth-floor window with immense satisfaction. She could spot the tiny figures of Fewsmith and the guards moving safely but slowly away from the armored car. Once her partner was definitely out of the chaos, she would leave behind the controls of the no-longer necessary big screen and hook up with him. But till then, she'd guard the room so that no one could halt the projection.

Polishing a small silver pistol on the cloth molding her pretty rump, Willadean thought of how best to dispose of Fewsmith, and when. Maybe after they got out of the country. Let him do all the driving, get exhausted and clumsy, and then he'd be good as dead. Sure, she'd lose the expertise with the gadget contained within his cooling brain, but who cared? A million large would last ol' Willadean a good long time. And she could be the belle of Baja as easily as the princess of Pine Mountain.

A solenoid latch clicked, and the outer door swung inward. Willadean trained her pistol on whoever was entering.

The intruder was a rough-edged, good-looking bruiser. Willadean felt her heart go thump-a-thump. Maybe this guy was another crook, out to share the score. If so, Willadean might have herself a new partner.

The guy's words broke Willadean's illusion. "Okay, I'm guessing you must be Fewsmith's woman. Better throw in the towel now, before anyone gets hurt. Your buddy's already captured."

Willadean risked a quick glance out the window and saw no confirmation of this joker's threat. She laughed. "Good try, pal. I was born on a Saturday, but not last Saturday. Now I think I'll measure you for a clay cabin."

"Wait! I've got something you want!"

Willadean's trigger finger eased back. "Now what might that be?"

The guy slowly moved his hand to his rear pocket and came up with a Palm Pilot.

"Just this!" he said, mashing a button.

Willadean tried to avert her eyes, but it was too late.

The sound of breaking glass was followed before too long by a muffled thump from street level.

Strine let loose a gust of relief. "I *thought* that was what 'defenestration' meant!"

* * *

The mesmerized guards halted when Fewsmith did, standing like toy soldiers in the *Nutcracker*. Parrish felt a brief surge of fear, thinking she'd become the target of their rifles. But apparently Fewsmith had not written that routine into the command set he had earlier instilled in them.

An obnoxious leer overspread the rogue scientist's face, and Parrish felt her fear displaced by cold anger against this little weasel.

"Well, well, well—if it's not the dull-witted Dr. Maxfield. Have you dropped by to see if you can coauthor a paper with me? If so, I'm afraid you're much too late."

As Fewsmith gloated, Parrish slinked her fingers into the purse slung from her shoulder. She knew she'd have to goad him into using the Palm Pilot and then precisely match his actions.

"I wouldn't want my name in the same journal as yours. You've warped an important discovery for selfish personal gain. Why, you're no better than that *Frenchman* who claimed to have discovered *N-rays*!"

Bristling at this vile scientific insult, Fewsmith raised his bandaged hand. "I think I'll let you have the fate I intended for your big dumb boyfriend. Look away if you want, but then of course I'll simply escape."

Parrish had her trump card in her fingers, held nearly out her purse. "Do your worst! I'm not afraid. And he's not dumb!"

Fewsmith triggered his deadly sequence just as Parrish whipped her mirror into place, shielding her own eyes.

A look of utter horror flashed over Fewsmith's face, as he was overwhelmed by his best composition: a mélange of images from *Go*, *An Affair to Remember*, *City on the Edge of Forever*, and *The Laughing Dead*. Then he was darting out into the street, looking frantically about for a moving car. Spotting a racing ambulance, he hurled himself beneath its wheels.

Once again, Parrish turned her eyes aside in time to miss the worst.

* * *

The cessation of the command sequence on the big public screen resulted in a gradual diminishment of the chaos in Blackmore Square, as the cycle of infection and reinfection ground to a halt, and even the most recently commandeered minds resumed their normal functioning. Trotting back to the center of the outbreak, alongside the incoming flood of EMTs, policemen, firemen, National Guard troopers, and reporters, Parrish knew then that Strine must have succeeded, and she experienced a little surge of pride in his accomplishments. The emotion took her by surprise, but her flexible intellect smoothly integrated the new feelings into her estimate of the man.

The crowd of stunned, disoriented, and embarrassed citizens was parting like wheat before a thresher, as someone bulled through the mass. Parrish caught sight of a bobbing baseball cap and speeded up to meet the detective.

Spotting her, Strine raced to her side. He hugged her, and she returned the gesture. But then he released her, a sober look replacing his joy at finding her unharmed.

"We've going to have some serious explaining to do to the authorities, once they make the inevitable connection between us and Fewsmith, so we'd better get our story straight."

"What do you mean?"

"Just look around you! The two people who caused this disaster are both dead—apparent suicides, luckily—but the cops will still want to know how they did it."

Parrish pondered the matter. "I think we should tell them Ron bragged to us about some sort of novel aerosol CBW agent. They'll discount the big screen images as just visual noise meant to distract the bank guards. Anything but the reality. Fewsmith's discovery is too dangerous to release. Can you imagine the kind of irresistible dictatorship that could be set up by some madman conversant in the grammar of Level Two? No, much as it pains my scientific soul to say it, this knowledge has to be expunged."

"But how?"

"I saw Fewsmith's Palm Pilot crushed under the ambulance. That leaves yours and the videotape from the control room. I assume you took the tape? Good! Give them to me."

Strine complied, and Parrish hammered the Palm Pilot against a nearby hydrant till it shattered. With Strine's help, she cracked the video case and unspooled the tape down a sewer grating.

"Now we race to Fewsmith's home before the cops even

figure out the address, then erase any traces of his invention we find there. *Et voilà*, the world is saved!"

Strine looked at her admiringly. "You don't have any desire to take over Fewsmith's invention and run with it? This could mean a Nobel Prize for you. It was only Fewsmith's greed and hatred that stopped him from getting the honors he deserved."

"Nuh-huh! I'm not strong enough to resist the temptation. Are you?"

Strine appeared to be considering the matter. "Well, there are a few things I'd change."

"Like what?"

"Well, the attitude of a certain beautiful woman toward a certain ex-ballplayer named Stingo Strine."

Parrish smiled. "No need to use a machine. Consider it done."

"Really?"

"On the level."

Writing "hard SF" is a challenge I don't visit upon myself often enough. Conceiving of new technologies and then rigorously and creatively extrapolating their impact on society is, of course, the quintessential science-fictional game. But as Bruce Sterling recently mentioned to me, "This is damn hard work!" The composition of this story inched ahead at a snail's pace until I fully visualized all the implications of Bash Applebrook's invention.

I'm particularly proud of one sentence here: "The station door hobermanned open." Ever since Robert Heinlein wrote, "The door dilated," SF authors have striven to emulate this blend of concision and cognitive estrangement. With my sentence—a reference to the Hoberman curtains employed at the most recent Winter Olympics—I felt I was contributing my little tile to the grand SF mosaic.

What's up Tiger Lily?

1. DUCK SOUP

The first indication received by Bash Applebrook that all was not right with his world happened over breakfast on the morning of Tuesday, June 25, 2029.

The newspaper he was reading turned into a movie screen.

Bash was instantly jerked out of his fascination with the current headline "MERCOSUR FREETER MAKES SPINTRONICS BREAKTHRU!" His jagged reaction caused some Metanomics Plus nutrishake to spill from his cup onto the tabletop, where it was quickly absorbed.

Looking at the clock on the wall—a display made of redacted fish scales whose mutable refractiveness substituted for ancient LEDs—as if to reassure himself that he hadn't been thrown entirely out of the time stream, Bash sought to gain some perspective on this alarming occurrence.

In itself, this transformation of his newspaper boded no ill. Such things happened millions of times daily around the globe, thanks to proteopape. And since Bash himself was the much-lauded, much-rewarded inventor of proteopape, he was positively the last person in the world to be astounded by the medium's capacity for change.

There was only one problem.

Bash had not instructed his newspaper to swap functions.

This impulsive, inexplicable toggling by his highly reliable newspaper scared Bash very much. Proteopape simply did not do such things. Eleven years ago, Bash had first engineered the substance with innumerable safeguards, backups and firewalls specifically intended to prevent just such herky-jerky transitions. In all the time since, there had been no recorded instances of proteopape malfunctioning, out of billions of uses. Even when sustaining up to seventy-five percent damage, proteopape continued to maintain functionality. (Beyond such limits, proteopape would just shut down altogether.) The miracle material that had transformed so much of the twenty-first century's media landscape simply did not crash.

And if proteopape were suddenly to develop a glitch— Well, imagining the immense and catastrophic repercussions from any flaws in the ubiquitous material raised shivers with the magnitude of tsunamis along Bash's spine.

Having assimilated the very possibility that his fabled invention could behave in nonpredictable ways, Bash gave his newspaper a shake, hoping to expunge this anomaly by the most primitive of engineering tactics. But the newspaper stubbornly continued to function as a movie screen, so Bash focused for clues on the actual movie being displayed across his ex-newspaper.

This particular sheet of proteopape, on which Bash had been reading his newspaper, measured approximately two feet by three feet. Possessing the stiffness and texture of heavy-bond dumb-paper, yet not quite as rigid as parchment, this sheet of proteopape had been folded in half vertically, producing four different faces, two outer and two inner. A bit old-fashioned, Bash preferred to read his newspaper on multiple pages, allowing him to refer backwards if he wished, simply by eyeballing a previous face of his newspaper. Of course, upon finishing with the fourth page of the paper, Bash simply turned back to the front, where the fifth page was now automatically displayed, with pages six, seven, and eight following.

But now every page revealed only the same movie, a quartet of active images. Bash turned the newspaper upside down, hoping to erase the unrequested show, but the inscribed sensors in the newspaper merely registered the new orientation and flipped the movie upright again.

Bash recognized the leering face of Groucho Marx, one of his father's favorite actors. Groucho wore some kind of ridiculous military uniform. *Duck Soup*, then. Now Margaret Dumont entered the scene, all dowager-haughty. But although the actions of the actors were canonically familiar, the conversation that followed bore no resemblance to any extant Hollywood script.

"So," said Groucho, in his familiar intonations that the MEMS speakers of the proteopape reproduced with high fidelity, "the little lady who wants to waste her mind and talents on artsy-fartsy stuff finally deigns to show up. Well, I'm afraid I've lost all interest in whatever crap you wanted me to watch."

"Okay, granted, I'm a little late," Dumont fruitily replied.

"But you did promise after the Woodies that you'd come with me again to hang out with my pals."

As this warped yet still meaningful dialogue from his personal life began to resonate with Bash, he started to feel queasy. He laid the newspaper nearly flat on the breakfast table, right atop his plate of auk eggs and fried plantains with mango syrup, and as the crease separating the half-pages disappeared, the movie redrew itself to fill the whole expanse of one side.

Groucho struck a mocking pose, one hand cradling his chin, the other with a cigar poised at his brow. "Well, a self-important louse like me can't be bothered with that bunch of crazy amateur *artistes* you hang out with. Such crazy ideas! So I've decided to abandon you and return to my cloistered sterile existence."

"Hit the road, then, you jerk! But I'll have the last laugh! You just wait and see!"

With that parting sally, Dumont and Marx vanished from Bash's newspaper. But the words and images that comprised Bash's regular morning blue-toothed installment of *The Boston Globe* did not reappear. The sheet of proteopape remained a frustrating virginal white, nonresponsive to any commands Bash gave it.

After his frustrated attempts to regain control of the newspaper, Bash gave up, reluctantly conceding that this sheet of proteopape was dead. He slumped back in his chair with a nervous sigh, admitting to himself that the origin of this sabotage was all too evident.

Why, oh why, had he ever agreed to a date with Dagny Winsome?

2. *THE BIG CHILL*

York and Adelaide Applebrook had gone bust in the big dotcom crash that had inaugurated the twenty-first century.

Their entrepreneurial venture—into which they had sunk their own lifesavings and millions of dollars more from various friends, relatives, and venture capitalists—had consisted of a website devoted to the marketing of Japanese poetry. Behind the tasteful, interactive facade of *Haiku Howdy!* had been nothing more than a bank of public domain images—Oriental landscapes, for the most part—and a simplistic poetry generator. The visitor to *Haiku Howdy!* would input a selection of nouns and adjectives that the software would form into a haiku. Matched with an appropriate image, the poem would be e-mailed to a designated recipient. Initially offered as a free service, the site was projected to go to pay-per-use status in a year or two, with estimated revenues of ten million dollars a year.

This rudimentary site and whimsical service represented the grand sum of the Applebrooks' inspiration and marketing plan.

The fact that at the height of their "success," in the year 1999, they named their newborn son Basho, after the famous master of haiku, was just one more token of their supreme confidence in their scheme.

When *Haiku Howdy!* collapsed after sixteen months of existence, having burned through millions and millions of dollars of OPM, the Applebrooks had cause to rethink their lifestyle and goals. They moved from Seattle to the less pricey, rural environs of Medford, Oregon and purchased a small pear orchard with some leftover funds they had secretly squirreled away from the screaming burned investors. They took a vow then and there to have nothing further to do with any hypothetical future digital utopia, making a back-to-the-land commitment similar to that made by many burnt-out hippies a generation prior.

Surely the repentant, simple-living Applebrooks never reckoned that their only child, young Basho, would grow up to revolutionize, unify, and dominate the essential ways in which digital information was disseminated across all media.

But from his earliest years, Bash exhibited a fascination with computers and their contents. Perhaps his prenatal immersion in the heady dotcom world had imprinted him with the romance of bytes and bauds. In any case, Bash's native talents (which were considerable; he tested off the high end of several scales) were, from the first, bent toward a career in information technologies.

Bash zipped through public schools, skipping several grades, and enrolled at MIT at age fifteen. Socially, Basho Applebrook felt awkward amidst the sophisticated elders of his generation. But in the classroom and labs he excelled. During his senior year on campus, he encountered his most important success in the field of moletronics, the science of manipulating addressable molecules, when he managed to produce the first fully functional sheet of proteopape.

Alone late one night in a lab, Bash dipped a standard blank sheet of high quality dumb paper into a special bath where it absorbed a tailored mix of dopant molecules. (This bath was the 413th reformulation of his original recipe.) Removing the paper, Bash placed it in a second tub of liquid. This tub featured a lattice of STM tweezers obedient to computer control. Bash sent a large file into the tub's controllers, and, gripping hold of each doped molecule with invisible force pincers, the device laid down intricate circuitry templates into the very molecules of the paper.

Junctions bloomed, MEMS proliferated. Memory, processors, sensors, a GPS unit, solar cells, rechargeable batteries, speakers, pixels, a camera, and wireless modem: all arrayed themselves invisibly and microscopically throughout the sheet of paper.

Removing the paper from its complexifying wash, Bash was pleased to see on its glistening face a hi-res image.

Depicted was a small pond with a frog by its edge, and the following haiku by Bash's namesake:

> *Old pond*
> *Frog jumps in*
> *Splash!*

Bash tapped a control square in the corner of the display, and the image became animated, with the frog carrying out the poem's instructions in an endless loop, with appropriate soundtrack.

Bash's smile, observed by no one, lit up the rafters.

Thus was born "protean paper," or, as a web-journalist (nowadays remembered for nothing else but this coinage) later dubbed it, "proteopape."

Bash's miraculous process merely added hundredths of a cent to each piece of paper processed. For this token price, one ended up with a sheet of proteopape that possessed magnitudes more processing power than an old-line supercomputer.

In effect, Bash had created flexible, weightless computers practically too cheap to sell.

But the difference between "practically" and "absolutely" meant a lot, across millions of units.

I^2—the age of Immanent Information—was about to commence.

A visit to the same canny lawyer who had helped his parents survive bankruptcy nearly twenty years ago insured that Bash's invention was securely patented. Anyone who wanted to employ Bash's process would have to license it from him, for a considerable annual fee.

At this point, the nineteen-year-old Bash went public.

By the time he was twenty-one, he was the richest man in the world.

But he had still never even ventured out on a date with any member of the opposite sex who was not his cousin Cora on his mother's side.

3. THE BREAKFAST CLUB

Dagny Winsome resembled no one so much as a pale blonde Olive Oyl. Affecting retro eyeglasses in place of the universal redactive surgery to correct her nearsightedness, Dagny exhibited a somatype that evoked thoughts of broomsticks, birches, baguettes and, given her predilection for striped shirts, barber poles. But her lack of curvature belied a certain popularity with males, attributable to her quick wit, wild impulsiveness, and gleeful subversiveness. Her long pale hair framed a face that could segue from calm innocence to irate impatience to quirky amusement in the span of a short conversation. Dagny's four years at MIT had been marked by participation in a score of famous hacks, including the overnight building of a two-thirds mockup of the Space Shuttle *George W. Bush* resting in a simulated crash in the middle of Massachusetts Avenue.

Bash stood in awe of Dagny from the minute he became aware of her and her rep. A year ahead of Bash and several years senior in age, yet sharing his major, Dagny had seemed the unapproachable apex of sophistication and, yes, feminine allure. Often he had dreamed of speaking to her, even asking her on a date. But he had never summoned up the requisite courage.

Dagny graduated, and Bash's following year was overtaken by the heady proteopape madness. For the next decade, he had heard not a word of her post-college career. Despite some desultory networking throughout the IT community, Bash had been unable to learn any information concerning her. Apparently, she had not employed her degree in any conventional manner.

So in Bash's heart, Dagny Winsome gradually became a faded yet still nostalgia-provoking ghost.

Until the day just two weeks ago, on June 11, when she turned up on his doorstep.

Women were not in the habit of showing up at the front entrance of Bash's home. For one thing, Bash lived in seclusion in a fairly well-secured mansion in the exclusive town of Lincoln, Massachusetts. Although no live guards or trained animals patrolled the grounds of his homestead, the fenced estate boasted elaborate cybernetic barriers wired both to nonlethal antipersonnel devices and to various agencies who were primed to respond at a moment's notice to any intrusion. Bash was not particularly paranoid, but as the world's richest individual, he was naturally the focus of many supplicants, and he cherished his privacy.

Also, Bash did not experience a steady flow of female callers since he remained as awkward with women as he had been at nineteen. Although not technically a virgin any longer at age thirty, he still failed to deeply comprehend the rituals of human courtship and mating. Sometimes he felt that the shortened form of his name stood for "Bashful" rather than "Basho."

Naturally, then, Bash was startled to hear his doorbell ring early one morning. He tentatively approached the front door. A curling sheet of proteopape carelessly thumb-tacked to the inner door conveyed an image of the front step transmitted from a second sheet of proteopape hanging outside and synched to the inner one. (When weather degraded the outside sheet of proteopape to uselessness, Bash would simply hang a new page.)

Imagine Bash's surprise to witness Dagny Winsome impatiently standing there. After a short, flummoxed moment, Bash threw wide the door.

"Dag—Dagny? But how—?"

Ten years onward from graduation, Dagny Winsome retained her collegiate looks and informality. She wore one of her trademark horizontally striped shirts, red and black. Her clunky eyeglasses incorporated enough plastic to form a car bumper. Her long, near-platinum hair had been pulled back and secured by a jeweled crab, one of the fashionable, ornamental redactives that metabolized human sweat and dead skin cells. Black jeans and a pair of NeetFeets completed her outfit.

Dagny said with some irritation, "Well, aren't you going to invite your old fellow alumna inside?"

"But how did you get past my security?"

Dagny snorted. "You call that gimcrack setup a security system? I had it hacked while my car was still five miles outside of town. And I only drove from Boston."

Bash made a mental note to install some hardware and software upgrades. But he could not, upon reflection, manufacture any ire against either his deficient cyberwards or Dagny herself. He was pleased to see her.

"Uh, sorry about my manners. Sure, come on in. I was just having breakfast. Want something?"

Dagny stepped briskly inside. "Green tea and a poppyseed muffin, some Canadian bacon on the side."

Bash reviewed the contents of his large freezer. "Uh, can do."

Seated in the kitchen, sipping their drinks while bacon microwaved, neither one spoke for some time. Dagny focused a dubious look on the decorative strip of proteopape wallpaper running around the upper quarter of the kitchen walls. A living frieze, the accent strip displayed a constantly shifting video of this year's *Sports Illustrated* swimsuit models at play in the Sino-Hindu space station, *Maohatma*. Embarrassed, Bash decided that to change the contents now would only accentuate the original bachelor's choice, so he fussed with the microwave while admiring Dagny out the corner of his eye.

Serving his guest her muffin and bacon, Bash was taken aback by her sudden confrontational question.

"So, how long are you going to vegetate here like some kind of anaerobe?"

Bash dropped into his seat. "Huh? What do you mean?"

Dagny waved a braceleted arm to sweep in the whole house. "Just look around. You've fashioned yourself a perfect little womb here. First you go and drop the biggest conceptual bombshell into the information society that the world has ever seen. Intelligent paper! Then you crawl into a hole with all your riches and pull the hole in after yourself."

"That's ridiculous. I—I'm still engaged with the world. Why, just last year I filed five patents—"

"All piddling little refinements on proteopape. Face it, you're just dicking around with bells and whistles now. You've lost your edge. You don't really care about the biz or its potential to change the world anymore."

Bash tried to objectively consider Dagny's accusations. His life was still full of interests and passions, wasn't it? He ran a big A-life colony that had kicked some butt in the annual Conway Wars; he composed songs on his full-body SymphonySuit, and downloads from his music website had hit an all-time high last week (53); and he was the biggest pear-orchard owner in Oregon's Rogue River Valley (the holding corporation was run by York and Adelaide)— Didn't all those hobbies and several others speak to his continuing involvement in the world at large? Yet suddenly Bash was unsure of his own worth and meaning. Did his life really look trivial to an outsider?

Irked by these novel sensations, Bash sought to counterattack. "What about you? I don't see where you've been exactly burning up the I^2 landscape. How have you been improving the world since school?"

Dagny was unflustered. "You never would have heard of anything I've done, even though I've got quite a rep in my field."

"And what field is that?"

"The art world. After graduation, I realized my heart just wasn't in the theoretical, R-and-D side of I^2. I was more interested in the creative, out-of-the-box uses the street had for stuff like proteopape than in any kind of engineering. I wanted to use nifty new tools to express myself, not make them so others could. So I split to the West Coast in '17, and I've mostly been there ever since. Oh, I travel a lot—the usual swirly emergent nodes like Austin, Prague, Havana, Hong Kong, Helsinki, Bangor. But generally you can find me working at home in LA."

The list of exciting cities dazzled Bash more than he expected it to, and he realized that for all his immense wealth he had truly been leading a cloistered existence.

"What brings you to stuffy old Boston then?"

"The Woodies. It's an awards ceremony for one of the things I do, and it's being held here this year. A local group, the Hubster Dubsters, are sponsoring the affair. It's kind of a joke, but I have to be there if I want to front as a player. So I figured, Bash lives out that way. What if I look him up and invite him to come along."

"But why?"

Dagny fixed Bash with an earnest gaze. "I won't pretend you meant anything to me at MIT, Bash. But I knew who you were, boy genius and all. And when you invented proteopape—well, I was kinda proud to have known you even a little bit. Proetopape is a real wizard wheeze, you know. It tumbled a lot of tipping points, sent some real change waves through the world. I admire you for that. So I guess what

I'm saying is I'd like to map your gedankenspace, and maybe help wake you up a little bit."

Bash considered this speech for a short time.

"You were proud of me?"

Dagny grinned. "Do porn stars have sex?"

Bash blushed. "So, when is this awards thing?"

4. VALLEY OF THE DOLLS

Some years back, Kenmore Square had been turned into a woonerf. The Dutch term literally meant "living yard," and referred to the practice of converting urban streets from vehicular to pedestrian usage. The formerly confusing nexus of several Boston avenues beneath the famed Citgo sign (now a giant sheet of laminated proteopape, like all modern billboards and exterior signage) had been transformed into a pleasant public venue carpeted with high-foot-traffic-sustaining redactive grasses and mosses and crisscrossed by flagstone paths.

On this early evening of June 12, the temperature registered typical for neo-Venusian New England, a balmy 92°F. The square was crowded with strolling shoppers, picnickers, café patrons, and club- and movie-goers. Children squealed as they played on the public squishee sculptures and underneath intricately dancing cyber-fountains. Patrolling autonomes—creeping, hopping, and stalking, their patternizing optics and tangle-foot projectors and beanbag-gun snouts and spray nozzles of liquid banana peel swiveling according to odd self-grown heuristics—maintained vigilance against any possible disrupters of the peace. A lone cop mounted on his compact StreetCamel added a layer of human oversight (the random manure dumps were a small price to pay for this layer of protection).

Bash and Dagny had parked Dagny's fuel-cell-powered Argentinian rental, a 2027 Gaucho, several blocks away. They entered the square now on foot from the south, via Newbury Street, engaged in earnest conversation.

"Mutability, Bash! Mutability rules! We're all Buddhists now, acknowledging change as paramount. Nothing fixed or solid, no hierarchies of originals and copies, nothing stable from one minute to the next. Every variant equally privileged. That's what proteopape's all about! Media and content are one. Can't you see it? Your invention undermined all the old paradigms. First editions, signed canvases, original film negatives— Those terms mean nothing anymore, and our art should reflect that."

Bash struggled to counter Dagny's passionate, illogical, and scary assertions. (Carried to its extreme, her philosophy led to a world of complete isotropic chaos, Bash felt.) But the novelty of arguing face-to-face with a living interlocutor had him slightly flustered.

"I just can't buy all that, Dag. Proteopape is just a means of transmission and display. The contents and value of what's being displayed don't change just because the surface they're displayed on might show something different the next minute. Look, suppose I used this store window here to display some paintings, changing the paintings by hand every ten seconds. That would be a very slow analog representation of what proteopape does. Would the canvases I chose to exhibit suddenly be deracinated or transformed by this treatment? I don't think so."

"Your analogy sucks! The canvases are still physical objects in your instance. But anything on proteopape has been digitized and rendered virtual. Once that happens, all the old standards collapse."

Their seemingly irresolvable argument had brought them to the door of their destination: a club with a proteopape display in an acid-yellow neon font naming it the Antiquarium. The display kept sinuously changing from letters into some kind of sea serpent and back. A long line of patrons awaited entrance.

A tall bald guy walking up and down the line was handing out small proteopape broadsides for some product or service or exhibition. Those in the queue who accepted the advertisements either folded the pages and tucked them into their pockets, or crumpled them up and threw them to the turf, where the little screens continued to flash a twisted mosaic of information. Bash remembered the first time he had seen someone so carelessly discard his invention, and how he had winced. But he had quickly become reconciled to the thoughtless disposal of so much cheap processing power, and aside from the littering aspect, the common action no longer bothered him.

Dagny turned to Bash and gripped both his hands in a surprisingly touching show of sincerity. "Let's drop all this futile talk. I think that once you see some of the stuff on display tonight—the awards ceremony features extensive clips, you know—you'll come around to my viewpoint. Or at least admit that it's a valid basis for further discussion."

"Well, I can't promise anything. But I'm keeping an open mind."

"That's all I ask. Now follow me. We don't have to stand in line here with the fans."

The stage door entrance behind the club, monitored by a chicly scaled Antiquarium employee, granted them exclusive entry into the club. Bash snuffled the funky odor of old spilled beer, drummer sweat, and various smokable drugs and experienced a grand moment of disorientation. Where was he? How had he ended up here?

But Dagny's swift maneuvering of Bash across the empty club's main dance floor gave him no time to savor his *jamais vu*.

Crossing the expanse, Bash saw the exhibits that gave

the club its name. Dozens of huge aquariums dotted the cavernous space. They hosted creepy-crawly redactives whose appearance was based on the Burgess Shale fossils, but whose actual germ lines derived from common modern fishes and crustaceans. In tank after tank, stubby-winged Anomalocarises crawled over the jutting spikes of Hallucigenias, while slithering Opabinias waggled their long, pincered snouts.

Bash felt as if he had entered a particularly bad dream. This whole night, from the tedious argument with Dagny up to this surreal display, was not proceeding as cheerfully as he had hoped.

Workers in STAFF T-shirts were setting up folding chairs in ranks across the dance floor, while others were positioning a lectern onstage and rigging a huge sheet of proteopape behind the podium. As Bash exited the main floor he saw the proteopape come alive:

FIFTH ANNUAL WOODY AWARDS
SPONSORED BY
MUD BUG SPORTS CLOTHES
NASHVILLE SITAR STUDIO
XYLLELLA COSMETICS
AND
THE HUBSTER DUBSTERS

Below these names was a caricature of a familiar bespectacled nebbish, executed by Hirschfeld (well into his second century, the 'borged artist was still alive and active in his exoskeleton and SecondSkin).

Now Dagny had dragged Bash into a dressing room of some sort, crowded with people in various states of undress and makeup. They passed through this organized confusion into the club's Green Room. Here, the atmosphere was less frenetic yet tenser.

"Bash, I want you to meet some special friends. Holland Flanders—"

Bash shook the hand of a well-muscled fellow wearing a wife-beater and cargo shorts, whose bare arms slowly seemed to be exuding miniscule flakes of golden glitter.

"—Cricket Licklider—"

The petite woman wore a suit of vaguely Japanese-looking crocodile-skin armor and blinked reptilian eyes. Contacts or redactions, Bash could not discern.

"—Roger Mexicorn—"

This wraithlike, long-haired lad sported banana-yellow skin and reminded Bash of a certain doomed albino from the literature of the fantastic.

"—Lester Schill—"

Bash thought this besuited, bearded guy the most normal, until he clasped Schill's palm and received a distinct erotic tingle from some kind of bioelectrical implant.

"—and Indicia Diddums."

Indicia's broad face cracked in a smile that revealed a set of fangs that any barracuda would have envied.

"These are some of the Hubster Dubsters, Bash. My fellow auteurs. They're all up for one or more Woodies tonight."

Bash tried to make sensible conversation under the slightly oppressive circumstances. "So, I have to confess, I had never heard of your special kind of, um, art before Dagny brought me up to speed. You guys, ah, mess with old films . . . ."

Schill frowned. "Crudely put, but accurate enough. Only the dialogue, however."

Diddums chimed in, her speech somewhat distorted by

her unnatural teeth. "Thash right. We practish a purer art than thosh lazy chumps who simply fuck with the images. They have their own awards anyway. The Zeligs."

Bash was confused. "Wait a minute. Your awards are named after Woody Allen, correct? Because he altered the soundtrack of that Japanese film over half a century ago—"

"*What's Up, Tiger Lily?*" supplied Dagny, as if coaching a favored but deficient student.

"But didn't Allen also make *Zelig*?"

"Certainly," Mexicorn said in a languid tone. "But just as the magnificent *Tiger Lily* preceded the feeble *Zelig*, so did our ceremony anticipate that of our degenerate rivals. We distinguish, of course, between the Good Woody and the Bad Woody."

"We're *writers*, you see," interjected Flanders, gesturing in a way that left a trail of body glitter through the air. "The *word* is primary with us."

Licklider doffed her angular helmet and scratched the blonde fuzz revealed. "And the artistic challenge arises in fitting our words to the established images, creating a startlingly different film in the process. Any idiot can paste King Kong into *Guess Who's Coming to Dinner*. But it takes real skill to formulate a new script that hews to the actions of the original film and the mouth movements and gestures of the actors, yet still completely detourns it."

Dagny said, "Well put, Cricket. There's our credo in a nutshell, Bash. Startling novelty born from the boringly familiar. But you'll soon see for yourself. Here, grab a glass of champagne. It's just the cheap stuff made from potatoes, but you'd never know from the taste."

Bash took the drink. Truthfully, it wasn't bad. Dagny went to talk to others of her peers, leaving Bash alone.

Cricket Licklider approached Bash. He shifted his

stance nervously and drained his glass. A bad mistake, as the potato champagne went straight to his brain.

"So," the woman said, "you're the brainiac who invented proteopape."

"Well, sure," Bash said. "That is, I did, but it didn't seem to require too many brains. After all, others had been messing with e-paper for a while, even if they weren't getting anywhere fast. It's not like I conceptualized the whole thing from scratch. The rest was just solid, if inspired, engineering."

"So why didn't anyone else get there first? No, you deserve all the luster, fizz." Cricket pinned Bash with her alligator eyes. "Tell me, you get much hot tail along with the royalties?"

"Uh, I, that is—"

"Well, believe me, you could walk off tonight with a double armful of proteopape groupies—of any of several genders. So just remember: if your date tonight doesn't come across like she should, there're plenty of other bints in the bleachers. And that includes me."

Cricket grinned broadly, then turned to leave. Bash said, "Wait a minute."

"Yeah?"

"Are you related to—?"

"My great-grandfather. And wouldn't he have sold my grandfather for a single sheet of proteopape?"

Dagny came then to reclaim Bash. "Let's go. We've got seats in the reserved section, but I want to be on the aisle so I can jump up easily when I win."

Bash followed Dagny out of the Green Room, which was rapidly emptying. Out on the main floor, fans were now swarming into chairs. The crush at the various bars was intense, and a palpable excitement filled the club.

Dagny managed to secure more drinks, and she and

Bash took their seats. Before too long, the lights dimmed and the ceremony began.

First came a few live song-and-dance numbers, each one in the spirit of the Woodies. Music and choreography replicated famous routines, but all the lyrics had been altered. The rumble between the Jets and Sharks from *West Side Story* now limned the current scientipolitical feud between the Viridians and the Dansgaard-Oeschgerites. Fred Astaire's acrobatic leaps from *Singin' in the Rain* now parodied the recent scandal involving Lourdes Ciccone and that prominent EU minister, Randy Rutger.

The audience applauded wildly for every act. Bash found himself bemused by this disproportionate reception to what amounted to some juvenile satire. Was this truly representative of the cultural revolution that proteopape had supposedly engendered? If so, he felt ashamed.

Finally, the master of ceremonies appeared, wearing a disposable suit cut along the lines of the famous oversized outfit often worn during shows of the last millennium by the singer David Byrne, whose octogenarian career had recently received a boost thanks to a sold-out tour with the Bleeding Latahs. Fashioned entirely from proteopape, the MC's outfit displayed a rapid-fire montage of subliminal images. The flicker rate made Bash's eyes hurt, and he had to avert them.

"Our first category is 'Best Transformation of Tragedy to Comedy.' And the contenders are Faustina Kenny for her *Casablanca*—"

A clip rolled on the big proteopape screen and on smaller screens scattered throughout the Antiquarium.

Bogart leaned over to Dooley Wilson as Sam, seated at the piano, and said, "Are those keys made from redactive ivory or wild ivory?"

Sam replied, "Neither, Rick—they're human bone from Chechnya. Can't you see how they glow!"

"—Engels Copeland for his *High Noon*—"

A stern Gary Cooper faced an adoring Grace Kelly and said, "Don't worry, Amy, the family jewels won't be damaged. My underwear is redactive armadillo hide!"

"—Jim Cupp for his *Lord of the Rings*—"

Frodo Baggins gazed deeply in Sam Gamgee's eyes as their boat drifted downriver and said, "Admit it, Sam, you ate the last damn antioxidant superchoc bar."

"—Lura Giffard for her *Blue Velvet*—"

A dissipated Dennis Hopper, breathing mask clamped to his face, muttered, "Why the hell did I ever volunteer to beta-test this new crowd-control spray?"

"—and finally, Dagny Winsome for her *Gone With the Wind*."

Cradling Vivien Leigh in his arms, Clark Gable said, "But Scarlett, if you go in for gender-reassignment, where will that leave me?"

"On the bottom," she replied.

"And the winner is—Dagny Winsome for *Gone with the Wind*!"

To a storm of applause, Dagny trotted onstage. Gleefully triumphant, she clutched the offered trophy—a bronze bust of Woody Allen with a blank word-balloon streaming from his lips—and launched into her acceptance speech.

"This was not a lock, folks! I was up against a lot of strong contenders. My thanks to the judges for recognizing that a femplus subtext does not preclude some real yocks. I'd just like to thank the California State Board of the Arts for their continued support, my parents for zygotic foresight, and Alex, my physiotherapist, for those inspirational, heated Moon-rock treatments. Oh, and let's shed some special luster on Basho Applebrook, the inventor of proteopape, who's with us tonight. Bash, stand up and take a bow!"

Utterly mortified, Bash got out of his seat as a spotlight zeroed in on him. Blinking, he turned to face the audience, essaying a weak smile. After enduring the noise of their clapping for as short a time as politely allowable, he gratefully sat down.

Dagny had returned to his side. She leaned in to kiss his cheek. Bash felt partially recompensed for his forced public exposure. But the rest of the ceremony quickly soured his mood.

"Best Transformation of Comedy to Tragedy" naturally followed the award Dagny had won. Then came "Musical into Nonmusical," and vice versa. "Subtext Foregrounded" and "Mockumentaries" were succeeded by the award for "Bomb Defusing," the object of which category was apparently to rob a suspenseful film of any suspense. "Idiot Plotting" featured all the characters exchanging moronic dialogue and offering the stupidest of motives for their actions. "Comic Book Narration" forced the actors to summarize aloud all their actions, and also to indulge in long-winded speeches during any fight scenes. "Gender Swap" found all the males dubbed with female voices, and contrariwise. "Ethnic Mismatch" covered the introduction of inappropriate foreign accents.

Bash's father had been born in 1970. During Bash's childhood, he had discovered a stash of magazines that York Applebrook had accumulated during his own childhood. Fascinated by the antiques, Bash had devoured the pile of *Mad* magazines, only half-understanding yet still laughing at parodies of movies old before he had been born. At the wise old age of ten, however, Bash had put aside the jejune drolleries of "the usual gang of idiots."

Tonight felt like being trapped in a giant issue of *Mad*.

Bash simply could not believe that all these supposedly mature adults felt that such juvenile skewings of classic films constituted a new and exciting art form. And somehow his invention of proteopape had catalyzed this stale quasi-dadaist display? Bash experienced a sense of shame.

He did not of course let Dagny know how he felt. Her pleasure in winning and in the victories of her peers prevented any such honesty. And, selfishly, Bash still thrilled to her kiss. The conversation with Cricket Licklider had made the possibility of post-Woodies sex with Dagny more vivid. No point in sacrificing the first likelihood of unmonied intercourse in two years on the altar of stubborn opinionated speechifying.

Finally the tedious ceremony ended. The assembled auteurs from around the globe split into cliques and adjourned to various other venues to celebrate or weep. Bash found himself accompanying Dagny, the Hubster Dubsters, and a pack of hangers-on to a bar called The Weeping Gorilla, whose decorative motif involved the lugubrious anthropoid posed with various celebrities. There, Bash consumed rather too much alcohol, rather too little food, and a handful of unidentified drugs.

Somehow Bash found himself naked in a hotel room with Dagny. Sex occurred in lurid kaleidoscopic intervals of consciousness. Afterwards, Bash remembered very little of the perhaps enjoyable experience.

But much to his dismay, he clearly recalled some boastful pillow talk afterwards.

"Hadda put a trapdoor in pro'eopape during testing. Lemme get inna operating system to debug. Still in there! Yup, never took it out, nobody ever found it neither. Every single sheet, still got a secret backdoor!"

Dagny, eyes shuttered, made sleepy noises. But, as evidenced by the subversion of Bash's *Boston Globe* on the morning of June 25, when his newspaper had played a symbolical version of their harsh breakup on the shoals of Bash's eventual honesty during their aborted second date, she had plainly heard every word.

5. *THE FUGITIVE*

Bash stood up from the breakfast table. His dead newspaper continued slowly to absorb the juices of his abandoned breakfast. The fish-scale wall clock morphed to a new minute. Everything looked hopeless.

Dagny Winsome had hacked the hidden trapdoor in proteopape, the existence of which no one had ever suspected until he blurted it out. Why hadn't he eliminated that feature before releasing his invention? Hubris, sheer hubris. Bash had wanted to feel as if he could reclaim his brainchild from the world's embrace at any time. The operating system trapdoor represented apron strings he couldn't bring himself to cut. And what was the appalling result of his parental vanity?

Now Dagny could commandeer every uniquely identifiable scrap of the ether-driven miracle medium and turn it to her own purposes. For the moment, her only motivation to tamper appeared to consist of expressing her displeasure with Bash. For that small blessing, Bash was grateful. But how long would it take before Dagny's congenital impishness seduced her into broader culture-jamming? This was the woman, after all, who had drugged one of MIT's deans as he slept, and brought him to awaken in a scrupulously exact mockup of his entire apartment exactly three-quarters scale.

Bash felt like diving into bed and pulling the covers over his head. But a moment's reflection stiffened his resolve. No one was going to mess with *his* proteopape and get away with it! Too much of the world's economy and culture relied on the medium to just abandon it. He would simply have to track Dagny down and attempt to reason with her.

As his first move, Bash took out his telephone. His telephone was simply a stiffened strip of proteopape. His defunct newspaper would have once served the purpose as well, but most people kept a dedicated phone on their persons, if for nothing else than to receive incoming calls when they were out of reach of other proteopape surfaces, and also to serve as their unique intelligent tag identifying them to I^2 entities.

Bash folded the phone into a little hollow pyramid and stood it on the table. The GlobeSpeak logo appeared instantly: a goofy anthropomorphic chatting globe inked by Robert Crumb, every appearance of which earned the heirs of the artist one milli-cent. (Given the volume of world communication, Sophie Crumb now owned most of southern France.) Bash ordered the phone to search for Cricket Licklider. Within a few seconds her face replaced the logo, while the cameras in Bash's phone reciprocated with his image.

Cricket grinned. "I knew you'd come looking for some of the good stuff eventually, Bashie-boy."

"No, it's not like that. I appreciate your attention, really I do, but I need to find Dagny."

Frowning, Cricket said, "You lost your girlfriend? Too bad. Why should I help you find her?"

"Because she's going to destroy proteopape if I don't stop her. Where would that leave you and your fellow Dubsters? Where would that leave any of us for that matter?"

This dire news secured Cricket's interest, widening her iguana eyes. "Holy shit! Well, Christ, I don't know what to say. I haven't seen her since the Woodies. She might not even be in town anymore."

"Can you get the rest of your crew together? Maybe one of them knows something useful."

"I'll do my best. Meet us at the clubhouse in an hour."

Cricket cut the transmission, but not before uploading the relevant address to Bash's phone.

Bash decided that a shave and shower would help settle his nerves.

In the bathroom, Bash lathered up his face in the proteopape mirror: a sheet that digitized his image in real time and displayed it unreversed. The mirror also ran a small window in which a live newscast streamed. As Bash listened intently for any bulletins regarding the public malfunctioning of proteopape, he took his antique Mach3 razor down and sudsed his face. Having been raised in a simple-living household, Bash still retained many old-fashioned habits, such as actually shaving. He drew the first swath through the foam up his neck and under his chin.

Without warning, his mirror suddenly hosted the leering face of Charles Laughton as the Hunchback of Notre Dame.

Bash yelped and cut himself. The Hunchback chortled, then vanished. And now his mirror was as dead as his newspaper.

Cursing Dagny, Bash located a small analogue mirror at the bottom of a closet and finished shaving. He put a proteopape band aid on the cut, and the band aid instantly assumed the exact texture and coloration of the skin it covered (with cut edited out), effectively becoming invisible.

Bash's shower curtain was more proteopape, laminated and featuring a loop of the Louisiana rainforest, complete with muted soundtrack. Bash yanked it off its hooks and took a shower without regard to slopping water onto the bathroom floor. Toweling off, he even regarded the roll of toilet paper next to the john suspiciously, but then decided that Dagny wouldn't dare.

Dressed in his usual casual manner—white Wickaway

shirt, calf-length tropical-print pants, and Supplex sandals—Bash left his house. He took his Segway ix from its recharging slot in the garage and set out for the nearby commuter-rail node. As he zipped neatly along the wealthy and shady streets of Lincoln, the warm, humid June air laving him, Bash tried to comprehend the full potential dimensions of Dagny's meddling with proteopape. He pictured schools, businesses, transportation, and government agencies all brought to a grinding halt as their proteopape systems crashed. Proteopape figured omnipresently in the year 2029. So deeply had it insinuated itself into daily life that even Bash could not keep track of all its uses. If proteopape went down, it would take the global economy with it.

And what of Bash's personal rep in the aftermath? When the facts came out, he would become the biggest idiot and traitor the world had ever tarred and feathered. His name would become synonymous with "fuck up."

"You pulled a helluva applebrook that time."

"I totally applebrooked my car, but wasn't hurt."

"Don't hire him, he's a real applebrook."

The breeze ruffling Bash's hair failed to dry the sweat on his brow as fast as it formed.

At the station, Bash parked and locked his Segway. He bounded up the stairs, and the station door hobermanned open automatically for him. He bought his ticket and, after only a ten-minute wait, found himself riding east toward the city.

At the end of Bash's car, a placard of proteopape mounted on the wall cycled through a set of advertisements. Bash kept a wary eye on the ads, but none betrayed a personal vendetta against him.

Disembarking at South Station, Bash looked around for his personal icon in the nearest piece of public proteopape and quickly discovered it glowing in the corner of a newsstand's signage: a bright green pear (thoughts of his parents briefly popped up) with the initials BA centered in it.

Every individual in the I^2 society owned such a self-selected icon, its uniqueness assured by a global registry. The icons had many uses, but right now Bash's emblem was going to help him arrive at the Dubster's club. His pocket phone was handshaking with every piece of proteopape in the immediate vicinity and was laying down a trail of electronic breadcrumbs for him to follow, based on the directions earlier transmitted by Cricket.

Beyond the newsstand, second pear appeared on a plaque identifying the presence of a wall-mounted fire extinguisher, and so Bash walked toward it. Many other travelers were simultaneously tracking their own icons with Bash. As he approached the second iteration of the luminous pear, a third copy glowed from the decorative patch on the backpack of a passing school kid. Bash followed the stranger until the kid turned right. (Many contemporary dramas and comedies revolved around the chance meetings initiated by one's icon appearing on the personal property of a stranger. An individual could of course deny this kind of access, but surprisingly few did.) The pear icon vanished from the pack, to be replaced by an occurrence at the head of the subway stairs. Thus Bash was led onto a train and to his eventual destination, a building on the Fenway not far from the Isabella Stewart Gardner Museum.

As he ascended the steps of the modest brownstone, Bash's eye was snagged by the passage of a sleek new Europa model car, one of the first to fully incorporate proteopape in place of windshield glass. He marveled at the realism of its "windows," which apparently disclosed the driver—a handsome young executive type—chatting with his passenger—a beautiful woman.

The car windows were in reality all sheets of suitably strengthened proteopape, utterly opaque. The inner surfaces of the "windows" displayed the outside world to the occupants of the car (or anything else, for that matter, although the driver, at least, had better be monitoring reality), while the outer surfaces broadcast the car's interior (the default setting) or any other selected feed. The driver and passenger Bash saw might have been the actual occupants of the Europa, or they might have been canned constructs. The car could in reality hold some schlubby Walter Mitty type, the president-in-exile of the Drowned Archipelagos or the notorious terrorist Mungo Bush Meat. (Suspicious of the latter instance, roving police would get an instant warrant to tap the windows and examine the true interior.)

Returning his attention to the door displaying his icon, Bash phoned Cricket.

"I'm here."

"One second."

The door opened on its old-fashioned hinges, and Bash stepped inside to be met by Cricket.

Today the woman wore an outfit of rose-colored spidersilk street pajamas that revealed an attractive figure concealed the earlier night by her formal armor. She smiled and gave Bash a brief spontaneous hug and peck.

"Buck up, Bashie-boy. Things can't be that bad."

"No, they're worse! Dagny is going to bring down civilization if she keeps on messing with proteopape."

"Exactly what is she doing, and how's she doing it?"

"I can't reveal everything, but it's all my fault. I inadvertently gave her the ability to ping and finger every piece of proteopape in existence."

Cricket whistled. "I knew you zillionaires bestowed generous gifts, but this one even beats the time South Africa gave away the AIDS cure."

"I didn't *mean* to pass this ability on to her. In fact, all I did was drop a drunken clue, and she ran with it."

"Our Dag is one clever girl, that's for sure."

Bash nervously looked around the dim narrow hallway full of antiques and was relieved to discover only dumb wall coverings and not a scrap of proteopape in sight.

"We should make sure to exclude any proteopape from our meeting with your friends. Otherwise Dagny will surely monitor our discussions."

Following his own advice, Bash took out his phone and placed it on an end table.

"Wait here. I'll run ahead and tell everyone to de-paper-ize themselves."

Cricket returned after only a minute. "Okay, let's go."

Walking down the long hall, Bash asked, "How did you guys ever end up in a building like this? I pictured your clubhouse as some kind of xinggan Koolhaus."

"Well, most of us Dubsters are just amateurs with day jobs, you know. We can't afford to commission special architecture by anyone really catalyzing. But our one rich member is Lester Schill. You met him the other night, right? The Schills have been Brahmins since way back to the 1950s! Big investments in the Worcester bio-axis, Djerassi, and that crowd. But Lester's the last of the Schill line, and he owns more properties than he can use. So he leases us this building for our HQ for a dollar a year."

"Isn't he concerned about what'll happen to the family fortune after his death?" This very issue had often plagued the childless Bash himself.

Cricket snickered. "Lester's not a breeder. And believe me, you really don't want to know the details of his special foldings. But I expect he's made provisions."

Their steps had brought them to a closed door. Cricket ushered Bash into a large room whose walls featured built-in shelves full of dumb books. Bash experienced a small shock, having actually forgotten that such antique private libraries still existed.

Close to a dozen Dubsters, assembled around a board-room-sized table, greeted Bash with quiet hellos or silent nods. Bash recognized Flanders, Mexicorn, Diddums, and the enigmatic Schill himself, but the others were strangers to him.

Cricket conducted Bash to the empty chair at the head of the table and he sat, unsure of what he needed to say to enlist the help of these people. No one offered him any prompting, but he finally came up with a concise introduction to his presence.

"One of your West Coast associates, Dagny Winsome, has stolen something from me. The knowledge of a trapdoor in the operating system of proteopape. She's already begun screwing around with various sheets of my personal protean paper, and if she continues on in this manner, she'll inspire widespread, absolute distrust of this medium. That would spell the end of our I^2 infrastructure, significantly impacting your own artistic activities. So I'm hoping that as her friends, you folks will have some insight into where Dagny might be hiding, and also be motivated to help me reach her and convince her to stop."

A blonde fellow whose face and hands were entirely covered in horrific-looking scarlet welts and blisters, which apparently pained him not a whit, said, "You're the brainster, why don't you just lock her out?"

Bash vented a frustrated sigh. "Don't you think that was the very first thing I tried? But she's beaten me to it, changed all my old access codes. She's got the only key to the trapdoor now. But if I could only get in, I could make proteopape safe forever by closing the trapdoor for good. But I need to find Dagny first."

Cricket spoke up. "Roger, tell Bash what you know about Dagny's departure."

The jaundiced ephebe said, "I drove her to the airport a day ago. She said she was heading back to LA."

"Did you actually see her board her flight?" Bash asked.

"No . . ."

"Well, I think she's still in the Greater Boston Metropolitan region. The time lag between coasts is negligible for most communications. Even international calls ricochet off the GlobeSpeak relays practically instantaneously." Bash was referring to the fleet of thousands of high-flying drone planes—laden with comm gear and perennially refueled in mid-air—which encircled the planet, providing long-distance links faster than satellites ever could. "But she wouldn't want to risk even millisecond delays if she was trying to pull off certain real-time pranks. Plus, I figure she'll finally want to pop out of hiding to lord it over me in person, once she's finished humiliating me."

The toothy Indicia Diddums spoke. "That raishes a good point. This looksh like a purely pershonal feud between you two. You're the richesht plug in the world, Applebrook. Why don't you just hire some private muschle to nail her assh?"

"I don't want word of this snafu to spread any further than absolutely necessary. I spent a long time vacillating before I even decided to tell you guys."

Lester Schill meditatively stroked his long beard before speaking. "What's in this for us? Just a continuation of the status quo? Where's our profit?"

Bash saw red. He got to his feet, nearly upsetting his chair.

"Profit? What kind of motive for saving the world is that? Was I thinking of profit when I first created proteopape? No! Sure, I'm richer than God now, but that's not why I did it. Money is useless after a certain point. I can't even spend a fraction of one percent of my fortune, it grows so fast. And you, Schill, damn it, are probably in the same position, even if your wealth is several orders of magnitude less than mine. Money is not at the root of this! Proteopape means freedom of information and the equitable distribution of computing power! Don't any of you remember what life was like before proteopape? Huge, electricity-gobbling server farms? Cellphone towers blighting the landscape? Miles of fiberoptics cluttering the sewers and the seas and the streets? Endless upgrades of hardware rendered almost instantly obsolescent? Big government databases versus individual privacy? Proteopape did away with all that! Now the server farms are in your pockets and on cereal boxes, in the trash in your wastebasket, and in signage all around. Now the individual can go head-to-head with any corporation or governmental agency. And I won't just stand helplessly by and let some dingbat artist with a grudge ruin it all! If you people won't help me without bribery, then I'll just solve this problem on my own!"

Nostrils flaring, face flushed, Bash glared at the stubborn Dubsters, who remained unimpressed by his fevered speech.

The stalemate was broken when a segment of the bookshelves seemingly detached itself and stepped forward.

The moving portion of the bookcases possessed a human silhouette. In the next second, the silhouette went white, revealing a head-to-toe suit of proteopape. This suit, Bash realized, must represent one of the newest third-generation Parametrics camo outfits. The myriad moletronic cameras in the rear of the suit captured the exact textures and lighting of the background against which the wearer stood, and projected the mappings onto the front of the clothing. The wearer received his visual inputs on the interior of the hood from the forward array of cameras. Gauzy portions of the hood allowed easy breathing, at the spotty sacrifice of some of the disguise's hi-res.

A hand came up to sweep the headgear backward, where it draped like a loose cowl on the individual's back. The face thus revealed belonged to a young Hispanic man with a thin mustache.

"My name is Tito Harnnoy, and I represent the Masqueleros. We will help you, hombre!"

6. *THE MANCHURIAN CANDIDATE*

Tito Harnnoy drove his battered, industrial-model, two-person Segway down Mass Ave toward Cambridge. Riding behind Harnnoy, Bash experienced a creeping nostalgia, not altogether pleasant, that grew stronger the closer they approached his old alma mater, MIT.

Although Bash, once he became rich, had given generously to his university, endowing entire buildings, scholarship funds, research programs, and tenured positions, he had not physically returned to the campus since graduation. The university held too many memories of juvenile sadness and loneliness blended with his culminating triumph. Whenever Bash cast his thoughts back to those years, he again became, to some degree, the geeky prodigy, a person he felt he had since outgrown. His maturity always a tenuous proposition, Bash felt it wisest not to court such retrogressive feelings. But now, apparently, he had no choice but to confront his past self.

Harnnoy broke Bash's reverie by saying, "Just a few smoots away from help, pard."

Indeed, they were crossing the Charles River into Cambridge. The scattered structures of MIT loomed ahead, to east and west.

Bash noted extraordinary activity on the water below. "What's happening down there?" he asked Harnnoy.

"Annual Dragon Boat Festival. Big Asian carnival today, pard."

Harnnoy brought the scooter to a gyroscopic stop nearly below the shadow of the Great Dome, and they dismounted. Walking into the embrace of the buildings that comprised the Infinite Corridor, they attained grassy Killian Court. The bucolic campus scene reflected the vibrant July day.

Several artists were "painting" the passing parade from various perspectives, employing smart styluses on canvases of proteopape. Depending on what programs each artist was running, their strokes translated into digitized pastels or charcoal, acrylics or oils, ink or pencil or watercolor. Some had style filters in place, producing instant Monets or Seurats.

Elsewhere, a kite-fighting contest was underway. Made of proteopape with an extra abundance of special MEMS, the kites could flex and flutter their surfaces and achieve dynamic, breeze-assisted flight. Tetherless, they were controlled by their handlers who employed sheets of conventional proteopape on the ground that ran various strategy programs and displayed the kites'-eye view. Curveting and darting, the lifelike kites sought to batter aerial opponents and knock them from the sky without being disabled in turn.

Elsewhere, sedentary proteopape users read magazines or newspapers or books, watched various video feeds, mailed correspondents, telefactored tourist autonomes around the globe, or performed any of a hundred other proteopape-mediated functions.

Conducting Bash through the quad and toward the towering Building 54, Harnnoy said, "I'm glad you decided to trust the Masqueleros, Applebrook. We won't let you down. It's a good thing we have our own ways of monitoring interesting emergent shit around town. We keep special feelers out for anything connected with your name, you know."

Bash didn't know. "But why?"

"Are you kidding? You're famous on campus. The biggest kinasehead to ever emerge from these hallowed halls, even considering all the other famous names. And that's no intronic string."

Bash felt weird. Had he really become some kind of emblematic figure to this strange, younger generation? The honor sat awkwardly on his shoulders.

"Well, that's a major tribute, I guess. I only hope I can live up to your expectations."

"Even if you never released anything beyond proteopape, you already have. That's why we want to help you now. And it's truly exonic that we managed to get a spy—me—into place for your meeting with the Dubsters. Those sugarbags would never have lifted a pinky finger to aid you."

Despite the worshipful talk, Bash still had his doubts about the utility and motives of the mysterious Masqueleros, but the intransigence of Cricket's friends left him little choice. (Ms. Licklider herself, although expressing genuine sympathy, had had no solid aid of her own to offer.)

"I really appreciate your help, Tito. But I'm still a little unclear on how you guys hope to track Dagny down."

"Cryonize your metabolism, pard. You'll see in a minute."

Descending a few stairs into an access well, they stopped at an innocuous basement door behind Building 54. A small square of proteopape was inset above the door handle. Harnnoy spit upon it.

"Wouldn't the oils on your fingers have served as well?" Bash asked.

"Sure. But spitting is muy narcocorrido."

"Oh."

The invisible lab in the paper performed an instant DNA analysis on Harnnoy's saliva, and the door swung open.

Inside the unlit, windowless room, a flock of glowing, floating heads awaited.

The faces on the heads were all famous ones: Marilyn Monroe, Stephen Hawking, Britney Spears (the teenage version, not the middle-aged spokesperson for OpiateBusters), President Winfrey, Freeman Dyson, Walt Whitman (the celebrations for his 200th birthday ten years ago had gained him renewed prominence), Woody Woodpecker, Sponge-Bob SquarePants, and Bart Simpson's son Homer Junior.

"Welcome to the lair of the Masqueleros," a parti-faced Terminator ominously intoned.

Bash came to a dead stop, stunned for a moment, before he realized what he was seeing. Then he got angry.

"Okay, everybody off with the masks. We can't have any proteopape around while we talk."

Overhead fluorescents flicked on, and the crowd of conspirators wearing only the cowls of their camo suits stood revealed, the projected faces fading in luminescence to match the ambient light. One by one the Masqueleros doffed their headgear to reveal the grinning, motley faces of teenagers of mixed heritage and gender. One member gathered up the disguises, including Harnnoy's full suit, and stuffed the potentially treacherous proteopape into an insulated cabinet.

Briefly, Bash recapped his problem for the attentive students. They nodded knowingly, and finally one girl said, "So you need to discover this bint's hiding place without alerting her to your presence. And since she effectively controls every piece of proteopape in the I^2-verse, your only avenue of information is seemingly closed. But you haven't reckoned with—the Internet!"

"The Internet!" Bash fumed. "Why don't I just employ

smoke signals or, or—the telegraph? The Internet is dead as Xerox."

A red-haired kid chimed in. "No latch, pard. Big swaths of the web are still in place, maintained by volunteers like us. We revere and cherish the kludgy old monster. The web's virtual ecology is different now, true, more of a set of marginal biomes separated by areas of clear-cut devastation. But we still host thousands of webcams. And there's no proteopape in the mix, it's all antique silicon. So here's what we do. We put a few agents out there searching, and I guarantee that in no time at all we spot your girlfriend."

Sighing, Bash said, "She's *not* my girlfriend. Oh, well, what've I got to lose? Let's give it a try."

The Masqueleros and Bash crowded into an adjacent room full of antique hardware, including decrepit plasma flatscreens and folding Palm Pilot peripheral keyboards duct-taped into usability. The trapped heat and smells of the laboring electronics reminded Bash of his student days, seemingly eons removed from the present. Several of the Masqueleros sat down in front of their machines and begin to furiously mouse away. Interior and exterior shots of Greater Boston as seen from innumerable forgotten and dusty webcams swarmed the screens in an impressionistic movie without plot or sound.

Tito Harnnoy handed Bash a can of Glialsqueeze pop and said, "Refresh yourself, pard. This could take a while."

Eventually Bash and Tito fell to discussing the latest spintronics developments, and their potential impact on proteopape.

"Making the circuitry smaller doesn't change the basic proteopape paradigm," Bash maintained. "Each sheet gets faster and boasts more capacity, but the standard functionality remains the same."

"Nuh-*huh*! Spintronics means that all of proteopape's

uses can be distributed into the environment itself. Proteopape as a distinct entity will vanish."

Bash had to chew on this disturbing new scenario for a while. Gradually, he began to accept Harnnoy's thesis, at least partially. Why hadn't he seen such an eventuality before? Maybe Dagny had been right when she accused him of losing his edge . . . .

"Got her!"

Bash and the others clustered around one monitor. And there shone Dagny.

She sat in a small, comfy nest of cushions and fast-food packaging trash, a large sheet of proteopape in her lap.

"What camera is this feed coming from?" Bash asked.

"It's mounted at ceiling level in the mezzanine of the Paramount Theater on Washington Street, down near Chinatown."

When Bash had been born in 1999, the Paramount Theater, one of the grand dames of twentieth-century Hollywood's Golden Age, had already been shuttered for over two decades. Various rehabilitation plans had been tossed about for the next fifteen years, until Bash entered MIT. During that year, renovations finally began. The grand opening of the theater coincided with the churning of the economy occasioned by the release of proteopape and also with a short-lived but scarily virulent outbreak of Megapox. Faced with uncertain financing, fear of contagion in mass gatherings, and the cheapness of superior home-theater systems fashioned of proteopape, the revamped movie house had locked its doors, falling once again into genteel desuetude.

"Can you magnify the view?" Bash asked. "See what she's looking at?"

The webcam zoomed in on the sheet of paper in Dagny's lap.

And Bash saw that she was watching them.

In infinite regress, the monitor showed the proteopape showing the monitor showing the proteopape showing . . .

Bash howled. "Someone's got proteopape on them!"

Just then, a leering Dagny looked backward over her shoulder directly at the webcam, and at the same time Bash's chin spoke.

"It's you, you idiot," Bash's epidermis said in Dagny's stepped-down voice.

Bash ripped off the smart band aid he had applied while shaving, and the image of the Masqueleros on Dagny's proteopape swung crazily to track the movement.

"Dagny!" Bash yelled into the band aid. "This has gone far enough! You've had your fun at my expense. Now give me your current password so I can make proteopape secure again."

"Come and get it," Dagny taunted. "I'm not going any-where."

"I will!"

With that bold avowal, Bash furiously twisted the band aid, causing the image of the Masqueleros on Dagny's proteopape to shatter. On the monitor screen she appeared unconcerned, lolling back among her cushions like the Queen of Sheba.

Bash turned to Tito. "Lend me a phone and your Segway. I'm going to nail down this troublemaker once and for all."

"Some of us'll go with you, pard."

"No, you stay here. Dagny won't react well to intimidation by a bunch of strangers. And besides, I need the Masqueleros to keep on spying on her and feed me any updates on her actions. All I can hope is that she'll listen to me and abandon this insane vendetta. If she doesn't— Well, I'm not sure what I'll do."

"No problemo, fizz."

Someone handed Bash a phone. He downloaded his identity into it, and then established an open channel to Harnnoy. After tucking the phone into the neckline of his shirt, allowing him to speak and be spoken to hands-free, Bash darted from the underground room.

7. *PHANTOM OF THE OPERA*

Bash made it as far as Killian Court before the first of Dagny's attacks commenced.

On all the canvases of the amateur painters, on all the individual sheets of proteopape held by the idling students, Bash's face appeared, displacing laboriously created artworks, as well as the contents of books, magazines, and videos. (Dagny had unearthed a paparazzo's image of Bash that made him look particularly demented.) And from the massed speakers in the proteopape pages boomed this warning in a gruff male voice:

"Attention! This is a nationwide alert from Homeland Security. All citizens should immediately exert extreme vigilance for the individual depicted here. He is wanted for moral turpitude, arrogant ignorance, and retrogressive revanchism. Approach him with caution, as he may bite."

This odd yet alarming message immediately caused general consternation to spread throughout the quadrangle. Bash turned up his shirt collar, hunched down his head, and hurried toward the street. But he had not reckoned with the kites.

Homing in on his phone, the co-opted kites began to dive bomb Bash. Several impacted the ground around him, crumpling with a noise like scrunching cellophane, but one scored a direct hit on his head, causing him to yelp.

His squeal attracted the eyes of several onlookers, and someone shouted, "There he is!"

Bash ran.

He briefly thought of abandoning his phone, but decided not to. He needed to stay in touch with the Masqueleros. But more crucially, giving up his phone would achieve no invisibility.

Bash was moving through a saturated I^2 environment. There was no escaping proteopape. Every smart surface—from store windows to sunglasses, from taxi rooftop displays to billboards, from employee nametags to vending machines—was a camera that would track him in his dash across town to the Paramount Theater. Illicitly tapping into all these sources, utilizing common yet sophisticated pattern recognition, sampling and extrapolative software, Dagny would never lose sight of her quarry. Bash might as well have had cameras implanted in his eyeballs.

Out on Mass Ave, Bash faced no interception from alarmed citizens. Apparently the false security warning had been broadcast only in Killian Court. But surely Dagny had further tricks up her striped sleeves.

He spoke into his dangling phone. "What's she doing now?"

Harnnoy's voice returned an answer. "Noodling around with her pape. She's got her back to the camera, so we can't see what kind of scripts she's running."

"Okay, thanks. I'm hitting the road now."

Once aboard the Segway, Bash headed back toward downtown Boston.

He obediently came to a halt at the first red stop light, chafing at the delay. But something odd about the engine noise of the car approaching behind him made Bash look over his shoulder.

The car—a 2029 Vermoulian with proteopape windows—was not slowing down.

In a flash, Bash realized what was happening.

Dagny had edited out both the traffic light and Bash's scooter from the driver's interior display.

Bash veered his Segway to the right, climbing the curb, and the Vermoulian zipped past him with only centimeters to spare. In the middle of the intersection, it broadsided another car. Luckily, the crash of the two lightweight urban vehicles, moving at relatively low speeds, resulted in only minor damages, although airbags noisily activated.

Bash drove down the sidewalk, scattering pedestrians, and continued around the accident.

Things were getting serious. No longer was Dagny content to merely harass Bash. Now she was involving innocent bystanders in her mad quest for revenge.

His ire rising, Bash crossed the Charles River. Beneath the bridge, huge jubilant crowds had assembled for the Dragon Boat races.

Bash took several wrong turns. Dagny had changed the street signs, misnaming avenues along his entire route and producing a labyrinth of new one-way streets. After foolishly adhering to the posted regulations for fear of getting stopped by some oblivious rule-bound cop, Bash abandoned all caution and just raced past snarled traffic down whatever avenue he felt would bring him most quickly to Washington Street.

Now Bash began to see his face everywhere, in varying sizes, surmounted or underlined by dire warnings. WANTED FOR CULTURAL ASSASSINATION, GUILTY OF SQUANDERING ARTISTIC CAPITAL, MASTERMIND IN FELONIOUS ASSAULT ON VISIONARIES . . .

The absurd charges made Bash see red. He swore aloud, and Harnnoy said, "What'd I do, pard?"

"Nothing, nothing. Dagny still at the Paramount?"

"*Verdad, compañero.*"

As he approached the Common, Bash noted growing crowds of gleeful pedestrians. What was going on . . . ?

The Dragon Boat Festival. Chinatown must be hosting parallel celebrations. Well, okay. The confusion would afford Bash cover—

A sheet of proteopape—spontaneously windblown, or aimed like a missile?—sailed up out of nowhere and wrapped Bash's head. He jerked the steering grips before taking his hands entirely off them to deal with the obstruction to his vision, and the Segway continued homeostatically on its new course to crash into a tree.

Bash picked himself up gingerly. The paper had fallen away from his face. Angrily, he crumpled it up and stuffed it into his pocket. He hurt all over, but no important body part seemed broken. The scooter was wrecked. Luckily, he hadn't hit anyone. Concerned bystanders clumped around him, but Bash brusquely managed to convince them to go away.

Harnnoy said, "I caught the smashup on the phone camera, Bash. You okay?"

"Uh, I guess. Sorry about totaling your ride. I'm going on foot now."

As Bash scurried off, he witnessed the arrival of several diligent autonomes converging on the accident. He accelerated his pace, fearful of getting corralled by the authorities before he could deal with Dagny.

Downtown Crossing was thronged, the ambient noise like a slumber party for teenage giants. The windows of Filene's claimed that Bash was a redactive splice between a skunk, hyena, and jackal. As Dagny's interventions failed to stop him, her taunts grew cruder. She must be getting desperate. Bash was counting on her to screw up somehow. He had no real plan otherwise.

Weaseling his way through the merrymakers, Bash was brought up short a block away from the Paramount by an oncoming parade. Heading the procession was a huge multiperson Chinese dragon. In lieu of dumb paint, its proteopape skin sheathed it in glittery scales and animated smoke-snorting head.

People were pointing to the sky. Bash looked up.

One of the famous TimWarDisVia aerostats serenely cruised overhead, obviously dispatched to provide an overhead view of the parade. Its proteopape skin featured Bash's face larger than God's. Scrolling text reflected poorly on Bash's parentage and morals.

"God *damn*!" Bash turned away from the sight, only to confront the dragon. Its head now mirrored Bash's, but its body was a snake's.

Small strings of firecrackers began to explode, causing shrieks, and Bash utilized the diversion to bull onward toward the shuttered Paramount Theater. He darted down the narrow alley separating the deserted building from its neighbors.

"Tito! Any tips on getting inside?"

"One of our webcams on the first floor shows something funky with one of the windows around the back."

The rear exterior wall of the theater presented a row of weather-distressed plywood sheets nailed over windows. The only service door was tightly secured. No obvious entrance manifested itself.

But then, with his trained eye, Bash noticed that one plywood facade failed close-up inspection as he walked slowly past it.

Dagny had stretched an expanse of proteopape across an open frame, and then set the pape to display a plywood texture.

Bash set his phone aside on the ground. "Tito, I'm going in alone. Call the cops if I'm not out in half an hour."

"Uptaken and bound, fizz!"

Rather vengefully, Bash smashed his fist through the disguising pape, and then scrambled inside.

Dagny had hotwired electricity from somewhere. The Paramount was well lit, although the illumination did nothing to dispel a moldy atmosphere from years of inoccupancy. Bash moved cautiously from the debris-strewn backstage area out into the general seating.

A flying disc whizzed past his ear like a suicidal mirror-finished bat. It hit a wall and shattered.

Dagny stood above him at the rail of the mezzanine with an armful of antique DVDs. The platters for the digital projectors must have been left behind when the Paramount ceased operations. The writing on a shard at Bash's feet read: *The Silmarillion.*

Dagny frisbee'd another old movie at Bash. He ducked just in time to avoid getting decapitated.

"Quit it, Dagny! Act like an adult, for Christ's sake! We have to talk!"

Dagny pushed her clunky eyeglasses back up her nose. "We've got nothing to talk about! You've proven you're a narrow-minded slave to old hierarchies, without an ounce of imagination left in your shriveled brainpan. And you insulted my art!"

"I'm sorry! I didn't mean to, honest. Jesus, even you said that the Woodies were a big joke."

"Don't try putting words in my mouth! Anyway, that was before I won one."

Bash stepped forward into an aisle. "I'm coming up there, Dagny, and you can't stop me."

A withering fusillade of discs forced Bash to eat his words and run for cover into an alcove.

Frustrated beyond endurance, Bash racked his wits for some means of overcoming the demented auteur.

A decade of neglect had begun to have its effects on

the very structure of the theater. The alcove where Bash stood was littered with fragments of plaster. Bash snatched up one as big as his fist. From his pocket he dug the sheet of proteopape that had blinded him and wrapped it around the heavy chunk. He stepped forward.

"Dagny, let's call a truce. I've got something here you need to read. It puts everything into a new light." Bash came within a few meters of the lower edge of the balcony before Dagny motioned him to stop. He offered the ball of pape on his upturned palm.

"I don't see what could possibly change things—"

"Just take a look, okay?"

"All right. Toss it up here."

Dagny set down her ammunition to free both hands and leaned over the railing to receive the supposedly featherweight pape.

Bash concentrated all his anger and resolve into his right arm. He made a motion as if to toss underhand. But at the last minute, he swiftly wound up and unleashed a mighty overhand pitch.

Dagny did not react swiftly enough to the deceit. The missile conked her on the head, and she went over backwards into the mezzanine seats.

Never before had Bash moved so fast. He found Dagny hovering murmurously on the interface between consciousness and oblivion. Reassured that she wasn't seriously injured, Bash arrowed toward her nest of pillows. He snatched up the sheet of proteopape that displayed his familiar toolkit for accessing the trapdoor features of his invention. With a few commands he had long ago memorized as a vital failsafe, he initiated the shutdown of the hidden override aspects of proteopape.

From one interlinked sheet of proteopape to the next, the commands raced, exponentially propagating around the globe like history's most efficient cyberworm, a spark that extinguished its very means of propagation as it raced along. Within mere minutes, the world was made safe and secure again for Immanent Information.

Bash returned to Dagny, who was struggling to sit up.

"You—you haven't beaten me. I'll find some way to show you—"

The joyful noises from the parade continuing outside insinuated themselves into Bash's relieved mind. He felt happy and inspired. Looking down at Dagny, he knew just what to say.

"Forget it, Jake. It's Chinatown."

Credits